AGE OF HEROES, ᴅᴏᴏᴋ 1

# Paladin's Prize

# GAELEN FOLEY

# Also By Gaelen Foley

**Ascension Trilogy**

*The Pirate Prince*

*Princess*

*Prince Charming*

**Knight Miscellany**

*The Duke*

*Lord of Fire*

*Lord of Ice*

*Lady of Desire*

*Devil Takes a Bride*

*One Night of Sin*

*His Wicked Kiss*

**The Spice Trilogy**

*Her Only Desire*

*Her Secret Fantasy*

*Her Every Pleasure*

**The Inferno Club**

*My Wicked Marquess*

*My Dangerous Duke*

*My Irresistible Earl*

*My Ruthless Prince*

*My Scandalous Viscount*

*My Notorious Gentleman*

*Secrets of a Scoundrel*

**Gryphon Chronicles**
**(Writing as E.G. Foley)**

*The Lost Heir*

*Jake & the Giant*

*The Dark Portal*

*The Gingerbread Wars*

*Rise of Allies*

**50 States of Fear**
**(Writing as E.G. Foley)**

*The Haunted Plantation*
*(Alabama)*

*Leader of the Pack*
*(Colorado)*

*Bringing Home Bigfoot*
*(Arkansas)*

*Dork and the Deathray*
*(Alaska)*

**Anthologies**

*Royal Weddings*

*Royal Bridesmaids*

# Credits and Copyright

*My good blade carves the casques of men,*
*My tough lance thrusteth sure,*
*My strength is as the strength of ten,*
*Because my heart is pure.*

~Alfred, Lord Tennyson, *"Sir Galahad"*

# Table of Contents

# Chapter 1
# Kiss of Life

The Golden Knight lay dying on the starlit field where he had made his stand alone against the bestial horde.

He had wreaked mayhem on the enemy, but had paid a terrible price.

Even now, the thirsty spring ground drank his noble blood like some dark pagan sacrifice to the old gods. Rainless rumbles from the dark sky, however, voiced the indignation of the deity under whose banner the paladin had won so many battles. Ilios, the Father of Lights, however, was not without *other* votaries in the area...

From the moment she had heard the distant clamor of the melee, the young healer had understood her mission and obeyed.

Shouldering her satchel of supplies, she had lifted the loose, wide hood of her gray gown, grasped her walking staff, and left her hermitage atop the mountain.

Twilight had darkened to nightfall while she trekked down through the wind-rippled woods, her tiny fey familiar hovering by her shoulder.

The lady Wrynne du Mere tried not to listen overmuch to the battle sounds echoing up from the farmer's field below as she went. Shouts. Roars. Ugly porcine squeals. The clatter of weaponry.

What would her parents say, she wondered, if they knew she was heading *toward* the danger rather than away from it? A small frisson of worry crept through her. For she knew what probably awaited her down there.

Everyone in Mistwood knew all too well about the Urmugoths rampaging through the countryside this past fortnight.

She was just glad the good-for-nothing king had finally yawned himself awake enough to send soldiers to deal with the beasts. Finally, somebody had bothered enough about their sleepy northern province to *do* something about the brutish raiders.

Whatever was happening down there, it reached a fairly swift crescendo. She only paused when a flash of brilliance suddenly lit up the night.

A thunderclap and a man's lionlike roar shook the whole valley. Her fairy shrieked at the sound and dove into her satchel, but Wrynne's very soul had gone quiet.

The hairs on her nape tingled as she sensed divine power in the air.

*Of course.* It could only be Sir Thaydor at the head of the king's troops, she thought in relief, still holding her breath. His devotion to the Light was said to flood the paladin on occasion with supernatural fighting ability, much like her healing.

And then he became practically invincible.

*Well, then.* An embarrassing flutter of giddy schoolgirl eagerness flitted in her belly to see the famous knight. There was obviously nothing to worry about.

"You can come out now," she told Silvertwig. "Don't worry, the king's champion is still undefeated, last I heard."

The Urms would rue the day they'd ever come crashing through the North Gate of the kingdom once they found Sir Thaydor waiting to put a stop to their bloody rampage.

Sure enough, the battle sounds had gone abruptly still.

*Victory as usual, Sir Thaydor?* she thought with a slight smile. She did not have the highest opinion of knights, in general. Most seemed thickheaded brutes who only lived to kill people and break things, but a paladin was another matter.

A paladin had a purpose and a code.

Reassured that he had matters well in hand, Wrynne told Silvertwig to hold on and banged her enchanted staff lightly on the ground, using a *hasten* spell to teleport the rest of the way down the mountain. There was no time to lose if she was to aid any of his men who'd been wounded in the battle.

Moments later, she stepped out of the woods onto the edge of her neighbor's pasture. It was now quite dark, but a few dropped torches burned here and there, and she shuddered at the carnage revealed by their eerie, flickering glow.

Dead Urmugoths everywhere. But where were the knights? Archers? Soldiers? *Anyone?*

Heart pounding, she scanned the field in confusion until the realization slowly sank in. It was not a troop of soldiers that had done this.

It was *one man*.

She stared across the battlefield, awestruck.

She had seen many things in her twenty-three years of life, but never so much death, and never such mad courage.

The Golden Knight had come alone.

Then she drew in her breath, for she saw that he had fallen—the hero of the kingdom, the favorite of the gods.

He was unmistakable in his bright armor, the silver steel of his breastplate, as well as his tattered white surcoat adorned with the sun symbol of Ilios in gold. By his position on a slight rise, surrounded as he was by the slumped, hulking bodies of Urmugoth warriors, she realized that Thaydor had not permitted himself to drop to his knees until every last foul thing sent against their people had been slain.

She started rushing out across the field, but unfortunately, some of the raiders were still clinging to life. She could sense the presence of evil ahead—or rather, brute malice, in their case.

A monstrous race of semi-primitive, nomadic barbarians, Urmugoths roamed the wastelands beyond the kingdom's northern border. Seven feet tall on average, clad in spiked armor, they adorned themselves with the bones of past enemies and wielded giant maces, clubs, and poleaxes. The stump tusks they sported on their lower jaws proved they were indeed descended from ogres, just like the nursery tales warned—to say nothing of their cannibalistic tendencies.

How a raiding party of some twenty Urms had got through the North Gates in the first place was the great mystery of the day, along with why the king failed to send troops to destroy them.

All Wrynne knew was that after somehow breaching the border, the Urms had raged across the countryside from farm to farm and village to village, plundering and killing, ripping the peasants apart, until, thank Ilios, justice had caught up to them this night.

Sir Thaydor had clearly lured them here, away from the people in the nearby hamlet and the people there, to fight them in this field.

Now all twenty of the hideous brutes were either dead or dying. Wrynne shook her head in wonder as she proceeded past them at a more guarded pace, just in case any of the beasts were still capable of attacking her.

As she walked by, she looked around at the litter of bodies and was still profoundly shocked at Sir Thaydor's obvious ferocity. He was known back in her hometown, the capital city of Pleiburg, as a decidedly gentle soul. Enemies might quake at his name, but at festivals after his victory parades, she had personally seen little children climb on him as if he were a great, tall, affable golden tree.

And now this bloodbath.

Well, she thought with a nervous shrug, the bards said the Paladin of Ilios could do this sort of thing when the power of the Light flooded him with a blinding, holy wrath and his famous blade, Hallowsmite, began to glow—but who believed bards?

It seemed they had been telling the truth for once.

*Go to him. Hurry. He needs you*, said the voice of the Light, deep within her heart.

Before going any closer to the dying Urms, Wrynne closed her eyes to the bloody scene before her and summoned forth the trancelike state of indomitable bliss that she would have to draw upon to heal whatever wounds the paladin had sustained.

That she do so was obviously the will of the god they both served in their two different, confraternal orders—he as the first of the Sons of Might, she as one of the Daughters of the Rose.

Ilios clearly wanted him alive, and no wonder. The man was a walking, talking force for good upon the earth, and she had a feeling in her bones that he was important to their country in ways yet to be revealed.

With a deep breath, Wrynne flicked her eyes open, ready to proceed. Her tranquil stare fixed on him, she set out across the battlefield, pulling more deeply into the peace within herself with every stride. He had used his gift to protect her and everyone who lived here; now she would wield hers to save him.

Time seemed to slow all around her. Ignoring the stench and severed limbs, the gore of spilt entrails, the low animal groans rising up here and there, and the baleful yellow eyes that watched her pass, she focused on the Light spreading through her body. The radiant path was the way of love and beauty...

The ugliness receded. The healing power unfolded within her like a flower, and at each spot where her bare feet trod the bloodstained ground, the crushed and trampled grass began to rise again, the delicate shoots of clover unbending.

The hem of her pewter-gray gown was edged with crimson by the time she knelt down beside him. "Sir Thaydor?"

No response.

She glanced at the arrow in his side, which had somehow found one small, vulnerable chink in his armor between his back and breast plates. She laid her hand gently on his chest and gazed at him in sorrow. Wrynne was a compassionate but not a sentimental woman. No healer could afford to be. One had to learn to steel oneself in order to work calmly and swiftly in the midst of human suffering.

But even she was shaken by the sight of the kingdom's greatest warrior lying defenseless on the ground, no one here to protect him now but her. She glanced around uneasily to make sure no more enemies were coming.

*Strange.* She could not shake the feeling that something was still out there that wanted him dead.

If they came back to finish him off, what could she do? She was no warrior.

*I have to get him out of here.*

With her tiny winged companion whispering anxiously in her ear, Wrynne took the rolled-up Aladdin stretcher out of her satchel. A rare and very expensive item, it had been a gift from her proud parents upon the completion of her healing studies. All the way from the exotic bazaars of Arabia, the magical floating stretcher had been made by djinn weavers from the strands of a flying carpet.

"Let's get him onto this," she murmured.

Silvertwig assisted as Wrynne hurried to unfurl the thick, tapestry-like cloth. Without it, she had no hope of transporting the warrior off the battlefield. His armor weighed a good four stone, and that did not include the solid muscle of the tall, broad-shouldered body underneath.

Oh, and they could not leave Hallowsmite behind. The longsword was heavy, too. She was a little afraid to touch it, just in case it had another thunderbolt stored in there somewhere, waiting to fly out.

*Don't be silly,* she thought. The power came from him, not from the sword itself.

Once the stretcher was unrolled, Wrynne used the golden strap of the hand-loop to make it rest on the ground.

Whether or not he could hear her, she gave her patient fair warning of the movement to come. "I'll try not to hurt you." It seemed an odd thing for a petite woman to say to a large man who had slain dragons, but she got to work anyway, quickly tucking it under the length of him.

Silvertwig fluttered her wings with all her might, helping Wrynne to budge his inert body upward on one side to get him onto the stretcher.

Unconscious, the heavy, powerful knight lay like a dead weight. Wrynne winced as the slight motion made the blood seep faster from around the arrow sticking out of his side.

Meanwhile, half a dozen of Silvertwig's tiny fey kinfolk had come flying out of the forest and gathered around to see what was happening. Even the fairies had been frightened of the Urmugoths, but now that they were dead, the curious little pranksters came out to gawk.

They twinkled like fireflies, hovering around the Golden Knight. Wrynne did not chase them off. Their colorful glow would help provide light for her next task.

Once she got Sir Thaydor onto the stretcher and ready to be evacuated to safety, it was time to assess his condition more fully.

Bracing herself, she took hold of his helmet. She could already see blood on the visor and a dent on the crown. If this was as bad as it looked, he might already be dead in there, but he did have divine protection, so…

"Shh," she whispered in surprise when he stirred a little, his metal-gauntleted hand reaching slowly but automatically for his dagger. "It's all right, Sir Thaydor. I've come to help you."

He groaned and dropped his hand back into the mud.

Carefully, Wrynne removed his helmet. Then she stared at him, ignoring the chiseled male beauty of his face in shock at the severity of his head wound.

Silvertwig sobbed and turned away.

He'd taken a chop from a poleaxe to the skull. It must have been a glancing blow, or it would have taken a chunk of his head clean off. Instead, he was left with a gaping skull fracture.

Wrynne took one look and felt slightly queasy. Oh, she could heal it, but it would take everything she had, and then what about the rest of him?

As her gaze moved over the fallen knight's imposing form, she felt her throat close when she saw the condition of his breastplate. The left side bore the dents of at least two full-force blows he had taken to the chest, possibly from a mace. Perhaps the blood running into his eyes from the head wound had blinded him before he could block them.

She let out a trembling exhalation. *This is so much worse than I thought.* Broken ribs and a collapsed lung would be the least of his worries. It was not just the blunt, shattering force of such massive blows themselves, but being encased in metal that made these types of injuries so devastating.

A great resounding blow on plate armor reechoed through the body with concussive force strong enough to rupture organs. Thus, if the head wound didn't kill him, the body blows would.

Sick with fear, she debated how to use her limited skills. She could choose one major wound or the other to heal immediately—the head wound probably being the more dire—but, unfortunately, then she would be spent, her magic depleted with nothing left to give him for at least an hour.

An hour Sir Thaydor didn't have.

That didn't even begin to address his lesser wounds, all of which were awful, starting with the arrow. The man was a mess.

Inspecting him, she also found his left leg broken below the knee, probably from a hideous side blow from a war hammer. Black streaks charred his left gauntlet and the vambrace protecting his forearm, where one of the Urmugoths must have clubbed him with a torch.

Wrynne found herself feeling slightly dizzy. Glancing up at the stars, she took a breath to steady herself. *Oh, Ilios, I fear you've picked the wrong healer.*

She had never dealt with such grievous battle wounds before. In her two-year tenure as local healer in this quarter of the province, she had stitched up many limbs from accidents with wagons and farming implements, made gallons of medicine, delivered dozens of babies, lanced boils, pulled teeth, performed a couple of sickening amputations, and even cured ten cases of the plague.

But nothing like this.

"He's a dead man," Silvertwig opined in the peculiar, chiming language of her people, like the jingle of tiny bells.

"No," Wrynne whispered, straightening her spine. "Not yet. Not if I can help it."

There was still *one* way to save him...

Heal all his wounds at once in a single, massive discharge of the most sacred and powerful magic she had ever learned at the Bastion.

But it would require a sacrifice on her part that she had not realized she'd be called upon to make this night.

The *Kiss of Life* was based on empath magic and was such a potent spell that a healer could only work it once in a lifetime. It was said to forge a deep bond of some sort between the two people involved, whether they liked it or not, and of course, there was always a price to pay when using magic.

It would leave her gift for healing others fully intact, but if memory served, it would strip her of her magical ability to heal *herself* quickly whenever she was sick or injured.

If she did this, she'd be vulnerable in the world in a way she had never been before. It was a frightening prospect.

Knowing she could cure herself at any time had ensured she never stopped to think twice about going in to help a fever-ridden village, for example. After this, she'd still have to go, only now, she might catch it like everybody else and there'd be no one to heal *her*. For a fleeting moment, she wrestled with herself—with a twinge of selfishness.

Maybe there was some other way. And what if he was already too far gone for even the mighty *Kiss of Life* to work? She'd end up sacrificing her self-healing power for no reason. That was hardly worth it.

"Sir Thaydor?" She touched his lips and still felt weak puffs of breath rising up to warm her hand. His skin was clammy but not yet cold unto death as she laid her hand on his cheek.

He startled her just then by opening his eyes.

Stark, brilliant blue eyes stared out at her from his blood- and grime- and sweat-streaked face. Eyes glazed with suffering, but keenly intelligent and aware.

*Sanctus solis,* what strength was in this man? she wondered. What tolerance for pain, that he could be the least bit conscious in his condition without screaming?

"I'm here," she said softly, taking his heavy steel hand. "You're not alone. Ilios sent me."

He was shaking as his agonized gaze took in the light-gray sackcloth of her simple pilgrim's gown and the pewter necklace of her order—a choker of delicate, coiled chain mail links, with a Celtic rose knot at her throat and a small sun pendant dangling down from it to her chest.

He stared gratefully at it, visibly comforted by the familiar holy symbols, and let her take his hand. "Sister," he forced out.

It was difficult to find her voice. "You've done well, my brother." Gently, she removed his right gauntlet and took his hand between her own, skin to skin. The healing was so much more powerful that way.

She knew in that moment that she would do anything to save his life.

The price was high, but how could she deny him? Sir Thaydor hadn't stopped to count the cost when he had thrown himself between the people and their enemies. Nor would she. "I know you're in massive pain right now, but I am going to help you."

He tried to shake his head. "No. Let me die."

"Thaydor," she chided softly. "We need you."

"Please," he rasped, staring at her in confusion, obviously concussed. "I can see Elysium… The portal's open. Can't you see it? Let me go."

"No. Stay with me." She ached for his suffering and placed her hand against his cheek. "Thaydor, listen to me. You've taken a bit of a knock to the head—"

He laughed, barely audible, at that.

"But I am going to fix it," she insisted, falling quite irrevocably in love with him from that very moment, she suspected.

For, honestly, how could the man laugh at a time like this, with his skull cleaved open and his brain peeking out?

*Divine madman. Holy warrior. Crusader.*

She shook her head at him with a chiding smile, then took the canteen out of her satchel and poured a small drip of water into his mouth. He welcomed it with parted lips. She wetted a bandage from her bag next and tenderly wiped the blood out of his eyes.

"There, now. Be as brave as you always are for just a little longer. In a moment, the pain will be gone and you'll sleep for a couple of days. I will take you to safety and attend you till you wake. No harm will befall you in my care, you have my word. Now, close your eyes, son of Light."

He either obeyed or simply passed out again. Probably the latter.

There was no time to lose. What she knew about using the *Kiss of Life* spell—what *she* would have to go through to take his wounds from him—frightened her, but she ignored her misgivings. Who could be more worthy of the gift than he?

Besides, this was obviously the whole point of why Ilios had led her to settle out here in the middle of nowhere in the first place, much to the vexation of her fashionable mother. Lately, Wrynne had started wondering herself what she was doing here, living like a hermit on some mountaintop.

Well, now she knew. Knew beyond all doubt.

Ilios had put her in place two years ago, lining up everything just right, making sure there'd be someone on hand who'd obey him when the time came to save his paladin.

She swallowed hard. This was a great honor…and a huge responsibility. With a sense of destiny sending chills down her spine, Wrynne vowed she would not fail.

But she couldn't do it alone. She'd need a little help from the only assistants on hand: the fairies.

This was not a terribly encouraging prospect. They were not known as the most dependable of folk. Of course, she knew she could rely on Silvertwig. She just hoped the other little tricksters would cooperate, because once she worked the *Kiss of Life* spell, she would be incapacitated for twelve to twenty-four hours.

Fortunately, the Aladdin stretcher made patients heavier than Thaydor light enough that even a child could maneuver it, simply using the golden hand-loops to guide it as it floated over the ground.

She glanced up at the cloud of small, winged onlookers. "Everybody, could I please have your attention? I need a favor. Sundew, Treegriddle, Plumbeam. You too, Mooncurl. Everybody listen. If you'll do what I ask, I'll make you a whole mound of saffron cakes tomorrow."

This got their full attention. They started cheering, zooming closer in excitement.

"Saffron cakes!"

"With honey?"

"Of course with honey," she said. "As much as you want."

"Hooray for saffron cakes!"

"I'm hungry!" Plumbeam whined.

"We want them now!" Treegriddle demanded.

"No, first you have to help me," Wrynne said.

"What do you want us to do?" the little lemon-yellow one, Sundew, asked.

"This man is badly hurt. He needs my strongest magic, a very potent spell. It will heal him, but he'll be out cold and so will I. This is where you come in. I'm putting Silvertwig in charge. Everyone has to listen to her."

"Aw!"

The others didn't like that, but Silvertwig preened and flew up higher, hands on her waist as she grinned at her cousins.

"As you can see, we got the knight on the stretcher. Once I do the spell, you'll all have to work together to float him up the path to my sanctuary. I know you know the way. Be careful with him," Wrynne said. "Don't get him caught on anything. And don't drop him. He's important.

Like a prince. When you get him up the mountain, put him in my bed. All right?"

They nodded and hovered around, wings whirring.

"Now, here's the important part," she continued. "After you've done all that, don't forget to come back for me. I'm going to be unconscious, too. And it's...not safe."

With an anxious gulp, she glanced around meaningfully at the dead and dying Urmugoths. Some of them still moved every now and then. Still groaned. Still watched her with murderous intent.

She turned back to the fairies with a twinge of desperation. "Please don't leave me here. Bring the Aladdin stretcher with you when you come back to get me. Shove me onto it and carry me home, just like you did with him. Promise you won't leave me here...with them."

Silvertwig patted her reassuringly on the shoulder. "I won't forget you, Wrynnay."

"Thanks. Then I might as well get started." She looked at Sir Thaydor and asked in nervous humor, "You ready?"

He was still unconscious, lingering at death's door.

*Elysium, indeed.* No doubt he'd earned a palace there in the celestial realm, an eternity of peace with no more enemies trying to kill him. Maybe it was wrong to drag him back into this life...

But the world needed such men so badly, especially in these dark times.

She went over the spell in her mind. She had an excellent memory, but she double-checked it in the book, considering she had never expected to use the *Kiss of Life* and would only have one shot to get it right.

Satisfied that she was ready, she cupped the paladin's cheek while the fairies looked on. He wasn't awake any longer, but she talked to him anyway. "I'll see you on the other side of all this, Thaydor."

*I hope.*

"I'll have to take the arrow out first before we begin," she went on. "It's probably going to hurt. I am sorry. Don't worry, though, it will all be over soon."

*Provided this works.*

Then she grasped the shaft of the arrow, nervously flicking her fingers around it. He groaned as she pulled it out of his flesh.

"I'm so sorry!" she whispered, while the blood began to pour afresh out of his side. Normally, she'd have a pile of bandages on hand and herbs to slow the bleeding, but this case was anything but normal.

The sacred incantations were already on her lips as she quickly borrowed Thaydor's knife, raised her left forearm, and cut herself. She clenched her fist, wincing, and felt the hot blood run between her fingers. She concentrated harder on the prayers, speaking the short lines over and over again, becoming them.

*"Vincit tenebris lux, amor vincit mortem..."*

Eyes closed, she began to sway slightly, the power of the Light intensifying as it took hold of her, tingling in her veins. When she unclenched her hand again and opened her eyes, still repeating the incantation, even she was amazed to see how the blood pooling in her palm glistened. The great red droplets glowed with ruby sparkles as the magic activated. She reached out her hand and let the light-spangled blood from her slashed forearm drip into Thaydor's open head wound.

Her blood mingled with his, an offering freely given. Now there was only one momentous step left, and after the tales she had heard, she was scared to do it, but she blocked out the fear, whispering the words over and over endlessly.

*"Vincit tenebris lux, amor vincit mortem..."*

*Light conquers darkness, love conquers death...*

Heart pounding, she lowered her lips to his and kissed him.

For a moment, she lingered with her mouth pressed softly to his, her warm breath mingling with his pained, shallow panting. Then she squeezed her eyes shut and willed all her healing power, her very life force, into him.

In the shattering blast of Light between them, the transfer took place. Radiance flashed out of all the places where he had been broken and torn while a wave of crimson pain washed through her. Wrynne gasped, sitting up with a small cry.

Nothing could have prepared her for the next few seconds as agony unfurled and then wrapped around her like a cloak.

She threw her head back, a scream tearing from her lips as the physical pain of Thaydor's wounds bloomed like evil flowers through her body, though she did not suffer the actual damage.

Even so, it was far worse than she could have imagined. First came the sensation of fire scorching up her left arm. Next, the arrow plunged into her side. She gasped at how real it seemed; she could almost feel the tip deep inside her innards. She tasted blood.

Third, a bone-cracking bash to the side of her leg knocked her to the ground. She felt his moment of panic, the loss of control as the enemies closed in—then blinding pain crashing down on top of her head.

Last, like the double knock of doom at the door, a sickening *thud, thud* to her torso that folded her over in agony, robbed her of breath.

The world started going black. Dark as the grave.

Obsidian terror swallowed her up.

Whether the fairies kept their word, whether the *Kiss of Life* spell had even worked, Wrynne did not know.

She simply passed out.

# Chapter 2
# Sanctuary

*ake up! Wake up, Daughter. Danger approaches…*
Wrynne paid the subtle inner warning no mind. Hours had passed, and she twitched fitfully on her pillow, absorbed in a strange dream.

The black-clad man knew no mercy, stealthy as the wind. Onyx eyes burned above the black scarf swathed across the lower half of his face as he slipped into the gate tower, climbed the winding stairs without a sound, and killed the sentries on duty, cutting the throats of some and coolly shooting others with arrows from the large bow he'd worn slung across his back.

*Hurry! He's coming.*

But she couldn't look away as the assassin, moving briskly and methodically, threw the sentries' bodies over the massive outer wall of the kingdom. The clatter of their landing got the attention of a band of twenty Urmugoths who'd made camp on the moors a few hundred yards out from the North Gates.

The assassin lit a final arrow off a torch on the wall, and with a taunting glitter of satisfaction in those jet-black eyes, he fired it up into the sky.

Wrynne watched it fly on a great burning arc through the night—and land at the Urmugoths' feet. The brutes looked up with belligerent grunts, snorts, and guttural curses. A few jumped to their feet.

*Oh, no, please don't,* she begged the ruthless killer with a whimper in her sleep. *Don't do it.*

Her protests were futile.

Flipping the bow behind him again, he marched over and seized hold of the great wooden windlass that worked the gates. Putting his back into it, the broad-shouldered stranger carried out a task that usually took three men to accomplish. He opened the gates of the kingdom and then got out of there.

Meanwhile, the Urmugoth band drew closer to investigate their open invitation into Veraidel.

Before melting back into the forest shadows, the assassin paused at the tree line to make sure his mission was complete. He tugged the mask down, and she glimpsed his face, beautiful but sinister, saw the grim curve of his half-smile as he watched the Urmugoths come storming in. Then he vanished into the night.

*Wake up, NOW!*

Wrynne sat up with a loud gasp, her heart pounding.

For a second, she blinked against the morning sun, not sure where she was, let alone why she had the sudden premonition of danger.

The day was sweet and cool. The birds filled the air around her woodland bower with their carefree piping, and although she felt as though she had been run over by an Urmugoth stampede, she realized, thank Ilios, she'd made it home safe.

With a groan, she fell onto her back again, still half-asleep, but the motion as she did so brought an unexpected clank of metal beside her.

*Thaydor!*

As the memory of last night's ordeal came flooding back in a rush, she flicked her eyes open only to find two wee fairies peering down at her, hovering like hummingbirds mere inches from her face.

"Awake!" one called to the others.

"Finally!"

The rest came zipping over, crowding so close about that she could hear the soft buzz of their wingbeats.

"Saffron cakes?" they pleaded.

"With honey!"

"Miss Wrynnay, you promised! Get up! We're hungry."

"Good morning to you, too," she mumbled, wanting to be left alone, but there was much to do. "Thanks for getting me home," she added begrudgingly. "Now, if you don't mind, it's early—"

"Please, please, we've been waiting ever so patiently! Saffron cakes, now!"

"With honey! You promised!"

"Right, right, I know. Very well. But first let me check on my patient."

She looked over at Sir Thaydor. Apparently, they had lain side by side all night on her bed, unmoving, she fully dressed, he still clad in his armor.

Like the sepulchral figures of a knight and his lady carved in stone atop their tombs, united in death forever, she thought with a snort.

The question was, *was* he dead or had the *Kiss of Life* spell actually worked?

She was almost afraid to look. She bit her lip and pushed up gingerly onto her elbow, trying not to shake the bed at all. The fairies retreated a bit.

"Thaydor?" she murmured.

He was still out cold, but his color looked decent. She put her hand in front of his nose and smiled in delight when she felt the air moving in and out of his nostrils.

A tiny hand tugged a length of her hair. "Saffron cakes! Now, Wrynnay!"

"Ow! Shh! In a minute. Say, I have an idea. Why don't you go pick some wild berries and bring them back. I'll cook them into the saffron cakes for you. It'll be even more delicious that way."

With small gasps and an exchange of startled glances, they seemed intrigued by this suggestion.

"Strawberries?"

"Blueberries?"

"Mulberries?"

"Elderberries?"

"Stinkberries?"

"There's no such thing as stinkberries," Silvertwig said, rolling her eyes.

"Any kind you want," Wrynne said impatiently. "Go now and see what you can find."

They zoomed off in all directions on this splendid treasure hunt, except for Silvertwig, who just grinned at her.

"I owe you one," Wrynne whispered to her familiar.

Silvertwig curtsied in midair, then twirled up into the rafters of Wrynne's airy, pavilion-like dwelling and crouched down to watch the proceedings from above.

Wrynne stretched with a wince, sore all over from the mere empathic echo of sharing the paladin's experience of being so savagely attacked. He might be used to that sort of thing, but her whole body felt as though she had spent the night on the torturer's rack.

Things could have been much, much worse, however. She was just relieved that the fairies had kept up their end of the bargain and got her home safely. As she shuffled around barefoot to Thaydor's side of the bed, she wryly noted that the Aladdin stretcher had got away from her helpers after they had dumped her off on her bed.

It was hovering up by the vaulted ceiling of her bower, and she wondered with a sigh how she was going to get it down from there.

Then she approached Thaydor—a little apprehensively, in truth. She couldn't believe the champion of the kingdom was passed out in her bed.

Gingerly, she inspected his head wound. Blood still caked his tawny, sun-streaked hair, but to her amazement, the frightful gash was closed. His skull fracture was now no more than a small cut as his body mended itself with shocking speed, thanks to the potent magic she had dispensed to him.

Stroking his brow lightly with her knuckle, she was so happy to see his improvement she could've kissed him again.

Instead, she closed her eyes and thanked their god from the bottom of her heart for saving him.

It was then that Wrynne remembered her dream and the premonition of danger that had woken her with such urgency.

Furrowing her brow, she left Thaydor's side and went outside, to the edge of her retreat. In a shaft of sunlight, she closed her eyes for a moment and found the weary center of peace within herself. Then she conjured a sanctuary spell, channeling the Light out through her raised hands.

A mirrorlike wall of invisibility encircled her dwelling, hiding her little, round, vine-covered pavilion behind a cover of deep forest. The magical concealment spread out to envelop the sunny glade where her apothecary garden thrived, as well as the mossy stone steps that led down to the secluded pool at the bottom of the waterfall.

Once she had the sanctuary spell in place, it was easier to relax. Still troubled by the dream and the momentous events of the night before, however, she took a moment to splash her face and swallow a few mouthfuls of sweet, clear water.

Thaydor could probably use some, too, she thought, so she carried the pitcher over to his bedside and poured some water onto a fresh bandage. With a fingertip, she parted his lips slightly, squeezing a few drops of water off the bandage and into his mouth.

As she cleaned some of the dried blood and grime off his chiseled face, she pondered the two Thaydors that she had now encountered. The first was the same public image of the Golden Knight that everybody knew, the second, the brutal warrior she had seen last night.

The first time she had ever seen him, he had been riding at the head of the army, leading the men home from the Krenian Wars in a victory parade that wound through the capital. Though just a young novitiate at the time, Wrynne had been as breathless as any young girl at the dazzling sight of the golden-haired paladin, with the sun glinting off his armor and the legendary blade at his hip with which he had felled a thousand foes. His white warhorse, Avalanche—who was almost as famous as his master—had pranced proudly underneath him.

The flower of chivalry, the people's champion had smiled modestly and nodded to the adoring throngs as they threw pink roses at his feet.

The other Thaydor was the one she had met last night, the savage warfighter in all the awful truth of his calling, far from the victory parades. Mud and death, blood and sacrifice, unimaginable suffering, despair, and the constant prospect of dying alone, far from home.

She was so glad she had been permitted to save him from that fate. If anyone had ever deserved it, Thaydor did.

Deciding to make him more comfortable, she began carefully removing his armor. She needed to see how his other wounds were coming along anyway. First, she unbuckled his sword belt and then pulled off the tatters of his proud white surcoat.

There were countless buckles and straps and leather lacings all over him holding the confusing harness of his armor in place. A knight could not do all the pieces by himself, which made her suddenly realize he must have been traveling with a squire.

She wondered where his knight-in-training could have gone—and their horses, for that matter. She hoped no harm had come to them.

As she slowly and carefully took apart the metal man, she piled all the form-fitted plates of steel over by the wall.

Next came the chain mail. The hip-length coat of small metal links protected all the vulnerable joints between his armor plates. Her attempts to pull his deadweight upper body into a sitting position so she could then lift the chain mail up and off over his head were almost comical. She thought for sure the clinking noise of it would wake him, but he was still in a magic-induced slumber, his head flopping against her shoulder like a drunkard's, his muscled arm resting across her shoulders, half his weight sagging against her.

"Whoa!" She pushed him toward the bed when he nearly rolled right off it onto the floor. "Thaydor, cooperate, would you?"

He slept on, deep in dreamland.

Finally drawing the heavy coat of chain mail off over his head like a mother undressing her sleeping toddler for bed, she carried the coat of mail over to the pile by the wall and blew a lock of her hair out of her face. She marched back resolutely to her patient.

Under his chain mail, Thaydor was wearing a very fine, red sleeveless gambeson over a loose linen shirt, black chausses, and simple black leather shoes. She immediately checked his broken leg and then rolled up his sleeve to see his burned forearm. Both limbs had been miraculously healed.

She stared, amazed.

*Good show, Wrynne,* she congratulated herself. But now for the real test—the body blows to his chest and the arrow in his side.

She swallowed hard, as it was a good deal more personal undressing the warrior from his actual clothes rather than merely his tough metal shell.

Fortunately, she was committed to virtuous principles and refused to think improper thoughts, no matter how beautiful he was. Or how many women in the kingdom would have liked to get their hands on him like this.

Briskly reminding herself that she was simply a healer, she began unlacing his gambeson, a hip-length, vestlike garment of luxurious red wool. Its heavily quilted design was intended to help absorb some of the impact of armored combat.

She winced at how all his clothes were stiff with the drying crust of heavy bloodstains. She tried not think too much about what would have happened if she hadn't come along, and kept her hands busy with her task.

"Almost there, my friend," she whispered.

Parting the gambeson at last, she was finally down to his loose, ivory shirt—though the natural color of the linen was now mostly stained a brownish red.

"Now, let's have a look and see how you're really doing, shall we?" With that, she lifted his shirt and cautiously touched his skin.

She held her breath as she inspected his side where the arrow had pierced him. Nothing. Pushing his shirt higher, exposing his sculpted abdomen and powerful chest to the morning air, she marveled. How many broken ribs and injured organs had he sustained last night? And yet now there was no more sign of damage than some light bruising around his ribcage.

She rested her hand on his muscled stomach and gazed in wonder at his face, wishing he would wake up so she could tell him what a miracle this was.

That handsome face arrested her for a moment. Tilting her head, she granted herself the indulgence of a moment to study the comely specimen that he was. He had a rectangular face, clean-shaven, with strong, gentlemanly features; deep-set eyes under thick, tawny eyebrows; a crooked nose that alone kept him from being too pretty, having been broken a few times; sculpted lips that bespoke an unexpected softness; and rather a large chin that gave his face an air of implacable determination.

It was a very nice face, she decided. *And a quite impressive body to go with it.* But she shoved off that wayward thought, merely glad he was in one piece and on the mend. What a shame it would have been to lose him.

She cupped his cheek with a fond, thoughtful smile. "You are really lucky I was there," she murmured, but on second thought, recalling the Urmugoths' killing spree, she added, "And we're all really lucky you were there. Thank you, Sir Thaydor."

She bent and pressed a light kiss to his forehead, wondering how she could already feel so close to a man she barely knew. It must be the result of all they had been through together last night—or that mysterious, bonding side effect of the *Kiss of Life* spell that she'd heard about. Even so, she anticipated his waking with a certain degree of shyness. He was the Golden Knight, for pity's sake. Scores of women fainted when he smiled.

As she slowly sat down on the stool beside the bed, she wondered how long the Urmugoths' orgy of destruction would have lasted if Thaydor had not shown up. Why was he the only one who'd come to the aid of their province, though?

Why had the king not sent troops?

Everyone around here had just assumed that help was on the way, though, obviously, there was some sort of delay. Maybe word of their plight had not yet reached Veraidel's capital city of Pleiburg.

No one had dared ask whether King Baynard was purposely letting the barbarians run rampant through their midst.

Why would he?

But when she recalled the dream from which she had just awoken, a dark hypothesis began forming in the back of her mind. The man in her dream had not moved like some ordinary brigand, but with the expertise of long military training.

*Was* it a dream, just some random concoction of her brain, or something more? Premonitions were not her main gift, but what if Ilios had sent along her first official vision, revealing to her actual events that had taken place?

But why would someone, especially the king, purposely allow the Urmugoths in through the gates? Who would do such a thing?

She looked at Thaydor, wishing he would wake up so she could ask him. He knew a lot more about dealing with evil than she did. Including evil in high places.

Thanks to regular letters from her mother reporting on all the society gossip from the capital, Wrynne had heard something about how Sir Thaydor had fallen out of favor with the court. According to Mother's letter, the king's longtime champion had been sent off from the palace and back out into the world again on various quests as a wandering knight-errant, for the great crime of speaking the truth in these dark times.

Word had it he had looked King Baynard right in the eyes and rebuked him for his recent lawless behavior. Putting his wife, Queen Engelise, aside and taking his new mistress under the very roof of Lionsclaw Keep was bad enough, but more importantly, he'd been ignoring the Earls' Assembly and certain basic tenets in the kingdom's Charter of late, making up laws as he pleased.

It had got to the point where somebody had to say something. Not too surprising, Wrynne mused, that it should have been Sir Thaydor who had finally taken it upon himself to speak out. He was, after all, descended from one of the illustrious warlords who had founded Veraidel centuries ago, and his father, Lord Clarenbeld, held his rightful place in the Earls' Assembly, as one of the kingdom's noble peers.

Alas, such honesty on the son's part was not quite politic.

His thanks in exchange for his concern for their country was to be sent on a string of increasingly dangerous suicide missions. Almost as if someone was trying to get rid of him... But the Paladin of Ilios feared no one, and thankfully, his polite banishment from court had left him free to come to the rescue of the people of Mistwood.

Staring at him sleeping so peacefully, she remembered last night when she had reached his side, how he had been entirely surrounded by the Urmugoths. As if the whole thing were all a trap arranged expressly for him—a man too powerful in the army and too popular with the people to be allowed to live…

At that moment, she heard a sound that jerked her head up sharply. Tearing her gaze away from Thaydor, she scanned the woods beyond her bower, her heart in her throat.

To her astonishment, a handsome, black-haired knight came walking up the forest path. He was looking around in all directions as he climbed the hill, his armor clanking as he neared.

"Thaydor?" he called. "Thaydor, man, where are you? Are you out there? Answer me! Are you hurt?"

His deep voice sounded concerned. So why, then, was she suddenly sensing the presence of something darker? Perhaps not evil, outright, but a dark, cold ruthlessness.

She studied the newcomer, a powerfully built knight, tall and rangy, with midnight hair and charcoal-gray armor trimmed in black and red. The white surcoat draped over his armor was adorned with the head of a crimson ram.

Wrynne gulped.

The emblem of Xoltheus, the war god.

*Well, you're rather a scary fellow, aren't you?*

But when he reached the top of the path and turned toward her, scanning the woods, her eyes widened. She went stock-still, holding her breath when she saw his angular face.

The black-clad assassin from her dream!

She stared at him in shock, her heart thundering so hard she was sure he must've heard it as he ambled closer. She prayed the sanctuary spell held, but she was not taking any chances.

If she was right—if all this was a plot designed to murder Thaydor— then she had to protect him. Unconscious, he was easy prey. Her dream had warned this man knew no mercy. If her sanctuary spell failed and he detected their presence, she had better be ready with something.

With a hard swallow, she rose silently from the bed and picked up Hallowsmite. She could barely lift the longsword, but gripping the hilt with both hands, she crept over to the edge of her bower.

She stood guard in front of Thaydor as the red knight came even closer, glancing all around with a scowl on his face. She could see the annoyance in his coal-black eyes.

"Thaydor!" he called again.

Shaking his head in disgust, he finally gave up. He turned around, confused, and headed back down the path.

Wrynne stood there trembling. She did not exhale until the black-haired man was out of sight.

Her heart was still pounding as she slowly lowered the blade.

* * *

When Thaydor opened his eyes dreamily, soft morning sunlight filtered through the gauzy bed hangings and flooded the whimsical room in which he lay.

*Where am I?* he wondered, but he felt too good, and frankly too lazy to care. He sensed no threats. Well, that was different. *Huh.* Then he closed his eyes again with a sound of pleasure and, for a moment, simply listened to the birdsong and the lilting waterfall outside, and savored the luxurious bliss of not being in pain.

His body felt lead-heavy and so very comfortable, but for a twinge of hunger. Probably a good sign. As waking cleared his mind bit by bit, he realized he not only wasn't in agony anymore, he felt *fantastic.*

Like he'd just had one of the best night's sleep of his life.

He let himself doze a little longer in lavish self-indulgence, then gradually stirred. When he finally opened his eyes once more, he found himself in some sort of enchanted bower, possibly of elven design.

The bed in which he had slept like the dead had a partial canopy above him, draped with gauzy lavender veils. Sunlight streamed through windows framed by tendrils of ivy. As his leisurely gaze traveled around the room, he saw his armor piled by the wall and suddenly gasped, remembering his horrific injuries.

At once, he curled upward, cautiously touching his middle. He lifted his shirt and looked at himself. Not a scratch! He touched his head and felt the crust of dried blood in his hair, but his searching fingers did not find any wound.

Another memory struck. *My leg!* He whipped the coverlet aside and looked down warily at his legs. Both were present and accounted for, yet he felt no pain. He wiggled his toes to make sure everything still worked.

*Sweet Ilios. How is this possible?* He distinctly remembered taking a crushing blow from an Urmugoth mace to his left lower leg. The instant fracture had knocked him off his feet, but it didn't even hurt now.

Furrowing his brow, he swung his legs over the edge of the bed, placed his bare feet on the cool flagstone floor, and stood. His left leg was just a little stiff but seemed perfectly able to carry half his weight, as it ought.

Then he was confounded. *What is this place? Where am I?* He had a vague memory of a woman…or an angel? A shocking thought suddenly struck him. *Am I dead?*

*Is this Elysium?*

It felt like it, what with the rosy sunlight and the waterfall…

He scanned the bright, airy chamber, noting shelves on the walls laden with books and vials and colorful apothecary jars. The dainty table under the shelves held a lavish offering of food and drink. His mouth watered at the sight.

But as his gaze traveled around the room, he finally spotted her.

*You.*

He had seen her in his dreams. A silver-eyed beauty with skin like cream and long, thick hair, dark as blackstrap molasses, cascading over her delicate shoulders.

He remembered her, her gentle touch. He remembered her gazing into his eyes and telling him everything would be well, and even though he knew he was already dead, he had believed her.

Whoever she was, she was presently fast asleep in a large, pillowed, cocoon-like chair that hung from the ceiling on woody, braided vines. Sleeping in a little bird's nest on the shelf near her was a tiny sylph—or wait, was it a fairy? He could never tell them apart.

The fairy stirred, her eyes widening to find Thaydor on his feet. He lifted his finger to his lips, requesting silence with a smile. He did not wish to wake his pretty doctor.

That he was alive told him she must be a healer of great power. She had obviously waged a mighty battle to save him. *Let her rest,* he thought.

But he wanted a closer look. He had no memory of how he had got here and could not fathom how he was alive, but one thing was certain. This sleeping beauty was the one responsible.

Sitting up in the bird's nest, the fairy watched him cross the room toward the girl without a sound. Crouching down in front of her, Thaydor gazed reverently at his fair savior, reliving some very difficult memories. What little he recalled from the night of the battle…

With death breathing down his neck and the open portal to Elysium shining before him, he had seen her and thought she was an angel at first. The mistake was understandable. She was as lovely as the dawn. But then, in his half-dead state, he had noticed that she wore the necklace of the sister order to the Sons of Might, the Daughters of the Rose. This had immediately told him that Ilios had sent her, and from that instant, he knew that he could trust her.

She was still wearing it now.

For a long moment, he could only stare in fascinated wonder at her beauty, though, for his part, he was still covered in dried blood and mud like a corpse that had fought its way out of the grave. If she woke now and found this reanimated, undead creature gawking at her, she'd probably scream, he thought. But, then... *No. Not this one*, he decided with a faint smile. She had proved as brave as she was beautiful.

He recalled her cool-nerved courage when she had come to his side in the horror of that night. Most of all, though, he remembered her kindness. *Strange...* He didn't even know her name, yet for reasons that he could not explain, he felt deeply and mysteriously bonded to this stranger. The sight of her, so innocent and defenseless in her slumber, moved him.

Thaydor dragged his stare away from her, startled by the desire stirring in his veins, considering what he had just been through. Glancing at his armor by the wall and seeing the dents and scars and bloodstains all over it, he went very still. Verily, it seemed he had done nothing but fight for so long, until the metal death suit had become him.

But this fair stranger had freed him from it. He looked at her again in deepening speculation.

Keenly aware of her beauty, he could not deny the hunger to touch her and affirm the life and strength that still flowed in his veins. He shook his head. Alluring as she was, he usually had expert control over such impulses, much to the annoyance of the many temptresses who crossed his path.

True, he tended to get a little...frustrated after a battle, yearning for release, but he had never admitted that weakness to anyone. While other knights celebrated victory with a visit to the fleshpots of the city, he preferred to tame his libido with prayer and fasting, save it like a fuel for the next inevitable battle. This girl, though...

He drew his hand back, fighting the urge to caress her cheek.

Perhaps it was understandable after his ordeal that he should wake up needy and confused. This time, he had nearly died, and today he felt all strange and…new.

*Hmm.* He was eager to learn her name, talk to her, and give her his thanks, but one thing was certain. No man could make a very good impression on a female in such a condition. His lips twisted in amusement. Alive though he was, the smell of death still clung to him. And sweat, and grime, and Urmugoth filth.

In short, the famous hero stank.

Rising to his feet, he winked at the wee silver fairy as he turned away, ready to rejoin the living.

The tiny creature watched his every move, wide-eyed. Stomach grumbling, Thaydor helped himself to the loaf of bread, hunk of cheese, and pitcher of cider that the girl had obviously left for him there on the table.

Piling it all into his arms, he stepped out into the dappled sunshine and paused to take in his surroundings. The picturesque woods. The funny little cupola-topped building behind him. The burgeoning garden in the bright glade.

*I could still believe this is Elysium,* he thought with a mystified smile. Then he took a large bite of the bread and went on his way, chewing as he headed down the rock-hewn steps to go and bathe in the waterfall.

# Chapter 3
## Temptation

A short while later, Wrynne awoke and found the bed across from her empty. She lifted her head from the pillow with a small intake of breath and glanced around the room.

Thaydor was gone.

She scrambled to climb—and nearly fell—out of her hanging cocoon chair, clumsy with nerves to find that the time had already come to meet her patient, who was obviously awake. She hadn't expected him to rejoin the world so soon! At least not for another day, but it seemed she hadn't counted on her patient's nigh superhuman strength. Her heart pounded at the prospect of finally making his acquaintance.

Patting her hair, wiping the sleep out of her eyes, she brushed her wrinkled skirts smooth and somehow recovered her usual air of serenity before she stepped outside.

She glanced around. No sign of him. She spotted Silvertwig tending the garden and lifted her hands in an inquiring gesture. *Where is he?*

The fairy pointed toward the waterfall.

*Oh, that makes sense.* Wrynne swept back inside and grabbed a couple of clean towels for him, along with her basket of homemade soap and lotions and such, then she went back out and started down the mossy woodland stairs.

But she went motionless when she saw him standing under the cascade, his sleek, muscled body gleaming wet…

A shiver ran through her, and she bit her lip as a wave of stupid, girlish infatuation ran through her. She steeled her resolve.

He was her patient. She shouldn't look at him like that.

*But he's Thaydor Clarenbeld. He's gorgeous. He's famous. And important. A hero. And he's, well…*

*Stark naked.*

Then all rational thought danced away from her when she noticed the man's unmistakable joy upon finding himself alive.

Arms flung open wide, his face thrown back to the water, he welcomed the cascade tumbling over him, the rejuvenating spray of the water splitting over stones and misting him from all directions, falling in foaming circles around his lean waist.

She knew exactly how that felt, having done the same thing many times herself. And his simple, wordless exultation filled her with emotions she could not explain.

Wrynne's flustered gaze softened, seeing him like that. Her initial awe at the sheer might and heart-stopping beauty of his honed warrior's body turned to something deeper. She felt such a kinship to this man.

After that, it was not difficult anymore to go down to him. If Thaydor wasn't going to be embarrassed of the Creator's fine handiwork in making him, neither would she. Besides, the pool was up to his waist, providing him with at least some modesty. She continued down the steps.

Moving out of the main gushing current to the edge where the water flow was lighter, Thaydor turned and saw her coming. He stepped out of the pounding waterfall, hurriedly wiping water off his handsome face, then pushed back his blond hair with both hands.

Wrynne gulped at the play of chiseled muscles rippling down his chest and abdomen with the careless motion.

"Good morning!" he called.

*Would you please act normal?* she begged herself, smiling, and trying to hide her breathless excitement at having the Golden Knight as her guest.

"Sir Thaydor," she answered graciously, speaking in a loud voice to be heard over the rushing waters. "How are you feeling?"

"Wonderful, thanks to you!" He dove underwater; she watched him come swimming toward her with long, leisurely strokes as she walked over and knelt down on the sun-warmed stones around the edge of the pool.

Surfacing, he flung water out of his eyes, and rested his elbows on the stone ledge beside her. "So, tell me, lady. To whom do I owe my thanks?"

His blue eyes mesmerized her.

"To Ilios, of course," she remembered to reply after a second of vacant staring.

"And?" he prompted. "What is your name, if it's not too much to ask?"

"Wrynne. Wrynne du Mere, o-of the Daughters of the Rose. But that part you already know."

"My lady, I owe you my life. I am in your debt forever." He captured her fingers in his strong, damp hand and pressed a reverent kiss to her knuckles, his cobalt eyes blazing with utter sincerity.

As he held her gaze, she could have fallen right into those earnest sapphire pools. Indeed, she was rather sure the very heavens stood still.

She blinked herself out of her daze as a blush crept into her cheeks. "No debt. Don't be silly. Y-you don't owe me anything."

Withdrawing her hand from his gentle grasp, she strove to lighten the unnerving mood of his chivalrous intensity with a jest. "I would appreciate it, though, if you'd try not to die for a while. Twenty to one odds, Sir Knight? That's a bit extreme, even for you," she said playfully, realizing she had succumbed to nervous chattering. But so be it. She was not used to the presence of a large, naked man. "Unless you were trying to commit suicide by Urmugoth?"

He smiled and stood up, stretching his neck and shoulders this way and that, the lower half of him still blessedly hidden by the shadowed water. She tried not to look at the glorious sculpture of his abdomen and chest and massive arms gleaming with wetness…

"There are worse things than dying, my lady. I sent for reinforcements, but they tarried." He shrugged. "It had to be done. Besides, I thought if nothing else—" His words broke off. "Ah, never mind."

"What is it?" she asked, intrigued.

He snorted and looked downstream to where the winding brook babbled away into the forest.

"Well?" she prompted, unable to take her eyes off him.

"I guess I thought that news of my death might, I don't know, shake some in our kingdom out of their complacency."

"Mmm." She smiled wistfully at him, startled not by his never-ending bravery but by his willingness to die to make a point. "The sentiments are admirable, but I fear that price is much too high, if it would even work. Unfortunately, many of our countrymen are sleeping harder than you were."

He sent her a sharp sideways glance, looking pleased and a bit surprised that she shared his opinion of the current situation in their country. "How long have I been here?"

"Only since last night."

"Really?"

She nodded. "We're just up the hill from where you had the battle."

"Did I win?" he asked with a roguish glint in his blue eyes.

She laughed. "Don't you always?"

"Well, usually," he admitted with a boyish grin, then dove under the water and swam away.

She couldn't wipe the mystified expression off her face as she watched him cross the pool. When he popped out of the water several yards away, she pulled a bar of soap out of the basket. "Don't take this personally, but here." She tossed it to him with a teasing smile.

He caught it. "Thanks!" He smelled the lavender-scented soap before he began rubbing it over his body.

Wrynne stifled a small groan of pained admiration and looked away.

"Du Mere?" he mused aloud a few seconds later as he continued washing himself. "Any relation to the Building Baron?"

"Ah, yes. That would be my father." She cringed slightly even as she smiled, waiting for his reaction.

But to her surprise, Thaydor looked impressed. "You must be very proud. There's not a town of any size in the realm that doesn't have a guildhall, tower, aqueduct, or palace that one of your father's companies didn't build."

"Oh, yes, he's everywhere," she said wryly. "No one haggles harder with the stonemasons' guild. He's the bane of the timber merchants, too."

Thaydor laughed. "I respect a man who knows how to get things done. Especially one who came up from nothing and built himself a merchant empire with naught but skill and hard work."

"That is *very* kind of you," she said, grateful for the generous words coming from one the kingdom's most prestigious citizens.

Many highborn people made fun of her loud, fat, coarse-mannered father. They neither knew nor cared that the Building Baron had a good heart. Only that he had the subtlety of a siege machine.

Wrynne had been but a child when Mother had made it her mission to parlay Father's fortune into a title through generous political donations.

With a sigh, Wrynne shifted to a sitting position. Pulling her skirts up to her knees, she slid her bare feet into the water.

Thaydor watched her every move.

"Father has the energy of a bull, I'll give him that. And the tact of one," she added in amusement as she kicked her feet idly in the water. Then she nodded at the hill behind her. "He donated this acreage and the building to the church. Wanted to make sure I'd have a decent place to live so far from home."

"It's beautiful here."

"It is. Father had his best elven architect draw up the plans for the pavilion. It does rather miss the whole point of a vow of poverty, though, doesn't it?" she added in ironic amusement. "Not that I'm complaining. My superiors said it was all right." She shrugged. "I have it all to myself for now. But it will remain for whoever the Bastion sends next, once my assignment here is over."

"What exactly do you do out here all day?"

"Local healer." She leaned back idly, bracing her hands behind her. "I grow my garden. I cater to the fairies when I must and pray the hours—for people who play fast and loose with their lives," she added pointedly, splashing at him with a little kick.

"Well, thank you for the prayers," said the great soldier, splashing her back. "Still, if you're from town and used to all that bustle and noise, don't you find it dull out here? Seems like it could get a little lonely."

"Not at all. It's peaceful," she said. Even if he was right, she was not about to admit something as personal as that to a naked man. "Believe me, I'm more than happy here. It's better than the life my parents would have chosen for me if I'd hadn't pledged a few years' service to the Daughters of the Rose and had stayed in town instead. Talk about boring!"

"Why? What did they have in mind for you?"

"Oh, the usual fare. Advantageous marriage, trying to get appointed as a lady-in-waiting at the court. That sort of thing." She gave him a dull stare and shook her head. "Frankly, I'd rather pull some beggar's rotten tooth out of his head than spend a day making sure the train of some royal woman's gown is in place."

Thaydor let out a bark of laughter, a merry twinkle in his eyes. "Pull a beggar's tooth, eh?"

"My parents mean well. Truly. They are just very caught up in the cares of this world. My father ever builds his fortune, and my mother's greatest wish is to enhance our family's social status." She paused a beat.

"Why am I telling you all this?"

He ignored the question, smiling at her as if he knew the reason: that, yes, very well, she *was* often lonely out here, and longed for some other, educated person to talk to.

His blue eyes twinkled. "I have to say, you do sound like a bit of a mismatch to your clan. Maybe someone left you in a basket on their doorstep as a baby. Have you asked?"

She couldn't help laughing. "It would explain a lot. I should show you my mother's last letter, reproaching me once again for not becoming one of the temple priestesses in the city so I could wear the golden gowns and the jeweled headdress on the high holidays."

He chuckled as he washed himself. "So that's the way of it, then."

"You should've heard our arguments when I told her I wanted to join the Daughters for a while before settling down. Lots of girls from fashionable families do as much!"

"That's true," he said. "It's not like the old days when girls weren't allowed to do anything."

She nodded emphatically. "For me, this was a natural fit. I've always had spiritual inclinations, but when I discovered I had some healing ability, too, I wanted to go to university at the Bastion to develop it. Thankfully, my father gave me his permission."

"Your mother finally gave in?"

"Begrudgingly." Wrynne did an arch imitation of the bejeweled baroness. "'I suppose it is customary for a genteel family to pledge a son or daughter to the church, if they have an extra one to spare.' Thank goodness I'm the spare. There are four of us—I'm the second child. Boy, girl, boy, girl." She caught herself. "Here I am, boring you to death when you just barely survived last night. Forgive me—"

"Nonsense! I want to know all about the woman who saved my life. And besides, do you know how rare it is for me that I get to be just a person for once, having a normal, human conversation? I am so glad not to be discussing military strategy or politics... So talk to me!" he ordered in a jovial tone. "Tell me about these brothers and sisters of yours. What are they like?"

She gazed at him, intrigued. Then she sighed and shook her head. "All I can say about my brothers is that they're both very silly young men. My sister Juliana, the baby of the family—well, let's just say, she's exactly like Mama. Juliana would *enjoy* straightening a royal lady's train all day."

"What about your father?" he asked, clearly enjoying this.

His genuine interest drew her out, overcoming her usual shy tendencies. "Ah, he's a good sort. Blustery, but kind. He's very busy, but he'll always drop everything for us when we need him. In fact, I am sure that if word of the Urmugoth incursion has reached Pleiburg, Papa is already in the process of hiring the fiercest mercenaries in the kingdom to come and retrieve me. Whisk me home to safety, while the people I came here to serve were left behind to get slaughtered." She shuddered. "Thanks to you, our nightmare here is over now."

"And thanks to you, I live to brag about it."

They smiled at each other from across the water.

"Come, Sir Thaydor," she said softly, "everybody knows you don't brag."

In that moment, neither could look away.

Wrynne did not know what was happening here. Thaydor didn't seem to know, either.

He lowered his head with an almost boyish air of innocent wariness, then glanced at her again, his lashes starred with water droplets. But a very adult, male hunger had begun to simmer in his eyes.

The awareness that charged the air between them almost overwhelmed her. Cheeks flushed, Wrynne looked away, casting about for the lighter mood of a moment ago before she was tempted to do something very foolish.

Like slip her dress off and join him in the pool.

She ignored her racing heartbeat and strove for a normal tone. If he wanted to talk, let him talk. "So, what about *your* family?"

He looked relieved by the question as he started rinsing the soap off his arms. "My father, the earl. My sister, Lady Ingrid, the pest. She's seventeen."

"Same age as my sister! And what about your mother?"

He stiffened a bit. "Sadly, she passed away when I was a lad."

"Oh…I'm so sorry."

There seemed a world of meaning behind his terse nod. "Thanks."

She quickly changed the subject with a smile. "And why is your sister a pest?"

"Oh, so many reasons." His easy air returned.

"Such as?"

"Well, she calls me 'Clank,' for starters."

"Ah, because of the armor?" Wrynne asked with a chuckle.

He nodded with a long-suffering smile.

"And your father? Earl Clarenbeld, is it?"

"Known as the War Hammer. But the only thing my old man usually hammers these days is tankards of ale," he said fondly. "I swear, he can drink a Viking warlord under the table. Even then, he still makes more sense than most people I know. We're quite close. Oh—and I have a grandmother with fifty cats." He gave her a look that said, *Beat that.*

She grinned as he finished rinsing.

For some reason, she hadn't expected a head-bashing warrior like him to have a sense of humor, let alone a family that sounded as ordinary yet maddening as her own, given his exalted lineage.

He might be a hero, but he was still just a person, she mused. One who'd lost his mother at a young age, too. That she hadn't known. As she got to her feet, she wondered what had happened to the countess, but she didn't dare pry further. Still, she couldn't help wondering if perhaps this early loss was part of what drove him to protect everybody.

"Here you are." She handed him a towel, then turned away politely while he climbed out of the pool and wrapped it around his waist.

"I really must ask," he said from behind her. "How did you do it? Save me, I mean."

She turned around, recalling the harrowing moments of working the *Kiss of Life* spell on him.

"It must have been some incredibly powerful magic," he said. "Because look at me…"

*Oh, I'm looking. Believe me.*

"I'm not just healed from the other night. Even my old scars are gone. I rather liked some of those scars," he jested, his smile fading as he gazed at her. "How did you do this to me?"

Wrynne decided on the spot not to burden him with the details of her own little sacrifice. He was already under enough pressure, with the fate of the kingdom resting on his shoulders every other week. With his chivalrous nature, she didn't want him to feel any sense of obligation to her.

"Ilios did it, Thaydor. I was just the conduit."

"A very powerful conduit. I have some healing ability myself, but nothing like that."

She shrugged, smiled, and avoided his gaze. "I don't know how it works. I was merely doing my duty. Oh, that reminds me. Your clothes. Wait right there."

She walked over and knelt down by the pile of dirty, bloodstained clothes he had left on the ground. He watched her as she closed her eyes and sought the peace within herself until she tapped into the power of the Light.

Given the Daughters' vow to love and serve others, the novitiates of Ilios were taught only that white magic that furthered their missions. *Feed the Poor* could conjure a single healthy meal for a hungry person, for example, and *Clothe the Naked* could restore a beggar's tattered rags to new condition, both for warmth and to give him back his dignity.

*Heal the Sick* had, of course, been the core of her studies, but there was also *Comfort the Sorrowing*, which calmed someone hysterical with grief or terror.

Such works, her superiors taught, were the proper use of magic, not the wild-and-woolly, anything-goes conjurings of sorcerers, nor the purely selfish manifestations of talented but irresponsible witches. Enchantresses who followed other schools of magic could wish into existence a glamorous wardrobe of silk and velvet gowns for themselves and never even notice the ragged children they strutted past in the streets.

Fortunately, only a small percentage of the population was born with magical ability, but it could be bestowed by one's god in exchange for a pledge of service. For those with a certain spark of natural ability, it could also be taught, though such knowledge was highly guarded.

Under strict instruction at the Bastion, the headquarters and small home city of the Ilian church, most clerics learned how to channel the Light into manifesting simple things for others. These tokens were always to be offered as gifts from the Creator and proof of his love for all his children.

She felt the power flow out easily from her hands in a short, sweet blast, and when she opened her eyes, she smiled to see Thaydor's clothes all neatly folded in a stack, not a mark on them.

She rose and turned to him. "I'll leave you here to dress. Are you hungry?"

"No, I ate what you left out." His eyes suddenly widened. "I hope that was for me!"

She chuckled. "Of course it was. I'm glad you made yourself at home," she said warmly. "You're welcome to stay as long as you like."

"Hmm, thanks. I do have to get out there and find my horse. Although he's usually pretty good about finding me."

"Avalanche?" she asked in delight. "I should like to meet him. What about your squire?"

Thaydor's face fell. Such pain passed behind his eyes at the question that she wished she had never asked. "He didn't make it. I told him to stay back. They never listen. So it seems I've lost another one." He shook his head. "Do you have a shovel I could borrow? I have to bury the poor lad."

"Yes, I keep one for my garden. I will help you."

"It's grim work, my lady. You don't want to see what the Urmugoths did to him. *I* do not want for you to see it."

"Leave you to face such an awful task alone, when you're the one who knew him, trained him? No, it's too sad. I'm coming with you."

He walked closer to her, heading for his clothes. "I've buried plenty of friends, believe me."

"I'll bet you have. I'm just glad *you're* still with us. That was a near thing, down there on that field."

"It must have been very frightening for you. Thank you for what you did for me. I don't know what I would have done if you hadn't come. Well, actually, I do know," he said wryly as he came to stand before her.

She gazed up at him, ignoring as best she could the water droplet that slid sensuously down his chest at about her eye level. "You said you saw Elysium," she murmured.

He nodded with an otherworldly glow in his cobalt eyes.

"What was it like?" she whispered.

Her heart skipped as he cupped her cheek in his hand. "It was a lot like this," he said softly. Then he quite startled her when he leaned down and kissed her chastely on the forehead. "My lady, you can say that I don't owe you all you please. But I will never forget what you did for me. If you ever need…*anything*, you just let me know."

After this solemn promise, he drew back and gazed at her with such unnerving intensity that Wrynne couldn't draw a breath.

Her pulse galloped like a cavalry charge.

Routed, she looked away, fumbling with embarrassment. "Well, um, your recovery is remarkable in any case." She cleared her throat and tried not to let him notice that she, sensible Wrynne, Mother's steady daughter, could have fainted like a nincompoop. "You really feel no side effects at all?"

"Well, I wouldn't say that," he admitted with a rueful smile, stepping back to put a safer distance between them, considering he was still wearing nothing but a towel. "Nothing's broken anymore. There's not a scratch on me. And bathing seems to have made me human again, but to be perfectly honest? I feel like I rolled down a mountainside strapped to a boulder."

She chuckled. "Aches and pains?"

"A bit," he said pointedly.

She nodded. *I had that, too. It was miserable.*

"All things considered, though," Thaydor said, "I'll take it."

"You might not have to."

"What, you've got a potion for me now?" he asked as she went to retrieve her basket with the soaps and things.

"Not exactly," she said with a laugh, avoiding his gaze and dismissing the cautionary alert that flared in her mind. *Dangerous territory.*

*Nonsense, this is for healing purposes only.*

Yes, she could admit there was some sort of powerful attraction here, but neither Thaydor nor she were the sort of people who would let themselves be swept away by sensuality.

Others might indulge such passions, but they were both committed to Ilian principles of virtue and surely could be trusted to behave.

Besides, if her earlier hypothesis was right and the king was out to get him, who knew what sort of threat might show up next? She needed to get her patient back to his full strength and fighting capacity as quickly as possible.

*How* she was going to broach the subject of the king's possible treachery, she had no idea, let alone *when*. The poor man had only just awakened from a death-sleep and still needed to rest. She longed to protect him from such dire news at least for a little while, so he could finish healing.

But it might not be possible to wait. That red knight, the assassin from her dream, had made it all the way to her doorstep. He might still come back.

She lifted a bottle out of the basket, still unable to meet his gaze. "Come, lie down on your stomach," she ordered. "Let's see what we can do about those sore muscles. This should give you some relief."

"What is it?" he asked warily.

She studied the bottle. It was easier than looking in his eyes and reading in them the same tug-of-war that she was feeling. Want versus virtue. Practicality versus lust.

"Oh, it's my own concoction," she said with a shrug, trying to sound nonchalant. "A liniment oil made with comfrey and leopard's bane, a tincture of rue, and a little salve of myrrh. It helps relax strained muscles and tendons. Speeds the healing of bruises and other injuries. It'll make you feel better..." She stole a sideward glance to gauge his reaction. "I promise."

* * *

*Oh, I don't doubt it.*

Thaydor searched her lovely face through narrowed eyes, his heart pounding.

He finally decided she was not trying to seduce him and shrugged. "All right." What did he have to lose? "Here?"

She nodded. "You'll be warmer in the sun."

*This is a bad idea.* But his senses thrilled to the prospect of her soft, lovely hands on him. With the towel still wrapped around his waist, he lay down on his stomach on a sun-warmed stone beside the crystal pool, rested his cheek on his folded arms, and closed his eyes.

He heard the light brush of fabric as she rolled up her sleeves, then his eyes widened as he felt her step over him and lower herself to her knees, straddling him.

With a silent gulp, he shut his eyes again, breathless to find out what this strange girl might do to him next.

The warm oil dripped all down his back, and then she set the bottle aside with a soft tap. Then a deep moan escaped him as she began caressing it into his skin.

"Does that feel good?" she purred in amusement.

"What kind of question is that?" he retorted in a mumble, smiling from ear to ear.

She laughed. She had the most entrancing giggle. He wanted to stay here with her forever, this fey enchantress...

He kept his eyes closed and let her do her work.

He sighed with pleasure as her hands glided over his back, smoothing out all the kinks and knots with rhythmic strokes. He knew she was not trying to arouse him, but it wasn't long before her ministrations had him throbbing and as hard as the rock on which he lay.

He cursed himself. He usually had such perfect control over his desires! But his flesh was so grateful to his beautiful healer that every inch of him wanted to thank her in the most primal fashion.

*Stop it,* he ordered himself, to little effect.

*Sanctus solis,* this was embarrassing. As her thumbs traveled down the taut cords of muscle alongside his spine, he strove heroically to act normal.

No, not *normal.* A normal knight would've probably had her on the ground right now, ravishing her whether she liked it or not, but he was Thaydor.

And while, by his own choice, he did not have very much experience with women, he was acutely aware at all times that he was the standard of chivalry the younger knights aspired to.

Just like he'd promised his mother on her deathbed that he would be when he grew up.

The one who could be counted on to thrash any of the young bucks who behaved in the old, barbaric manner.

So, no. He must not entertain such thoughts. If the Paladin of Ilios, of all men, could not control his lust, then who the hell else would even bother trying?

He was ashamed of what he was feeling right now toward this obviously virtuous young woman. The possibilities running through his mind were anything but honorable.

*Either get yourself under control, man, or get the hell out of here now. This isn't you.*

Of course, if he married her, then he could...

"Thaydor?" she murmured, interrupting his silent argument with himself. "There's something I have to tell you."

"Uh, yes?" he rasped as she ended the massage, a fact that caused him a simultaneous pang of denial and a private sigh of relief.

As she went to wash the liniment oil off her hands in the pool, he took a deep breath to try to clear his head and shifted his position to conceal the evidence of his appreciation. His body was thankfully calming down, having let him know, in no uncertain terms, that he was very much alive. And more human than he liked to admit.

He cleared his throat. "What is it, Mistress Wrynne?" he asked, trying to focus and failing when he noticed the fetching shape of her backside as she leaned forward beside the pool and finished washing her hands.

"While you were asleep, I had a dream," she said. "Or possibly a vision. I'm not sure which."

"Oh?"

"I dreamed of a man all dressed in black, with black hair and coal-black eyes. He slipped into the gate tower, killed the sentries, and purposely let the Urmugoths into Veraidel."

He arched a brow.

"The only reason I am telling you this is because he then showed up here, in the flesh. The same man from my dream."

"Really?"

She nodded. "He came walking up the path calling for you. He seemed like a friend trying to find you, but I sensed a darkness in him. So I hid you and this place with a sanctuary spell."

He stared at her. "You dreamed of him, and then he appeared?"

She nodded.

"Has this sort of thing ever happened to you before?"

"No. There is one more thing," she said. "He wore the scarlet insignia of a ram emblazed on his surcoat."

"Oh!" Relief flooded him. "Don't worry, that was just Sir Reynulf, then. Sounds like the reinforcements I sent for finally arrived." He snorted. "A little late, boys. Wonder what took 'em so long."

"Sir Reynulf?"

"Second in command. The Bloodletter of Xoltheus. Sort of like a paladin, only, well, for the war god," he said in mild disapproval, leaving her to draw her own conclusions about what that might entail. "Reynulf probably saw the Urmugoth remains down there and wondered what the devil happened to me."

"So this man is your friend?" She stared intently at him. "Are you sure about that?"

"I don't know if I'd call him a *friend*. More of a colleague. Acquaintance." He frowned, puzzled. "Why?"

"Is he capable of doing what my dream showed?"

"Well, tactically, of course. It's not that difficult. The sentries are common soldiers, and by the middle of the night, anybody's tired. Plus, their attention is fixed on looking out over the walls, not watching for someone coming up behind them."

"Devotees of the war god are known for being ruthless," she said meaningfully.

"Yes, but they're loyal. The perfect soldiers. For them, virtue consists of victory and following orders, period."

"Exactly," she said, still staring at him, seeming to will him to put the pieces together on his own, but he would not.

Not when they made a shape that he stubbornly refused to consider. Reynulf was not what anyone would call a *good* man. He actually rather delighted in being a bit of a bastard, but no one could be that dishonorable. Not someone who had fought by his side many times in the past.

So he just furrowed his brow and shook his head at her obtusely. "What are you trying to say, Wrynne?"

Frustration flashed in her gray eyes. "Very well, since you're too chivalrous for your own good. I *do* think my dream was real and that this Reynulf *was* following orders. Someone told him to let the Urmugoths in on purpose, knowing you would come, and then held back the reinforcements that you asked for. Don't you see what this means?"

He just looked at her.

"Thaydor, I think the king is trying to kill you."

# Chapter 4
## Grim Work

Thaydor stared at her for a long moment. It wasn't as though the thought had never occurred to him. He had merely refused to entertain it.

Now that she had spoken it aloud, however, he simultaneously knew deep in his bones that it was true—and still refused to believe it.

He shook his head. "No."

"Thaydor, it's one thing to be loyal and another to be willfully blind," she said, gazing up at him.

"Why would the king want to kill me?" He stirred his finger in the air impatiently, gesturing to her to turn around so he could get dressed.

She did. He let the towel fall and reached for his braies.

"I heard you yelled at him," she said.

"I never yell. Well, except in battle."

"He's a king! You must have said *something* he didn't like."

He scoffed at her suggestion. "Do you think in all the years I've served His Majesty we've never exchanged harsh words before? I've never been one to bow and scrape or merely tell him what he wants to hear. Baynard knows that. He doesn't always like what I have to say, but he knows my opinion is usually valid. He trusts me."

Her back still to him, she rested her hands on her hips. Waves of her dark, silky hair danced down her back as she shook her head with a long-suffering air.

"Furthermore, I am the Paladin of Ilios," he clipped out, drawing on his chausses next and angrily lacing them. "I am bound by sacred oath to represent the just might of God upon this Earth. To strike at me—and in such a cowardly fashion!—is as good as a slap in the face to the Almighty himself."

"I'm not trying to upset you—"

"I'm not upset!" he insisted. "What you're saying cannot be true, that is all. Not after all I've done for him." He reached for his magically cleaned and mended shirt.

She sighed. "Let me ask you this," she said, obviously trying another approach. "When you were on your way here, did you hear of the king sending troops to our aid? Did you see any soldiers on the road?"

"No," he said defensively.

"And the knights that you sent for didn't come?"

"They were delayed! I'm sure there's a perfectly reasonable explanation."

"All right, then," she said, her patience fraying, "why were you sent away from the court? I've heard the gossip, but why don't you tell me in your own words so we can sort this out."

"It wasn't Baynard's fault." He scowled at her slender back. "It was because of his new advisor."

"Aha!" She spun around as he was lacing up the loose V-neck of his shirt.

"Aha, what?" he retorted in amusement.

"Who's his new advisor?"

"The Lord Hierophant, Eudo Vecbarin, also known as the Silver Sage." Thaydor curled his lip in disgust. "Ever heard of him?"

"Of course. High priest of the cult of Harmonium, worshippers of the false goddess, Efrena."

"Right." Thaydor was heartened but not surprised by her disapproving tone.

There were many religions in Veraidel, but to the followers of Ilios, theirs was the only true one.

The pagans regarded the Creator as the father figure in the pantheon of gods, but stalwart crusaders like Thaydor scoffed at the existence of any other deity. The other so-called gods were silly, made-up delusions, and the vapid cults they spawned were downright unhealthy, in his view.

However, since mercy and tolerance, charity and goodwill to one's fellow man were all principles of the Light, Ilios did not mind other faiths existing. Every human being had to find the truth for him or herself. So taught the church. Father Ilios was a big enough deity to be patient with his children and much too gentlemanly to force his worship on anyone.

Of course, it was not always easy for people with radically different values and views of the world to get along in society. There was inevitable friction that sometimes came to the surface. But it helped, in Thaydor's view, that Veraidel—and many other surrounding kingdoms—had long since adopted the Ilian church of the Light as the state religion. It had been the exclusive faith of a long line of Veraidel's kings, and explained the close alliance between the military arms of church and state.

His own order, for example, the Sons of Might, was aligned with the church, but pledged an oath of fealty to the king. When Thaydor rode into battle for Veraidel, he went with knights of other faiths arrayed around him, and he was glad to have them.

The red knights of Xoltheus, the war god, led by Reynulf, were particularly useful in combat. They were not afraid to die.

Of course, privately, to Thaydor, there was no such thing as Xoltheus. If he existed at all, he was probably a demon masquerading as a god. But Thaydor knew full well it was not his place to say so. In public, the servants of the Light were instructed to treat all men with brotherly respect.

The followers of Ilios were not *so* very virtuous, however, that behind closed doors they never complained or aired their exasperation with all these ridiculous idols their countrymen bowed down to.

The bloodthirsty war cult of Xoltheus, and its sister faith, the sex cult of Fonja.

The gloomy, self-flagellating hermits in the desert, followers of the sorrowing god, Irditay.

The mysterious wizards of Okteus, Lord of Shadows.

And of course, the cynics who believed in nothing at all.

But none were so obnoxious in his view as the condescending followers of Efrena the Silver, hermaphrodite goddess of harmony.

She—or he, on certain feast days—was called "the One" and depicted as a silver mist that symbolized the blurring of the boundaries between good and evil, male and female. She was neither; she was both. Silver or gray were her colors, because to her followers, nothing was ever simply black and white.

Indeed, that they had transcended good and evil was the Harmonists' most cherished fantasy. The silver cult was terribly popular with philosophers and thinkers like Lord Eudo—those who deemed themselves wiser than the common man and didn't deal much in the real world.

Thaydor didn't like them.

As pacifists, they certainly didn't get their hands dirty fighting wars, and why should they, when, to them, there was no such thing as an enemy?

They "loved" everyone without judgment, even the Urmugoths, whom they claimed were just misunderstood. After all, hadn't Veraidel once belonged to the Urmugoths before the warlord founders of the kingdom drove them out? Perhaps the Urms had a right to be angry.

Such was the nonsense the Harmonists spouted, Thaydor mused. Sometimes the Harmonists even sent missionaries out to the Urms to see if they could establish some sort of rapport. The fools were usually never heard from again. *Probably served up as supper.* He shook his head. He had often wondered if they regretted their good intentions while they were turning on an Urmugoth spit.

But so be it. They were entitled to their views, however unrealistic. To them, all was good, all was permissible, and if you disapproved of anyone's behavior, that was merely your biased, small-minded opinion. Those who clung to right and wrong as independent absolutes were merely rigid, backward remnants of a narrow-minded age on the wane.

Like the followers of Ilios.

It was rather amusing, though, he thought. Despite the Harmonists' bland protestations of loving all men the same, they couldn't *stand* the Ilian faithful, because the Light's adherents were not shy about refuting their dangerous desire to conflate good and evil. Ironically, the only real sin to a Harmonist was offending someone's *feelings* by, for example, speaking a hard truth.

In a forceful tone of voice.

Like Thaydor had done to the king and, indeed, to the Silver Sage himself.

"Surely you're not telling me the king has converted to Harmonism?" Wrynne asked darkly.

"I wouldn't say His Majesty's *converted*. At the end of the day, I don't think he really believes in anything." Thaydor sat down heavily on the stone stairs to put on his shoes. "I don't know how much you've heard about recent events in the city way out here, but the trouble started when His Majesty added the worship of Efrena to his faith in the Light. The first king in generations to do anything like that."

"Yes, that much I knew," she said, nodding. "But I never heard why he did it."

"Lord Eudo convinced him that showing a more open attitude would make him more popular with the people. So he bit."

"What does he care about being popular with the people when he's king?"

Thaydor shook his head. "He cares. He's thin-skinned, vain. Criticism of any kind stings him. A petty weakness, if you ask me. But Lord Eudo spotted it and found a way to take advantage of it. I've been away for quite some time now, but I'd imagine his influence over the king is probably near total at this point."

Wrynne brought over his gambeson and held it up for him to slip his arms through. "Perhaps we shouldn't be too surprised. Efrena's probably the perfect religion for those involved in politics," she said cynically as he shrugged the vestlike garment into place and began buttoning it. "No good and evil? The ends justify the means? Gives people the liberty to do whatever they want with a clean conscience."

"Well, Baynard obviously didn't think the thing through," Thaydor replied. "Because once he had bowed down to Efrena, then, by the very nature of the Harmonists' open philosophies, he was trapped. All the other cults suddenly started clamoring to be shown the same respect. He didn't want to give offense. The red warriors demanded similar homage paid to Xoltheus, and the king hardly dared cross that lot. So he trotted over and paid his respects at the Temple of War." He shook his head, still struggling to believe the words himself.

"That was all the harlots of Fonja needed to see before they, too, were clamoring for His Majesty to come and participate in their unseemly rites. From what I hear, he went happily."

"Not Fonja, too!" she cried, paling. "They're so base! And he's married! It's bad enough he has a mistress in the castle... Oh, poor Queen Engelise."

"I'm sure Lord Eudo cleared away any niggling guilt His Majesty might've felt about cheating on his wife by reminding him of the Harmonist view that marriage is outmoded. No person can 'belong' to another and all that. Last I heard, Queen Engelise was leaving Veraidel for a while to visit her parents in Aisedor. Frankly, we'll be lucky if the King and Queen of Aisedor don't recall their ambassadors after this insult to their daughter. I can't say what Baynard might be thinking. But I suppose few think men think clearly around the likes of Sana. The royal mistress, after all, *is* a top temple prostitute of Fonja."

Wrynne's jaw dropped. "The *mistress* is a Fonja cultist? Heavens, I didn't know *that*." Her words were barely audible, she was so shocked.

He nodded. "When he's not wasting the day away in that little schemer's bed, he's got the Silver Sage whispering in his ear, telling him what to think about everything."

"What of the Golden Master?"

It was the title given to the oldest, wisest, highest-ranking priest and prophet of the Light—the Ilian church's spiritual leader. Golden Masters had been guiding the kings of Veraidel for ages, and most of the surrounding kingdoms, too, like the queen's elegant homeland of Aisedor, to the west.

Thaydor shook his head. "His Excellency has been shut out of court affairs. They don't dare send him packing, but they never seek his counsel."

Wrynne shuddered, staring at the ground as she pondered all he had told her. "I had no idea things had got so bad."

"Well, they have, and to answer your original question, that's why I had to say something, had to speak up. And that's why I got thrown out. Suffice to say the Silver Sage and I don't get along." He paused. "From what I've seen traveling around on the *stupid* assignments and futile quests I've been given for the past few months, the people are already starting to follow the king's idolatrous new example. They'll bring divine wrath down on all of us if they're not careful," he muttered.

Wrynne dragged her hand through her hair and shuffled over to sit down beside him on the cool stone step.

They looked at each other matter-of-factly.

"So with all this going on," she said, "with the king bending laws to suit himself, worshiping idols, sleeping with a temple prostitute, and the whole moral order of the kingdom turned upside down, you can't bring yourself to believe that someone in the palace might want you dead?"

He grumbled out a sigh, propped his elbow on his knee, chin on his fist. Then he looked at her skeptically. "Tell me why. Because I don't deserve this."

"Of course you don't deserve it! But you're a threat all the same."

"No one is more loyal to this kingdom than I am! I have my faults, but I am nothing if not steadfast."

"Exactly! You're from a long line of patriots, and as paladin, you're the representative of Ilios on this Earth—"

"No, the Golden Master is."

"He's not the one the people can relate to," she insisted. "You're the king's champion—"

"*Was*, I think," he interrupted. "I'm actually not sure if I still am or not."

She went on as if he hadn't spoken. "Moreover, people know you've often been the voice of reason in the kingdom's affairs. Remember that time the Krenian Wars nearly broke out again, and you managed to talk both sides out of it?"

"It was a stupid misunderstanding that would have needlessly cost lives," he said with a dismissive wave of his hand.

"A man of war with a heart of peace," she said, staring at him and rather embarrassing him with her frank remarks. "When you talk, the kingdom listens. All the other *knights* listen. The army listens." She laid her hand on his shoulder. "You're dangerous, my friend, and I'm not talking about your skill with a sword. If I were the king and I didn't want to hear criticism of my new life, I'd want to kill you, too. Sorry," she added with a shrug.

Thaydor clenched his jaw and sat back, resting his elbows on the stone step behind him. "So, what, then?" he mused aloud a moment later. "The king told Reynulf to open the gates and let the bloody Urms in, knowing I would come?"

"Or the Silver Sage told him to do it."

"Because that's treason," he said through gritted teeth. "Innocent people died. If this was done deliberately, someone needs to hang."

"I'm sorry," she said, and hesitated. "I've never had a vision before. I probably shouldn't have brought it up so soon. You just survived a terrible ordeal, and we don't have any proof yet. Aside from Sir Reynulf showing up here, it's all just conjecture at this point."

"You don't have to soften it for me. I appreciate your honesty and your...looking out for me." He put his arm around her and pressed a quick, brotherly kiss to her head. "Thank you."

He released her and stood. "Think I'll go have a look around the North Gate. There could be witnesses out there who saw what happened the night the Urms got in. That might be able to either corroborate or disprove your vision."

*Of course, if it is Reynulf's doing,* he thought, *he wouldn't leave survivors.* He wouldn't be that careless.

Wrynne put her hand out, and Thaydor pulled her up. "I'm coming with you. Just let me get my boots. I'll bring the shovel," she said as she sprang up onto the next step. The higher step put her on eye level with him. "We can bury your squire on the way."

"My lady, I cannot allow you to put yourself at risk—"

"Nonsense, we're in my territory. I know the people here. They're country people, Thaydor. They don't easily trust outsiders, even famous heroes," she said, giving him a playful poke in the chest. "If there *are* any witnesses out there, they're likely terrified, but they'll talk to me. You need me. Besides, I know the way—Clank!"

"How now!" he protested with a playful frown as she borrowed his sister's nickname for him.

She turned around, skirts spinning gracefully, and ran lightly up the steps.

"I'm beginning to think you're a bit of a pest, too," he called after her.

Her airy laughter trailed down to him. With a mystified smile, Thaydor shook his head, barely knowing what to make of her.

\* \* \*

As it turned out, Thaydor was right. She did *not* want to see what had happened to his squire. But it was too late now. His name had been Eadric of Hazelmore, nineteen years old, and his body had been strewn about in six main pieces across the far end of the farmer's field.

It was the first stop on their day's errands, and more horrible than Wrynne had anticipated, but at least there was no sign of Reynulf or his men.

The Urmugoths, however, were far larger by the stark light of day than she had realized. Sweet Ilios, if she had been able to see them clearly that night, she doubted she would have had the courage to go to Thaydor's side, especially since a few of them had still been alive then.

Wrynne braced herself. The only thing uglier than an Urmugoth, she decided as her stomach churned, was one three days dead—bloated and discolored, pecked upon by ravens and crows, its entrails hanging out.

The black birds swirled back, fluttering off as Wrynne walked out onto the field alongside Thaydor. Both shielded their noses from the ghastly stench—she with her scarf, he with his sleeve.

"I'll get some of the men to burn the bodies when we go down to the village," she said.

"I'm surprised they haven't already done so," he answered. "It's not healthy."

"They've probably been busy burying their own," she said sadly.

"As must I." He shook his head in bitter regret, eyes narrowed as he scanned the field. "I told him to stay back," he muttered. "They got a hold of him over there." He pointed across the otherwise green, growing field of alfalfa to the far end where a wild apple tree grew. "You should go back and wait at the edge of the woods. This won't take long." He took a step forward, but she stopped him with a hand on his arm.

"I'll get him. You dig the hole." She handed him the shovel; he looked at her in astonishment.

"No."

"Thaydor, please." She gave him the spiky-rayed metal sun sculpture—a symbol of Ilios—that she had taken off the wall of her home to mark the boy's grave. Whisking off her cloak, she balled it up and set it aside on a clean patch of ground. "I cannot let you do this. It's too much."

He scoffed. "You're a lady—"

"I'm a *doctor*," she shot back, and despite her own doubt, added firmly, "I can do this. Now pick a spot to bury him and dig."

He arched a brow at the order.

Brooking no more argument, she set off across the field with the boy's makeshift burial shroud tucked under her arm—one of the old, donated, wool blankets that she kept on hand to give to the poor.

Fixing her scarf across the lower half of her face, she pulled on her old pair of gardening gloves as she marched toward the tree where his squire had been murdered.

From behind her, she could feel Thaydor watching her with incredulity. But when she glanced defiantly over her shoulder, he shrugged, shook his head, then idly twirled the shovel like a weapon, as though waiting to see if she would actually get through the gruesome task.

Leaving her to reap the fruits of her own stubbornness, he glanced around for a good gravesite, chose one by the edge of the woods, and glanced at her again and started digging, his foot braced atop the spade to help break up the soil.

*Humph*. Wrynne looked forward again, steeled herself, and, upon reaching the far end of the field, spread the blanket out on the ground. This done, she willed her stomach not to revolt as she went about the task of gathering up the pieces of poor, young Eadric.

With her pulse pounding in her ears and prayers spinning through her dizzied head, she got through it by pretending the arms and legs in various locations were just logs she was clearing off the field, stacking into a pile on the blanket. She refused to let herself notice the teeth marks where the Urmugoths had bit off chunks of him, probably just for spite.

She looked at the head from the corner of her eye, but wasn't ready to collect that yet. Her breath came in jerky little gasps. It was hard enough getting herself to grab the bloodied torso by its belt. It was heavier and messier than the logs, but there was no way she was letting Thaydor do this. He had already been through enough.

Besides, she owed him. Everybody, all of Mistwood, owed him. He was the only who had cared about them. Not even their own king, to whom they paid their bloody taxes, gave a fig. The knight ought to be spared at least this much.

She had dragged the squire's torso halfway to the blanket before she had to step away, whirl around, and drop to all fours, retching her guts out.

Not that she had anything to vomit. Once she had realized this task awaited, she had wisely decided to skip breakfast this morning.

She closed her eyes, so absorbed in trying to steady her stomach that she didn't notice Thaydor until he'd stalked past her, grabbed the torso roughly by its belt, and heaved it onto the pile of body parts.

Wrynne gagged at the wet, squishy thud it made when it landed.

"Where's his head?"

"Over there." Wrynne had not even noticed she was crying until she looked up, pointing with a sob. She started to stand. "I'll get it. You shouldn't—"

"Ridiculous woman!" he exploded at her. "Go sit down before you *fall* down."

She stopped crying abruptly, quivering with nausea. "I was only trying to help."

"That's what he said," he growled.

Thaydor walked away, picked up the head, and stoically laid it on the pile. Wrynne buried her face in the crook of her arm and turned away, weeping. With quick, efficient motions, Thaydor wrapped the blanket around the lad's remains, then bound the gory package with the garden twine she had brought for that purpose.

She was left alone as he picked up the macabre bundle, and, using the knotted twine as a handle, carried it off to the hole like it was no more than a sack of laundry.

Sitting on the ground, queasy and still crying a little, Wrynne pulled off her old garden gloves and threw them, then drew her knees up to her chest. She wrapped her arms around her bent legs and rested her forehead on her knees, wishing there was a way to wipe those images from her mind.

Meanwhile, Thaydor lowered the bundle into the grave. A rivulet babbled nearby, just inside the woods, and ran along the bottom of the mountain. He went over to it and washed his hands.

Remaining there for a moment, he splashed his face. Then he stood and walked back out to Wrynne, bringing her some water so she could do the same. He poured what little was left in his cupped hands when he reached her across her brow. It ran down over her eyelids and her cheeks like tears.

"I should have never let you..." he started. "I didn't think you'd really do it!"

"I was trying to spare you for once!" she sobbed out.

"I'm a knight, Wrynne. Death is my stock in trade. How are you feeling?"

*Awful.* It was strange and unsettling to realize that she couldn't heal herself anymore because of the decision she had made on this very field. "I-I'm all right."

"Then why are you crying?" he asked softly, smoothing her hair with a cool, damp, comforting hand. "You didn't even know him."

Fresh tears welled up in her eyes as she met his gaze. "It could have been you."

He pulled her into his arms when she started crying again at the horror of what the boy had gone through. Hushing her, he stroked her back and held her for a while. "I appreciate the gesture, demoiselle," he said at length, "but don't do me any more favors, all right?"

She pulled back and smiled ruefully at him through the last of her tears. *If you only knew.*

* * *

A while later, the body had been sprinkled with garden lime and the hole had been filled in. They marked the grave with the sun of Ilios, then knelt side by side next to it and prayed aloud the prayers for the dead.

They had no sooner finished reciting the solemn verses commending the squire's soul to Elysium when they heard the rhythm of galloping hoofbeats approaching from behind.

Wrynne instantly thought of the red knight and glanced over her shoulder in dread, but Thaydor rose to his feet with a grin and gave a loud whistle. Over the rise, cantering toward them, was the most magnificent white horse Wrynne had ever seen.

"There he is! Good boy!"

Avalanche nickered to Thaydor as he swept across the field, his ivory mane and tail streaming out behind him. Barreling at them like he'd run them down, the white stallion practically bounced to a halt right in front of the tall man and began to nuzzle him.

Thaydor greeted his trusty steed with an affectionate caress on his snowy-white muzzle and a pat on the neck. "Where've you been, boy? Out having fun?"

Wrynne hung back, awestruck. "He's beautiful."

"Come," he said, gesturing her forward. "He won't hurt you. You said you wanted to meet him."

The towering horse snorted but stood docile as Wrynne stepped toward him, venturing a touch on his shoulder.

"Avie," Thaydor said, "this is Lady Wrynne."

She smiled. "He's so soft. Why isn't he wearing any tack?"

"I ordered Eadric to set the horses free once this fellow did his part. Avie helped me lead the Urms away from the village. They can't resist a chase." He scratched the horse affectionately behind the ears. "Fast as he is, he got me a good head start. I jumped off and got into position. No point fighting on horseback when the Urms' favorite weapon is the poleaxe, after all. Before they caught up, I sent the horses off with Eadric. If anything went wrong, I didn't want my ol' mate ending up as the Urms' supper."

She winced at the thought.

Thaydor glanced around. "I wonder what happened to Eadric's bay. Where's Polly, Av? Is she alive? Did someone steal her?"

In reply, the warhorse rested his chin on Thaydor's shoulder like a giant dog. Wrynne laughed. Thaydor chuckled and gave the horse an affectionate, one-armed embrace.

"Silly old thing. You should see him in battle. You'd think it was a different horse. Vicious. His capriole can knock out four enemies at once." He flashed a smile. "Less work for me."

"I don't want to talk about battle anymore, please." The terse words escaped her rather more rudely than she had intended. "Sorry," she mumbled.

"No, *I'm* sorry." He sent her a regretful glance. "I'm a fool. Let's get out of here, shall we?"

She nodded.

Life was for the living.

* * *

Their next stop was the tiny village of Buckby, less than a mile away.

"I'm going to go talk to my neighbors," Wrynne said. Thaydor nodded, glad to see her color back to normal. Those nauseating moments in the field had left her quite ashen.

"I had Eadric hide our supply wagon in the woods beside the road down that way when we first arrived. I'll go find it, saddle Avalanche for our trip to the North Gate, and join you in a few minutes."

She nodded, and they went their separate ways. Avalanche followed him.

It did not take Thaydor long to find the wagon parked among the trees and hidden with some greenery. Usually Eadric's bay, Polly, served as their draft horse, but his squire had unharnessed the mare when they had arrived, and now she was nowhere in sight.

What mattered, though, was that neither the Urmugoths nor the locals had discovered his store of supplies. The wagon's wooden bed was loaded up with Thaydor's other weapons and a couple of spare shields, the horses' tack and feed, the men's bedrolls, extra clothes, and various other supplies, such as food and water. They had a couple of holy books, as well as a small purse of gold coins.

He moved the supplies he needed out to the grassy edge of the road, then carried Avalanche's saddle over and set it down, too. From this vantage point, he had a clear view up the road into the hamlet, where he saw Wrynne surrounded by traumatized peasants.

He paused and watched from a distance as the frightened, weeping people gathered around her. He was mightily impressed to see her calming and comforting them, as if she had not been in tears herself twenty minutes ago. It was the sort of thing his mother would have done.

While Wrynne tried to pass along the solace of the Light, Thaydor found that their weeping only made him sadder and angrier.

*If she's right and you did this to these people, Reynulf, I will make you pay.*

With an ache in his heart for what those poor country folk had been through, he turned his attention to the task of brushing and then saddling his horse. The animal's warm, steady presence helped him recover from his own private ordeal. Returning to the site of his near-death had been a little more difficult for him than he had let on. He had hid it from Wrynne, but he felt sad and sick and rather miserable after revisiting the gory scene, and facing up to the depressing fact, once again, that this was his life.

Every battle took a little piece of his soul. A part of him mourned for every life he snuffed out, even if the enemy deserved it.

The greatest mystery to him was why he always survived. The only explanation seemed to be that Ilios must have some sort of plan for him. Glancing toward the town again, he wondered if that plan involved Wrynne. It really was remarkable, how natural it felt to be with her. As if she were already a part of him somehow.

Too bad the people around him tended to die.

No, she was better off without him.

*Unless more Urmugoths get through the gate*, he thought, furrowing his brow. In which case, the safest place for her was right by his side so he could protect her. Provided she did exactly what he said at all times.

*And how likely is that? She's as stubborn as I am.*

Besides, if she was right and the king *was* after him, then he was a target. She should keep away from him for her own good.

He returned to the wagon, dug a small, leather-bound book of poetry out of his pack, and tucked it inside his gambeson. It was the only thing that ever really helped when he got into this dark, troubled mood. Then he wasted no more time and went to her aid in the overwhelming task of trying to comfort and encourage the entire ravaged community.

When she turned and saw him approaching, relief flickered in her deep gray eyes.

"Here he is, our hero," she announced as Thaydor walked into the village, leading Avalanche by the reins.

The title made him flinch, because if only he had got here a little sooner, maybe he could have saved more of their family members. But he gave no sign the word bothered him. These days, people needed something, someone to believe in.

He knew what was expected of him.

He summoned up a reassuring smile as he greeted them, but as the mourning peasants crowded around him with tears and thanks, he soon found that both he and Wrynne had their work cut out for them here.

Wrynne had not expected Thaydor to be as good with people as he was with a sword, but she quickly learned that he was even more of a knight *out* of his armor than in it.

He gathered the peasants of Buckby close with comforting words. As they huddled round him, he put his big, strong arms around their shoulders as if he could hug twelve of them at once. He dried an old lady's tears. He let the shaken men recount every detail of how the Urmugoths had ransacked the place before he had drawn them away.

While Wrynne went from cottage to cottage healing people who had been injured, Thaydor helped the men lift a roof beam of a wrecked house back into place. He let the youngsters pet Avalanche, and then, at one mother's shy request, he knelt down and had a little talk with the children who'd been having nightmares ever since the Urmugoths had stormed into their lives on that terrifying night. Many feared they might come back.

"I promise you, I got them all. Every last one of 'em," he told his wide-eyed audience. "Want to know how I did it?"

Wrynne leaned in the doorway of the cottage where he'd gathered the children for their official meeting, listening.

"With this. Hallowsmite." He pulled his sword partway out of its scabbard.

The children oohed and ahhed.

"'Tis a holy blade filled with white magic and blessed by the Golden Master himself. You see? Those ugly brutes didn't stand a chance." He looked earnestly from face to face and cupped one little girl's apple cheek. "You have nothing to be afraid of anymore. Those monsters are all gone now. I killed 'em dead, and next, I'm going to send for a retinue of the warrior monks to guard the gates forever. They'll keep you safe, and so will I. You do believe me, don't you?"

The room was quiet. The children seemed in awe of him.

"Everybody knows the Golden Knight would never tell a lie," Wrynne spoke up serenely from her post in the doorway.

The wee ones pondered this, but they must have felt better, for they started fidgeting and bouncing around where they sat.

"Sir Thaydor, did you really kill a dragon once?" a boy of about ten piped up in the back.

"Well, yes, but it wasn't very big."

"What color was it?"

"Green. With horns."

Wrynne smiled as the wee ones proceeded to interrogate the Golden Knight on his various adventures. He answered half a dozen questions good-naturedly, but he clearly did not know what he was in for. He soon learned the children's curiosity knew no bounds. As the interview dragged on and on, he sent her a glance over his shoulder that said, *Help!*

She just grinned roguishly and left him to bear the burden of his fame, slipping outside again.

There was one more home she had to visit. Yasen, the desperate husband, met her outside the door to his tiny thatch-roofed cottage, waiting anxiously for her.

"It's my wife, Britheva. I had to restrain her." His eyes filled with tears. "She tried to take her own life after those monsters killed our little Sunnhild. Can you do something for her?"

Wrynne froze and looked at him, taking the news of the infant's death like a knife in the heart. "Sunny's...dead? I-I hadn't heard." She had delivered that babe a mere three months ago. "How? W-what did they...?"

"I didn't see it, thank Ilios," he whispered, trembling. "The neighbors tell me one of the creatures hurled the babe against a wall. She fell and died instantly. Her neck was broken." He looked away. "At least she didn't suffer."

Wrynne closed her eyes and leaned against the house, taking a moment to steady herself.

Oh, for a minute, how she wished she were a knight and could have slain those monsters herself. What on earth was she to say to poor Bri?

Laying hold of all the faith she possessed, she took a cautious step into the one-room cottage, ready as she'd ever be to face the infant's shattered mother.

The hollow-eyed woman, her bandaged wrists tied to her bedposts for her own safety, took one look at her and turned her face away in despair. "Get out. You're not welcome here."

"Oh, Britheva—"

"Get out, I said! Your god has abandoned me! I curse him! He's a liar, and he doesn't care..."

Wrynne went over to her anyway, made sure there was nothing on hand that she could use to harm herself, and untied her. "I am so sorry," she whispered.

Britheva crumbled. Wrynne embraced her and wept with her, begging her not to hurt herself.

"But why?" the woman wailed. "Why did Ilios do this to me? To punish me? To teach me something? What kind of a lesson could there possibly be in—"

"Ilios didn't do this! No, Bri. Listen to me. You must never think that! It was evil that did this to your child. Don't let it destroy you, too."

"It already has."

"You've got to fight."

"How? Who? With what? I have nothing."

"Defy the darkness with Light. Conquer evil with love. That is the only way." She gripped her hands, both women in tears. "All is not lost. Sunny is with Him now, safe in His care. And you still have five more children and a husband who need you. Love them with all your heart, even if it's broken. That is how you win," she whispered, trembling. "That is how you hold up your daughter's precious little light. You don't give up—ever."

"I miss her so much."

Wrynne held her as she worked the *Comfort the Sorrowing* spell to grant the woman some relief in the still-raw shock of her unspeakable loss.

She left Britheva sleeping peacefully when she stepped outside, but she herself was in tears once again and feeling wholly inadequate.

Thaydor was waiting outside the cottage for her, and looked taken aback when he saw her face. A few more people asked for healings for small cuts and bruises, but he waved them off.

"Lady Wrynne has had enough for one day. She's done all she can do. She'll be back in a few days, perhaps. Good luck to you all now. We must be going."

\* \* \*

Thaydor knew it was time to get her out of there, now. To him, Wrynne looked lost, drained, and utterly wrung out. These people would use her up until there was nothing left of her, and he could not allow that to happen. He had come to collect her anyway, but had not realized she had saved the most painful task for last.

Though her tears had stopped, she was pale and quiet as he lifted her up onto Avalanche's withers and then swung up into the saddle behind her. He secured her with his arm around her waist as she settled into place, seated sideways across his lap.

The people waved goodbye as he hurried his horse out of the village at a fast walk, heading north on a green path between two fields.

They rode in silence that was only broken when Wrynne had to tell him to turn right at this path, and left at that huge old oak tree, and then cross through those woods. Other than that, they were too drained to talk. Their physical contact was enough. Indeed, if he had been wearing his armor, he would never have been so attuned to her softness.

But on that sunny afternoon, riding through the dappled woods, there was no safe casing of steel to separate their bodies. He could feel every line of her and she of him.

After a time, she laid her head on his shoulder and closed her eyes, seeming to take as much comfort from their close embrace as he did. To be sure, the warm, supple yielding of her body was something more potent than poetry for drowning out his anguish.

He savored it, seeing no need to discuss the practicalities he'd seen to in her absence. He had convinced some of the men from Buckby to go burn the Urm bodies. It needed to be done, plus, he had a feeling it would make them feel better—some small measure of revenge to put the filthy creatures in the ground.

They would be keeping an eye out for his other horse, too. Actually, he had a sneaking suspicion that somebody had already tried to claim Polly as the no-longer-needed property of the deceased. Now that they knew Thaydor was looking for the horse, he was confident that whoever had taken the bay mare would bring her back.

He had also asked if anyone had heard anything about how the Urms had got through the gates. The villagers had no information on that point, but they did say that Reynulf had been there with half a dozen soldiers asking if anyone had seen him. They had told the Bloodletter about his arrival three nights ago and his mighty battle against the invaders, but given that no one had seen Thaydor since, they had nothing more to tell.

They had agreed not to mention his visit to Buckby if Reynulf came back. The men had nodded with knowing looks in their eyes. Since Thaydor had shown up at the village with Wrynne, they had accepted him, but he had seen for himself that she was right. It was not their way to open up to outsiders.

That should work in his favor, anyway.

As they passed through a small, picturesque stretch of woods, Wrynne finally seemed to be perking up.

"What a day," she said, letting out a sigh. "I'll definitely be weeding my garden tonight."

He looked at her curiously. "Haven't you already done enough work?"

"That's not work. Tending my garden is how I stay sane."

"Ah, I see."

She looked up at him. "You can help if you want. It really works."

"I have my own preferred method, but thank you," he said. "I'll tell you if you promise not to laugh."

"I would never laugh at you."

"Very well." Smiling, he reached into his gambeson and handed her his book of poetry. "Here. It's easier than weeding, anyway."

She looked at it, then at him, as if she thought it was adorable. He shrugged and felt a little foolish.

She smiled, studying him. "You know, you were wonderful back there."

"So were you," he countered, pausing to guide Avalanche across a small brook. Then he glanced at her again. "You would have gone and faced all that by yourself days ago if you hadn't been looking after me. Am I right?"

She nodded. "But I'm glad you were there. It made the whole thing a lot easier. And everybody loved you."

*I only care what you think about me.* The stray thought surprised even him.

When he glanced at her again, he found her watching him and got distracted when he noticed that her eyes matched the soft gray of the forest shadows around them.

"You're very beautiful, Wrynne," he blurted out. "That is— I mean— You are a credit to your order."

He frowned, and she smiled at his awkward botch of a compliment and gave him another look that said, *Adorable.*

He glanced away self-consciously and mumbled, "I read the poems, I don't write them."

She laughed softly and tucked the book back into his vest for him, her hand grazing his chest.

"What happened at that last house?" he asked at length. "I could tell it really hurt you. If it helps, you can talk to me about it."

"Oh, Thaydor." She shook her head sorrowfully. "The Urms killed that woman's baby. A beautiful, healthy girl, only three months old. I delivered her myself. And they bashed her little life out against a wall like she was nothing."

A fiery gust of rage poured through him to hear of this new low of Urmugoth barbarity, but he tamped it down. He had already killed them. What more could he do? Besides, it would only upset her if he let his fury loose. "I see."

"That poor woman. You don't recover from something like that," she remarked. "Not really. What do you say to a grieving mother?"

He glanced at her in misery. "You tell me. I must write a letter to Eadric's mother tonight."

With a soft sound of sympathy, she curled her fingers in the back of his hair where her hand was draped around his neck. He shook his head, met her gaze, and then nuzzled her face tenderly with his own, for there were no words.

He held her a little tighter as they rode on, but hatred coursed through his veins, not just for the Urmugoth rot, who were too stupid half the time to know what they were doing, but for the Silver Sage, who might just be the true source of all this.

*Let him come here and look into the faces we saw today,* he thought bitterly. *Then he can teach his followers that evil is just an illusion.*

Fortunately, the North Gate and its towers were in sight when they emerged from the woods. He urged Avalanche into a smooth canter and crossed the grassy field approaching the walls. He hailed the current sentries from below, calling up to them. He told them who they were and received permission to come up and talk to the guards on duty.

Given his fame, the soldiers were all too happy to meet him and very willing to tell him what they knew. Indeed, they seemed relieved to have a seasoned, authoritative warrior to talk to about the distressing events in the province of late.

First, however, Thaydor decided that his fair companion had heard enough talk of murder and mayhem for one day and asked her to wait a short distance away. She seemed glad to escape the guards' bloody descriptions of how they had found their companions on the night the Urmugoths had first got in.

Her hair and cloak blowing around her, Wrynne wandered off down the windy rampart to wait for him. As she leaned on the crenellated battlements, gazing out at the view, Thaydor did his best to ignore the curve of her backside, which was thrust out a bit in her idle pose.

He strove to focus on his questions for the men. They were locals and not terribly well trained in fighting. Their skill level was usually sufficient, for the miles of high walls that had been built around the borders of Veraidel decades ago kept the barbarians out most of the time.

Thaydor gathered the sentries around and questioned them together. As he had suspected, not a man on duty had been left alive on the night of the breach to tell how it all had happened.

The men explained how the fourth watch had arrived for duty at three a.m. as usual, only to find the horrifying sight of the gates wide open and their companions of the third watch dead, their throats cut. Two had even been tossed out over the wall.

A few seemed to have had time to put up a fight, but they had clearly lost.

"Were there any teeth marks on the bodies?" he asked.

"Only on the two poor bastards who were thrown over the wall," the sergeant said. "They gnawed 'em good."

"But not the men up here?"

"Right."

"Hmm," said Thaydor. "And you say they had their throats cut?"

"Yes, sir."

Not the Urms' preferred method of dispatching their victims. If the typical Urm could get close enough to cut a man's throat, they'd just as soon twist his neck. The deft use of a knife required more dexterity than the ogre descendants possessed.

The guards answered everything Thaydor could think to ask, and even offered their best guess on how it had played out. They theorized that the twenty Urms must have somehow got their big, gray hands on some grappling hooks and ropes strong enough to support their heavy weight. A few must have climbed the walls in an unguarded spot and then come up here to open the gates for their friends.

"I think it would be wise to see if you lads can find the spot where this might have happened," he suggested. "I'd start by going along the walls and checking the parapets for any fresh gashes or scratches that could have been made by grappling hooks. If this is how they got in, it would be good to confirm it. Did you find any footprints of Urm size inside the gatehouse?"

"No, only out on the road," the sergeant said.

"Sir, you don't think more will try it, do you?" one asked.

Thaydor glanced around at them, realizing in surprise that the men looked nearly as shaken as the children had at the prospect of it happening again.

He smiled and gave them the same reassuring promise—that he'd write immediately to the warrior monks of the nearest monastery of Ilios to come out and reinforce them.

They thanked him profusely, then admitted that a quarter of their garrison had stopped reporting for duty. The cowards had fled rather than risk meeting a similar fate.

Apparently, the usually dull job of sentry did not pay well enough for that.

He asked to see the rest of the gatehouse, and they showed him around, but he found no useful clues.

Upon returning to Wrynne on the ramparts, he joined her in gazing out at the bleak beauty of the wastelands. Little grew out on those boggy moors but sphagnum moss, heather, and sedge. An occasional craggy-limbed, blighted-looking tree stood here and there, but in the pink light of the setting sun, the lonely landscape held a certain wistful allure—at least when it was empty.

No Urmugoths were in sight, but it would be dark soon.

"What did you find out?" Wrynne murmured.

He shrugged, at a loss. "Not a whole lot."

She turned to him, her gray eyes troubled. "Thaydor? If I'm right about the king, what will you do?"

He shook his head wearily. "I don't know yet. I'm sure I'll think of something."

She took his hand. "Come. At least you'll be safe at my place tonight."

He glanced hungrily at her, pondering the night ahead. *But will you be safe with me?*

# Chapter 5
# Glow

valanche carried them up the mountain path to Wrynne's bower, with two hours of daylight left before dusk.

When they arrived, she could already hear the fairies bickering in the rafters, and wondered aloud what to make for supper as Thaydor reined in.

"It will be nice to have a guest for once."

"Don't go to any trouble on my account," he said as he dismounted.

"Nonsense, we've got to eat! You must be starved. It's a late meal as it is."

"Can I help?" he offered as he helped her down and set her on her feet. "I could make the fire for you."

"If you like—or catch a couple of fish. They're already confined with nets in a section of the brook. But really, you should just relax."

"I'm happy to do whatever's helpful. Just give me my orders," he said with a winning smile.

"No, it's all right. I'm picky about my cooking. The fire can't be too high. Trout roasts best on a low flame."

"Well, if you think of anything that I can do, just tell me. My lady?" he added as she turned around and headed for the pavilion.

"Yes?" At once, she paused, glanced back, and found him gazing at her with a wistful frown. "What is it?"

"I'll be leaving in the morning."

She tried to hide her disappointment. "Are you sure you feel well enough? I really think you need more rest."

"I'm all right. I think a good night's sleep tonight will have me back to my old self by tomorrow."

"You can take the bed. I'll sleep in my hanging chair."

"Certainly not. I'll sleep on the floor."

"It's fine! I take naps there all the time. I'll be very comfortable. Please, I insist."

"I've already imposed on you so much. As if it wasn't enough you saved my life."

"It's not a problem." She chuckled and took a step closer. "It's been nice having you here. You're welcome to stay."

"No… I think I'd better be moving on. As long as your neighbors hand over my other horse, I'll have her hitched and be on my way by midmorning."

Wrynne smoothed the wrinkles out of her skirts after the long horseback ride and struggled not to argue. "Where will you go?" she asked in a measured tone.

"South to the capital. I think it's time I go and have a talk with King Baynard."

She jerked her head up to meet his gaze. *"What?"*

"I'm not going to run and hide. I've been thinking about it the whole way here, and I've concluded that the best course is simply for me to go and meet him face-to-face. I'm sure we can sort this out like reasonable men."

"You can't be serious," she said. "Thaydor! He's trying to have you killed!"

"We don't know that for certain. Things looked a bit suspicious at the gates, I grant you, but we have no proof that His Majesty is the one behind it. In fact, he may need my protection. He's still our king, even if he's gone off course."

She stared at him. "Your protection?"

"Between the Silver Sage breathing down his neck and his new mistress keeping him intoxicated round the clock, he may not even know what's been happening. I might be the only one now who can help him. Free him from their foul influences."

"But Thaydor—"

"Don't worry, my lady. At the moment, the only person we can tie to any of this is Reynulf, and if I see him, I'll know to be on my guard, thanks to you."

She gazed at him for a long moment. "So you've made up your mind to return to the city."

"Yes."

"Very well. I'm coming with you," she informed him, and pivoted to start gathering her things for their departure in the morning.

"Er, my lady, I don't think that's such a good idea."

"Too bad!" She spun around and glared at him. "I went to a lot of trouble to save your life! I'm not going to stand by and do nothing while you go and throw it away."

He tilted his head with a droll expression. "Give me a little credit, Wrynne. I'm not a fool."

"You give others too much credit! Thaydor." She took a step toward him. "You're so good and fair-minded yourself that you can't fathom those you consider allies being wicked. But they are. I feel it in my bones."

"I'm not naive," he said, bristling a bit. "I simply choose not to cast people down without facts, without proof. You cannot come with me, demoiselle. I am sorry."

She narrowed her eyes at him. "Why not?"

"Because." He stared at her.

"Because *why*?" she demanded, exasperated. "Are you finally admitting it *is* dangerous?"

"No, it's not that."

"Well?"

His cheeks flushed. "Are you going to make me say it?"

"Say what?" she exclaimed. "I don't know what you're talking about. I can do as I please, anyway. If I want to come with you, then I shall. You have no authority over me."

"Actually, I do—in the hierarchy of the church, anyway."

"Oh, pulling rank on me, Paladin? Very nice."

He shrugged. "Sorry, but it's for your own good. Besides, your people need you here."

"And what of the will of Ilios, hmm? Maybe He prefers that I go with you. To protect you!"

His eyebrows rose slowly. He couldn't hide the grin that crept across his face. "Protect *me*?"

She nearly stamped her foot in vexation. "Well, you have to sleep sometime! I could keep watch. You have no squire now. How will you even put on your armor to fight?"

"If you haven't noticed, dear lady, my traveling companions have a tendency to die. Besides, you don't know the first thing about squiring for a knight. You can barely lift my weapons, and I doubt you know the proper way of putting armor on a man."

"Well, I took it off you handily enough," she shot back.

His blue eyes flared at this bold reminder of how she had undressed him. Then he looked away and suddenly seemed to lose his train of thought.

Wrynne folded her arms across her chest. A pleased little *humph* escaped her.

He shook his head as if to clear it. "So where do you keep the kindling?"

"I told you, never mind. I can make the fire. Why don't you see to your horse?"

He looked at Avalanche as though he had forgotten all about him. With a terse nod, he got to work unsaddling his steed. Wrynne remained a moment longer, watching him in dismay.

"I don't understand," she said at length. "Am I such dull company? Because I thought it was rather pleasant today, the two of us working together."

He sent her a piercing glance as he set the saddle down. "That's the problem. Because contrary to rumor, my lady, I am not a saint."

Wrynne blinked, finally grasping the source of his objections. "Oh," she said in a slightly strangled tone. "I see."

"Do you?" he taunted in a low tone, eyeing her in a most un-paladin-like way, just to make the point. As if she didn't realize he was very much a man.

She looked away, cheeks burning. It suddenly seemed prudent to stop arguing.

"I'll go make supper," she mumbled, but as she hurried off, she felt his eyes on her body all the way to the fire pit that lay between her bower and the stream.

Unnerved, she kept her back to him as she fetched some dry kindling out of the tinderbox and tucked it under a couple of small logs in the fire pit. She fumbled with the flint, hands trembling after his blunt admission.

As she tried to strike a spark, he suddenly appeared beside her, startling her. He leaned down, and stilled her hands with his own much larger ones, gently cupping them with a warm touch.

"Let me do it," he murmured by her ear. Then he took the flint and the fire steel and set the wood ablaze.

He did not look at her, nor she at him. Acute awareness charged the air between them, but they both stared at the growing bonfire.

"Thank you," she said after a moment, stealing a wary sidelong glance at him.

He met her gaze and nodded, looking just a little too long into her eyes. He cleared his throat and rose. "What shall I do next?" Hands on hips, he awaited her command.

*Heady thought.* Wrynne chased off wayward imaginings. "Oh, nothing. Make yourself comfortable, please. I'll let you know when supper's ready."

"Are you sure?"

She nodded. "It'll only be about half an hour."

"If you're sure you don't need me, I should clean up my armor a bit before it rusts."

She sent him a poignant smile at this reminder that he had no squire now to carry out such tasks for him. Thaydor went back into the pavilion and gathered up as much of his armor as he could carry in one armload. Clanking away, he carried it down the stone steps to wash off the caked-on blood and grime in the brook below the waterfall pool.

She shuddered at the memory of how wet and red and sticky it had been on the night she had found him. Then she shook her head, wondering how long it would be before he ended up like that again. How could the man refuse the help she was offering?

At least now she knew why. Of course, he was worried she'd end up dead, like his series of past squires, but there was more to it than that. He desired her, and it disturbed him.

She blushed and thrilled to the thought at the same time. His admission only made her want to go with him all the more. How could she bear to stay here, left behind, knowing he was out there, in danger?

What he felt—what they both felt—was natural enough. The attraction was no excuse for refusing her help when his life was at stake. With unknown enemies out for his blood, who else could he trust the way he could trust her? They shared the same beliefs, the same values...

She blew on the fire and poked at it in frustration, sending Silvertwig a morose look as her familiar flew over to her. Having witnessed their whole exchange, the fairy shook her head and folded her arms across her chest as she hovered in midair.

"Have you ever seen anyone so stubborn?" Wynne whispered, glancing around to make sure her guest was still down by the lower stream. "He thinks he can do everything himself. What does he think, that I'm incompetent? Just a helpless damsel?"

She huffed and rolled her eyes, while Silvertwig lifted her eyebrows as if about to say that Wrynne, actually, was often that stubborn.

Wrynne didn't give her the chance. "Maybe I ought to remind the great paladin that I had the same basic fighters' training at the Bastion as every other cleric and layperson. I even have some light armor," she whispered, "*and* a weapon. Not that I've ever had to use it on a living thing. Target practice mostly," she admitted. "But the point is, I *can*! I was trained for the armies of Light just like him, and I'm willing!"

She shot to her feet and set her hands on her waist, staring at Silvertwig in indignation. "Does he think me a child?"

The fairy shrugged.

"Or does he fear that if he lets me come along, I might try to seduce him? Dent his precious honor? Because that would be absurd." She scoffed, blushing. "Yes, it's true that Sons of Might and Daughters of the Rose are often encouraged to, um, marry. But what woman in her right mind would ever marry a knight and worry every day for the rest of her life? Besides, I'm bound by the same standards of behavior as he is. So what if he...fancies me..."

It was almost too wildly flattering a thought for her to wrap her mind around.

"It doesn't mean we have to act on it. And honestly, even if he lost control, which I doubt would ever happen, I'd rather he ravished me—twice!—than let him go out there with who knows how many people trying to kill him and no one to watch his back!"

"Twice, eh?" Silvertwig chirped with a knowing grin. "Quite a sacrifice, mistress. Really big of you."

"Oh, shut up," Wrynne mumbled. "I didn't mean it like that. He's important to the whole kingdom. And to Ilios!" she insisted while Silvertwig snickered.

Scowling, Wrynne stomped off, red-cheeked, to catch a couple of fish for their meal.

By the time she had the trout cleaned and roasting on the spit a few inches above the fire, she had made up her mind that she was going to help Thaydor whether he liked it or not. Of course, there was no need to tell him so flat-out. Why alert him of her true intentions when he would only forbid it? She'd simply have to work around his protective nature.

*It isn't lying outright,* she insisted to herself. That would have been a sin. But she was not above, well, finessing him a bit. Delaying full disclosure until it was more difficult for him to say no.

Mother did it all the time with Father, and while the Building Baron almost always blustered in the short term, he always realized later that his wife was right.

Just so would she handle Sir Thaydor.

And she had a fair notion of how to get the stubborn mule headed down the right path, too. He was a hero; let him help her, then. Poor, defenseless damsel that she obviously was in his eyes.

"Supper's ready!" she called down to him from the top of the waterfall ten minutes later.

"Be right there!" he yelled back.

His handsome, chiseled face wore a troubled look when he joined her on the broad, flat boulder beside the stream where she had set up their picnic a few feet above the waterfall.

"Well, this is very pleasant," he said with an appreciative glance as he sat down on the edge of the blanket across from her. "It smells delicious, too."

"Wait until you taste it. Fish from right over there. Vegetables and herbs straight from my garden." She nodded over her shoulder at it, then smiled at him.

"You spoil me," he teased.

They said the customary prayer of thanks before meals, then Wrynne poured a wooden goblet full of the rustic local wine and handed it to him. "I only have the one cup. We'll have to share," she said with a pert smile.

"You first, my lady."

"How gallant."

He chuckled. "You did all the work."

She took a sip and then handed it to him. "It's not the fine Aisedorian vintage you're probably used to, but it's not half bad."

"It's good," he said after taking a swallow.

They ate, enjoyed the food, and chatted about nothing in particular. When they had finished their plates, however, Wrynne poured them a second cup of wine, noticing he still had those indigo shadows lurking in his eyes.

The wine had loosened her tongue and dulled her inhibitions enough to pursue the matter. "So, tell me. What's bothering you?"

She could tell he was about to deny that anything was, but when she offered a knowing smile, he frowned and shook his head. "It's not a suitable topic for the table...even if the table is a rock."

"We're done eating. It's all right now."

He stared at her, his brow furrowed. "My armor," he said. "So much blood. I can't believe I'm alive."

"'Tis a miracle," she agreed, glossing over the how of it. "But why are you surprised? You of all people know the power of Ilios. He looks after his own."

"Yes, I suppose," he said, but he still looked confused. He took another swallow of wine. "That reminds me. I still have to write my letters to Eadric's family and the warrior monks at the monastery about twenty miles from here, on the edge of the Scythe Valley. Could I possibly trouble you for two sheets of paper and some ink before we lose the rest of the light?"

"Of course. Come inside. I'll clean this up while you get that over with."

"Thanks."

They rose, and he followed her inside, where she set him up at the table with writing supplies and a candle. Her bower seemed so much smaller when he was in it. His big, powerful body barely fit on her dainty wooden chair when he sat down to begin, but he insisted he was comfortable. She lit a couple of hanging lanterns around the place and took one with her when she went to clean up after their meal.

This was quickly done, though the cut on her forearm which she'd made for the *Kiss of Life* spell stung a little when she got it wet. Rolling her sleeve up higher to check the bandage, she shrugged off the slight pain and dried the dishes by the stream.

When she brought the dishes back inside to put them away, Thaydor was blowing a bit of drying sand across the first completed letter. "Making progress?" She crossed behind him and put the dishes, cup, and utensils away in the cabinet.

"The one to the monastery's done. Now for the hard one."

She caressed his shoulder before leaving him alone again. "You'll get through it. Then you'll have earned this." She set his poetry book down on the table by his hand.

He smiled ruefully at her.

She resisted the urge to run her fingers through his golden hair. "I'm going to go weed my garden."

"Have fun!" he called in a sardonic tone as she danced lightly out of the pavilion. "But don't overdo it, now. All pleasures in moderation, my lady."

She shot him an arch look over her shoulder and traipsed off to her garden, still smiling as she passed the grassy area where Avalanche grazed contentedly, his coat pearlescent in the gathering twilight.

She let herself in through the willow-lattice enclosure that protected her raised beds from rabbits and deer and other forest creatures. She was rather tired and it was getting dark, but she raised the lantern and forgot all about the day's troubles as she perused the vegetable beds and the medicinal herbs, tugging out scraggly shoots of weeds here and there as she went. There weren't many, since she tended to yank them out as soon as they appeared, but just being in her garden soothed her spirits.

Yet a heaviness still hung over her heart after the events of the day. All the suffering she'd seen. She'd given all she had and it hadn't felt like nearly enough. And then there was the lingering horror of her stubborn attempt to gather up Eadric earlier today…

And still, all of that, as hard as it had been, did not feel like the true cause of her restlessness tonight.

As she looked around at her garden and then slowly scanned the lovely woods, where the night birds had begun to call and the fairy lights were beginning to twinkle, she realized the source of her bittersweet mood. She'd be leaving this place on the morrow and might never come back.

Her superiors had warned her that she would sense it when the time came for her to move on. They had said she'd feel a stirring in her heart that she would have to follow if she was to stay on the path of the divine will for her life.

She knew that time had come.

It was both scary and exciting. She had not been expecting this at all, and yet it was not as difficult as she would have thought to let it go. She'd been here long enough.

*I have been very happy here,* she thought, staring around at her peaceful abode, where she had learned so much about love and beauty and kindness and peace—the things that truly mattered in life. *But it's time to say goodbye.*

Time to take what she had learned in her hermitage out into the wider world, where it could do some good.

The thought of leaving to start down some new, as-yet unknown path in life frightened her a little—until Thaydor stepped out of the pavilion and came striding toward her with a smile.

What on earth was there to be afraid of with the Golden Knight by her side? She was most assuredly not helpless, but just in case she ran into any trouble, she knew he'd keep her safe.

*Well, then,* she thought with a slight tremor at the momentousness of her realization. Saving the paladin from death appeared to have changed her fate, as well.

It seemed he wasn't the only one who needed to write a letter to the Bastion. She'd have to let Mother Superior know that she was leaving…

"Do try to contain yourself from all this hilarity," the big knight teased as he joined her in the garden. But he frowned when he saw the strange expression on her face. "What's wrong? You don't look like you're having much fun, after all."

She sighed and summoned up a smile. "All the weeds are already pulled." Then she peered at the book in his hand and tapped on its leather cover. "Maybe you should try your way instead. Read me a poem?"

"I'd love to, if you're sure you've given up on the weeding festivities?"

When she nodded in amusement, he sat down on a large rock inside the enclosure and opened the book. "Ah, here's one. Are you ready?" He glanced at her, his blue eyes twinkling.

"I think so."

He cleared his throat and read in a thoughtful tone:

*"When the nightingale sings,*
*The woods waxen green,*
*Leaf and grass and blossom springs,*
*In April, to be sure;*
*But love is to mine heart gone*
*With one spear so keen,*
*Night and day my blood it drinks,*
*Until my soul cannot endure."*

He looked at her to see how she liked it.

"That makes you feel *better*?" she exclaimed with a saucy grin and a hint of a self-conscious blush to have a paladin reading her poetry. "Sounds a little depressing to me."

He smiled wryly at her comment and continued:

*"Sweet lady, I pray thee*

*For one gentle word of love*
*While I live in this dark world,*
*For thou alone art pure.*
*With thy touch, my sweet beloved,*
*My bliss thou couldst achieve;*
*A sweet kiss of thy mouth*
*Might be my only cure."*

Wrynne went very still, taken off guard by that last part. She looked warily at him, her heart pounding all of a sudden with the guilt of her little benevolent secret.

*Does he know somehow about the Kiss of Life spell? I thought he was unconscious. Does he remember somehow...?*

He avoided her gaze, perhaps abashed or perhaps merely contemplating the wildly romantic words. Or perhaps waiting for her to come clean on just how far she had gone to save him.

"It's pretty, isn't it?" he murmured, glancing at her. "Perhaps a little overdramatic, considering some half-hysterical bard probably wrote it. Still, it makes me wonder..." His words trailed off, his eyes full of unspoken yearnings.

"Wonder what?" she asked softly, still unsure.

"What it must be like to love someone so much."

Her tension eased at his sweet words. Relief flowed through her. He didn't know. He just liked the poem. Quite a coincidence...if there was such a thing.

"It is very pretty," she concurred as she sat down beside him. She couldn't resist teasing him a little, though. "Who'd have guessed the fierce Golden Knight possessed such a romantic soul?"

"Don't tell the Urmugoths," he said drily.

"Or the dragons," she added. "They'd never let you live it down."

"Or the boys in the barracks."

She laughed and clapped him fondly on the thigh as she stood up again and wandered back to her beds to hunt for any stray weeds, more moved by his chivalrous heart than she could say. If she did not distract herself—quickly—she might well be tempted to do something foolish.

She avoided looking at the beautiful man for fear he'd read her own daft longings in her eyes. Instead, she turned her attention back to a subject. *Hmm, who can I get to see to my garden once I'm gone?*

Thaydor snapped the book shut and followed her. "So, what are we growing, then?"

She pointed out the many vegetables, the few flowers, and then the medicinal plants. "Mugwort, chamomile, comfrey, lavender, agrimony, nightshade—"

"Nightshade? Should I be worried? They do say poison is a woman's weapon."

"May I remind you I am one of the few people *not* trying to kill you," she pointed out in mock indignation. "And before you judge me a witch, allow me to explain that a tiny bit of poison is a crucial ingredient in many a medicine. Say I want to cure someone of worms—"

"Ugh, let's not."

She laughed at his grimace and changed the subject. She didn't want to bore him. "Did you finish your letters?"

He nodded with a melancholy smile.

"You look like you need more poetry."

"There's only so much it can do," he admitted. Then he sighed. "Another boy is dead and it's my fault."

She tilted her head back and studied him in the fading light. "Do you really feel that way?"

His simple shrug was far sadder than his easy smile of earlier had let on. He shook his head and said nothing.

She took his hand, vaguely aware that she had started doing that quite often in their brief acquaintance. It had begun to feel almost second nature. She just couldn't seem to help touching him. His hands were so big and strong and warm, and besides, she had already undressed the man, had she not? As his healer. But though she had mended his physical injuries, she could see in his wistful blue eyes that his heart was still hurting.

"I have an idea," she whispered. "I'll be right back."

She gave his hand a squeeze and then released it, leaving the garden enclosure. Dashing into the pavilion, she returned a moment later with two tiny, almost-spent candle nubs in her hand and a surprise for him rolled up under her arm.

"Here. Hold these," she instructed.

He arched a brow as she gave him the stumpy candles, then she carried the lantern over to find a few large oak leaves. She picked them, then wove them together by their stems into what looked like two fairly sturdy little rafts.

She nodded toward the stone steps. "Come on."

As the night's darkness deepened from pearl gray to indigo, she led him down to the waterfall pool, holding the lantern up as she walked down the steps. On the flat flagstone area below, the pieces of his armor were still laid out to finish drying. Moonlight gleamed on the once-again bright steel and glistened on the rippling water.

Thaydor followed her over to the edge of the pool and joined her as she bent down, setting the lantern between them. She opened its delicate side door, took the wax nubs from him, and lit both from the flame within. She set each candle in one of the little green leaf-boats, giving one to him and taking one for herself. Then she nodded to him.

He stared at her, the tiny flickering light in his hand catching the blue fire in his eyes.

"Is there anything you'd like to say to honor Eadric's memory?" she asked in a soft tone.

He shook his head, at a loss. Clearly, he had not expected this, had not realized what she was up to.

"I will, then." Wrynne turned to the pool where the starlight danced, reflected in the water. She bent down, holding her candle-raft above the surface for a moment.

"Eadric, we never met, but you gave your life protecting us, the people of Mistwood. You made the choice not to retreat as ordered, but instead held your ground, trying to aid the warrior you admired and emulated. You were a brave young man, and we thank you for your sacrifice. You've earned your rest and a hero's laurels in Elysium." She released her floating candle into the pool and then turned to Thaydor.

He seemed to struggle, the angles of his face taut in the flickering candlelight as he leaned toward the pool. "You were a good lad," he forced out gruffly. "Courageous and loyal. You believed in our cause. You'd have made a fine knight. I'm sorry," he added barely audibly.

She laid her hand on his shoulder with tears in her eyes as Thaydor pushed the second little green boat toward the center of the pool.

In silence, they watched the tiny glowing lights drift slowly toward the brook that flowed out the other end of the pool. She caressed his arm, but when her touch stilled, he covered her hand with his own.

After a heartbeat, he lifted it to his lips and kissed her knuckles. "Thank you," he whispered. "You truly are the kindest person I have ever known."

She held his gaze in wonder. But she hadn't brought him down here to earn his praise. Only to cheer him up.

She glanced toward the candles moving steadily toward the brook, then brushed the tears off her cheeks and smiled at him. "Let's follow them."

"Huh?"

"Follow the lights. Let's see how far they make it."

He shook his head in regretful amusement. "I don't feel much like hiking, to be honest."

"That's not what I meant." Her smile widened. "Behold!" She sprang up and suddenly unfurled the Aladdin stretcher.

"What in the...?" he murmured, staring as she smoothed out the wrinkles while it floated three feet off the ground. "*What* is that?"

"Magical stretcher. The latest thing in the healing arts! I use it for my patients. Hold on to it, would you? Don't let it get away. I need to fetch the pole."

"It flies?" He grasped the edge of the mysterious floating tapestry while she dashed over to the hillside by the steps.

"Not very high. It's only partly made from magic carpets." She grabbed a walking stick that she left leaning by the steps for her occasional use.

Returning with a grin, she took over the task of holding the Aladdin stretcher steady. "All right! Get on."

"Get on?" he echoed.

"Fine, shall I show you how it's done? Here." She put the walking stick in his hands. "You're in charge of punting."

"What in the world...?" he uttered, then he laughed, watching her ease carefully onto the floating cloth.

"See? It's very simple. Come on, let's go! Our candles are about to spill over the edge of the pool, Thaydor, hurry!"

"I'm not getting on that thing," he retorted.

"Oh, yes, you are."

"Can it even hold me?"

"Thaydor. You've been on it before," she chided. "It's how I brought you up from the battlefield. Now, come on, it's fun! Let's go for a ride."

"My lady, with all due respect, we need to reexamine your definition of the word *fun*. Weeding? Now this?"

"Have you got something better to do? Come *on!*"

He snorted and shook his head at her. But finally he gave in, laughing, and slung his leg over the long cloth as if it were a horse. "If we end up in the water..."

"Oh, don't be a baby. We're not going to end up in the water!"

"So you say." He steadied himself, his feet dangling off both sides, while Wrynne sat cross-legged between his sprawled thighs.

"Get settled already! Are you on?" she asked.

"I'm on. What do I do?"

"Whoa!" she cried as the whole thing lurched to the side.

"Sorry! Don't move around so much," he scolded.

"I didn't! That was you." They were both laughing like children. "Just push off the ground with the stick, you big dolt. Don't worry, it doesn't go very fast. It just glides, nice and gentle. I promise, you'll be perfectly safe."

"It's not like I'm afraid, you little loon." He settled more comfortably into his seat. "So I take it you've done this before?"

She looked over her shoulder at him and grinned. "A few times. Oh, I admit it, you were right. It *does* get a wee bit boring out here sometimes. One has to amuse oneself somehow."

"Apparently." He shook his head. "You're mad."

"Would you get going? We have to keep up with our candles!"

He harrumphed. "This is the silliest thing I've ever done."

"You need more silliness in your life, Clank. Now let's go!"

"Aye aye, cap'n," he said affably. Then he pushed off with the walking stick and the Aladdin stretcher glided out across the waterfall pool.

He quickly used the stick to push them several inches higher above the water's surface to avoid getting his feet wet.

Wrynne laughed in madcap delight as he straightened out their course and headed for the brook. "You're doing great!"

At that moment, the candles on their little green rafts spilled over the edge of the pool and began traveling swiftly down the winding brook.

The two of them followed.

\* \* \*

Feeling as though she had put him under a spell, Thaydor pursued the tiny lights, using the meandering path of the stream as their silvered road.

A few feet over the water's surface, they floated along through the fairy woods, laughing, joking, teasing each other—and a strange thing happened.

In trying to keep up with the candles, he forgot all about his earlier sorrow and somehow escaped his grief, unable to resist the dreamy enchantment of the starry night with her.

*How can I leave this girl tomorrow?* he wondered. *I know we only just met, but I feel as if I've found my other self.* He had never experienced such a deep and instantaneous bond to anyone before.

When the candles eventually winked out of sight far ahead of them, they turned around and floated back the way they had come, docking at last at the same landing.

Tired as they both were after the incredibly difficult day, they stayed up talking half the night on the rock where they had picnicked, lying side by side near the top of the waterfall, and watching the constellations rotate round the sky.

She asked how he had been chosen as the paladin, and he told her about the final test the Sons of Might had to endure after all their training—forty days and nights of silence and fasting in the Scythe Valley.

"Ooh, that sounds painful! Daughters of the Rose only have to fast for ten days as our final test, and I hated it. I kept dreaming of cake."

"Well, near the end of our trial," Thaydor said, "an elderly shepherd came hobbling down into the valley, asking all the knights if we had seen his lost sheep. We hadn't, but of course, by that time, we were all hallucinating from hunger so badly that my brethren probably would have eaten the poor thing raw if it had wandered into our midst. We were all so starved, exhausted, and demoralized that nobody wanted to help the old man. But for some reason, I felt sorry for him, so I scraped up what little strength I had left and set out to help him search for the thing."

"Did you find it?" she asked, rolling onto her side next to him. She leaned her elbow on the rock and propped her head on her hand.

"We did. It was stuck by its little white fluff in some brambles. I got it out and put it in the old shepherd's arms."

"So you didn't eat it?" she asked, eyes twinkling.

"No," he retorted, "though that was a near thing. When I led the old man back past our camp to see him off, I had to hold some of my fellow knights at bay. They screamed at me. Some of them wanted to fight me just so they could tear the little animal apart."

She grimaced.

He shook his head. "They were ready to throw aside all the progress they had made, but I prevented them, and fortunately, the shepherd and his lamb escaped the valley unscathed."

"Thanks to you," she said with a smile.

"Well, as it turned out, the old shepherd hadn't been a man at all, but a celestial emissary of the Light in disguise."

Wrynne gasped. "An angel?"

Thaydor nodded slowly, still amazed at the encounter. "His true mission was the find the next Paladin of Ilios, and for this, he came cloaked as a mortal." He paused. "In the morning, I awoke to find Hallowsmite lying on the ground beside me."

Just like many paladins before him had.

"The magical sword of the Light." Wrynne searched his face with a mystified gaze. "What does it do, exactly?"

"I'm not really supposed to discuss it. But I think I can trust you with some of its secrets," he added with a wink.

"Oh, you don't have to tell me if you don't—"

"No, I want to. Just keep it to yourself."

"You have my word."

He could tell she was pleased that he was confiding in her. "One of my favorite features is the percussion wave Hallowsmite can produce when I drive it tip-first into the ground. It works a little like this. Watch." He reached for a nearby stone and sat up. "You'll notice at the moment that the rock strikes the surface of the water, a wave of energy flies out in a perfect circle all around it from the point of impact."

He tossed the rock into the water to demonstrate.

She looked askance at him. "Yes, I am familiar with this phenomenon," she said rather wryly.

"Well, my sword can do that—only with energy. Whoosh! It just flies out in all directions from my blade, strong enough to knock every enemy around me off his feet."

"How very handy."

"It's saved my life more than once." He hesitated, not sure how much he should say, but she looked impressed, and he was only human. Shrugging off his wariness, he gave her a confidential smile. "Sometimes, when my enemies get me really angry, and the percussion wave doesn't seem quite enough, I can make it send out a ring of fire. I don't like to use that, though, unless I have to. Burning to death…" He shook his head. "That's a bad way for anyone to go."

"You have mercy even on your enemies."

"Some," he said with a prudent nod.

"Well, I think it's marvelous you were chosen for who you are as a person, not what you can do as a warrior," she said as he reclined again on his elbows, watching a bat go flapping by overhead.

"It's a great responsibility, being Paladin," he admitted. "But I always knew something like this would happen to me, even when I was a boy."

"Why do you say that?"

"I don't know... I always felt a bit different from others." He watched a firefly that landed on her knee and glowed there for a moment before it flew away again. "Even as a lad, I was always very serious. My mother was the one who put the notion in my head, I think. She told me a man must be good before he can be great, and she was very fond of saying we only get one chance at this life, so make it count."

"Ah, very true."

"She was beautiful and wise and I adored her. We all did. I didn't have much time with her, but I know she made me what I am. What she said to me on her deathbed is what set me on my path."

She touched his shoulder with a comforting caress. "What happened to her, Thaydor?"

"She caught a wasting fever while caring for the poor the winter I turned twelve. Before she died, she made me promise to take care of everyone and always try my hardest to do what's right. I gave her my word, and here I am."

She made a soft sound of sympathy. "Poor boy. I'm so sorry you lost her. I wish I could've been there to heal her for you and your family."

He smiled at her. "That's kind of you. There aren't many people with your abilities, to be sure, but back then, you'd have only been a child."

"I could heal when I was little."

"Could you?" He smiled at her in kinship. "I could fight."

She chuckled. "I guess we were born to be what we are, then."

He sighed. "It would seem so."

"How did it start for you?" she asked, gazing warmly at him.

"Well, I was always meant to be a knight because of my father. An earl has military duties, so he made sure to start my training very early. I think Father realized something was different about me, though, when I was eight and thrashed a bully twice my age for picking on my little sister. What about you?"

"I healed a bird's hurt wing by accident when I was six."

"Six!"

"It couldn't fly when I found it in the garden. I picked it up and petted it for a while to comfort it, and didn't realize until years later that my touch was what had enabled it to fly away. I thought it just got better on its own."

"That's adorable," Thaydor informed her.

She grinned and blushed a bit, and they chatted a while longer. But as the night sounds of the woods surrounded them, Wrynne eventually dozed off with her head resting on his chest.

Smiling to himself, he kept his arm around her to prevent her from rolling off the boulder into the brook. He was rather astonished, himself, at how he'd opened up to her. She had a soothing presence and was so easy to talk to. She made the world seem right again after all the darkness he had faced of late.

"Thaydor?" she mumbled sometime after he'd thought she was asleep.

"Yes, demoiselle?"

Her starry eyes opened to slits, and her voice came out as a drowsy purr. "Could I at least ride with you in your wagon tomorrow as far as Toad Hollow?"

"What's a Toad Hollow?" he murmured in amusement.

"Market town. It's on your way, and I need to purchase some supplies."

"Of course you may. Certainly," he said, relieved that she wasn't asking to come with him in a general sense, given the danger. "The longer I can enjoy your company, the better."

She smiled dreamily and snuggled closer to him. "Thank you."

"Does this town have a decent travelers' inn?"

"Mmm, the Blind Badger. Why?"

"You must let me buy you supper before we part ways. A token of my thanks for your hospitality here and the small matter of your saving my life."

"I'd like that." She tilted her head up to see his face. "Our last meal together?"

"Oh, I don't think so," he whispered.

Her eyes opened wider as she looked at him in question.

He kissed the tip of her nose. "What if I promised to come back and see you again soon?"

She pushed up onto her elbow beside him. "Would you?"

He nodded, unable to take his eyes off her. The river kept flowing all around their rock, but Thaydor was quite sure that time stopped, at least for a heartbeat.

"I'd like that," she breathed.

"Then consider it done."

Whose idea it was, or if they both decided mutually, he could not say, but inch by inch, their faces drew closer. The next thing he knew, his lips were pressed to hers with aching sweetness; his hand cupped her nape in a gentle hold.

His heart thundered against the quiet, musical babbling of the brook that wrapped around them while the stars looked on.

*How can this be?* he wondered in amazement. *Is this what falling in love feels like?*

As he ended the kiss, she looked into his eyes with complete trust. He stroked her cheek and marveled at the silken beauty of her skin, but neither of them made a move to take it any further than this one exquisite moment.

Not when they both knew that tomorrow they must part.

He flinched at the thought and dropped his gaze, capturing her hand to press another light kiss to her knuckles. "We should probably say good night," he whispered.

Even the Golden Knight had limits to his chivalry, after all, and it took all he possessed to fight the fire that burned in him for her.

She nodded, and he helped her up, then walked her back to her pavilion with his arm around her waist. He tucked her into her strange little hanging nest of a chair and covered her over with the quilt lying there.

"Good night, you," he whispered.

She laughed, half-asleep already, and brushed his knee with a clumsy parting caress as he stepped away from her and took off his gambeson as he returned to her bed.

With a sigh, he lay down, folded his arms beneath his head, and refused to look again in her direction, for every fiber of his being told him she would have come willingly to him if he had asked her to.

Their longing filled the whimsical round room, but Thaydor studied the ceiling and reminded himself repeatedly that he was the Paladin of Ilios, and a true knight did not ravish his future wife until the ring was on her finger.

And *that* he would most assuredly be bringing back with him on his next visit here.

He was no scholar, just a fierce, brute soldier when it came down to a fight, but he knew to trust his instincts, and he wasn't stupid enough to let his perfect woman get away.

Wrynne didn't know it yet, but she would be his. As soon as possible. *Nay, sooner.*

Just as quickly as he could sort out the headache of who was trying to kill him this time, he'd be back to claim her for his own. She'd be safe here until he found and fixed the problem, anyway. Until then, the last thing he wanted was to drag her into the net of treachery that he had to admit he sensed was already closing around him.

*Funny, though,* he mused, feeling much better about life in general as he closed his eyes. He never would've imagined that nearly getting killed would turn out to be one of the best things that had ever happened to him.

The amount of blood he had cleaned out of his armor made it plain he should have died.

Somehow he hadn't, and yet it seemed he had found Elysium anyway.

# Chapter 6

# Wanted

Sure enough, the next morning, a dozen men from Buckby arrived in the field below Wrynne's mountain to burn the Urmugoth bodies, as Thaydor had suggested.

They sent a boy up the winding footpath to let him know they had "found" his bay mare, hitched her to his wagon for him, and brought the whole lot to their hero, for his convenience. Horse and wagon waited at the bottom of the mountain path.

Wrynne and he exchanged a glance of wry amusement at this change of heart on the unknown horse-thief's part, but all was forgiven, as long as nothing was missing from the cart.

Thaydor left to take his now cleaned but still dented armor down to the wagon, letting the awestruck boy help by carrying a few of the smaller pieces of his armor.

When they had gone, Wrynne hurried to make her final preparations for leaving her hermitage. She bathed in the waterfall pool, dried off, and dressed again in fresh clothes, then changed the bandage on her arm where she had cut herself to work the *Kiss of Life* spell.

As she packed her things, she discussed her decision with Silvertwig. Though her little familiar was sad about their leaving this very pleasant assignment, Silvertwig had agreed to take Thaydor's letter to the warrior monks to secure their help at the border gates. Wrynne had folded the letter up for her into a tiny square small enough to fit in the fairy's satchel.

"You're sure you know the way to the Scythe Valley?"

Silvertwig nodded, and though Wrynne knew her fey friend was quite resourceful, she frowned with worry all the same. Twenty miles was a vast distance to cover for someone who was barely six inches tall.

"Find me when you can," Wrynne instructed. "I'm not sure where I'll be... In fact, you should probably just go to my family's house in Pleiburg and wait for me there. Let them know I'm safe."

The fairy nodded sadly.

"I'll miss you, Silvertwig," she said softly. "Please be careful."

"You too, Wrynnay." Silvertwig landed on her shoulder and pressed a wee kiss to her cheek, then wiped away a tear and flew off on her mission.

Hands propped on her waist, Wrynne glanced around to make sure she had everything she needed. She had donned good, sturdy boots and would wear her cloak and carry her staff, as well as her large satchel full of healing supplies.

Into this she also tucked her most vital reference books for healers, an extra set of clothes, and—perhaps most importantly—her small, light crossbow with a slim quiver of ten mistletoe darts.

She filled a crate with all the food that would merely spoil if she left it behind and went to put it in the wagon, along with her satchel. She used her staff and the *hasten* spell to teleport herself down the mountain in a trice. Since she was a healer rather than a mage, her ability with spells was limited. *Hasten*, for example, was a low-level travel spell only suitable for short distances. Though it tended to leave her rather dizzy, it made life easier sometimes.

Whooshing back into materiality near the bottom of the forest path, she immediately winced at the stench near the battlefield.

She peeked out of the woods to check on Thaydor's whereabouts before taking her burdens over to the wagon. Fortunately, he was standing by the men out in the middle of the field.

The villagers were working on digging the mass grave in which the Urms would be burned before their bones were covered over. She grimaced, glad to be getting out of here. The whole field now stank terribly of death, and it wouldn't get much better until the fire had consumed all that was left of the monsters.

As she carefully hefted her two packages into the wagon, she saw there was still plenty of room in back to hide her things. The real trick would be getting her armor loaded into it without Thaydor noticing. If he saw that, he would know she was up to something. Whispering the *hasten* spell once more, she banged her staff on the ground again and returned to materiality up by her bower.

Her armor was stored in a compact leather trunk and was not

anywhere near as elaborate as Thaydor's. She hadn't even worn it since the ceremonial day of her class's graduation from their training at the Bastion, for even the young women who pledged a few years or a whole lifetime of service to Ilios were taught the rudiments of warfare. As they well knew, the forces of good must always be ready to do battle against the forces of evil. Everyone had a part to play.

Opening the case to make sure her armor was still in good order, she closed it again, and just as quickly conveyed it down the mountain. She tucked it in the wagon and hid it somewhat from view amid all the baggage and supplies.

*He'll never notice,* she thought, glancing back out at the field.

Thaydor hadn't moved. Arms folded across his chest, he stood in a kingly pose, chatting away with his rustic compatriots.

She shook her head fondly, impressed at how the warrior son of an earl and heir to one of Veraidel's most prestigious families could get along with anyone. Then she whisked back up the mountain and made a last visit to her garden.

When Thaydor had finally returned, saddled Avalanche, and was ready to go, Wrynne closed and locked the wooden shutters all around her bower, her heart pounding.

The time had come.

She had put the fairies in charge of her garden and made them promise to let the villagers know they could take from it what they needed when it bloomed. There was nothing left to do.

"Ready?" Thaydor asked with a smile, suspecting nothing.

She nodded wistfully. "I think so."

She looked around at her bower one last time and said a silent goodbye to it, to the peace and safety she had known here. She didn't know when she'd be back.

If ever.

Then she joined him. They walked down the mountain path together, he leading his horse rather than taxing the stallion with a steep downhill ride. When they reached the field at the bottom, Thaydor tied Avalanche to the back of the cart, then handed Wrynne up onto the driver's box. He checked Polly's harness one last time, then vaulted up onto the seat beside Wrynne and took up the reins.

And so they set out for Toad Hollow, rolling along in the clunky jug of a wagon.

The sadness of leaving her home wore off quickly in the excitement of the road ahead. She was a young woman on an adventure. The day was bright and clear, she was with the man she was fairly sure she had already half fallen in love with, and now she could personally make sure he stayed safe.

The farther down the road they rolled, with Avalanche trotting along behind, the lighter Wrynne's heart lifted. She noticed that Thaydor kept a couple of weapons close to hand, though—Hallowsmite sheathed at his side and the hilt of a dagger peeking out the top of his boot. He was obviously ready to deal with enemies, but, trusting soul that he was, he did not think to look inside her satchel. Otherwise, he might have discovered that his traveling companion was equipped for a much longer journey than a mere day's trip to the market town.

Having got this far, Wrynne was already growing a trifle anxious about how and when to make her request about continuing on with him. She didn't want him to get angry... Perhaps during their meal at the Blind Badger?

There was one approach that would probably work, though she hated to manipulate him. Since he was going to Pleiburg anyway, she could probably charm him into taking her to the city under the pretense of going home to visit her parents. After all that upsetting business with the Urmugoths, of course, he would understand.

And since he insisted on seeing her as a damsel in distress anyway, he wouldn't think twice if she implied that she needed her mother's comforting embrace. But she wasn't sure she *wanted* a man of such courage and strength to view her that way—weak and needy—especially after she had shown him how strong she could be. His opinion of her mattered a great deal to her, she had to admit, given her own enormous admiration of him.

Unsure yet how to gain his agreement, she pushed the matter out of her mind for now and just enjoyed being with him at this, the official start of their quest.

Leaving the green shadows of the woods, they followed the dusty lane as it meandered through the patchwork countryside. A small, lively river ran parallel to the road and widened as it went, and farms nestled in the dips between the hills. At length, they reached a fingerpost pointing the way: TOAD HOLLOW – 1 MILE.

"How exciting," Thaydor jested.

"Not really," Wrynne drawled, making him chuckle. "You'll see."

Outside the provincial town, a riverside mill kept its waterwheel busily churning. Beside it, gray wisps rose from the pointed roof of a little round smokehouse where some delicious-smelling meat was curing.

The town was alive with sound as loud, metallic blows rang out rhythmically from the blacksmith's forge and livestock lowed and bleated in a nearby pen. On the water, three men poled a ferry downriver, crates and barrels piled atop the low, flat barge.

They entered the town by driving over a stone bridge and through open gates overlooked by a single sturdy tower. Toad Hollow was not large, but it was busy, a warren of winding, cobbled lanes with a jumble of half-timbered houses and all manner of shops. In the middle of the largest intersection, the market vendors sold their wares from wooden stands and handcarts, shaded by a hodgepodge of draped canvas tents and colorful striped awnings.

"There's the inn." Wrynne pointed at the hanging wooden placard for the Blind Badger, an L-shaped coaching inn, painted white with black shutters. It had a tavern on the ground level and guest lodgings all around the galleried upper story.

"Looks good," Thaydor replied with a nod. "We should get your shopping done first. Then we can leave your things in the wagon while we eat."

She nodded vaguely, since she didn't really need to buy anything. He drove the wagon into an out-of-the-way spot at the edge of the innyard. He gave the young attendant there a coin to watch the horses and the wagon so they could go peruse the market.

Suddenly feeling a bit guilty, Wrynne was beginning to rethink the wisdom of being less than forthright. The Paladin of Ilios probably had a stricter-than-average response to people telling him untruths. *Little late to worry about that now.*

"Let's keep our eyes open, just in case," he murmured, his hand resting on the hilt of his sword.

She nodded and stayed alert as she walked with him into the open-air market, wondering if she should come clean right then. Drifting among the vendor stalls and donkey carts, she noticed a few townsfolk looking curiously at Thaydor.

*No wonder*, she thought. He stood a head taller than most of the men and was as beautiful as a demigod. The women eyed her enviously while the men simply stepped out of his way.

Oddly enough, it was a child who was the first to recognize him for who he was. "Mama, look!" The boy pointed. "It's the Golden Knight!"

The youngster broke away from his harried-looking mother, who was in the midst of haggling with a costermonger.

"Sir Thaydor!" The boy came barreling over to them, craning his neck to peer up the man. "I knew it was you! I saw you at the tournament last summer!"

"Did you, now?" Thaydor bent down and gave the lad a jovial smile. "Did I win?"

"Of course you did! You always win. You're the royal champion! And guess what? The knight you beat in the joust is here, too—Sir Reynulf! Are you going to fight him again?"

Wrynne looked at him in alarm.

At that moment, a deep voice boomed across the square. *"Thaydor!"*

The tone was anything but friendly.

Thaydor straightened up, bristling, his hand resting on the hilt of his sword.

The crowd parted to reveal the red knight in full armor.

"Reynulf," he greeted his fellow paladin, his tone even.

The Bloodletter of Xoltheus wore the same smirk Wrynne remembered from her dream, his dark eyes blazing. Flanking Reynulf were a dozen of the king's soldiers in round helmets, chain mail, and blue-and-white surcoats with the royal insignia.

Wrynne put a hand on the boy's shoulder and murmured, "Go back to your mother. *Now.*" The child started to protest, then saw her blistering glance and fled.

Thaydor did not move. "Wrynne," he said very calmly under his breath, "can you drive a wagon?"

"Certainly."

"Go and move it outside the gates. I'll meet you there shortly."

She glanced at him in wild uncertainty. *Sweet Ilios. Walled town. We're trapped.*

"I'll be fine," he said softly, his stare pinned on the black-haired knight. "Go. Eadric failed to listen to me. Remember what happened to him?" he reminded her in a low tone when she lingered, torn.

"Very well." She swallowed her uncertainty and nodded. "Be careful." Then she slipped away, blending into the crowd and heading down one of the market aisles, her heart pounding.

Before leaving the market for the innyard, she paused just long enough to see what happened next. People fled out of the way, clearing a path as the soldiers clomped toward him in formation. The red knight hung back. Reynulf was the only man there who was Thaydor's size, but the foot soldiers had the numbers…and their orders, it seemed.

She could hear their captain shouting. "Sir Thaydor Clarenbeld! Thaydor, son of Thaydon War Hammer!" the man yelled at him in a tone of guarded respect. "Stop right there, sir! Would you put your hands up, please, where we can see them? Don't touch Hallowsmite! You need to come with us."

Another dozen troops hurried onto the scene, streaming into position from the other end of the market to surround him.

Wrynne's stomach twisted with a dreadful knowing as she glanced again in Thaydor's direction. This degree of treachery could only come from the palace. Just as she had warned him.

"What is the meaning of this?" Thaydor demanded.

"Sir Thaydor Clarenbeld, you are under arrest!" the captain shouted.

"Arrest?" he thundered in astonishment. "For what?"

It was the war god's paladin who answered him with a cold smile, but Wrynne was too far away to hear Reynulf's reply. All she saw was the rage that filled Thaydor's face, then the ripple of shocked murmurs as the gawking shoppers whispered to one another. Much to her frustration, she could not make out their words, only see their incredulous expressions.

But the shock on Thaydor's face told her that he knew in that moment beyond all doubt that he had been well and truly betrayed. Given his own high rank, the warrant for his arrest could not have been issued unless the king himself had signed it.

"You know these are lies," he said loudly to Reynulf.

The red knight shrugged. "I have my orders."

Thaydor shook his head, his stare fixed on Reynulf. But when he drew his sword, against the captain's warnings, Wrynne's breath caught, her hand flying to her mouth. *Don't…*

Lowering his head, Thaydor charged straight at Reynulf and tackled him. Ramming him with his shoulder, he knocked his rival off his feet and sent him crashing to the ground in a clatter of metal. Still dressed in street clothes, Thaydor was too quick and agile to go down with the heavily armored knight.

Instead, he stepped on Reynulf's chest as he leaped over the red knight and ran a few steps out into the square, eluding the soldiers who had surrounded him and moving clear of the crowd of innocent bystanders.

Wrynne could not tell what exactly he intended to do. Fleeing was obviously not in the man's nature, but if he hurt or killed any of the king's men, he would only be making it worse for himself.

She could not bear to walk away and leave him to his fate, but he had given her his orders, and she knew she had to trust in his experience and skill. Hoping no one had noticed them come into the town together, she ran the rest of the way to the wagon and dismissed the boy who'd been guarding it.

As she climbed up onto the driver's seat and took up the reins, she paused for a second, wondering if she should free Avalanche to gallop to his master's side and get him out of there. He was trained to do so, judging by how he had gone running to Thaydor yesterday in the field.

But no, she decided. If the king's men captured his mount, Thaydor would be absolutely furious at her.

Then, to her horror, one the king's men bellowed to the sentries on the tower. *"Shut the gates!"*

Wrynne clapped the reins over Polly's back and managed to get the wagon moving. The way Thaydor had left it parked, backing up would have been too long and arduous an ordeal, so her only choice was to go forward and circle all the way around the inn before turning back out onto the street.

As she squeezed through the narrow drive that wrapped around the inn, she could not help but notice the array of signs, leaflets, and handbills nailed up all along the tall wooden fence. She ignored postings of the tavern's menu and countless advertisements for the town's various shops, but her gaze homed in on a freshly inked *Wanted* poster nailed up in a prominent position.

It featured a very poor sketch of Thaydor's face.

With a furious glare, she leaned out from the driver's seat and tore it off the wall as she passed. She glimpsed the words *Bounty, Urmugoths* and *Beware! Armed and Dangerous*, before she spotted the most shocking word of all along the bottom. *Treason.*

"What rubbish!" she cried aloud, enraged. Folding it roughly in half, she tucked it under her backside to keep it from blowing away. She'd examine it later. There was no time right now to learn the details of whatever trumped-up charges they had dreamed up against him, but it didn't look good.

She couldn't believe it. The king's champion, the most honorable man in Veraidel was now a fugitive with a bounty on his head?

Then she urged Polly out onto the street and turned left toward the town gates. The soldiers were already trying to close them, shooing people either out or in. Obviously, they wanted Thaydor trapped within the town walls so they could corner him. Wrynne felt sick just thinking about it.

She did not know what she was going to do. But the first thing was to obey his orders and get this wagon outside the gates. Pedestrians, but no carriages, blocked her way as she hurried Polly onto the bridge.

"Let me through!" she hollered as the gates, still wide, swung slowly toward each other.

"Sorry, mistress, you'll have to wait!"

"I can't wait! I'm a healer. There's an outbreak of fever down in Butterdale! I'm on my way to help them. I just stopped into town to buy some medicine. Now, let me go to them or people are going to die!"

He eyed her simple clothes and spotted the necklace identifying her as a Daughter of the Rose and gave in. "Oh, very well. Hurry up!" He waved her through impatiently. Distracted by all the excitement of everyone looking for Thaydor, the sentry did not notice the very fine white warhorse trotting along behind the humble carriage.

Unhappy about lying *again*—though once more, she'd had no choice—Wrynne held her breath as she drove over the bridge, glancing back to ensure Avalanche made it through, as well. To her relief, the towering gates closed inches behind the horse's swishing ivory tail.

Turning off the bridge and back onto the road, she picked up the pace, urging Polly into a trot. She looked over her shoulder in distress, wondering how Thaydor was ever going to get out of there, past that heartless assassin.

Whether or not her dream about Reynulf was true, it was no mystery why he would've been willing to carry out this deceitful warrant. Of course, he was only following orders, but every knight had ambition, and with Thaydor out of the way, Reynulf would finally be the top knight in the kingdom. She would bet he'd already been promised the role of royal champion.

Eyes narrowed, she shook her head angrily and finally slowed the carriage, pulling over to the side of the road about a half-mile south of the town.

*Now what do I do?*

It was hard to think clearly in her rattled state. Even if he had already escaped, which she doubted, he would still have to find her and the wagon.

*Unless I go find him.*

She'd brought her staff. Using the *hasten* spell three times in a row could have her back inside the town walls.

*I can get him out of there.*

It was not the most appetizing prospect, and he might not like seeing her there again. Eadric had come after him on the battlefield, after all, which was how he had ended up in pieces. However, she knew it would work.

She briskly decided this was the best plan, perhaps the *only* plan at this point. Scanning the woods alongside the road, she picked an opening between the trees wide enough to fit the wagon.

She jumped down off the driver's seat and took hold of Polly's bridle, murmuring assurances to the bay mare as she led her on foot into the forest. Avalanche followed with the cart. Once she had walked the horses several yards into the woods, she tied Polly to a tree. She stilled her mind as best she could under the circumstances and cast a sanctuary spell to hide them.

Making sure the horses were content, she got her staff off the back of the wagon and then walked out to the road. From this vantage point, the horses and wagon were invisible. The only evidence left behind were the wagon tracks where she had left the road. She kicked dust over the telltale tracks, then memorized the location, marking the spot in her mind by the half-fallen pine tree that appeared to have been hit by lightning long ago.

*Hold on, Thaydor. Don't get yourself killed again, my friend. I'm on my way.* With that, Wrynne closed her eyes, gripped her jewel-headed staff, banged it lightly on the ground, and whispered, "*Hasten.*"

Landing about a thousand feet up the empty road, she took a breath to steady the slight vertigo, then she did it again. The third jump would put her inside the walls of Toad Hollow. She thought for a moment about where to land, then bumped her staff on the ground once more and whispered the command.

*Poof!*

She was dizzy when she popped back into materiality in an alley across from the market. With a queasy groan, she clutched her stomach.

*Ugh, I really need to learn a proper travel spell.*

*Hasten* was really just intended for very short distances—emergency escapes and the like. Even so, her little spell had got her there faster than even Avalanche could have carried her, and fortunately, no one had seen her arrive.

Trying to regain her balance, she strode out of the alley and looked around amid the still-seething chaos.

"Thaydor?" she shouted, searching the scene before her. She checked the market, striding past the aisles to see if he was in there somewhere, but no. She peered into the surrounding streets, as well, then suddenly spotted him running across the rooftops, sword in hand.

A little taken aback, she shook her head to herself. *So that's how he means to get over the wall. Madman.*

Thankfully, the blade of Hallowsmite was not yet bloody, but still bright and clean from what she could see.

She shifted her gaze down to the ground where the soldiers chased after him, swarming the adjoined buildings atop which the Golden Knight dashed, sure-footed as a cat. How he balanced atop the peaked roof ridges, she had no idea.

But his escape plan wasn't going to work.

From where she stood, she could see what he could not yet—a large gap lay between the houses and the top of the wall. It was too wide to jump. Even for him.

The soldiers were yelling at him to come down and at one another, reporting which way he was going. Reynulf looked on in amusement, leaning by a post out of the way and casually drinking a tankard of ale, as though he merely meant to let the soldiers wear their quarry out before he stepped in to take Thaydor into custody.

*What infuriating arrogance!*

Wrynne glared at Reynulf, then scowled to see that his men had shackles at the ready. Closing in on Thaydor from both sides on the ground, they had even brought out a man-catcher on a long wooden pole.

*How dare they?*

The hero of the kingdom, and they'd clap that contraption around his neck as though he were a rabid dog? Wrynne thumped her staff angrily on the cobblestones and magically whooshed up onto the roof a few yards ahead of him.

Thaydor, running straight at her, nearly fell off it in his astonishment. "Wrynne?"

"Hullo, dear. Having fun?" she inquired as she used her staff to steady herself atop the narrow roof ridge.

"What are you doing here?" he cried, waving his arms to catch his balance.

"Rescuing you, Sir Knight. Take my hand." Fighting the dizziness that came with the spell—and probably with the simple fact of standing on a rooftop—she stretched out her hand, waiting for him to reach her. Below, the soldiers fell into ever-greater chaos at this new arrival.

"A sorceress!" someone shrieked. The whole town gawked at her, some of the people falling back in fear.

"Look, sir! He's got a witch helping him!"

She had got the red knight's full attention. "Who is that?" Reynulf demanded.

One of the market vendors squinted. "I recognize that woman! It's the Maid of the Mount! She's got Ilian magic!"

Reynulf snorted. "Kill her," he ordered. "He's the only one we need alive."

"Archerrrrs!" the captain bellowed, waving his arm to signal his men.

"Thaydor!" Wrynne cried, only to lose her balance when she jerked too fast to look at the archers taking aim at her.

"Wrynne!" Thaydor caught her hand as she teetered wildly, planting his foot atop a dormer to save them both. He yanked her to his chest, then turned to the soldiers, his sword raised in a frantic gesture of surrender. "Don't shoot! Hold your fire! Let her go! I'm coming down!"

"Oh, no, you're not!" she muttered, clinging to him.

"What are you do—" His words broke off and he cursed as they both started falling in earnest, their arms wrapped around each other.

"*Hasten!*" Wrynne clunked her staff awkwardly on the roof tiles as they plunged earthward.

*Whoosh!*

In the twinkling of an eye, they landed on their rear ends in the middle of the dusty road well outside the town.

Thaydor sat up immediately, shaking his head to clear it. He looked at her, saw she was safe, then glanced over his shoulder at the distant town walls.

He let out a slightly dazed laugh. "Well, that's new."

"Oh, I'm a girl of many hidden talents. Come on, we're not there yet." She grasped hold of his arm again. "*Hasten.*"

# Chapter 7

# Bonfire

The rain drummed on the forest trees and dripped off the mouth of the secluded cave where they had taken shelter for the night. Having laid out the two bedrolls across from each other, Wrynne was working on building a fire from the dry kindling that they'd had the foresight to stop and collect when they'd seen the dark clouds gathering.

Thaydor had gone to cover the wagon with an oilskin stored among his provisions. Since the cave had plenty of room, they had brought the horses in, as well. Avalanche and Polly were contentedly slurping their water and munching their grain. To be sure, the two had earned the extra handful of oats.

Between Wrynne's *hasten* spell and the trusty horses' willingness to pull the cart at a gallop for as long as Thaydor had dared push them, they had managed to outrun Reynulf and his men.

Thaydor had bitterly agreed that, considering Wrynne and he were now both fugitives, there was no point in talking to the king. Instead, they were heading to the Bastion to consult the oracle and hopefully receive some guidance and at least temporary sanctuary.

Wrynne was worried about the paladin. Ever since she had handed him the *Wanted* poster, he'd had a lost, stunned look in his blue eyes. He seemed to be in shock. So was she, in truth. She could not believe they were now both outlaws.

The poor man had read that dreadful piece of paper so many times he must have memorized it by now, as if it might start making sense to him if only he studied it hard enough. He had not looked this disturbed even on the night he had nearly died.

She blew on the spark she'd created to get the campfire started. The mundane normality of the task helped to calm her.

"They're blaming *me*?" he had uttered when she had first showed it to him. "Unbelievable! *I* let the Urmugoths in? *I* killed the sentries? How can they possibly justify such a ridiculous claim? Whyever would I do such a thing? So that I could win my way back into the king's good graces? As if I care for his opinion! Sweet Ilios, is that what people actually think of me? That I'm some bootlicking toady?"

"No, of course not, Thaydor," she had reassured him, sitting down beside him in the cave. "Trust me, anyone who knows you or even knows *of* you will realize at once you are not capable of this. Such a cruel, deceitful scheme would never even occur to you, let alone would you ever carry it out. All Veraidel know this is a lie, then everyone will realize the king's lost his mind."

"I hope that's all it is... Madness. I-I don't understand." He had shaken his head, genuinely at a loss. "How can they spread these lies about me? I've done nothing wrong. They want to destroy me just because I spoke out?"

Wrynne had only been able to shrug, tears springing into her eyes for him. "I'm so sorry."

"No, it's not for myself that I'm angry," he'd answered absently, staring at the cave wall in thought. "It's because of what it means."

"What does it mean?"

He'd been quiet for a long moment before he'd finally said, "It means that the kingdom has gone quietly into tyranny while no one was paying attention. That's what it means."

His words and his grim, quiet tone had made her blood run cold.

"I didn't want to believe it was possible...or acknowledge what that I sensed in the palace. Something off... But the truth was there, gnawing at me, despite my insistence to myself that Baynard could be trusted. A cold feeling in my gut. Yes, I'm afraid I've felt this coming for a long time now."

"What are you saying?"

"The kingdom is in danger. Everybody's grown so complacent. They're asleep." He had looked at her, his eyes ablaze. "If the rule of law means nothing... If we're no longer free to speak our minds... If false accusations can be issued from the highest seat in the realm and cast far and wide, to be acted on with the full force of the law... If the Crown itself can attack a loyal citizen without cause... Then we have all become slaves, Wrynne. It's just that nobody else has noticed yet...because they came after me first.

"But of course they did," he had murmured, more to himself than to her. "They knew I'd never allow it. So that's where all of this was going. Now it all makes sense. *Sanctus solis*, you were right, Wrynne." He'd looked at her grimly. "They *were* trying to kill me. But it's worse than even *you* thought."

"How?" she had whispered.

"This is not just some vain retaliation for the king's wounded pride, because I rebuked him for this public dalliance with his mistress. No. The Baynard I know wouldn't bother. If you ask me, this comes straight from Lord Eudo, and I'd bet you anything he's setting up a coup. Get rid of me, get rid of the king. Damn it, how could I be so stupid not to see it until now?" he had suddenly exploded. He let out a curse and walked out of the cave. "Excuse me."

"What are we going to do?" she'd shouted after him.

He had paused, his back still to her, fists clenched by his sides.

"Fight it!" he had growled. Then he had strode out, mumbling something about going out to cover the wagon with the oilskin so their things didn't get wet.

For a quarter hour or so, he stayed outside, keeping to himself. When he returned presently, his blond hair looked a shade darker from the rain, but the same fury remained in his eyes. He had a bow and a quiver of arrows slung over his shoulder. "I'm not hungry, but I'll go get you something to eat if you—"

"No need! Stay." She swept to her feet. "I brought food. It's in the wagon. I'll go get it."

He furrowed his brow. "Did you buy something in the town before we fled?"

She paused. "No, I brought it with me from my bower." She pulled on her cloak and lifted the hood. "Come. Maybe I have something that can tempt you."

"I daresay," he answered under his breath, and gave her a swift glance that made her blush.

She looked away, abashed. "You really ought to eat. You'll need your strength," she warned, then hurried out into the rain.

"Wrynne," he said softly after she brushed by him at the cave's mouth.

"Yes?" She turned and found him gazing at her with a look of anguished intensity on his handsome face.

He shook his head. "I'm so sorry I brought all this upon you. You saved my life and I've ruined yours."

"Ah, don't be daft." With a fond, chiding smile, she took a step back in his direction. "You haven't ruined anything."

"I should've never let you come with me to town. This is all my fault."

"Stop it. You've got enough enemies against you out there without also pummeling yourself, especially not for my sake. Now, you listen to me, Paladin. Everything is going to be all right," she promised, the rain misting her face. "You are Sir Thaydor Clarenbeld, the Golden Knight, and you will fix this. I have total faith in you. As for me, well," she admitted, "I sort of *knew* what I was getting into when I climbed in the wagon with you this morning. Call it woman's intuition."

"You told me they were after me," he agreed, hands in pockets. "If only I'd have listened."

She smiled at him. "That's why I tagged along. In case you got into a scrape. Oh, come, I didn't really need any supplies from the market," she finally confessed. "I just wanted to stay with you, make sure you'd be all right. That's why I brought all this. Look!" she said brightly.

Going over to the wagon, she pulled up the edge of the oilskin and pointed at her cluster of baggage tucked away behind the horses' unused saddles and some large sacks of Thaydor's various supplies. She beckoned him over. "Why don't you put those muscles to work helping me carry some of these things into the cave? I'll make you something to eat, and perhaps we can restore your cheery nature," she teased.

He furrowed his brow and left the cave's mouth, striding out into the rain with her. Joining her at the back of the wagon, he frowned at the tidy heap of her baggage, once she had heaved aside Polly's saddle and Avalanche's extra blanket.

"What is all this?"

"The crate's full of food." She shrugged. "It was extra. I didn't want it to go to waste. The satchel's got my healing supplies, clothes and things."

"And this leather case?"

"My armor?" she said, then bit her lip and glanced up at him.

He paused before turning his head and giving her a hard look. "So you lied to me."

"I only wanted to help…"

He just looked at her. He didn't have to say it. *Familiar words.* She had acted on the same impulse that had got Eadric killed. More importantly, she had ignored his express wishes.

His blue eyes turned steely. He shook his head, picked up the crate of food, and turned away. "Don't ever lie to me again," he warned in a low tone, then headed back to the cave.

Wrynne's heart pounded. Flustered by his disapproval, she couldn't leave it at that. "Thaydor!" she protested. "Come, I didn't really *lie*."

"That's exactly what you did," he replied as he marched ahead of her toward the cave.

"What choice did you leave me?" she exclaimed, feeling defensive and embarrassed as she hurried after him through the steady rain.

Ahead of her, he walked into the cave and put the crate down near the fire. Carrying her satchel, Wrynne frowned as she approached. She had no desire to stay out in the sopping wet forest. It was getting dark. But on the other hand, she was not overly eager to go in there and face him, either.

He was not having a good day as it was, and she was the only person on hand at whom he could vent his understandable anger at the world. Besides, she somewhat deserved it, she conceded with a scowl.

But considering that she had saved his neck, stubbornly, she had no interest in backing down. "I asked you yesterday if I could come with you," she reminded him tersely when she joined him in the cave.

"And I said no," he countered, leaning down to warm his hands by the fire.

"You wouldn't even listen!" She dropped her satchel on the ground in irritation and tore off her cloak. "Anyway, I don't answer to you. You have no authority over my life. I can do what I want and go where I please."

"No authority? Do you really want me to pull rank on you in both hierarchies—church and state? Because that is not the point, Wrynne! You manipulated me!" he exclaimed, straightening up and turning to her. He loomed over her, exceedingly tall, muscular, and annoyed. "Pardon if I seem a bit perturbed about all this, but it's been rather a bad day for finding out I've trusted the wrong people!"

Her jaw dropped. "Don't lump me in with them! Thaydor!" she protested. "Oh, fine! Very well, yes, I could have been more truthful. But don't put me in the same camp as those who betrayed you, because I would never! Surely you don't doubt that at least I'm on your side?"

He was silent for a moment, still unwilling to let her off the hook, much to her surprise.

Sweet Ilios, he was lawful.

"Lying is not a small thing, Wrynne. Not to me. Not even for a good cause. All right? So don't do it again."

"I heard you the first time," she muttered, hating being scolded like a child. She folded her arms across her chest, scowling at the mossy rock wall.

He stared at her, but now she was the one refusing to look at him.

"From the first moment I saw you, I trusted you instinctively," he said. "How could I not? My life was in your hands. And you saved me. Nobody ever saves me. I'm always saving everybody else. But you... Now I find out you tricked me and played on my trust just to get your way—"

"So I could *help* you!"

"It doesn't matter. A lie's a lie. Don't you understand what that does to someone like me, whose whole existence is usually a matter of life and death, from one quest to the next? I'll tell you what it does," he said crisply before she could insist that he was overreacting. "It plants a seed of doubt that we cannot afford to have between us, especially if our lives are going to depend on each other...as they apparently are, now that we're both being hunted."

She shook her head at him, amazed. "I don't believe you. You're questioning my loyalty? Whether or not you can trust me, rely on me? After I saved your life? Twice?"

"No. I'm questioning if you can follow orders. Like Eadric should have done. Like a good soldier."

"I'm not Eadric, and I am not a soldier—"

"Precisely why you shouldn't even be here!"

"Still, let's not forget that you'd have been clapped in a man-catcher, shackled, and thrown in a prison cart today if it wasn't for me. Honestly! Pardon me, Paladin, if I am not as virtuous as you and chose to keep my own counsel on my true plans this morning. So sorry! What was I to do? Let you go tearing off alone to get yourself killed?"

"You can't even go home now because you followed me!" he shouted, gesturing angrily in the direction of Mistwood. "You were seen by countless witnesses aiding a fugitive. A man the king himself has singled out as an enemy of the Crown. Don't you see? You've put yourself and possibly your whole family in danger for my sake. All I wanted, Wrynne, was to protect you. So I could come back later and we could be together—"

"Wait. What?"

"But now, because of this, I have no idea what will become of either of us. There's nowhere safe for you until I fix this."

"And you *will*. And I'll help you. That's why I'm here." Striving for a conciliatory tone, she moved closer, privately stunned by his professed wish to be with her.

His admission gave her the courage to ignore his intimidating anger; she fingered the front of his coat and attempted to cajole him into forgiving her. "I wasn't trying to deceive you. Please don't be angry anymore. Listen to me. I do have training, you know, the same as everybody at the Bastion. I won't get in your way, and I promise, you don't have to worry for me so much. I'm not some delicate little damsel in a tower. I can take care of myself. I'm not worried about being safe. I just want to be with you." She looked up at him through her lashes. "What need have we to wait until later, when we can be together now?"

He grasped her wrists lightly and stilled her caresses on his chest. "You could have been killed today," he said, his eyes deadly serious. "Reynulf doesn't play games, and now you've made an enemy of him. Me, I can take him. But he'll use you against me. I've got to hide you somewhere..." He looked away, pondering. "Maybe at the Bastion."

*"No."* She pulled free of his gentle hold and backed away, losing patience with him. "You're not getting rid of me, you big, bullheaded Clank. You don't have to save the world alone. Let me help." She folded her arms across her chest. "I really think you need me."

He ignored her. "I suppose I could send you to my father..."

"I am not leaving your side. Clearly, it's the will of Ilios that we face this together." She lifted her chin. "Why else would He lead you to battle the Urms on my very doorstep? Maybe He told me to go with you this morning and look after you. Did you ever think of that?"

He arched a brow. "Ilios doesn't tell people to lie."

She lost her temper again, nearly spooking the horses as she kicked her satchel out of her way. "You want to know the truth? Very well. I hated your plan! Go and talk to the king? Oh, indeed. Well, I'm sorry, Thaydor, but when somebody's trying to kill you, you don't sit down with them for tea."

"No, that would be too honest, wouldn't it?" he needled her with a sardonic smile. "You know—not to brag, my lady—but I do have considerable experience in matters of strategy."

"And absolutely no fear."

He snorted. "You say that like it's a bad thing."

"Blast it, you're my responsibility now! I didn't yank you back from the jaws of death just so you could go rushing out and get yourself killed! I gave up too much to save you—" She snapped her mouth shut abruptly, but it was too late to call the words back.

"What did you say?" he asked, his stare homing in on her.

Her heart pounded, and she faltered.

"Wrynne?" he demanded, leaning closer.

"Never mind," she mumbled, turning away.

"No, do tell, my lady. What did you mean by that? What did you give up to save me?"

"It doesn't matter."

He clasped her elbow firmly and turned her around to face him once more. "It matters very much to me. Tell me, now."

She clamped her mouth shut.

The paragon lost patience. "Speak, woman!"

"I will not. It's none of your concern." She yanked her arm free and glared up at him.

"On the contrary, I think it concerns me directly. This has to do with the method you used to save my life, doesn't it? How *did* you bring me back, anyway? I've noticed you have not been terribly forthcoming about that, and I have a right to know."

"You're alive. That's what matters."

"But how? Humor me. I know full well my wounds should've killed me. I saw the amount of blood in my armor and my helmet when I cleaned it. What did you do to me?"

Suspicion crept into his face. Doubt.

She let out a huff of indignation. She couldn't believe how he looked at her all of a sudden, as though he was wondering what else she might have lied about.

"Well, it's nothing nefarious!" she cried, aghast at his leeriness of her.

He backed away from her a little. "Don't tell me you actually *are* a sorceress, like those yokels said back in the town?"

"No, of course not," she said in exasperation.

"Did you use some kind of unsanctioned magic on me?" he demanded, looking rather spooked.

"No! Thaydor. It's sanctioned. I swear, you can trust me."

"Oh? Then start talking."

He had her cornered.

Wrynne heaved a sigh and looked away. She had tried to spare him, to avoid the reaction she could guess he would have, but he wanted honesty? *Very well.*

"It's called the *Kiss of Life* spell. I learned it at the Bastion, so please, calm down, it's fully sanctioned by the church. You were going to *die*, Thaydor. I'm just a mid-level healer. I wasn't powerful enough to save you any other way."

"*Kiss of Life?*" he echoed.

"Have you ever heard of it?" She eyed him anxiously.

"Heard of it, yes. Don't know the details. Explain…please."

She took a deep breath in an attempt to calm herself. "It's fairly straightforward. Whoever designed the spell knew how hard it is to think when someone's dying right in front of you, so, thankfully, they kept it simple. First, there's a short but weighty incantation: *Vincit tenebris lux, amor vincit mortem.*"

He touched his stomach vaguely, as though he had felt his very flesh respond to the sacred power of the words that had healed him. "Light conquers darkness," he translated in a low tone. "Love conquers death?"

"Yes. While saying that chant, I had to let my blood drip into one of your wounds." She pulled up her sleeve and lifted her bandaged left forearm to show him the proof of what she said. "And then I had to kiss you. On the lips. And then you were healed. Do you remember any of this?"

"No."

"You slept for two days. Then you woke up; I found you in the waterfall, and all the rest you know. You see? Nothing wicked. And I'm in perfect health," she assured him. "My blood is clean of all ill humours, so don't worry that I mixed it with yours."

"Huh." He folded his arms across his chest and touched his chin in thought. "But even white magic comes with a price. So what did you have to give up in exchange for my life?"

"It's no great thing. I don't regret it in the least. I was happy to—"

"Stop trying to delay and just tell me!" he burst out in exasperation.

"Before the *Kiss of Life*, I could have healed this cut magically for myself." She lifted her arm and showed the bandage again. "Now I can't." She rolled her sleeve back down quickly. "That was the price. I can't heal myself anymore. Just other people."

His face fell as he stared at her, his blue eyes filling with compassion…and regret. "Oh, Wrynne…"

"I don't care! Trust me, it's fine. I don't miss it. I was only doing my duty, just like you."

He tilted his head, the anger fading from his face. Something much softer was taking its place as he gazed at her.

"Please, don't look at me like that," she said. "I'm not some hero. You're the hero. And for me, it was well worth it to see the Paladin of Ilios preserved to fight another day."

He was gazing at her tenderly but looking rather pained. "Then it seems I am indeed in your debt." He stepped closer, but she backed away in vexation.

"No, you're not! Ugh, this is exactly why I didn't want to tell you! There's no debt. You don't owe me anything. Please. I didn't really do it for you, anyway; I did it for Ilios. Does that make you feel better? As I said, it was my duty. Nothing personal. I didn't even know you then."

"A kiss on the lips of a dying man? Sorry, demoiselle, but it doesn't get more personal than that."

She looked up at him, at a loss. "I gave it to you freely."

"And now look where it's led you." Taking hold of her wrist, he drew her closer. This time, Wrynne did not resist.

Gently pushing up her sleeve, he examined her bandaged forearm by the firelight. "May I?" He glanced at her face and whispered, "Let me do this for you."

She made no objection as he pulled out the tucked end of her bandage and then began unwrapping it from around her arm. She stood, docile, as he turned her palm up; her cheeks filled with heat at his soft, careful touch on the delicate skin near her cut. He took a deep breath and let it out slowly, closing his eyes, his angular face sculpted in the fire's orange glow. He opened his eyes again and cupped the air a couple of inches over her wound with his open hand.

A sweet warmth began to glow from the heart of his palm, focused on her cut, but spreading with a lovely tingle up her arm and down to her fingers. She marveled at being on the receiving end of a healer's magic for once. Paladins were the only sort of knights who had the power.

Slowly but surely, her torn flesh began to mend. It only took about thirty seconds and the cut disappeared. But then, when her arm was once more perfectly unscathed, Thaydor made contact, laying his hand on her skin.

And at that moment, a strange thing happened.

Wrynne drew in her breath, closed her eyes, and gasped as a shock of unimaginable pleasure ran like lightning from the place where he touched her all throughout her body, down to her toes. A soft, sensuous cry of confusion escaped her as it flashed, lingering especially strong and hot in the core of her womanhood; she bit her lip and shuddered.

Thaydor had to reach out and catch her around the waist to stop her from fainting headlong into the fire. "Are you all right?" he asked quickly.

She sagged against him, panting. "What was that?"

"I-I don't know."

She swallowed hard, striving for clarity. It passed just as quickly as it had seized her.

"Wrynne?"

*Sweet Ilios.* She looked at Thaydor in astonishment. *Did I just have a...?*

*Gracious!* She suppressed a giggle. *Well, that was rather naughty.*

*Not my fault,* her conscience defended.

*How is that even possible?* She looked at him, wide-eyed. *Why, he is a man of the most remarkable talents...*

"Answer me. What's wrong?" Bewilderment replaced the worry on his face when Wrynne glanced at him, mischief dancing in her eyes.

He had no idea that he'd just made her come.

"So, er, you really *can* heal," she commented awkwardly, her cheeks flushing.

"Yes, as I told you. Simple injuries like that. Did it hurt when I—"

"No." She cleared her throat and casually inspected her arm, unable to look at him without yearning to devour him. "Not at all. Thank you."

"Are you sure you're all right?" he asked, staring at her apprehensively again as he ran a hand through her hair.

"Oh yes. Ahem. Thaydor? Did you...do something *different* to me? Something else...besides healing?"

"No. Why?" His blue eyes searched hers innocently.

*You are beyond adorable,* she decided, trying not to laugh. "No reason."

He was eyeing her strangely. "Perhaps you should sit down."

"Yes."

Solicitous as ever, he steadied her as she took a seat on one of the bedrolls.

*Whew.* She chuckled to herself and leaned back on her hands, stretching her legs out before her and crossing her ankles. Still tingling a bit, she suddenly felt lovely, if perhaps rather scandalized at herself, and she was glad Thaydor did not seem to realize what he had just accidentally done to her.

Not that she minded one bit.

He crouched down beside her and stared into the fire for a moment. Darkness was descending outside, but the rain poured on, running in rivulets off the cave's arched entrance.

Wrynne sighed and dropped her head back luxuriously for a moment. "I should see about our food now."

He didn't seem to hear, his gaze fixed on the bonfire. "Maybe you were right," he said at length. "Maybe, having brought me back, you *are* now responsible for me in some odd way. But I'm responsible for you, too. We have to stick together." He sent her a matter-of-fact sideways glance. "I think our path is clear. We have to marry."

*"What?"* She sat up straight, her eyes widening.

"It's obviously the path that Ilios has set for us. As you said, why else would he have so clearly brought us together? More to the point, 'tis my duty to ensure your safety after all you've done for me, all you've sacrificed for my sake."

"Thaydor—"

"You must be protected, and since it's my duty to see to that, you must stay by my side. Given both our roles as servants of the Light who must behave as examples to others, our traveling together cannot be seen as improper or scandalous in any way. After all, if the likes of you and I cannot act honorably, then no one else will even try. So, what say you?"

He looked her up and down. "Marry me when we get to the Bastion tomorrow. It's the right thing to do."

Her eyebrows rose slowly. The stiff, pragmatic marriage proposal from the Golden Knight had flabbergasted her.

His lips twisted in amusement. "Very well. You have until tomorrow to decide. But I suggest you make your peace with it, for I'm afraid I must insist."

"Thaydor..." she finally managed again.

"Yes, Wrynne?" he asked in a tone of lavish patience.

She cast about for reason. It wasn't easy after the experience of a moment ago.

"Is this all because of the *Kiss of Life* spell?" she asked, suddenly fearful his care for her was purely concocted by her own magic. She didn't want that kind of marriage.

"Darling, you gave up your ability to heal yourself for my sake. Then you lost your sweet little woodland home and now your peace and your good name, all for helping me. Honestly, what did you think I was going to do? If you understood my nature at all by now, and I think you do, you should've seen this coming and thought it over before you followed me this morning. Am I some dishonorable cur to let a woman give up everything for me, and then just walk away from her?"

She stared into his eyes, at a loss. He really was a bullheaded Clank. But he was so, so hard to say no to. "I appreciate your concern for me, truly, but I am not marrying you out of obligation. As I told you, you don't owe me anything. So, thank you, but no."

He tilted his head, studying her in perplexity, then he looked at the fire again. "Very well… Perhaps it's my turn for a bit of uncomfortable honesty."

He bit his lip and sent her a sidelong glance.

"What is it?"

"I'm not asking out of simple obligation, Wrynne. I like the notion of having you for my wife, because of your own…qualities."

"Because I'm a healer?"

"No. Not for your powers." He let out a breathy laugh, sounding almost nervous. "I like…being around you. You make me feel more…comfortable than women usually do. You're beautiful and kind and warm and brave. You care about others, and I think we're very compatible. I'm sorry if this shocks you or if it's too fast, but in my mode of life, hesitation isn't usually wise. I prefer to find my target, follow my instincts, and take action. Experience has taught me you don't always get a second chance."

"Is that what I am? A target?" she asked, arching a brow.

"Of a sort, yes." He smiled, holding her gaze. "I think you and I would suit each other very well. That's why I said I would come back for you. I had already made up my mind on it last night."

Her eyes widened. "You did?"

He nodded. "I planned to bring a ring. It was supposed to be a surprise, but since our plans have obviously changed… Well, do you really think I'd let a woman like you get away?"

She stared at him in amazement. She had never been on the receiving end of such words from a man before.

He held her gaze and seemed to hold his breath. "There's also the fact that I sort of fell in love with you last night."

"You did?" she breathed, tongue-tied.

He looked deeply into her eyes. "You know full well I did," he whispered. "And I think you fell at least a little in love with me, too."

Wrynne couldn't speak to confirm or deny. She held his stare, incredulous with pulse-pounding joy.

But slowly, her heart sank as she remembered there was a logical explanation for what they were feeling. The very reason she had said no from the start.

She longed to just say, *Yes, of course, I'll marry you.* What woman in her right mind would give any other answer?

But she had to tell him. The man deserved to know.

She lowered her head. "Thaydor, there's something else you need to know about the *Kiss of Life* spell. In the interests of total honesty...since that matters so much to you."

He furrowed his brow, a renewed flicker of wariness in his eyes. "Yes?"

She winced to have to break the news, unsure how he'd take it. "I've heard from other healers that the *Kiss of Life*...can create the sense of a powerful bond between the two people involved," she said gingerly, her face burning. "I think it's possible that what we seem to be feeling for each other...could be, um, just a side effect of the magic."

He leaned closer, pinning her with an avid gaze. "So you feel it, too?"

"Of course I do," she whispered in a strangled tone, well aware that the man of her dreams could slip through her fingers, thanks to too much tiresome honesty. But that was what he obviously needed from her, and so be it.

"Perhaps I should've mentioned it before, but I-I didn't know it would be this strong. And I didn't want to burden you after all you'd been through. Most of all, I did *not* want you to feel obligated to me. I knew you would, and now you do, and I hate it. So, no, my darling knight," she said with a sorrowful gaze, "I cannot take advantage of you when you might be under the influence of magic. We don't know if this is real or illusion. It could wear off in a week, a few days... Until then, it wouldn't be fair to hold you to this offer. So, I'm sorry, Thaydor. My answer must still be no. Despite what I feel right now."

Frustration flickered in his eyes. "You don't understand. This sort of thing doesn't happen to me. I've never felt this way before. I want you…so deeply."

"And I you." Watching her fingers as she let them go traveling up his arm, she struggled to give an answer she did not want to give and one he clearly did not want to hear. "But while we both might be feeling this way now, marriage is forever. These effects might wear off—"

"Not for me. I know myself, Wrynne, and these aren't side effects. I was meant to find you and make you mine."

She clung to reason as best she could, though the passion emanating from him intoxicated her. "I could do more research at the Bastion, try to find out more about the spell. How long these residual effects might take to wear off—"

"I don't *want* it to wear off! I won't let it." He cupped her nape and stared into her eyes. "Please just say yes. Be my wife. You think I'm a good knight? I'll be an even better husband, I promise. I'm loyal. I work hard. I don't lie. I'll never abandon you. I'll never let anybody hurt you. I'll do everything I can to make you happy."

"I know you'd do that all." How she didn't swoon outright was the only question. *Is this indeed the perfect man?* she wondered. And he could be hers. She lifted her trembling hand to touch his hair, still damp with rain. "Oh, Thaydor, my golden angel, why must you tempt me so?"

His eyes flickered with heat at the question. "Darling, I haven't even begun to tempt you yet," he whispered as his lips inched closer to hers.

Breathless with want of him, she did her best to fight this losing battle, resting her hand against his rock-hard chest, trying only halfheartedly to hold him at bay. "It's just that if I agreed and the spell wore off and you regretted marrying me, I would die. I mean it."

He shook his head in fond amusement, so close she could feel his warm, moist breath on her face. "Never."

"Think!" she pleaded. "Please don't just charge in for once, I beg you. This is my heart. I am nobody, and you are the hero of the kingdom—"

He stopped her with a finger over her lips. "Never call yourself a nobody again in my hearing. And by the way, haven't you heard? I'm not a hero anymore," he whispered as he flashed a roguish grin. "I'm an *outlaw*."

And then she really did swoon, letting out a small sigh of yearning distress.

He tugged her closer with a knowing, crooked smile. "Marry me, demoiselle, and do you know what you'll achieve? You'll give me the proper incentive to clear both our names and put all this to rights." He shook his head, his blazing eyes full of zeal. "They go after me, it's one thing. They go after my wife, I'll give them a war."

She looked at him breathlessly and did not know what came over her. She suddenly threw her arms around his neck and kissed him. He seemed surprised but pulled her closer, his large hands sliding around her waist.

Heart pounding, she broke the kiss and rested her forehead against his. "You say you want the truth? Very well," she admitted in a shaky whisper. "I've never wanted anything more than I want to be with you. I think I've loved you ever since I first saw you years ago from a distance in the city. If this is what you truly want, then I'll marry you. But if a day ever comes when you regret it, know you'll break my heart."

"I never will. Believe me, sweet, you're safe in my keeping. I am nothing if not steadfast."

She looked at him in soft surrender. "Then I'm yours."

A leonine glow stole into his eyes and a seductive half-smile of anticipation curved his lips. "Finally," he purred, softly teasing her. "Shall we seal our troth with another kiss?"

"Maybe one," she conceded, her cheeks warm with the flattery of his interest. Her heart pounded with crazed joy. She could hardly contain herself at the thought that she was actually going to marry Thaydor Clarenbeld.

She slid her arms around his granite shoulders as he pulled her flush against his body. He nuzzled her nose with his own and, cradling her in his embrace, eased her onto her back on the bedroll. Wrynne watched him, riveted, allowing him to do with her what he willed. He slowly moved atop her, bracing himself on his hands while his mouth descended to hers with feather-light softness.

A blissful sigh escaped her as her eyelids fluttered closed. At first, his heated lips brushed hers with tender reverence, his urgency carefully restrained. But when she moaned and pulled him closer, desperate for more, he parted her lips with a stroke of his tongue and tasted her in dreamy intensity.

With a sound of pleasure low in his throat, he deepened the kiss. She drank it in, thrilling to the dominance and demand building in the rhythm of his mouth on hers. Her legs parted slightly to let him lie between them, though they were both still fully clothed.

She planned to keep it that way but gave herself freely to the passion of his kisses. She buried her fingers in his thick hair and consumed his delicious tongue swirling against hers. He tasted of rain. Indeed, their clothes and hair were both still damp, but the moisture turned steamy in the heat of their newfound desire.

Warrior that he was, it would have been easy to be intimidated by the sheer size and might of him in such a situation. Well over six feet tall and built for combat, he was a lot of man to contend with. Her breasts were pleasantly crushed against the muscled planes of his chest. She could feel the taut force of his thighs, the leanness of his hip brushing hers. His hard body imprisoned her, but she had no desire to escape.

She was his for the taking if he changed his mind and gave her no choice. If he did let her choose—and of course, he would never do otherwise—she wasn't sure she had sufficient will to say no.

Her heart slammed in her chest as he paused in kissing her and slowly ran his hand down the center of her chest to her midriff. Arousal sang through her veins as he set about familiarizing himself with all that would soon belong to him, touching her, learning her.

"You are so damned beautiful," he said tenderly after a moment. Then he lowered his head and kissed her throat, nibbling it lightly.

She panted, arching her back as he kissed his way down her neck, loosened the small front tie of her bodice and caressed her breasts. She looked down and watched him touch her where no one ever had. His warm, wet mouth soon followed where his hands had gone. Her whole body throbbed as his tongue explored the rosy tip of each breast, and he made her writhe with pleasure while the bonfire crackled nearby and the rain pattered steadily outside.

"Tempted yet?" he whispered knowingly, leaning on his elbow beside her.

"More than I can say."

"It's right that it should be like this tonight," he whispered. "The two of us together here. Seems it's you and me against the world."

"Why don't you take this off?" Lifting a trembling hand to his chest, she ventured to begin unlacing the front of his gambeson. "Let me make you more comfortable."

She plucked the cords free until her fingertips found his bare chest. He stared at her the whole time.

"There's no one I'd want by my side more than you, Wrynne."

"No place I'd rather be. Except perhaps a bed," she confessed with a shy smile. "But only if we're both there."

"I'll give you a bed," he teased as he slipped the garment off his strong shoulders, then peeled his shirt off over his head and cast it aside, muscles rippling down his abdomen. "Hell, I'll give you a palace when all this is over."

She laughed breathlessly, rapt with the sight of his magnificent, bronzed body sculpted by shadow and flame. "I don't care about a palace."

"Precisely why you deserve one." He pulled her astride his lap, and clutching at her skirts, inched them higher up her thighs.

She moaned, her lips skimming his velveteen shoulder. "Darling, we can't. You know we mustn't."

"Why not? We'll be married tomorrow," he said as he slipped his hand under her gown, kneading her hip. "Day after at the latest. I don't know if I can wait. I need you with everything in me. I feel like I've been waiting for you forever."

She thrilled to his touch, to his longing for her. "*You* want to break the rules? For me?"

He groaned, half in jest. "Can't I please, just once?"

She smiled against his fevered skin. "You'd never forgive yourself. Besides, if we stray and incur guilt—"

"What, for the sin of *lust*?" He cast her a devilish half-smile. "Guilty as charged, love."

She laughed and nipped playfully at his earlobe. "That makes two of us. All the same, we both know where we get our powers from. What if going astray even for one night diminishes our gifts just when we need them most? Your fighting skills. My healing. We're going to need all we've got to battle what we're up against."

He paused and scowled. "That is a good point. Damn you," he added in jest.

She hugged him with a soft chuckle. "It'll be worth the wait. For now, it's enough just to kiss and touch...isn't it?"

"Ah, you drive me mad." He tilted his head back as she began to stroke him. He sank back on his bedroll and let her do to him as she pleased.

She leaned atop him with a wicked smile. She whispered in his ear what had happened to her earlier.

He laughed aloud.

"Hmm, I could have some fun with that," he murmured.

And he did.

As the night moved on in unbearable temptation, they learned the secret of the extraordinary pleasure a healer's hands could bestow, gliding all over each other's bodies.

"Your touch is amazing," he panted, looking almost drunk with sensation. "You have no idea what you do to me."

His frank sensuality made her bold. Just once—over his clothes—she rested her hand on his bulging nether regions and stroked him. With a naughty smile, she sent her knight's long, rigid lance a pulse of the same warm, glowing energy that she had used so many times to heal.

She had not meant to bring him to climax. But she found—triumphantly—that she had. He surrendered to her ministrations with a gasp of such sweet agony she realized too late that he had been trying with all his might to hold back. But it seemed the paladin *was* capable of losing a battle, after all.

And then he was adorably embarrassed—though he laughed and said his bad day had certainly taken a good turn. And *then*, with an azure gleam in his eyes, he claimed his wicked revenge by paying her back in kind.

Several times.

Well, they needed it, she supposed. Both of them had so much hunger pent up inside from a lifetime of trying so hard to be so very good.

As she moved under him, still fully dressed, she could hardly wait for him to take her in their marriage bed. Tomorrow night seemed too far away. But slipping a finger, and then two, inside her, he satisfied her for now beyond her wildest dreams.

When she was spent, dazed, breathless, and emptied of all care, he held her in his arms for the rest of the night and kept her warm while the rain drummed on. She cast her arm across his chiseled abdomen and slept, her head nestled on his bare chest. It felt like the most natural place in the world for her to be.

*Elysium, indeed.*

# Chapter 8
# Oracle

The white tower gleamed in the brilliant midday sun, dominating the plain below the ridge where Thaydor halted the wagon for a moment.

Having set out from the cave early this morning, their half-day's journey was almost at an end.

They had reached the outer edge of the many thousands of acres controlled by the Ilian church and were approaching its official headquarters. The Bastion comprised a tiny, semi-independent city-state within Veraidel, and was under the kingdom's protection.

But given that His Majesty's spies were probably already posted around the perimeter awaiting his arrival, he and Wrynne were wearing their simple gray pilgrims' cloaks with the hoods drawn up to prevent them from being recognized. Thaydor had even put Avalanche under harness beside Polly to try to make his famous warhorse blend in as well.

His enemies would no doubt expect him to come here sooner or later, seeking guidance and practical support from his strongest allies in the church hierarchy. Perhaps he had beaten them here, he mused as he scanned right and left. If not, he should be able to slip in unnoticed. Either way, he was not unduly worried. Not even Reynulf would launch an attack on holy ground. All they had to do was get there. It wasn't far.

A world away from the troubles that besieged them, the busy, sprawling complex around the white marble Lux Aeterna Tower on the plain below bristled with lofty spires and soared with seemingly weightless flying buttresses.

Countless gargoyles kept watch from the eaves of an ornately carved collection of large, honey-colored sandstone buildings in the Gothic style, many with stained glass windows to dazzle the eyes of the faithful and lift their aspirations to eternity.

In the center of it all, the massive white marble tower reached toward heaven. Swans drifted across the large lake that cast the tower's mirror image up to the ever-watchful eyes of the Almighty and his armies of angels.

Wrynne and Thaydor exchanged an intimate smile at the sight of the place where they would soon be wed. The Bastion had shaped and molded so much of who they had become, from the university halls with their cloistered dormitories to the chapter houses of both their confraternal orders, from the military training fields where he had learned to fight to the sprawling physick gardens where she had learned to nurture and grow the apothecary herbs used in the healing arts.

They'd be safe here at least for a day or two, until the oracle told them what to do next. No one in all of Veraidel's long and colorful history had ever dared attack the Bastion, for even those who did not believe in Ilios were unwilling to risk waking the golden dragon who lived at the bottom of the lake.

None in living memory had seen the mighty Talath, but in bygone centuries, she had been known to rise up out of the depths in all her terrifying glory and roast any forces sent against the place. As ancient guardian of the Bastion, the mighty beast answered to no one but Ilios, Thaydor supposed. If she was real.

In any case, Thaydor knew the Golden Master himself would grant them sanctuary—and not even Lord Eudo would chance a public confrontation against the old holy man of Ilios. Still, neither he nor Wrynne wished to risk provoking any sort of political retaliation against the church for harboring them. So while they would seek brief solace here, they'd be on their way again as soon as possible.

He glanced at his alluring companion, eager to get her to safety. "Shall we?"

She nodded with a smile of relief.

He clapped the reins over the horses' backs and drove on past the green swathe of crops, pastures, and orchards. They passed the stables and the dairy farms, where the nuns' famous cheese was being made, and the vineyards and the winepress and the acres of hops being grown for the monks' award-winning ale, past the quaint brewery.

Nearer in lay the impressive Ilian hospital and the tidy rows of almshouses for the elderly poor, as well as the orphanage, with the little play yard for the children. Closer still to the busy, golden beehive of the

Bastion's inner circle stood the several palaces of the highest-ranking clerics in the church hierarchy, known as the Venerables.

Other buildings housed the orders of teaching monks and nuns who ran all branches of Veraidel's only university, also here at the Bastion. Other divisions of church scholars kept the great library and worked tirelessly in the scriptorium, penning beautiful illuminated manuscripts. The most erudite order of clerics worked as observers and cataloguers of nature. They spent their time studying creation, researching everything from the stars shining through the domed observatory to the lowliest of life forms growing in the dirt.

Everywhere was order; everyone had his place. And given the chaos of his life over the past few days, Thaydor welcomed the return to sanity with all his orderly, disciplined soul.

Driving along the edge of the meditation gardens further lifted his mood. The gardens were most beautiful, with colonnades, terraces, and fountains. Winding paths through the exquisite, ornamental acres offered contemplative walks, with regular stopping points to sit and think or pray.

As they went by the chapel beside the gardens' gateway, swirling strains of polyphonic chorus floated to them on the breeze, ethereal and bright as the sunlight itself. Wrynne looked over at him and took his hand. Seeing wonder mingled with anxiety in her beautiful gray eyes, he suspected she was thinking about their wedding.

He regretted that it had to be so hasty, that their families couldn't come. Ingrid would wring his neck when she found out she had lost the chance to be a bridesmaid, and what Wrynne's mother would say, he barely dared wonder.

For his part, marrying a girl without first asking her father's permission bothered him exceedingly, even though she was of legal age to make her own decisions.

But as much as this seemed out of order, he knew it would not be proper for them to continue traveling together in their current state— especially now that they had lost the fight to keep their hands off each other. Besides, it would not be safe for their kinfolk to be around them until this storm blew over, anyway.

He took his hand back from Wrynne's light hold in order to turn the wagon to the right at the intersection ahead. This put them on the broad, triumphal avenue leading straight up to the foot of the tower and the heart of the complex.

As the main approach to the little city, the so-called Avenue of the Sun was lined on both sides with tall white banners bearing the golden sunburst crest of Ilios. Sunflowers were planted along the parade route, as well, as a secondary symbol of the Light.

At last, he drove into the cobbled courtyard of the chapter house of the Sons of Might and reined the wagon to a halt. He let out a sigh, pulled down the hood of his cloak, and looked around.

"Anybody home?"

* * *

"Thaydor!" a deep voice shouted.

Wrynne looked over to find a burly, bearded friar striding toward them, a hearty grin on his beefy face.

A thick-bodied bear of a man, he wore a brown robe with a rope-belt cinched across his potbelly. With a burst of carefree laughter, he held his arms up at his sides. "Welcome, brother! We've been expecting you!"

"Brother Piero! Ah, it's been too long!" Thaydor jumped down from the wagon and clasped the friar's outstretched forearm. The man greeted him in the same fashion.

Though Brother Piero was fat and rather messy looking, something about the wild glint in his dark eyes told her he must be one of the warrior monks. Sturdy as he was, he looked like he could do some damage once he put his armor on.

"I take it you've heard my interesting news?" Thaydor drawled.

"What, that you're suddenly the kingdom's most infamous outlaw?" Piero laughed and clapped him on the shoulder. "What tripe! Aye, I saw one of those *Wanted* posters. Took it with me to the garderobe this morning and used it to wipe my arse. Er…beggin' your pardon, lady." He pressed his hands together as in prayer and bowed to her.

Wrynne's lips twitched. "Don't mind me. Greetings, brother."

"Who is your companion, lad? Ah, one of our fair Roses, I see," the friar said with a broad smile, gesturing to her necklace.

"My lady, Brother Piero has been a fixture at our chapter house since the days when I lived here as a student," Thaydor explained.

"You make me sound so old!"

"You *are* old."

"I am not yet fifty, you impertinent whelp! I daresay I can still trounce you with the quarterstaff."

"Maybe with the quarterstaff," Thaydor conceded. "I never had much patience for it."

"You always liked a bladed weapon better."

"That's true."

"Ahem," Wrynne said in amusement. "Pleased to meet you, Brother Piero. I am Wrynne du Mere and I would like to either get down from this wagon or continue on to *my* chapter house. So what are we doing, hmm?"

She gazed expectantly at Thaydor, but something about her rather wifely tone of voice must've startled Brother Piero.

He looked from Wrynne to Thaydor in astonishment. "Are you two…?"

"She saved my life," Thaydor said with a nonchalant grin, then changed the subject, clasping the older man's shoulder. "I crave your patience, brother, but we need to consult the oracle and receive whatever counsel the Venerables can bestow about our situation."

"Of course! Come. Fret not, children. We will look after the both of you." He beckoned to Wrynne, and Thaydor handed her down from the wagon. "Oh, and Bartholomew! See to the horses!" he called to someone in the chapter house stables. "Ha, Avalanche!" Piero patted the steed's neck. "How's he doing?"

"Very well," the paladin answered. They followed the friar into the chapter house. "But I'm afraid I have bad news about my latest squire."

Piero winced as he held the heavily carved oak door open for them. "Not another one, man!"

"Eadric of Hazelmore has gone to Elysium," Thaydor said quietly.

Genuine sadness filled his dark eyes. The burly monk paused, shook his head, and looked at the ground. "Ah, well, so may it be. Ilios sees all. I figure he knows what he's doing."

"I'm counting on it," Thaydor agreed. "I do wish they'd stop sending me squires who aren't ready, though."

"They all volunteer! They want to *be* you."

Thaydor harrumphed.

Wrynne poked his stomach. "Maybe your new fame as the Villain of Veraidel will dim their hero worship."

"That would be one good thing, at least." He cast his arm around her shoulders and pulled her near in chummy fashion.

Piero seemed intrigued as he glanced from Wrynne to Thaydor, both of them looking much too happy for two people who were being hunted.

"Fear not, you two," he resumed. "These lies of the darkness cannot withstand the Light shining upon them. We just have to figure out how best to do that. And we shall, never you fret. This way."

He led them up a dark, carved, turning wooden staircase. "Your rooms are up here. Sister, I'm afraid we don't have much in the way of accommodations for ladies, but we do have one bedchamber for visiting female relatives."

"I can go to my own chapter house—"

"No. You'll be much safer here," Thaydor interrupted as they stepped into the upstairs hallway. "We don't know who else might be working with the king in this. I want you within shouting distance of me at all times."

She shrugged. "As you wish. But I would at least like to visit them before we leave."

"Of course. Later."

The corridor was lined with doors to the private quarters of the Sons of Might members currently in residence. They followed Brother Piero to the door at the end of the hallway. He opened it. "Here you are, my lady. Our female guestroom. I take it you'll want the room across the hall from her," he said to Thaydor, gesturing at it.

Thaydor nodded and went into her room, where he glanced around to make sure everything looked acceptable. After spending the previous night in a cave, the well-appointed chamber was more than Wrynne expected.

"Thank you," she said, setting her satchel down on the nearest chair. "This will be perfect."

"Would you like me to send word over to the Temple of Prophecy that you need an appointment right away?" the friar asked.

"I should think they already know," Thaydor said, flashing a smile.

"Ha! Good point." Piero laughed. "I'll do it anyway so they can clear their schedules for you, under the circumstances. And the Venerables, too. I don't know how many of them you'll get, but I'm sure they'll want to speak with you."

"Thanks. Oh, and tell the priestesses at the Temple of Prophecy that we'll both want a chance individually to consult the oracle," he said, tilting his head in her direction. "I *should* do it, since I'm the one slated for destruction, but Wrynne may have better results. She's already shown something of a gift for visions and such. That dream you had of Reynulf," he reminded her.

She nodded. "Whatever I can do to help." Then she looked at the friar. "Thank you, once again, for all your help, Brother Piero."

"My honor, lady." He bowed to her. "Just promise me I'll be invited to the wedding?"

They looked at him and then each other in slightly guilty surprise.

"Are we that obvious?" Thaydor murmured.

"Ah, you don't have to be an oracle to know when two people are in love. I have eyes! I trust you will behave yourselves under our roof, eh? Ilios sees all." He arched a bushy eyebrow at them as he turned to go, chuckling as they blushed and mumbled their chagrined compliance.

"Piero?" Thaydor asked as the large, portly whirlwind of a man started striding off, dwarfing the narrow hallway through which he passed.

"Aye, lad?" he said, turning around.

Thaydor gazed at him affectionately. "Of course you are invited to the wedding. And the sooner the better."

"Ha! I knew it! I was only teasing, but when I saw the way you looked at her... Finally! Ah, I am delighted for you both." He ran back and congratulated them properly, pumping Thaydor's hand and then nearly breaking Wrynne's ribs with his big bear hug.

"You two are just...beautiful together. You're going to have the most extraordinary children! Look at you. All Elysium will rejoice. Amen, I say! Take good care of him, my lady," he warned, misty-eyed as he set her down on her feet again. "He's the best we've got."

"I know he is. I will," she promised, hoping he didn't crush her fingers as he held both her hands in his two big paws.

"As for your wedding, leave it all to me!" Piero announced with sudden zeal. "Yes, yes, I know you're on the run for your lives, but this is *love* we are talking about here! The greatest gift of Ilios! No, don't fret, 'tis no trouble. With everything you two are dealing with, all you'll have to do is show up. Leave it to me! I will personally make sure you two have the perfect wedding."

"You are more than kind." Wrynne pressed her lips shut and dropped her gaze to the floor to avoid laughing, while Thaydor mumbled his rather astonished thanks.

Who'd have thought a burly, celibate warrior monk would be so keen to plan a spontaneous wedding for his friend? Perhaps the rugged friar harbored a secret romantic streak, bless him.

After Brother Piero had gone rushing off on his many, sudden wedding-party errands, she and Thaydor exchanged a twinkling glance.

"This should be interesting," he whispered.

She shook her head, smiling. "As long as I end up with the right groom, that's all I care about."

"No worries on that point, lovely. You're all mine. Or soon to be." He sauntered over and kissed her, but with Piero's reminder to behave ringing in their ears, they parted, biding their time for now.

Thaydor did, however, send her a playful leer from the doorway before retreating to his room across the hall. It was time to prepare to see the oracle.

* * *

Except for a few noisy birds calling from the fruit trees around the large building, the domed Temple of Prophecy was an especially quiet place. Wrynne and Thaydor followed the cloistered walkway through the afternoon shade to the arched door beneath the sunburst window, where they entered.

Inside the dim, silent vestibule, they followed the usual procedure and, at once, removed their shoes. Then one of the prophetic sisters greeted them. She was draped in plain white robes with a gold clasp at her shoulder and her hair piled in tendrils on her head.

They bowed to her and murmured their thanks for so quickly being seen. With barely a word, she nodded and turned away. "Follow me."

As the oracle's attendant led them deeper into the temple, they began to hear the vibratory tones of meditative chimes resonating on the air as they were softly struck, while the scent of incense burning wafted toward them. It helped create a very soothing mood, but Wrynne was still nervous.

She glanced at Thaydor. Never had she dreamed that one day she'd be visiting the Temple of Prophecy with the Paladin of Ilios.

*Let alone marry him.*

She had never been so happy and so scared at the same time in all her life, but she pushed her anxiety aside as the woman in white gestured for them to sit. There were benches in the large, serene anteroom just outside the center courtyard where the oracle received her petitioners.

They were the only ones there.

"Sit. Make yourselves comfortable. Breathe deeply for a few minutes and think of the matter that brings you here. In your heart, tell the Father of Lights that you seek his guidance and form your question clearly in your mind. Which of you will go first?"

Wrynne pointed at Thaydor.

The woman nodded and continued her recitation of the instructions given to all visitors, whether they had ever been there before or not.

"Whenever you feel ready, go to the table there." She nodded at the long, waist-high countertop that ran the length of the wall. "Take one of the small squares of parchment provided and write your question on it in as few words as possible. If you cannot read or write, one of us will write it for you. Simply ask.

"Then roll your parchment into a tiny scroll or fold it as you wish and bring it with you to the doorway." She pointed to the door gracefully. "From there, I will take you one by one to consult the oracle. When your parchment is burned, she will read the shape of the smoke and the ashes, and give your answer privately. What you do with the information, or with whom you choose to share it, is entirely up to you unless she tells you otherwise. Any questions?"

They had none, so she left them to carry out the simple instructions. Unfortunately, for whatever reason, Wrynne found it difficult to clear her mind *or* concentrate while sitting next to Thaydor. His big, powerful presence was still just too thrilling to her in so many ways. She feared she was a little obsessed with the man, especially after last night.

The way he had touched her… She shuddered with pleasure at the vivid memory.

She stole a glance at him. He was of course doing as he was told, breathing slowly and meditating on his weighty questions and probably wondering how to pare it down to just one. Since his eyes were closed, Wrynne stole a moment to gaze at him.

How beautiful he was. How good. How reassuring to be next to him and to know that Ilios himself had ordained their match, bringing them together…

Thaydor must have sensed her study, for he opened his blue, blue eyes and sent her a curious glance, as if to say, *What?*

She just smiled, caught staring.

The way he arched his eyebrow at her in wry reproach nearly made her burst out in inappropriate laughter, given the solemnity of the place.

She got a chiding elbow on the side for that, and he sent her a twinkling scowl that said, *Don't make me laugh, you rascal.*

"Sorry," she whispered, then closed her eyes with determination, though her smile wouldn't dim. Couldn't a soon-to-be bride feel a little giddy on her wedding day?

She still couldn't concentrate, distracted by her acute awareness of the irresistible man who would deflower her tonight.

Only when he rose and went to write his question could she begin to settle down. *You'll have the rest of your life to dote on him,* she scolded herself. *Now pay attention.*

Finally, she managed to clear her mind, but even so, she watched Thaydor with pleasure when he finished writing and walked over to the arched doorway, still rolling his parchment into a tiny matchstick for the oracle to burn.

The white-clad assistant met the tall, princely paladin there and offered the open base of a bronze censer in which to place his question. He did so, then followed the woman out of view into the central courtyard open to the sky.

Consultations with the oracle usually only took about a quarter hour, giving Wrynne time to calm down. At length, she rose in a relatively serene state and walked over to the table. She took a piece of parchment and picked up a stylus.

As she dipped it in the ink, she puzzled over how to word her question. With her entire life having been turned upside down, she decided to leave it up to Ilios to tell her whatever he thought best. Sometimes a mere mortal didn't even know the right question to ask, so she left it open-ended: *Father, what is Your will for me?*

She trusted that somehow Ilios would let her know how she could best help Thaydor and the kingdom, which was all she really wanted. It might take time, but she believed whole-heartedly that good would win, that their names would be cleared and justice restored to the kingdom.

The one thing she really couldn't say was whether the Almighty would send down divine retribution to punish the whole kingdom on account of King Baynard's offenses. The maker of the universe was not one to be trifled with, after all. He was patient, long-suffering, and kind, but like any king, he would only tolerate so many insults.

It was frightening to contemplate what kind of fully deserved scourge he could bestow upon the kingdom if he chose to turn his back on them and leave them to their folly. Without his protection, they'd be left wide-open to any sort of evil—plague, fire, war. But they'd have brought it on themselves...

When Thaydor came out from the inner courtyard at the heart of the temple, his brow was furrowed. He looked a bit confused and more than a little annoyed. Wrynne did not stop to talk to him, however, as the assistant nodded to her and beckoned from the doorway.

She went right over, put her parchment in the base of another empty censer, which the woman held up, then followed her across the quiet stone corridor. Through another Gothic arched doorway, the priestess gestured to her to proceed into the center courtyard.

Wrynne went.

It was common knowledge that most oracles went quite mad on account of all their talking with the gods. But the middle-aged woman seated on a stool in the middle of the round, white-pillared colonnade did not look too terribly insane, just a little weary and glassy-eyed and somewhat unkempt. She was older than her assistant but wore the same uniform of white robes and ringlets piled atop her head with a bandeau. Only her hair was wilder, gray and frizzed out in all directions.

She did not make eye contact as Wrynne sat down on the stool across from her. Meanwhile, her helper brought the censer over and hung it on the low metal shepherd's hook planted in the ground before the oracle.

"Are you ready?" the assistant murmured to the older woman, who nodded, staring fiercely at nothing in the most disturbing fashion.

She appeared already half in trance, perhaps from having just given Thaydor his predictions.

Wrynne was dying to find out what sort of prophecy or guidance he'd been given, but with her own answers about to be revealed, she nervously watched the process unfold.

The priestess assisting the oracle murmured prayers of intercession under her breath as she took a long, slender twig for a match and lit it from the coals burning in the golden brazier beside the oracle's chair. Cupping her hand to protect the tiny flame at the end of the match, she transferred the sacred fire to the contents of the censer and set Wrynne's parchment alight. She quickly replaced the bronze lid of the censer and blew out the match, bowed, and then withdrew.

It took a moment for the parchment to start burning well, but then the smoke began to rise up through the sunburst shape of holes and slits in the lid. The oracle stared at the smoke as it spiraled upward, twisted and gathered and wafted into a small cloud, only to disperse and drift away. Wrynne's heart pounded as she waited to learn what the oracle was seeing in the ever-shifting shapes of the smoke. What Ilios was telling her.

"Yes, yes…" the prophetess mumbled to herself. "And then…?"

She narrowed her piercing eyes, leaned closer, tilted her head to the right and the left, searching the smoke for its secrets.

Wrynne was ready to burst. "What do you—"

"Shh! Don't speak." The oracle blinked hard and then stared again at the smoke. "You will betray him."

"What? No," Wrynne said. "Who? Ilios? Never—"

"Your husband," she whispered. "The golden one."

Wrynne turned white, staring at the woman. "Not possible."

That was the problem with prophecy. Sometimes it brought news you couldn't bear to believe. The last thing in the world you'd ever thought you'd hear.

Heart pounding, she strove to press past the horror of the woman's words. "How can I avoid it?" she asked quickly.

"Stay by his side."

Wrynne had no time to contemplate how specifically she meant this. The smoke was fading. "What sort of betrayal?"

The oracle shook her head, gazing at the tendrils of rising gray. "I cannot see it. But you will hurt him." She nodded. "You will hate him. Even as you love him. You alone can destroy him. You will hunger for his death."

"You are mad," Wrynne breathed, recoiling. "That is impossible!"

"It will be."

"Then I will change my fate! I won't marry him."

"Yes, you will. Ilios commands it. You must."

Her head was spinning. "If I refuse?"

"Then he will die at the hands of Xoltheus on the new moon. And the kingdom will fall." The oracle said it as though Thaydor was the only thing still holding Veraidel together.

Maybe he was.

Wrynne looked away, stricken, as the last of the smoke faded upward into the sky. She looked at the seer again, on the verge of tears. "It's my wedding day. Surely there must be one good thing you can tell me?"

The oracle made eye contact with her, but only briefly, as she leaned forward. Carefully lifting the lid of the censer, she inspected the ashes now that the smoke had stopped. She searched deeper.

Wrynne's heart pounded as she waited for the verdict, desperate for any shred of good news.

The woman's lined mouth twisted as she continued studying the ashes. "Ilios was pleased with your question. It shows obedience. So he leaves you a gift."

Wrynne raised her eyebrows hopefully and waited.

The madwoman's smile grew, and even though it was genuine, it was still rather ghastly. "Oh yes." She nodded to herself. "I see it now…"

"Yes?"

"Tread your way with care, Daughter. If you remain on this path, the blessing I see will become, but it can still be lost. You must tell no one."

Wrynne nodded eagerly. "I promise. What is it?"

To her surprise, the oracle reached out and grasped her shoulder with a claw-like grip and stared into her eyes. Her voice was a whisper. "You will give birth to a mighty king."

The old woman let her go without warning, and Wrynne nearly fell off the stool, she was so shocked.

"Go. That is all. You are done!" The eccentric seer shot to her feet and, without further ado, fled out the other end of the courtyard.

Wrynne stood up, dazed. She needed a moment to gather her thoughts. She was not yet ready to face her beloved after what she had just been told.

*Betray Thaydor? Never! Not me. Anyone but me. I love him…*

But just in case there was some grain of truth to the oracle's seemingly impossible words, at least she had given Wrynne the key of how to avoid it: *Stay by his side.*

*Very well, I won't let him out of my sight.*

With that, she lifted the hem of her gown, whirled around, and marched back to rejoin him with all due haste.

He rose when he saw her coming. Wrynne rushed right into his waiting arms and slipped her own around his waist. As she pressed her cheek against his chest, she vowed to herself that she would never let anything come between them.

"How did you fare?" he murmured, wrapping his sheltering embrace around her shoulders.

She wasn't sure what to say. It had all been rather monumental, but she wasn't allowed to tell him much.

He tipped her chin upward with his fingertips, drawing her gaze up to meet his. "What did she say?"

"Not much," she said cautiously, shrugging. "'Tis the will of Ilios that we marry…and I am to stay close to you."

"Ah, I like that prophecy," he said with a guileless smile. "It's a lot better than mine, anyway."

"Why? What's wrong? Did she say something bad about your fate?" she asked quickly.

"No, not *bad*, just…vexing," he answered with a mild scowl. "She said, and I quote, *To restore justice to the land, you must first find the Trumpet of the Runescar Highlands.*"

Wrynne blinked. "What's that?"

"Not a what, it's a who. It's that thrice-exasperating bard, Jonty Maguire."

"Oh…right!" Wrynne exclaimed as Thaydor turned her toward the door and steered her toward the exit, his arm draped over her shoulders. "I thought that name sounded familiar."

"You've heard of him? Even so far away as Mistwood?"

"Yes, even in Mistwood," she retorted with a smile. "Well, he is one of the most famous bards alive. What's he got to do with anything?"

"I don't know, but her instructions were clear. If we want to solve this, we have to track him down."

"Any idea where to find him?"

He snorted. "Probably under the table in some disreputable tavern, cavorting with unmentionable women."

"Oh dear," Wrynne said in amusement as they returned to vestibule where they had left their shoes.

They put them on again.

"So he's a wayward soul, eh? Fond of the drink?" she asked.

"Aren't they all? Bards. Useless beggars. Sit around groaning all day about their fine *feelings*. And they call that work!"

"Oh, come, you don't really mean that. I happen to know you have a secret fondness for poetry," she whispered, "and that is also the realm of the bards. Personally, I love listening to them of an evening. They make life so much more interesting."

"With their lies?" he asked in disdain, dropping a donation in the metal box by the door.

"They're called *stories*, Thaydor." She seized hold of his coat and drew him closer, smiling. "Don't be such a Clank."

"I know. You're right," he grumbled, leaning down to kiss her. "But I'm sorry. That chap bothers me."

"Why?"

"Everything's a joke to him, the arrogant jester." He hauled the door open for her. "Why he is so sought after, I have no idea. The queen's ladies-in-waiting weep at his silly, tragic love songs, and every knight in the barracks is continually begging the scoundrel to come along on his latest quest so the bard can witness all his derring-do and write the ballad of his deeds. Not me! I can't stand the fellow," he declared. "Thinks he's funny. Such a wit. Frankly, it's a wonder nobody's cut out his tongue yet. All he ever does is mock everything and everyone!"

"Ah, I see. Including you, Paladin?"

"Especially me," he grumbled as they stepped outside. "I think he enjoys testing my patience."

Wrynne chuckled. "Well, if the oracle says the bard is this important, we had better find him."

"I'll see who I can get working on the task of locating the fool. He shouldn't be that difficult to find," he added as they walked through the cloister. "The dates and times of his performances are usually posted in advance. If he's not in some lord's manor house, he likes to play in pubs."

"Hmm, I can hardly wait to meet a man who'd dare take his life in his hands by poking fun at the mighty Golden Knight," she teased.

"Why? You do it all the time," he retorted, and looked askance at her with a twinkle in his eyes.

From there, they hurried on to their next appointment, entering the base of the great white tower. Hopefully, the wise, old Venerables would have further advice on how they should proceed.

Wrynne was nervous about being called before this small conclave of the highest-ranking elders in the church. She had shaken hands with one of them at her graduation, but she had been only one beaming student out of hundreds that day.

Thaydor, however, looked perfectly at ease. Indeed, he already knew the way to the Solarium. He had mentioned earlier that he had been called to meetings with the Venerables on many previous occasions, due to his role as paladin. He assured her they didn't bite.

As they approached the Solarium, a robed cleric serving as chamberlain greeted them in hushed tones outside the door. As he prepared to show them in, briefing them on protocol, Wrynne was shocked and rather terrified to hear that the Golden Master himself had popped in using a magical transport spell and was waiting with the others to receive them.

Her heart thumped at this unexpected honor. It was too much. Just as the Paladin of Ilios was elected by all the other knights to be their leader, so the Golden Master was elected by the Venerables as the best among their number. The ancient holy man's decisions guided the entire church, just as Thaydor's strategies guided the knights in battle.

She had never expected to be formally introduced to the chief representative of Ilios on Earth or she'd have worn her better gown. There was no time to change.

Everything was happening so fast.

Wrynne hung back shyly by the door as they were shown into the Solarium while Thaydor marched ahead toward the robed elders. He bowed to them, then knelt before the old man on the center throne and kissed his ring.

"Rise, my son. It is good to see you again, Thaydor." The frail, white-bearded ancient clasped his hand, then frowned, slowly looking past him. "Ah, now where is your cooperatrix, hmm?"

Thaydor rose smoothly and turned, holding out his hand to her. "Wrynne?"

"Come forward, child," the Golden Master rasped.

She smoothed her dress. Heart pounding, she joined them and followed suit, bowing to the Venerables and then kneeling to kiss the old man's ring.

This done, she went and stood beside Thaydor in front of all of them.

"Now, then. I hear tell you both have run into a spot of trouble," the old relic said serenely.

"Someone let a band of twenty Urmugoths into the North Gate in the hopes of getting rid of me," Thaydor informed him. "They knew I would come. The creatures nearly killed me, but the Lady Wrynne du Mere, a Daughter of the Rose, saved me with the *Kiss of Life* spell."

"Indeed? That is a powerful magic. And you went through all the pain?" the old man asked her.

Thaydor looked at her sharply.

She winced in apology. She hadn't mentioned that.

"Yes, Your Excellency," she said.

"And now I hear you are to marry?"

"Yes, sir," Thaydor answered in a strong, unhesitating voice.

The Golden Master's rheumy eyes were shrewd, his nod slow and deliberate. "Good, then. So may it be. You went to consult the oracle, yes? Do you both feel clear about the answers you received?"

They nodded, glancing at each other. Wrynne lowered her gaze to hide her conflicted reaction to the messages she had been given—one inspiring awe, the other filling her with dread. She was not allowed to share the wondrous part about their future son, and she had no desire to reveal the ludicrous assertion that one day, she'd betray the man she loved.

"As it happens," the Golden Master said, "I have a word of knowledge for each of you, myself."

"Thank you, sir. We are honored," Thaydor said in earnest.

The ancient held up his bony hand. "Kneel for the blessing."

They did.

The old man stared searchingly at the handpicked champion of their god. "Thaydor, first among the Sons of Might, you are a mortal honored even by the warrior angels of Elysium for your commitment to justice. But you are still a man, prone to all the weaknesses of the flesh. You are warned against wrath and pride and all forms of vengeance. You can and shall be angry, but remember mercy and forgiveness in the day of wrath. Do not let your just rage lead you into hatred or you will become all that you despise."

Thaydor held his gaze, seeming to absorb the words for a moment, then lowered his head to accept the warning in humility.

"Wrynne." The Golden Master turned his attention to her, his gaze softening. "Gentle Daughter of the Rose. You are cautioned against the weakness of dishonesty and too much love of peace. I know, child, as a softhearted healer, you cannot bear to hurt any living thing, but even a well-intentioned lie born of kindness can lead to disaster. A cure often hurts. Remember that. I see in your heart that you learned much wisdom in your hermitage—the sweetest kind, rooted in love. That wisdom will be needed. So do not be silent in an effort to keep the peace at any cost. Even when you know it will sting, you have a duty to speak up. Your lord may need your counsel in the future…even when he doesn't want to hear it."

She nodded with a murmur of gratitude.

"Bow your heads, now. I declare the Light's brightest blessings on your match. Be joined in love forevermore. So may it be."

"So may it be," they both whispered, and Thaydor took her hand.

# Chapter 9
# Vows Unto Death

Their hands were joined once again as they stood before the altar at sunset in the chapel next to the gardens. The evening light shone through the round sunburst window at the front of the church. It burnished the brass buttons down the front of Thaydor's ceremonial dress uniform—a belted, white, hip-length doublet over dark blue chausses and smart black boots. An ornamental sword with a jeweled hilt gleamed at his side.

Wrynne's visit to the Daughters of the Rose chapter house had left her bedecked in a breathtaking wedding kirtle of white satin with a charming heart-shaped neckline, a lavish train, and long lace sleeves that stretched down to elegant points on her hands.

The slim-fitted gown hugged her curves but flared out below the hip in full, trailing skirts, with a slit up the front to show the sky-blue underskirt beneath. She wore a jeweled belt about her hips, and the gauzy veil that covered her head was topped with a wreath to hold it in place.

Through the wispy fabric, Thaydor could see that she wore her sable hair long and loose, flowing over her shoulders. He was simply dazzled, unable to take his eyes off her. She had walked in carrying a bouquet of red, pink, and white roses but had since set the flowers aside for this crucial moment of the ceremony.

He gently clasped her fingers as she stood beside him and, heart pounding, finished repeating the priest's words. "I will be your shield and love you always."

Everything was a bit of a blur.

Next Wrynne echoed the traditional promises of the bride: "I will be your water and quench your heart's thirst all my life."

Then Thaydor followed the order to place the ring on her finger. *Gladly.* He smiled, gazing into her dove-gray eyes as he did so. The simple gold band was temporary. A large, polished diamond handed down through his family awaited her in the vault of his father's castle.

"And so," the priest went on, "before this gathering of friends, and with the blessing of the Father, I now pronounce you man and wife, forever as one."

"So may it be," the people said.

The priest closed the holy book and smiled at Thaydor. "You may kiss your bride."

When Thaydor turned and lifted her veil, he discovered tears welling in her eyes. He brought her hands to his lips and kissed each one, then he bent and caressed her lips softly with his own. He felt her tremulous wonder in this moment, and his heart clenched when two crystal teardrops spilled from beneath her lashes and fell onto his hands.

"Those had better be tears of joy," he whispered fondly.

She brushed them away and nodded with a quick, endearing sniffle.

But when he turned to face their guests, lifting her hand to present his prize to all in the thronged pews, the thunderous applause made her blush and laugh, and then she was all right again.

*Sweet Ilios, I love her.*

Bursting with pride, he tucked her dainty hand into the crook of his arm and escorted her out of the chapel and under the arch of swords his brother knights had created just outside.

There were congratulations all around from the Sons of Might. From there, the party poured out into the gardens, where Brother Piero had arranged for musicians to play for them and the refreshments of a traditional bride-ale, including a fine wedding cake and a steady flow of wine.

They both embraced the wearied warrior monk when they saw him, and abashed him with their profuse thanks.

"It was just as you promised," Wrynne said warmly. "Everything was perfect. We owe it all to you."

With a sheen of sentimental tears already in his eyes and a beefy arm around each one of them, he smiled from ear to ear. "Just enjoy yourselves. And be happy."

*While you can.*

He did not say that part aloud, but he and Thaydor exchanged a guarded look, for they had been both thinking it since yesterday, when they had found out where they'd have to go to get a hold of Jonty Maguire.

"Ah, calamity!" Piero cried suddenly, looking into his empty cup. "I need more ale!"

"Have at you," Thaydor jested, slapping him on the back. The big friar went bustling off to refill his cup and see to their guests, leaving him to ponder briefly the next leg of their quest.

According to the information he had received late this afternoon, the wild bard had gone and got himself thrown into the Blackport Dungeon. On what charges, nobody could say.

Well, whatever the merry scapegrace had done now, it struck Thaydor as more than a little ironic that in order for him to carry out the oracle's advice, he—the most wanted fugitive in the kingdom at the moment—was going to have to break *into* a dungeon.

But all that trouble could keep until tomorrow. Tonight, the only place he wanted to go was straight to bed with his luscious little bride.

His awareness of her was intense, even as she introduced him to several of her friends from the Daughters of the Rose. Though he smiled and nodded politely, it was hard to pay attention.

As twilight deepened into darkness, he was admittedly growing just a tiny bit nervous about the wedding night. He had never deflowered a girl before, and the truth was he did not have the most experience in the world when it came to women—by choice, by course.

Women threw themselves at him everywhere he went; some even showed up uninvited in his bed. But they were easy to refuse when he knew full well that they were either married or only there to try to manipulate him with some sort of lustful power game.

The unspeakable harlots of Fonja were the worst of all. They seemed to find it terribly amusing to try to seduce him. He'd heard there was some kind of running wager among them to see who could make him break his vows of chivalry and upright, honorable conduct.

He found them all repulsive.

Wrynne, however, was as dedicated to righteousness as he was…and had even less experience.

Well, if he was terrible, at least she wouldn't know any better, he thought wryly. Somehow, the thought did not give him any comfort. Truly, it was hell sometimes having to live up to his own daunting reputation for being excellent at everything.

He sighed and downed a swallow of wine, rather amused at his own idiotic mix of almost virginal anxiety and crazed eagerness. All he wanted was to give Wrynne the perfect first time she deserved.

Yes, he doted on her, but he was still very much a battle-hardened warrior, more than a foot taller and a good six stone of muscle heavier than she was. What if he hurt her, or scared her unintentionally? The girl had suddenly become everything to him and his only wish was to make her happy. He did not want to make her, of all people, bleed.

But he must.

He finished his goblet of wine with a terse command to himself to calm down. He did not get this worked up before even a battle!

At least she had made it easy on him with what had happened that night in the cave. The fact that they had already begun to explore each other's bodies took some of the pressure off. To be sure, he already knew that he could give her pleasure. She had been more than game for it.

At length, they bade their guests adieu and retired to their accommodations for the night—not at the chapter house tonight. For this special occasion, they were granted the use of the private guest apartment at the top of the white tower usually reserved for visiting dignitaries.

An opulent, high-ceilinged bedchamber with gilded trim and velvet drapes awaited them, bathed in candlelight. Through a pair of arched doors, the opulent room let out onto a small square courtyard on the roof of the tower, open to the sky. From there, they could see for miles in all directions.

Wrynne's white bridal veil, now hanging down her back, blew and billowed in the wind at that elevation as they stood together by the waist-high wall and savored the soaring views. Between the little fountain and the stone urns full of flowers, there were low chairs built at a steep reclining angle so that guests could lie back and gaze up at the stars. They were eager to try them, but first Wrynne said she needed to change out of the elaborate gown. She wanted to give it back to the Daughters of the Rose in the same pristine condition in which it had been lent to her.

Done trying to move gracefully in the yards of fabric, she scooped up handfuls of the voluminous gown, flopped the long train over her arm, and marched into the bedchamber.

"Could I get your help, husband?" she called in a flirtatious tone.

"My dear," he said as he sauntered after her with a smile, "if your first request to me is to help you undress, I am *really* going to like being married."

She grinned and took the wreath off her head, setting it aside. Next, she gingerly removed the veil and held it out to him. "Would you do something with this?"

He took it from her, put it on his own head, and presented himself to make her laugh.

"You could start a new fashion," she said, her gray eyes twinkling.

He took the veil off and found a clothing hook on the wall, where he hung it up. Returning for the gown, he swept her long hair forward over her shoulder and could not resist kissing her exposed nape.

She let out a sweet sigh, lifting her shoulder happily. Then he set about slowly unlacing the white ribbons down her back.

"You look absolutely…celestial," he whispered as he parted the back of the bodice, exposing her creamy skin and the top line of her thin white chemise. He kissed each of her shoulder blades and the curve of her neck, then took hold of the ends of the long, tight lace sleeves of the gown and held them so she could draw her arms out.

These he also kissed when they were bare, moving down onto his knees beside her amid the pool of puffy white fabric. In a trancelike state, he breathed in the intoxicating scent of her skin as he let his lips wander from her palm and wrist all the way up her arm, taking particular care to nibble the sensitive flesh in the crook of her elbow.

When his attentions roused a moan of desire from her lips, he rose and lifted her off her stockinged feet into his arms, carrying her over to the ornate canopy bed, where he laid her down.

Their stares locked as he caressed her stomach through the crisp layer of linen just for a moment before taking off his belt and coat. He tossed them aside, his dress sword clattering to the floor.

"Take off your shirt," she whispered with a come-hither stare.

He smiled and obeyed.

She bit her lip at the sight of his body.

"Do I please you?" he whispered.

"No," she said. "You drive me wild."

With a half-smile, he leaned down and planted his hands on either side of her on the mattress, and then kissed her, hard.

Her marvelous, healing hands stroked up and down his sides as she opened her mouth, hungry for his kiss. Her passionate response to him lit the already-banked fires in his blood. He realized she was more ready for him than he had expected with all his fretful, overprotective worrying. Perhaps even as eager as he, though that seemed impossible.

He wanted her so much.

He had thought they'd sit awhile outside together, have more wine perhaps, and warm up gradually to the night's main task to be accomplished—the official consummation—but her undulating body, her heaving breaths, and turgid nipples raking his bare chest made it clear she was ready to go.

Enthralled by her passion, he peeled the white shift off her, then pulled the covers back and slid her under them. Kissing her all the while, he hastened to rid himself of chausses and braies. His trembling fingers fumbled with the lacings until she assisted. Her touch made him groan— she wasn't even using magic.

Naked at last, he climbed into bed with her and pulled her on top of him in a wordless effort to let her know that she would be the one to decide the moment when he would take her. Surely it was no small thing for a woman to allow a man into her very body. Far be it from him to rush her. He could wait until she gave the signal even if it killed him.

Wrynne seemed to be enjoying her command of the situation and stretched out flat atop him, belly to belly. His thunderous erection throbbed between them, and her night-dark hair hung down around him like a veil, cloaking them in their own little world. He tucked it behind her ear.

He felt her lips curve as she kissed him. "Husband?"

"Yes, wife?" he whispered.

"I am very happy right now."

"Good. So am I," he answered.

"Yes, I noticed," she teased in a breathy purr, moving her hips to tease his cock with the silkiness of her lithe, nubile body.

He closed his eyes with a groan of pleasure. "Don't do that," he rasped.

"Thaydor?" she breathed.

"Yes, you hot-blooded little minx? What is it?"

"I'm really not sure…what to do."

"Oh, I see," he murmured, sliding his hands down the sinuous curve of her back to cup her charming buttocks firmly in his hands. "Would you like me to show you?"

"Very much," she answered with a shy, rosy blush.

"It isn't difficult. Don't be nervous."

"Oh, I could never be nervous with you. I know you'd never hurt me."

He gazed into her eyes. "You melt me when you say things like that."

"How I love you," she said softly. "All steel on the outside, with a poet's heart tucked away behind the armor."

He felt a little sheepish at such honeyed praise, but she had never outright said that she loved him until now.

The words made him go still. He cupped her nape and held her gaze for another moment in wonder, as if he could see into her very soul.

"What is it?" she whispered, touching his face.

"I love you, too," he said. He couldn't believe he was one of the fortunate few who had actually managed to marry for love and not just practicality. His heart full unto bursting, he kissed her as he smoothly switched their positions, rolling her onto her back and easing atop her.

Beneath him, Wrynne wrapped her arms around his neck and slid her legs around his hips as he entered her tenderly, kissing her all the while. Deeper he pressed into her dreamy wetness until he met with her maiden barrier.

He paused in kissing her as he broke through it with a thrust of his hips. "I'm sorry," he whispered at her low cry, shaking all over with need.

"No, it's all right. I love you," she panted, petting his chest and shoulders and struggling to gather herself.

He held still for her somehow, though he was breathlessly close to exploding. He waited, mentally saying the Greek alphabet in reverse to distract himself from the exquisite pleasure of her body's warm velvet grip.

Resting on his elbows, he traced little shapes across her forehead with his fingertip, taking his time until he felt her relax under him again. "Does it hurt?" he murmured worriedly.

"It doesn't matter. I'm glad. It means I'm yours now forever."

"And I'm yours." Overwhelmed by his sheer adoration, he did not know how to hold back anymore.

Thankfully, she pulled him down to kiss her, nicely recovered, it seemed. Her embrace as she clutched him to her bosom and fed upon his fevered kisses asked silently, cautiously for more. His heart slammed in his chest as he resumed the motion, making love to her with slow, careful strokes as gently as he could.

Her building moans filled his ears with the most gratifying music, but he could feel his control slipping away. At least her intoxicating cries assured him his bride had reached *some* modicum of pleasure in her deflowering, along with the pain. As for him, thanks to their perch atop the tower, *all* the surrounding kingdoms probably heard his roar of release as he surrendered to her completely, filling her womb with his seed.

*So may it be.*

# Chapter 10
# Dungeon

"**J** hope that oracle knows what she's talking about. Because this doesn't make any sense at all to me," Thaydor grumbled three days later.

They crouched down behind a shallow rise about a mile outside the forbidding walls of the brooding Blackport Dungeon. He shook his head. "I don't see why I can't just crash the front door down and go in and drag the idiot out."

"For obvious reasons, darling," Wrynne said, shaking her head. Everything about the bard had made him rather grumpy. "It's a *dungeon*."

"So? I've laid siege to worse."

"Listen to your wife, lad," Brother Piero urged, his head now draped in a hood of chain mail, his white surcoat pale in the waning twilight. He and two of the other Sons of Might from the chapter house had come along to provide them with some extra hands for their mission.

"You are not going in there, I forbid it," the stouthearted warrior monk continued. "Not with all the king's men scouring the land to arrest you. Why make it easy on them? All they'd have to do is back you into a cell and you're doomed. Don't let love cloud your common sense. She can do this much more easily than we can, and without bloodshed."

"Thank you, Brother Piero," said Wrynne.

He sent her a wink. "You're welcome, dear."

"I hate this," Thaydor mumbled.

"Oh, I'll be *fine*, husband," Wrynne said with a chuckle while her large, armor-clad paladin scowled in the direction of the infamous prison. "Trust me. I'll go in as a humble sister on a charity mission and offer healing to the sick within. When I see the bard, I'll figure out a way to get near him and then use my *hasten* spell to get him out. It worked to save you once, didn't it?"

He merely growled.

"And you all must be ready to ride—and probably fight—as soon as we appear," she instructed. "I'm sure the guards will give chase."

"But if you do this, then you'll be a fugitive in earnest like me," Thaydor said.

"I'm your wife. We face everything from now on together." She laid a hand gently on his shiny silver breastplate.

At the Bastion, his armor had been restored to its former glory after the Urms' damage. Hallowsmite hung in his scabbard at his waist, its blade newly sharpened.

"You have to let me help when I am able," she added. "This is for the best. I'm a lot less recognizable than you. You cannot argue that."

"Well, you can't wear your armor, then." Thaydor's unhappy gaze flicked over her. "It'll only rouse their suspicions. And what if they don't let you take your staff in? They might strip it from you as a possible weapon. If that happens, all this is a waste of time."

"I'll just have to sweet-talk them somehow."

"That's your plan?" he retorted.

She ignored her scowling husband and turned to the brothers. "I trust you fellows have mastered the *Feed the Hungry* spell?"

"Certainly, mistress," Brother Piero said with a nod.

"A few nice charity cakes or pies or loaves of some sort would help to get me in the door." She lifted her arm and started unbuckling the straps of her brushed silver breastplate.

While the three warrior monks proceeded to conjure a variety of tempting edibles that she could offer the prisoners and the guards, Thaydor helped her take off the few pieces of armor, which she had donned at his insistence when they had left the Bastion.

He grumbled over the task all the while. "It should be me going in there. I don't like you having to lie your way into that place, either, after the Golden Master specifically warned you about dishonesty."

She looked over her shoulder at him as he undid a strap she couldn't reach. The oracle had also warned her about not leaving his side. Did this count?

"I know," she finally said, hiding her uneasiness. "But this is the easiest way. Besides, from the sound of it, the bard hasn't even committed a crime. I suspect that, given the influence he wields with his art over all the people, high and low, he probably has as many high-placed enemies as you do. Well, almost as many."

"If you ask me, it's probably his big mouth that got him into this. Oh, never mind. Just promise me you'll be careful. I need you, you know."

"How sweet," she murmured, turning to him. "Do try not to worry so. I'll be back before you know it."

"How can I not worry? Look at that place! You're my wife! What kind of husband lets his lady enter such a hellhole?"

"One who respects her abilities! Calm down," Wrynne ordered, losing patience. She was already nervous enough about this, and his misgivings were starting to make her doubt herself. "You know the Daughters of the Rose regularly visit prisons as part of our good works. I've done this before—not here, but elsewhere. The point is, when the guards see me, it won't seem strange to them at all. Your showing up on their doorstep would be another story entirely."

"But the sisters rarely go alone," he pointed out.

"I am honestly going to throttle you! Are you trying to make me lose my nerve?"

He just looked at her, and, the dear man, she could see the genuine distress in his eyes. "Of course not."

Marriage and a couple of days of lovemaking before they'd had to leave had only strengthened their bond and deepened their engrossment in each other. If their love was merely a side effect of the *Kiss of Life* spell, it still showed no signs of wearing off.

"Don't you believe in me?" she asked.

"I do. I just…want to keep you safe."

"Listen," she said softly, "I'll let you in on a little secret that should make you feel better about this. I *know* I'm not going to die in there, because the oracle informed me I have a destiny to fulfill further off in time."

"Wait, what? You didn't tell me! Destiny? What did she prophesy about you?"

"I'm not allowed to say."

"Oh." He paused, brow furrowed. "Was it good or bad, at least?"

"Good. Very good. Now give me a kiss for luck, because I'm doing this. I have to go."

He bent down and brushed a quick kiss to her lips, though the scowl never left his face. She couldn't help but smile dotingly. He was so amusing, her Clank.

"This should do," Piero said, nodding at the stack of a dozen pies the men had created out of thin air.

"Excellent." Pulling up the hood of her gray cloak, she rested her staff lengthwise across her shoulders like a yoke, then told them to tie one of the cloth bundles of stacked pies on each end.

"Are you sure it's not too heavy for you?" her new husband asked once they did so.

"Thaydor!" she said in exasperation.

"Fine," he muttered. "Go."

With that, Wrynne left their hiding place and walked the mile up the dusty road. The hulking dungeon loomed before her, looking even more ominous as darkness descended. Her heart pounded, butterflies tickled in her stomach, and she felt very alone, but she refused to cower. The bundles of food swung gently with her every stride.

It was somewhat reassuring to know that Thaydor and the others were watching over her with bows drawn to cover her if there was any sign of trouble, but she was soon out of range.

At last, she reached the brooding stone barbican at the dungeon's entrance, where the outer portcullis was raised. Half a dozen guards were already waiting for her there with narrowed eyes and bristling stances.

They had seen her coming. A few took no interest, leaning casually here and there around the gatehouse, but she had seen a couple of them watching her approach for the past few minutes.

It was too dark for them to tell from a distance who or what she was, so their wariness was understandable. When she stepped into the edge of their torches' glow, however, they relaxed. One little woman on her own was clearly not enough to worry six big, armed men.

"Greetings in the name of Father Ilios," she called, loud enough for them all to hear as she walked up to the mouth of the building.

"Mistress," one of them greeted her warily.

They allowed her to step past the raised outer portcullis under the archway and into the torch-lit shelter of the squat stone building that guarded the dungeon's entrance.

"What brings you out alone at this hour, lady?"

She let out a large sigh. "The hour of my arrival was by accident, believe me. Getting here took longer than I thought." She set her burden down with a weary smile. "I've come to offer the consolation of our god to the prisoners within."

The guard's skeptical glance flicked to her packages. "What's in the bundles?"

"A donation of food from our chapter house."

"Captain?" the guard called to his superior, who then joined them.

A lean, swarthy man in his thirties, the captain was distinguished by the brown leather armor shaped to his chest, with plain pewter rivets on his epaulets marking his rank. He looked her over with a businesslike nod. "You one of them Rose ladies?"

"Yes, sir." She lifted her chin and showed him the necklace around her throat, proof of her affiliation.

He seemed satisfied, though suspicion of everyone and everything seemed bred into him after dealing with criminals all day. "We don't see much of your kind around here."

She nodded. "That's why I was sent. We realize we've been neglecting your establishment for too long. I was chosen to be sent here because I am also a healer. If I can be of service to any of your prisoners— or yourselves—please allow me to honor the Father by sharing the gift he has bestowed upon me with any of your people who are seriously injured or ill."

Some of the guards paid no attention, already digging into the food, but the first one still looked skeptical.

"Why would you want to come to a godforsaken place like this, pretty thing like you?"

"My god commands it," she replied.

He shrugged. "Why?"

"The Creator loves all his children, even those who have sinned badly enough to end up here. My order operates our prison ministry because Father Ilios wishes those here to know they have not been forgotten. They can always repent, and He will still take them back."

The impatient flick of his eyebrows told her she had already bored him with such talk. "I prefer Fonja, myself. No offense."

*I'll bet you do*, she thought. *If you call going to a brothel a religion.*

The temple prostitutes, both male and female, promised they could help believers obtain their desires through the use of sex magick.

"None taken," she said pleasantly.

"Right. Well, we'll still have to search you."

"I understand." She raised her hands and waited. "But I advise you to not make free with my person, or the god who protects me at all times may roast you where you stand."

*And if he doesn't, my husband will probably cut you in half.*

The captain merely smirked, ignoring both her warning and the rascally grins of his men. They watched him in lewd humor as he bent to skim his hands down her sides. Thankfully, however, he merely did his duty and did not insult her.

"Go to the warden's office and tell him she's unarmed," he confirmed to the others over his shoulder. "So, you really are a healer, eh?"

"Yes, sir."

"Maybe you could show us. Fix Gorland's broken finger?"

"I'd be glad to," she said, well aware he was asking her to prove her status before they'd let her in.

"Gorland, get over here!"

Wrynne then got her first inkling of the true unpleasantness of the job she had set for herself. A large, lumbering prison guard came over to his captain. He had dull-witted eyes and a homely, brutish face, and though he was no threat to her, she sensed the cruel streak in him.

Somehow she forced a smile, hiding her distaste. "Let me see it."

Gorland held up his right hand and stretched out his fingers. The pinkie was obviously broken.

"Oh, that's nasty. What happened?"

He grunted. "Eh, busted it keeping some son of a bitch in line."

"Language, man!" the captain exclaimed. "She's a bloody nun!"

*Not exactly,* Wrynne thought as luscious memories of last night with Thaydor flashed in her mind.

She cleared her throat and let them believe whatever they liked. But if the guard had come out with a broken finger, she wondered how much worse the prisoner might have fared. She hoped it hadn't been the bard.

"Well, this will only take a moment, then you'll be right as rain." *And ready to bash more prisoners with that fist.* "Close your eyes and try to clear your mind."

The big oaf glanced worriedly at his superior.

"Do it. We'll watch her," the captain said.

Gorland obeyed and shut his eyes. No doubt it made him jumpy to do so, given the nature of his post.

Wrynne cupped her right hand a few inches above the man's broken finger. It was swollen to twice its proper size and crooked at a wrong angle. Nervous as she was, it took her a little longer than usual to find the serenity in her core. But at last, she settled down into her gift and concentrated until she felt the Light flowing through her.

"Ow!" Gorland mumbled in surprise as the bone shifted into place of its own accord and began knitting itself back together. His eyes popped open. "Hey! That actually feels better!" He lifted his hand up and wiggled his fingers. "How about that!"

He laughed aloud, and his mates seemed impressed, nodding to one another.

Wrynne smiled. The demonstration was enough to get her in.

"We'll watch these packages for you, mistress," the other guards said, hording the baked goods on their rough wooden table while the captain rang a bell to summon the warden.

"Save some of that for me!" Gorland hurried over to join his mates, taking a large chunk of pie that the men were already tearing apart.

"That was supposed to be for the prisoners," she chided gently.

"Oh, we'll make sure they get some," one lied through a mouthful of saffron cake. Fortunately, they were all so excited about the unexpected treats that they never even thought about her walking staff.

The warden joined them then and listened while the captain apprised him of the situation. Older and more grizzled than the others, the warden was a small man but seemed exceedingly tough—short, stocky, and balding, with a patch over one eye. He wore leather armor like the captain's.

"I'll take her in," the warden said. "I could use a break from doing figures for our monthly supplies. You searched her?"

"She's clean."

"This way, Sister!" He beckoned her over.

As Wrynne hurried to join him by the closed inner portcullis, he shook his head at his men crowding around the table.

"Hoy! Look lively!" he barked at Gorland, gesturing impatiently to the heavy metal grate barring their way into the prison.

"Yes, sir!" The big guard, still chewing, hurried to crank the windlass, putting his brawn to good use. The razor-sharp portcullis slowly retracted upward.

Wrynne followed the warden under it.

"I'd hide my face if I was you," he said, a ring of keys jangling at his side. "The scurvy rubbish in these cages ain't seen a pretty lass in years, some of 'em. They got no manners on a good day as it is."

"Thank you for the reminder. I will." She drew her light gray scarf across the lower half of her face, but even this concealment did nothing to deter the prisoners' interest as she followed the warden down the dark, dank central aisle.

He had unhooked the truncheon from his belt and gripped it in his hand as he marched ahead of her with a bellicose stride. With his good eye, he glanced over his shoulder every now and then, as though making sure none of the human flotsam and jetsam in the cells had grabbed her.

The place made her skin crawl and her stomach turn. The hideous stench of human waste was overpowering. She had no idea how many patients awaited her in the prison's infirmary, but she did not see how *anyone* could be healthy here. Rats scampered along the dripping stone walls, from which torches jutted here and there. Their dim, flickering illumination filled the corridor with writhing shadows, and the shadows, in turn, made the forlorn, mad, and hostile faces that peered out at her from behind the bars all the more frightening.

The foul-mouthed prisoners filled the air with the deafening noise of their depravity, shouting such obscenities at her that Thaydor, had he heard it, would have surely unleashed the earthshaking magic bound up in Hallowsmite and rocked the whole prison to its foundations.

She did her best to block out the taunts and disgusting, futile propositions.

"Shut up!" the warden bellowed, but there was no way he could stop the indecent clamor swarming around her. "Just ignore them, mistress."

"I am."

Two prisoners tried to spit on her but missed. Not all of them were human. One aisle the warden led her down was reserved for inmates of other races. Here the bars were especially thick, doubly reinforced.

Inside were monsters.

She saw a couple of lumbering Urmugoths, a minotaur, and even a young cyclops nearly eight feet tall. She shuddered. Blackport Dungeon really was as notorious as its reputation.

*Poor bard.*

The warden knew the way well, marching through the dark labyrinth of his domain. She hurried after him, furtively scanning the cells for the famous redheaded Highlander as they passed.

Her bald, stocky escort made a right ahead, returning to aisles lined with cells with human prisoners. The men's reactions to her were the same here—if they could still be called *men* in their debased states.

*What have I got myself into?* A chill ran along her spine. She was going to have to treat some of these creatures. Touch them.

She tried not to recoil as they waggled their tongues at her, made obscene noises, and reached through the bars trying to stroke her. Though she managed to keep her panic at bay, she could not hide her distaste. How long did it take, she wondered, for such a place to warp a man beyond recognition? To think they wanted to put Thaydor in a dungeon like this …

Of course, if he got caught, then she'd get caught, too. There were similar establishments for women. She could not bear to think about it right now.

She suddenly shrieked when a bearded, rail-thin man with crazed eyes clawed at her with a garbled roar from behind the bars of his cell. Startled, she lurched away from him and tripped, inadvertently getting too close to the cells on the opposite side. The matted, dirty creature in the cage behind her grabbed the hood of her cloak and yanked her closer, trying to bite her face.

The warden was there in a heartbeat, clobbering the wiry arm holding on to her shoulder. "Don't you dare!"

The prisoner let go, but only out of pain. While the warden screamed at him and swore to make an example of anyone who tried that sort of thing again, Wrynne stood trembling in the center of the aisle while they jeered at her from every direction.

"Silence!" the warden insisted. "This woman is protected by the gods, and moreover, you stupid filth, she's come to help you! Anyone who tries another trick of that sort will be put on the rack! Do you understand me? Maybe I'll just put you there for fun!"

For a moment, the whole row went silent.

"Thank you," Wrynne whispered, sounding as shaken as she felt.

He snorted. "Your god's mercy and your own is wasted on these vermin. You still want to do this, lady?"

She pressed her lips shut to avoid saying how she really felt and nodded. "To be honest, though, I don't know how long I might last, so please take me to only your most serious cases first."

He nodded. "We keep 'em in the infirmary. This way." She heard him grumbling under his breath as he trudged ahead. "Never let no daughter o' mine join the church if this is what they make 'em do…"

Then the clamor started up again, but at least now, none of the prisoners tried to grab her. Yet, as Wrynne hurried after him, the warden's mention of having daughters suddenly made her wonder what her springing Jonty Maguire from jail would mean for the warden himself. And the captain, and the other guards. They would probably be punished…

*Oh, Ilios.* They had done nothing wrong, simply trusted her. Believed her lies.

And for that matter, what about the Daughters of the Rose? Would there be consequences for her entire order because of what she was about to do, helping a high-profile prisoner escape?

Just when she was on the verge of losing her nerve and aborting the rescue mission, she heard a song floating down the corridor.

A rich male voice with a hint of a melancholy Highland brogue bounced off the stone walls, its strong, deep timbre weaving like the threads of a gorgeous magical tapestry, a note of beauty and sanity in a madhouse reaching out to steady her through the noisy assault of the other prisoners' lustful obscenities.

> *"As I dreamt upon a night,*
> *Forsooth I saw a seemly sight:*
> *I beheld a maid so bright,*
> *A rose she bore in hand…"*

Her heart instantly lightened at the sound, for she knew she had just found her target.

The famous bard was in a cell ahead. Though she could not yet see his face, she saw his hands gripping the bars—somewhat cleaner than the other prisoners' were, with the long, tapered fingers of a musician. He sang out in the darkness for all he was worth, and his music had its effect, stilling the savage foulness aimed at her by the other inmates.

> *"Her eyes, they were so lovely!*
> *Her countenance so sweet.*
> *Of all my care and sorrow,*
> *She made my pain abate."*

"Stop that!" the warden scolded, giving the bars of his singer's cell a good whack as he strode ahead of her. He glanced back over his shoulder. "Never mind that one, mistress. Merely the latest addition to our mad zoo. Thinks he's something special. I'm sure he just wants your attention."

"But I do! Verily! Pray you, sweet lady! Fair one! Angel of mercy, a moment of your time, I beseech you! Take pity on me…in the name of Ilios!"

*Oh, you're clever,* she thought in amusement. *As if you give a fig for Ilios when you're known for wine and women. Nice flattery, though.*

As Wrynne stepped alongside his cell, she paused, taking her first look at the wayward soul she had secretly come to rescue. Jonty Maguire was lean and sinewy, tall—though not the height of her towering paladin. He was dressed in a loose linen shirt that hung unlaced across his chest, and a Highland kilt so grimy it was impossible to identify the colors of his clan. A wild tangle of dark auburn hair hung to his wide shoulders, and his jaw was covered in a rugged reddish scruff.

"Please—dear lady." He clung to the bars, his intelligent emerald eyes locking on to hers in soulful desperation. But not even the squalor in this place could dim the bard's charisma. He was a good-looking man, full of fire and intensity, with an angular face that showed his every emotion, from roguery to despair—and even a blend of both, if that were possible.

"You sing well, sir."

"Of course I do," he said impatiently, speaking at a rapid pace, as though well aware the warden wouldn't give them much time. "A month ago, 'twas royal ears that listened to my songs. Now I sing for the damned. I am Jonathon Maguire, lady. You've probably heard of me. Or not—it scarcely matters. I hate to trouble you, but can you get a message out for me? There seems to have been a terrible mistake—"

"No mistake," the warden interjected, looking placidly amused. "They all say that at first. This one, though, he's a right proper gentl'man. I'll give him that."

"Thank you so much for that, master warden," the fiery bard said as though he could barely contain his sarcasm.

Wrynne fought a smile and gave him a soothing "Blessings of Ilios upon you, master bard."

"Yes, yes," he said, all knife-hilt cheekbones and dramatic dark eyebrows as he flicked his highly trained fingers once more around the bars and fixed her with a pleading gaze, hunching his tall frame down to try to cajole her. "I can give you gold if you like…a donation to the church!"

"Leave her alone," the warden said in bored annoyance. "Come along, Sister. Your patients are this way."

"Wait! I have another verse!" he pleaded, reaching through the bars of his cage, not in a threatening manner like the others had, but on a sudden inspiration, Wrynne pretended to be outraged when his famous lyre-stroking fingertips grazed the back of her hood.

"How dare you?" she bit back, pivoting and lowering her scarf angrily. *"Lugere aegritudine! Hic sum ut liberem te."*

"What?" His emerald eyes widened with abrupt astonishment.

"You heard me," she said coldly, as though she had just given him the most withering of educated set downs.

He stared at her, then bowed to hide his grin. "My humblest apologies, lady."

"Humph!" she said, turning on her heel. "You were right," she told the warden as they marched on. "No manners a'tall."

"What did you say to him?"

"I rebuked him, of course. Told him it's one thing to be ogled by cretins such as these, but a gentleman ought to know better."

Another lie.

The Golden Master would not be happy with her.

In actuality, her Latin words to the bard had been a terse command: *Feign illness! I am here to rescue you.*

* * *

"What's taking so long?" Thaydor muttered, his armor clanking softly as he paced.

"Calm down, she'll be fine. Maybe they had more sick in the dungeon than we expected."

"Aye, and what if she catches it?" he retorted.

"Then you'll heal her," Piero said in an ever-so-reasonable tone.

Thaydor frowned toward the dungeon. "If anyone lays a hand on her, I'll burn the place down."

"Stop pacing and get into position," his old friend scolded. "She could pop into view with the bard at any moment. We've got to be ready to run as soon as they appear."

"I'm looking forward to meeting him," one of the younger monks remarked.

Thaydor stifled a sardonic reply. Ilios wouldn't approve of his unbrotherly sentiments toward the bard. He didn't really *know* Jonty Maguire very well, after all.

It was just that some people had it so easy in life. Free to roam wherever they pleased—no cares, no commitments, no responsibilities— while he carried enough for ten men and had obeyed orders since he was old enough to walk.

He supposed if he were at liberty to do whatever he pleased, even *he* might manage to be charming once in a while.

Or not.

Ah, well. Sitting around playing music would probably bore him to death.

*Come on, sweeting. Where are you?* Crossbow resting on his arm, he got into position with the others and waited in case she needed cover.

He suddenly wondered if Wrynne would think the bard charming. His frown deepened. Well, this was a new emotion...

*Jealousy.*

He scoffed at himself and shook his head. But if Jonty Maguire ridiculed him in front of his wife and made a fool of him, Thaydor feared he might temporarily turn into an Urmugoth and tear the merry scapegrace limb from limb.

*Don't push me, mate,* he thought, staring at the prison. *I'm a paladin, not a saint.*

* * *

"I rather wish you wouldn't have told me that," Wrynne said, glancing from the warden to the evil-eyed prisoner who was strapped down in the next infirmary cot, waiting to be healed.

The warden shrugged. "Wasn't sure if it mattered. Don't worry, he's been castrated since he hurt all them girls."

*Still,* Wrynne thought. She tried for a few moments longer, but the Light would not flow—the aura of evil around the pox-ridden man was too overwhelming, and maybe, deep down, she did not really *want* to heal him.

She gave up, shaking her head. "I'm sorry. I can't. I tried. It won't work."

"It worked for all the others, bitch! Try harder!" the patient ranted.

"Don't you dare talk to her that way!" the warden thundered, menacing him with his club.

"It's all right," she said, hiding how rattled she had become while facing her criminal patients at close quarters.

*Forgive, forgive...*

Thaydor would be furious if he could see what manner of people she had been treating.

Thankfully, they soon left the infirmary. Still a bit unnerved, she glanced at the warden as they walked back down the corridor by which they had come. "Why is that last one still alive? I thought hanging was the penalty for such crimes."

"Ach, he's related to some duke."

"Oh." Even curing a murderer of jaundice had not revolted her the way the rapist had. She couldn't wait to get out of this place. She just hoped she'd succeed in taking Jonty Maguire with her.

As they neared the bard's cell, tension tightened the knots in her stomach. She had already aided—nay, married—a fugitive, and she was about to break a prisoner out of jail. Thinking about the possible consequences was too terrifying. But having met him, she couldn't leave him here to rot. Not now. She knew in her bones that he did not deserve this.

Somehow she ignored her fears, following the warden as they retraced their footsteps through the mazelike dungeon. She kept watch for Jonty's cell, then fought a smile when she heard his mournful groaning coming from up ahead.

"Help! Please!" the magnificent voice wrenched out, though they could not yet see the man. "My guts are all twisted. I'm sick. Chills. Fever!"

"Oh, shut up," the warden muttered as they came alongside his cell once more.

"Sudden onset, I daresay," Wrynne remarked.

To her relief, the warden stopped there and glanced at her sardonically. "Obviously, he's faking, mistress. I'm no healer and even I know that."

Jonty groaned. He was lying on his cot clutching his stomach. In the dim torchlight, they could see his grimace and his admirable shaking.

"He's a trained playactor! Don't the bards' guilds make their members learn this sort of thing?"

"Hmm, I don't know. Do you mind if I talk to him for a moment just to be sure? My vows require I do not turn my back on anyone who is truly suffering."

The warden shrugged. "Suit yourself."

Wrynne stepped nearer to the bars.

"Did this just start now?" she asked skeptically.

"No, of course not!" he snapped, playing his part well. "I didn't complain before, but two nights ago, the stomachache began. It's only grown worse. Please help me, Sister!"

"Could he have been served spoiled food?" she asked the warden, who was now also wincing in disgust.

"Well, we don't give 'em what you might call *fine cuisine*, but look around. None of the others are sick with this. They all eat the same food. Fakin'," he repeated.

"You're probably right. But perhaps I should have a look at him. Abdominal pain could mean typhoid fever. It's very contagious."

That got the warden's full attention.

"I don't need an outbreak in my jail," he said a trifle nervously. He backed away from Jonty's cell and covered his mouth and nose with his hand. "Had a bout of typhoid fever here two years ago. Killed thirty, including five of my guards."

"Well, don't be too alarmed just yet," she soothed. "It could simply be his appendix has burst. That's fatal, I'm afraid."

"Oh, save me!" Jonty wailed, clutching his stomach and rolling on his cot.

"Fatal?" The warden frowned. "I'm not allowed to let him die."

"The pain! The pain!" Jonty moaned.

"You believe him?" the warden asked, squinting at her.

She shrugged. "Better safe than sorry. It will only take a moment, like the others."

"Very well. If you're fakin' in there, I'll have you flogged till you lose that famous voice of yours from screamin'."

The warden lifted his mass of keys and started unlocking the cell.

"Ought you to shackle him first, sir? For my safety. Is he dangerous?"

"Nay, he's in here for debts and disturbin' the peace."

"They sent him to a place like this for such small crimes?"

"I reckon somebody wanted to teach him a lesson. I don't ask questions. But after havin' him here for the past month, I can understand why someone would want to try to shut 'im up—though from what I've seen, it's impossible."

Wrynne smiled at the warden. As he opened the door to Jonty's cell for her, she hoped nothing too bad happened to him for what she was about to do. He seemed a decent man with a very hard job.

"The Father of Lights sends his blessings upon you," she said, offering the same formal greeting she had used with the other inmates as she stepped into Jonty's cell.

Heart pounding, she clutched her staff and walked the few short paces toward the cot where the bard lay theatrically writhing.

"Your abdomen, you say? Let me see."

With the warden right behind her, she had to stall for just a little time.

"Can you pull up your shirt, please? I need to see if your stomach is swollen."

He paused and glanced at her, the wicked twinkle in his green eyes at odds with his show of suffering. "You want me to undress for you? Odd request from a nun."

She gave him a stern look. "I'm not a nun. I'm a Daughter of the Rose."

"You're very pretty."

"Would you shut up?" she said through gritted teeth.

"Aye, milady." The wild bard obediently pulled up his loose shirt and revealed a sharply chiseled stomach, though not as impressive as Thaydor's. Also, he smelled like a dungeon.

"Now tell me if it hurts when I touch it," she instructed, crouching down beside his cot.

"Touch it all you like. Please," he whispered.

Wrynne scowled at him.

He groaned again. "Mother!" He pretended to sob like a sick child, chin trembling.

She fought not to laugh at his charade as she went about her inspection.

"Yowww," he purred in roguish mischief when she laid her hand on his stomach and palpated him, the warden looking on.

"Please, sir, I'm a doctor. And I'm married," she added under her breath.

"Tragedy," he whispered. "Then again, tragedy is one of my favorite art forms…"

"Well?" the warden asked, hovering nearby. "Fakin'?"

"Actually…" Wrynne gripped her staff in one hand and kept her other planted on Jonty. He held on to her arm, curling upward smoothly into a sitting position. "There's only one thing I can say for certain."

"What's that?"

Wrynne bumped her staff on the ground.

"Cheerio, mate!" Jonty grinned at the warden, waving goodbye as Wrynne whispered, "*Hasten.*"

In the twinkling of an eye, they were gone.

They landed in a field about a thousand feet outside the walls of Blackport Dungeon, collapsing in a heap. Jonty rolled onto his back in the cool, tall grass in gales of raucous laughter.

"Shh! They'll hear you." As Wrynne sat up, sputtering and shaking the usual *hasten* spell dizziness out of her head, the bard caught sight of the sky and drew in his breath at the beauteous stars.

"Oh!" He sat up suddenly, craning his neck to view every possible constellation. "The sky…"

"Admire it later, friend. We have to teleport again a few more times to join our party. They'll be waiting."

"Party?" He jumped to his feet and offered his hand, pulling Wrynne up unceremoniously.

"Of course. I wouldn't attempt this on my own."

"Well, whoever you are, I could kiss you."

"Not if you value your life," she said with an arch smile. "I wasn't lying when I said I have a husband."

"Oh? Who's the lucky fellow? Tell me. I know everybody."

"You'll see. *Hasten.*"

This time, they managed to land upright when the spell carried them another thousand feet toward the others. She was glad of that. She did not think her husband would have appreciated seeing her lying on the ground in a tangled pile of limbs with another man.

Not even one who smelled like a dungeon.

She steadied herself and glanced at her fellow traveler. "You all right?"

He glanced down at himself, saw that all his parts had arrived in their proper places, and grinned. "All here."

"Here we go again."

There were five jumps in a mile, so they were both rather woozy by the time they reached their waiting companions, but at least they got there fast. It had taken only seconds.

"Wrynne!" a strong voice called from out of the darkness. She looked across the landscape just ten yards off and glimpsed moonlight gleaming on armor as Thaydor marched out from behind the men's cover and strode toward her.

"They made it. Quickly, to the horses!" Brother Piero commanded the two other warriors, while Wrynne nodded to Jonty to follow.

She rushed ahead, running into Thaydor's embrace. His hands descended firmly onto her shoulders, and he searched her face worriedly for a moment. "Are you all right? Any problems?"

"Everything went smoothly. I'm fine."

"Praise be to Ilios," he murmured, and tipping her chin up with a gentle press of his fingertips, he bent to brush a brief kiss to her lips. "Well done, darling."

"Oh, you have *got* to be joking!" Incredulous laughter filled the air as the bard joined them. "Golden Boy? *You're* the one behind this?"

Wrynne turned to Jonty. "Allow me to present my husband, master bard. I believe you two already know each other."

Thaydor scoffed. "You could say that."

Jonty turned to her in mirth, laying his hand on his heart. "Oh, dear lady! You must be a piece of perfection, indeed, to have been selected by this one. The great, the glorious Sir Thaydor Clarenbeld!"

"She is, actually. Now stop looking at her," he said with a cool, aloof smile.

"Boys," Wrynne warned. "Jonty, you've been in prison for a while, so you probably haven't heard. My husband is the most wanted outlaw in the kingdom right now. I daresay I'm the *second* most wanted at this point, and in about five minutes, you're about to be the third. So I suggest we all make a timely egress."

"Wait, they're after him, too?" Jonty asked, squinting. "How is that possible? He practically *is* the kingdom. They turn against me, that's one thing. I piss off everybody. 'Tis my gift. But you?" he asked Thaydor. "And pardon, but I still can't wrap my head around the marriage part! I thought you were some sort of priest!"

"Hardly," Wrynne purred, her arm around her husband's steel-clad waist.

Jonty shook his head, looking amused and nonplused. "I can have some fun with this."

"I don't suggest you do," Thaydor said mildly.

"A Daughter of the Rose," Jonty mused aloud. "But of course. This one wouldn't have any but a she-paragon. Well, who'd have thought a lover's heart beat all this time inside this great, shiny chunk o' metal standing before us?"

"Watch it."

"Can we go before we all get arrested?" Wrynne asked impatiently.

Thaydor looked at her and then at the rascally bard, and seemed to remind himself he was the bigger man. "We brought you a mount, Maguire. I hope you can ride in that skirt." He pivoted and walked away, heading for the horses.

"Hoy! Respect the kilt!" Jonty called indignantly.

"Come on. We have to keep moving," Wrynne said.

They both followed Thaydor up the shallow rise, behind which the horses were hidden.

"He's taken the hero routine to a whole new height while I've been locked up, hasn't he? Rescuing people he doesn't even like?"

"Actually, the oracle in service to our god told us you have some sort of information on which the fate of the whole kingdom rests."

"What? Me?" Jonty stopped and looked at her incredulously. "Shite in a bucket!"

"Language!" Thaydor huffed from over by Avalanche's side. "You are speaking to a lady!"

"Apologies."

"Get on your horse, Wrynne. Maguire, the chestnut's for you."

"Thank you. All of you. Even you, Clarenbeld. I mean it—truly. Much as it pains me, I am in your debt."

Thaydor shrugged, but Wrynne smiled reassuringly at the newcomer. "You're welcome."

Then they hurried to the horses, but as she set her foot in the stirrup to mount up, a long, bone-chilling howl suddenly split the night.

Everybody turned to look.

It was instantly followed by a clamor of frenzied barking in the distance.

"And here come the guard dogs," Piero murmured in a tone of dark humor.

Jonty snorted. "Try dire wolves."

"Dire wolves? Are you jesting?" Thaydor demanded from beside Avalanche.

"No, they loose them on any prisoner who tries to escape."

"How many are there?"

"Six, from what I've heard."

"What are dire wolves?" Wrynne asked, wide-eyed.

"Death in fur," Jonty replied.

"What do we do?" she cried.

"Ride like hell, I should think," he muttered.

"No," said Thaydor. "We'll never outrun them. We have to make a stand and kill them."

The younger monk stared toward the prison. "Judging by the sound, I'd say we've got a minute and a half to decide."

"We could climb into the trees," Wrynne started. "Pick them off with crossbows from above—"

"While they tear the horses apart? No," Thaydor said. "We must defend our animals."

"Would a sanctuary spell work?" she countered urgently.

"They'd still smell us," said Brother Piero. He looked askance at Jonty. "Some more than others."

The bard arched a brow.

"Yes—that's it! Maguire, take off your shirt. We need an article of clothing that smells like you to draw the dire wolves. Wrynne, *hasten* yourself and the kilt out of here. I'll meet you five miles due north as soon as this is finished."

"I don't want to leave you," she protested, recalling the oracle's warning. "Can't we all just get on the horses and ride? If we go right now—"

"Dire wolves can last much longer over distances than horses," Thaydor said, pushing her staff insistently into her hands while Jonty lifted his shirt off over his head. "We'll never outrun them. The pack will hunt us cross-country until the horses are exhausted, then they'll move in for the kill. Horses are their natural prey."

"He's right," Jonty said as he tossed Thaydor his dirty, crumpled-up shirt. "Dire wolves don't take no for an answer. Wild ones still roam the Highland forests where I come from. I saw one once as a boy. Smoke gray, six feet long from nose to tail, probably weighed as much as him." He nodded at Thaydor. "Fangs like daggers."

"Would you shut up?" her husband exclaimed. "You're terrifying her!"

"I'm not terrified! I want to stay and help," Wrynne pleaded. "I brought my crossbow—"

"Wife, no. We discussed this," Thaydor said sharply. "You agreed to do as I say. That was my only condition for allowing you to come along. Otherwise, I'd have left you at the Bastion. Now be gone, both of you. We need his information. Figure out what he knows while you're waiting for me."

He sent the monks an absent glance full of effortless command. "Gather the horses together. We'll form a ring around them."

They hurried to do so, steadying the animals. The horses were already showing signs of panic, hearing the howls and smelling their dreaded predators.

The knights would be lucky if their own mounts didn't kick them from behind while they battled the dire wolves ahead.

"Swords or pikes?" Piero wondered aloud.

"Both should come in handy." Thaydor hesitated, his hand on his steed's pearly neck. He turned to Wrynne.

For a moment, his blue eyes looked almost boyish with worry. "I don't suppose you could *hasten* Avalanche to safety?"

She shook her head. "One passenger at a time. Either the horse or the bard. Which one would you rather I take?"

"Hmm." The fleeting look of vulnerability vanished as he drew his sword. "Tough choice."

"Thanks a lot," Jonty retorted.

"I could come back for a second trip," she offered.

"Don't you dare come back here! Absolutely not. Even if we tarry, you stay away from here. Remember what happened when Eadric disobeyed me."

"Very well," she said, crestfallen. "Please be careful."

"We'll be fine."

"Five miles north?"

He nodded. "Soon as I can."

"Do it swiftly," she warned. "Remember, the guards will be right behind these creatures. Don't let yourself be taken. I can't bear for you to end up in that place."

"I won't. Now go!"

"They're in the field!" the other knight reported. "Thirty seconds."

"Get out of here, Wrynne." Thaydor backed up against the frightened horses, sword at the ready.

"Thaydor? I love you," she whispered, clutching her staff while she gripped Jonty's arm.

"And I you. Don't worry, wife," he said softly before slamming down the visor on his helm. "What's a few man-eating wolves after twenty Urmugoths? All in a day's work."

Piero let out a short, hearty laugh at that, while he and his brothers got into position, encircling the horses.

"And you—behave yourself with my wife."

"Can't I at least have a weapon if one of these monsters gets past you?" Jonty asked urgently.

"They won't. But here." Thaydor tossed him an extra sword.

Jonty caught it deftly by the hilt, tested the blade with a few figure eights in the air, and slipped the weapon through the leather belt holding up his kilt. "That's better. Don't worry, I'll keep her safe."

"Ten seconds!" shouted the monk.

"Run along, children!" Piero said, hefting a nasty-looking pike.

"Shall we?" Jonty offered her his arm.

*Ilios, protect them.* Reluctantly taking the bare-chested bard's naked elbow, she bumped her staff on the ground in distress. "*Hasten.*"

As the magic started to dissolve them, she saw the first huge, bristling dire wolf leap up onto the rise and bare its fangs at the men. Thaydor roared and lifted Hallowsmite as the yellow-eyed beast launched itself at him.

The horses screamed. One tried to rear. More dire wolves flooded over the rise. There were far more than six.

But the horrifying tableau disappeared in the next heartbeat as the *hasten* spell whisked her and Jonty off to safety.

# Chapter 11
# Bard

**J**onty was worried about the girl.

Each time the moonlight caught the dread in her beautiful gray eyes, he feared love would drive her to do something rash, like transport herself back to Signore Perfect's side. Love, in his experience, had a habit of wrecking people's lives.

So he kept talking to distract her, even though he got the feeling he was only annoying her.

They used the *hasten* spell again and again until they had gone about three of the five miles Thaydor had specified. Unfortunately, the fifteen consecutive, jarring blinks through space had left them both utterly nauseated.

"Ugh, I really need to learn a better travel spell," the girl groaned.

"Aye, you do," he agreed, weaving on his feet. He felt as queasy and drunk as if he had guzzled a whole bottle of Irish *uisge beatha* without pausing to take a breath.

Which he had done more than once in his wasted youth. Life of the party, him. 'Twas a curse.

At least the chill of being naked from the waist up helped clear his head. He turned to his mysterious, fair companion. "Perhaps we should go on foot for a while."

She nodded, looking dazed.

They walked and jogged by turns for another two miles, but Jonty only started to relax once they were out of earshot of the terrible snarling sounds, human shouts, and equine screams coming from the direction of the knights' battle against the dire wolves.

*Bad business, that.* He suggested they get off the road in case the prison guards came along. She agreed. They picked their way carefully into the thick, ancient forest flanking both sides of the road.

"We should probably climb a tree in case any of the dire wolves get past them," she said, glancing over her shoulder at him, as somber as an owl. "One where we can see the road so my husband doesn't miss us when he comes along."

"Very well. You choose the tree."

She seemed so nervous, barely holding herself together in fear for Thaydor battling monsters, that Jonty was glad to give her this little assignment to distract her.

She picked a mighty, gnarled oak hundreds of years old for their watchtower. He gave her a boost up into its branches, then followed, warning her to mind her step in the night's blind darkness.

Only a little moonlight filtered through the thick canopy of forest leaves. Birds warbled, startled at their incursion into their domain at this late hour. Before long, they found a fat, comfortable branch to sit on, with a thinner bough in front of them on which to rest their arms. Using the latter to hold themselves securely in place, they had an excellent view of the road as they sat side by side.

And so they waited, their feet dangling in midair some three stories up, like two children who had escaped their studies for the day and were hiding from their tutor.

He turned to her. "You do realize you haven't actually told me your name yet?"

"Oh." She smiled despite her agitation. "Sorry. It's Wrynne du Mere—I mean, now Clarenbeld, I suppose." She looked amazed to say this aloud, then added, "Pleased to meet you."

"No, the pleasure's mine, Lady Clarenbeld, believe me." He offered his hand. "I don't know how I can ever repay you, truly," he said as she shook it with a quizzical smile. "Shall I sing something pleasant for you while we wait? You look like you're in agony."

"I am. But no, thank you. The dire wolves might hear you."

"Ach, don't worry about them. They won't get past your braw laddie. He eats dire wolves for breakfast. I take it you've never actually seen him fight?"

"No, but I've seen him half-dead, and that, I don't *ever* want to see again." She tilted her head and gazed at him curiously for a moment. "I hear you two don't get along so well. Why doesn't he like you?"

"Ah, I suppose because I give him a hard time now and then," he conceded with a grin.

"Why is that?"

"Don't take it amiss, but nobody's that good."

"Thaydor is. He's the genuine article, Jonty. Believe me. He really is exactly what he seems. He's good and true, and gives all he's got to what he believes in. And anyway, you should go easy on him." She swung her feet as she talked. "He's got enough trouble to deal with now that he's the most wanted man in the kingdom."

"How in the world did that happen?"

While she filled him in on the treachery from that bastard, Reynulf, the *Wanted* posters, and the Urms, she avidly watched the road for any sign of her beloved.

Jonty was too cynical to be surprised by the news. Corruption had been simmering in the capital for months now. He had run afoul of it, himself, which was how he had ended up in Blackport.

What did *astonish* him, however, was to think that the pompous paladin was actually in love.

*Wonders never cease,* he thought in cynical amusement.

But, hell, if even a great, head-lopping brute like Thaydor Clarenbeld could fall in love, then maybe there was hope someday for a wayward, womanizing bard.

Not smelling like this, of course.

"So, Jonty?" Wrynne asked, turning to him.

He gazed at her for a moment and decided he liked her very well. With her night-dark hair, pale skin, and dove-gray eyes, she was quite fetching, but not enough so to make her arrogant. On the contrary, Wrynne was unpretentious and easy to be around, with a gentle quality of sheltered innocence, as though she had grown up in a convent. And yet, beneath her whisper-soft demeanor, he had certainly noticed that the girl possessed a spine of steel.

"Yes, my lady?" he asked indulgently.

"While we're waiting, we should try to figure out what the oracle meant by her prophecy about you."

"Ah, yes. What exactly did she say?"

"She told Thaydor the fate of the kingdom rests on him finding the Trumpet of the Runescar Highlands."

"May all the gods help us, then," he muttered.

"Well?" She searched his face impatiently. "You must know something useful."

"That's all we have to go on?" he exclaimed.

She nodded.

"Bloody hell. I don't know… Let me see. This seething brain of mine, I've a lot of knowledge rattling around in this head. Hmm. It could be anything. Could you at least point me in the right direction?"

She thought for a moment. "Thaydor believes that all this trouble is coming from Lord Eudo rather than the king. Do you know who I mean? The Silver Sage?"

"Oh, indeed. He's the one who had me thrown in jail."

"Why? Did you make fun of him, too?"

"Aye," Jonty said with a snort. "Turns out the bleeder's got no sense of humor whatsoever. As you may have heard from certain paladins of our acquaintance, I rather enjoy poking fun at the rich and powerful."

She gave him a chiding smile. "Yes, I had heard that. But why?"

"Keeps 'em honest. Plus, it's fun. When they're constantly surrounded by arse-kissing courtiers and toadies, it's good for these people to be reminded that they've still got feet of clay just like the rest of us and that we see it. That we're not afraid of them. That we're *watching* everything they do. You don't take your eyes off a would-be predator unless you fancy getting eaten."

"A predator? That's how you see Thaydor?"

"He could be if he chose to be. Would you trust Reynulf with power?"

She lowered her gaze. "I see your point."

"So long as they can still laugh at themselves," he continued, "then I figure it's probably still safe for the rest of us. Once they get too proud to take a joke, to me, that's a sign that they could start getting dangerous."

"You're an interesting man, Jonty."

"Aren't I, though?"

"I had no idea being a bard was such serious business. I thought you all were simply entertainers."

"That is a useful fiction." He gave her a wink. "For that very reason, we bards can get away with saying things other people can't. Sometimes people equate us with jesters. Pah!" He scowled. "Vile slaves. Bootlickers of tyranny."

"How's that?" she asked, arching a brow at him in surprise.

"Jesters only exist to make the *kings* laugh. They make fools of the common man for the court's amusement. Kick the weak and those who have no voice with which to speak up for themselves. Bards are just the opposite. At least proper bards. Our mission—those of us with spines—is to keep the mighty in check, using no sharper weapon than our sharp tongues and sharp wits."

"So that's why you make fun of Thaydor."

"Darling, he could be a nightmare beyond imagining if he chose to go that way."

"Worse than Reynulf?"

"Worse than ten Reynulfs! Reynulf's a lone wolf. Thaydor's a born leader. Everybody trusts him—and there's the rub. He could get away with horrors, and everyone would believe it was the good and right and moral thing to do."

"You needn't fear that. That's not who he is, and besides, I wouldn't let him."

He picked up her hand off the branch and pressed a quick kiss to her knuckles. "I like you."

She laughed. "The feeling is mutual, master bard."

"Have you got any water?"

She reached into her satchel and offered him her canteen.

"Ah! I love a woman who's prepared. Pity it's not something stronger, but my thanks anyway, lady." He took a swig and then continued. "So, anyway, about Lord Eudo. Seeing him wormin' his way through the court, workin' to enlarge his circle of influence, you can be sure I was keeping both eyes on him. Naturally, I started having a bit o' fun at his expense. He didn't like that. But, come on, if anyone ought to be able to laugh at himself, it ought to be the leader of the Harmonists, wouldn't ye fancy? What, with all their talk of getting along with everybody? No such thing as an enemy and all that rot?" He shook his head. "But he couldn't do it. Takes himself *much* too seriously, and believe me, that perked me ears up. So I pushed harder."

"Jonty!"

"The people loved it! My lines were getting picked up and repeated everywhere. Milady, the man's a total fraud. Him and his mask o' virtue! He doesn't even follow the philosophies of his own church! He says one thing in public and the opposite behind closed doors. I talked to people, trusted sources of mine around the palace and the city, and I soon drew my own conclusions. The Lord Hierophant of Efrena, for all his lofty talk, is just a typical court schemer driven by the lust for power. He's using the Harmonist cult to get whatever he wants."

"Which is?"

"That I don't know, on account of how I've been in prison. He had to shut me up, y'see. The light I was shinin' on him must have started interfering with whatever plans he's got up his sleeve."

"You're lucky he didn't have you killed," she said, stealing another glance toward the road to watch for Thaydor.

Jonty flicked a mosquito off his bare arm. "I'm sure he would've liked to, but he couldn't, or he'd risk the whole kingdom catchin' on. First Thaydor being sent away, and then me? Even the most dull-witted peasant would have begun to suspect things were not normal in the king's court. What really surprised me, though, was that the people who loved my jokes about him the most were Lord Eudo's own servants. Turns out the bleeder is not very popular with his own domestic staff."

"Oh, really?"

"One of his housemaids came over to me one night at a pub after one of my performances. She was tipsy enough to tell me I was more right about 'the old goat' than even I knew. It was the perfect chance for me to pry. I bought her a pint and started asking her questions. People like to talk to me, which probably isn't wise unless they want their stories to end up in a tale. But wouldn't you know, I learned something highly enlightening from that little housemaid. Servants always know what's really going on."

"What did she say?"

"About a year ago, he came back from the Harmonists' annual retreat at Silvermount, a shrine to Efrena, and he was a changed man." Jonty shrugged. "She said from then on, he started acting 'weird.'"

"Weird?"

"Distracted. Irritable. Aloof. He left off his daily private worship at home, and then developed a nasty temper. The head of the church of Harmony *beat* one of his footmen bloody with a fireplace poker for forgetting to clean the ashes out of the hearth. The whole staff was shocked, she told me. Publicly, he could keep up the charade. But in private, she said it was like he had slowly started going mad. Talking to himself. Keeping odd hours."

"So something happened to him at Silvermount?"

He nodded, narrowing his eyes. "That was the servants' theory, but they had no idea what it could've been. When they saw him pressure the king into paying homage at the Harmonists' shrine to Efrena, *then* they got frightened. She said they couldn't believe nobody else noticed how off the Silver Sage seemed. But everyone treats him with such deference, who would dare point it out?"

"You, apparently." Wrynne shook her head. "It sounds like he was exposed to some sort of evil influence out there."

"What, magical, you mean? It was over a year ago. Most spells would have worn off by now, surely."

"Maybe a curse."

"Demonic possession?" he suggested.

"Jonty," she retorted, "I'm sure it's nothing that exotic. Maybe he had a fight with someone he cared about. Lost some important relationship in his life. Or perhaps a crisis in his faith. Maybe his mind actually *is* ill."

"Maybe he did something naughty at Silvermount for which he is now being blackmailed," he suggested, arching a brow.

"You do have quite an imagination, don't you?" She sent him a charming little smile and then shrugged. "I suppose it could be anything."

"Well, I can tell you this. I was on my way out the door to go have a look around at Silvermount when I got arrested. What a coincidence, eh? I thought I might find something there. Do a little investigating. But I never got the chance."

"Sounds like we have our next destination sorted. This has to be what the oracle was talking about."

"Agreed. Maybe I can get someone to talk to me up there. Somebody *must* have noticed something. Once we know what changed him so much, perhaps we'll be able to deduce what he's up to and how to stop him. And by the way...look who's coming." He smiled and nodded toward the road.

She drew in her breath, peering through the branches. "Thaydor!"

He was riding Avalanche at an easy canter and leading two of the other horses by the reins.

"Oh no!" she murmured. "He's alone. Where are Piero and the brothers? I hope nothing's happened to them!"

"Let's go."

They scrambled down the tree. Twigs and leaves crunched underfoot as they dropped onto the forest floor and hurried through the thicket toward the lonely, moonlit road.

"Thaydor!" Wrynne called as loudly as she dared, waving her arms as they stepped out a hundred yards ahead of him. "We're here!"

When he reined in before them, she hurried over to Avalanche's side and tilted her head back, scanning her husband's face while worried questions tumbled from her lips. "Are you all right? Where's Piero? And the others? Was anyone hurt? Are the dire wolves dead?"

"Yes. Everyone's fine. We split up to throw the guards off our trail. They'll be along shortly. We need to keep moving. Mount up."

She seemed loath to leave his side, clinging to his hand. "I'm so glad you're safe, darling. Those wolves looked ferocious."

"So am I when the occasion calls. Everything go all right with you two?"

Jonty nodded.

Thaydor met his gaze with a terse nod of thanks, man to man. "Good. Let's find some shelter for the night, get the horses settled, and determine our next move."

"I think Jonty and I made some good progress on that point," she said eagerly. "We'll tell you all about it."

"Later. First we need to get out of sight." He nodded as Wrynne and Jonty swung up onto their still-agitated horses. "Follow me."

In spite of himself, Jonty did.

\* \* \*

As Wrynne galloped Polly half a stride behind Avalanche, she gave thanks for Thaydor's safety with every yard of ground they covered. But even her unasked-for prayers were answered when, lo and behold, about fifteen miles up the road, they came upon a fanciful stone travelers' inn.

Horse heads peered out of the stable at the back of the cobbled yard. Nearer by, warm light and lively music poured from the ground-floor tavern.

They reined to a halt in the shadows and gazed at the place longingly.

"I smell food." Jonty sniffed, nearly floated off his horse's back, but the wavering melody of the shawm, the wild strumming of the gittern, and the rhythmic, silver jingle of the timbrel seemed to beckon to his music-starved soul even more than the food lured his body.

Wrynne glanced at Thaydor. "Do you think we can chance it? We could all use a rest."

He shook his head in regret. "Remember the *Wanted* posters? They've probably got one displayed in there, too. You two could probably go in, though."

"I'm not going to leave you behind," she said.

"Hold on," Jonty murmured, squinting at the placard hanging above the doorway in the darkness. "The Spicy Cup... I know this place!" He suddenly laughed aloud. "They love me here!"

"That was before you were an escaped convict," Thaydor pointed out. "Tends to change the opinions of others."

"Nay, these are good people. We can trust 'em," Jonty said.

"Really? What are their names?"

"How should I know? I canna be expected to remember the names of everyone I meet when I'm constantly on the move from place to place, tourin' about. But I do remember this: whoever they were, they liked me here. They'll be glad to see me. Oh, enough of the steely stare, knight! Not all of us have the strength of ten. I need some food, a fresh shirt, a good cup o' mead, and a bath."

"I don't disagree, especially on the last, but the guards will surely look here by the morrow if they don't come tonight."

"Thaydor," Wrynne spoke up, "why don't we let him try? If you could've seen the awful conditions he endured in that dungeon... The bard at least deserves a decent meal after all he's been through."

He frowned, weighed it, and shrugged. "I don't like it, but if you insist. Make it fast. My lady and I will make camp in the woods off the road, there. Find us when you're ready. You can leave your horse with us. And Maguire? Do not. Get. Drunk. We need to keep our wits sharp."

"My wits are sharper'n yours when I'm asleep," Jonty shot back. "Don't worry about me, laddie." He jumped off his horse. "Just look after your girl."

"Be careful in there," Wrynne warned, also dismounting and taking the chestnut's reins from Jonty.

"I'll see what I can do for you two, as well," he promised.

"Don't mention us to them!" Thaydor whispered as loudly as he dared, but Jonty ignored him, already striding in his half-naked state toward the lively establishment.

Wrynne wondered what sort of reception he'd get. She turned and looked at Thaydor in question. He shook his head with a long-suffering look. Then they withdrew from the road and picked their way into the woods.

It was good to have him all to herself again, now that the danger was past for the moment. "Maybe we can find a cave for the night," she said with a note of flirtation in her voice.

He glanced over his shoulder and flashed a grin. "Now there's a plan I like."

But there was no cave, just a flat patch of ground under a huge pine tree that looked acceptable. There was room enough for the horses, and the inn was visible through the trees in case Jonty ran into trouble. They could watch the innyard from there to monitor the arrival of any search party from the Blackport, as well.

Moving with efficiency, they unrolled their blankets to set up camp, but as they spread them out over the thick bed of fragrant pine needles under the tree, Thaydor sent her a smoldering look that told her he had urgent expectations of her that night.

Wrynne felt the thrill of his hungry glance down to her toes and bit her lip as she turned to secure the horses. *Thank you, dire wolves.* It was a curious thing she had noticed about her warrior husband. Any sort of battle seemed to get his blood up. With all his instincts on high alert, he craved release afterward—some equally physical way to burn off the aftermath of violence in his veins. She was more than happy to oblige.

As she helped him take off a few pieces of his armor, she was already anticipating the feel of his hands on her body and the taste of his tongue in her mouth, when suddenly, a loud crackle of twigs snapping underfoot barged in on their intimate arrangement.

Thaydor turned to face the intruder, reaching for a knife and gently shoving Wrynne behind him.

Heart pounding, she glanced toward Polly, wondering if she had time to pull her little crossbow out of the saddlebag.

"Not very subtle, whoever it is," he murmured, glimpsing the glow of a lantern through the trees.

"Is it Jonty?"

Before he could answer, a loud whisper called, "Halloo? Sir Thaydor, be ye here?"

A plump old woman in an apron waddled into view, holding up a lantern. "Oh, bless me! There ye be."

Thaydor lowered his blade as she let out a cheerful laugh. Wrynne stepped out from behind him with a cautious tilt of her head.

"A good night to you, gentles. I am Mistress Margaret of Galssop, landlady here." She laughed as she spoke. "The dear mad bard told me who ye be—privately—so I could come out and let you know 'tis all right to come inside if ye will."

Thaydor frowned warily. "We'd rather not."

"Nay, this won't do!" she scolded. "I'll not have the Paladin of Ilios and his bride sleepin' in the woods like a pair of common beggars when we got warm beds inside waitin' for ye. Come in and take yer supper, both o' ye."

Thaydor and Wrynne exchanged a guarded glance.

"Thank you, Mistress Margaret," he said darkly, "but perhaps you are not aware there is a bounty on my head?"

"Pshaw! You think I'd turn you in, sir? Nay, not enough gold in the ground to make me or any of my house betray you after all you've done for our people."

Wrynne was touched when she saw Thaydor's face soften at the old woman's words. She sent him a glance that said, *You see? They still believe in you.*

"Besides," Margaret added, "you brought my son William back safe and sound from the Krenian Wars, and for that, 'tis the least I can do. Now you young folk come in and take shelter." She was beckoning and shooing them toward her establishment like an old hen. "I won't hear of havin' it otherwise."

Wrynne sensed no hidden malice from her and, apparently, neither did Thaydor.

"Mistress, if the king's men learn you gave us succor, there could be consequences for you," he warned.

"Pah! That lout don't know his arse from a hole in the ground anymore. If it comes to it, we've got hiding places in the walls—priest holes. Now come and put your horses in the stable. Our boy will see to them."

"You're very kind," Wrynne said.

"And ye both are very welcome, lady. Come now! No dawdling. 'Tis late, and the fairies don't like folk botherin' their woods after dark. No tellin' what they'd turn you into if you slept out here, anyway. A pair of toadstools, likely."

Wrynne bit back a giggle. *I love her,* she mouthed to him as the old woman waddled ahead of them through the thicket.

"I told Maguire not to tell them who we are," Thaydor grumbled nonetheless.

"Oh, I think it's safe to say that Jonty does what Jonty deems best."

"Harrumph."

She smiled at his frown and started gathering up the bedrolls. "Don't worry, husband. It'll be all right. We'll sleep with one eye open."

"If we sleep at all," he breathed with a wicked smile.

They didn't, much.

While Jonty had his mead and his food and all the attention he'd been starved for, entertaining the whole taproom with his tales and a lyre under his arm, Wrynne and Thaydor landed in the promised bed with the chamber door locked and no thought of dire wolves or dissipated kings.

Soon, they were completely absorbed in sensation. Thaydor showed her positions she had not known existed. Positions that might well be a sin. She didn't care. He took her from behind on all fours, he took her from below, he took her from above, with her leg thrown across his shoulder. Wrynne gave herself to him completely in the unfamiliar bed, while the hearth's light played across his gorgeous, velveteen skin.

She heaved under him, her skin damp with perspiration as he took her to new heights of pleasure and left her nearly sobbing with release. He growled like he'd become the ravenous dire wolf when he came the second time, and then he finally collapsed atop her, shaking and sweaty.

"Oh, Thaydor," she groaned in blissful exhaustion.

He kissed her brow and eased his heavy weight off her, blowing out a long, satisfied breath. His work done, he crashed onto his back next to her and took her hand, lifted it wearily to his lips.

"Very well," he panted at length. "Every now and then, the bard has a good idea."

Wrynne burst into laughter at this admission and punched him softly in the chest. He scooped her into his arms and pulled her atop him, kissing her once more.

"Mine," he said as he held her.

"Always."

"You are beautiful. And very good at this," he whispered.

"Am I really?" she asked, rather gleeful at the latter.

He nodded with an almost pained look of pleasure, flicking a glance down to her breasts. "Oh *yes*."

"So are you, Sir Thaydor," she purred.

"No, I need more practice," he protested. "Lots and lots of practice. Daily. Nightly. Any free moment, really…"

She laughed. Caressing and speaking lovers' nonsense to each other, they had not even bothered to discuss yet what Jonty had revealed.

But tomorrow would be another day, and with the authorities on the hunt for them, Wrynne was learning to enjoy the moment.

Even more surprisingly, Thaydor was, too.

As it turned out, her mighty paladin was not *all* business. All he had lacked was the right playmate.

*Until now,* she mused as she stroked him in contentment. Then she pressed a tender kiss to his hard jaw, hopelessly smitten.

*Hate him?*

*Impossible.*

This man was the love of her life.

# Chapter 12
## Pagans

"Well, that's unexpected," Jonty said the next day, when the three of them were suddenly forced to rein in their horses.

A thick iron chain had been strung across the lonely wooded road leading up to Silvermount, the Harmonists' retreat.

DANGER! KEEP OUT! read the wooden sign hanging from it, with a skull and crossbones painted beneath the words.

*But why?* Wrynne glanced around uneasily. The woods seemed very still.

Though the area felt remote, in actuality, the mountain shrine to Efrena, goddess of harmony, lay just ten miles north of Veraidel's bustling capital city of Pleiburg.

She turned to her husband. "Should we be worried?"

"Perhaps." Brow furrowed, Thaydor sat astride Avalanche beside her, contemplating the ominous placard.

He was dressed as a civilian today, too recognizable in his suit of armor. But considering the number of people trying to kill him, she was glad that he still wore his short coat of chain mail hidden beneath the dark blue gambeson that he had paired with black braies.

When he glanced at her, she could not help noticing how the indigo shade of his coat made his eyes look as deep and blue as the sea.

He shrugged off the nominal barrier before them. "Maybe they just want to scare people away."

"Or maybe this means they *are* hiding something, just as I suspected," Jonty chimed in.

He, too, looked much better after their brief respite at the Spicy Cup. He'd eaten enough for three men at the inn—and had drunk enough mead for half a dozen. He'd had a bath and washed the stench of

Blackport Dungeon off him, shaved, washed his wild mop of dark auburn hair, and tied it back in a queue.

Having shed the kilt that made the famous bard so readily identifiable, he was now dressed in the set of fresh clothes that Mistress Margaret had sold him. The landlady had been glad to make the trade— her grown son's Sunday best in exchange for a few of Thaydor's gold coins.

The striking Runescar Highlander looked more presentable but a lot less exotic in brown braies and a dark green wool coat, with a brown belt around his waist, clean boots, and a charcoal cloak hanging from his shoulders. Thaydor had given the bard his choice of weapons from his extensive traveling armory, as well. Jonty had chosen a good sword and a dagger. Other than being armed to the teeth, they looked like three ordinary travelers.

Unfortunately, of course, they were still being hunted by the law.

"Let's leave the horses here so we can approach more stealthily," Thaydor suggested. "The Harmonists claim to be pacifists, but who knows? We may run into any opposition. Wrynne, can you hide the animals for us with a sanctuary spell?"

She agreed, and they dismounted. They led their horses off the road and tied them up, then she concealed the animals. Returning to the road to go the rest of the way on foot, she felt her heartbeat quicken with uneasiness over what they might find at the top of the hill.

She had never been to a Harmonist religious site before. It was not forbidden to set foot in one, but the Ilian church generally frowned on such commingling.

"Let's keep our eyes open," Thaydor advised in a low tone as he assisted her in stepping over the chain.

Then they proceeded up the winding drive, weapons drawn. Walking between the men, Wrynne scanned both sides of the narrow country lane continually, her small crossbow at the ready. There was nothing to see but woods.

Until they reached the crest of the hill. Then the colossus of the hermaphrodite goddess Efrena came into view. A huge white marble nude of "the One" towered at the end of an avenue made of white and silver-blue pavers.

On both sides of the promenade, stately white columns stood, only reaching about as high as the massive Efrena's hip.

The pearl-white statue, with breasts and phallus bared, had blank, serene eyes and wild, coiled hair barely tamed by a circlet crown. One hand was raised, pointing upward, the other pointing down. Around its huge bare feet were braziers for burnt offerings, but the low, round pedestal on which the colossus stood was encircled by a stone lily pond.

*Fire and water paired*, Wrynne mused as she studied it. Obviously in keeping with the Harmonist philosophy of all things as balanced pairs of opposites.

Beyond the marble shrine itself, lush green gardens stretched out with mathematical symmetry on both sides. It was obvious to Wrynne's horticulturally trained eye, however, that the once-tidy beds and garden walkways had lain untended for many months.

Tucked away behind the trees, she could just make out the sprawling, domed villa where the Harmonists who came here on their annual retreat here would be housed.

"I wonder if anyone's home," Thaydor said as they stepped gingerly onto the promenade.

"I doubt it. The whole place looks abandoned," Jonty said.

He was right. There was not a soul in sight, and the only sound was the wind lightly strumming the Aeolian harps that graced the gardens here and there, and the wind chimes hanging from the trees.

Wrynne did not even hear any birds singing, though it was a fine spring morning, and the orchard nearby would be burgeoning at this time of year with all the fruits and seeds and nuts their little hearts could desire. So where were they?

"Eerie," Jonty said, looking around, his green eyes narrowed.

"Something's definitely wrong here," Wrynne agreed in a wary murmur. "I sense the presence of some sort of evil."

"As do I," Thaydor said. "Not sure if it's human, though…"

"You two and your tricks. Must be nice to have that gift," Jonty muttered.

"Quiet. Whoever—or whatever—is here, we don't want them to hear us. Stay sharp." Thaydor scanned ahead, keeping Hallowsmite angled before him as they slowly moved deeper into the Harmonists' sacred place.

Efrena seemed to stare down her haughty Roman nose at them.

Jonty kept watch behind with agile steps, his borrowed sword at the ready.

Wrynne stayed between the two men, surveying the beautiful but overgrown grounds. Her crossbow rested on her forearm, already loaded with a mistletoe dart.

The quiet was unnerving. But there was nothing to see but a haze of yellow pollen and dandelion fluff drifting on the air.

She searched the shadows of the shrubs and the branches of the trees with every step, grateful for the flat expanse of lawn on either side of the marble avenue. If someone or something charged out at them from the leafy cover of the garden, at least they'd see it coming.

"Do you get the feeling we are being watched?" she asked, a chill running down her spine.

"Aye," Jonty said. "But by what? Or whom?"

"Hard to say," Thaydor mumbled, his gaze continually moving over the landscape.

Still, they saw no one, which certainly seemed to lessen the need for stealth. Her heart beat faster as they proceeded up the promenade, past the shadows of one column after another striping the marble pavers.

"Should we go to the villa?" she asked.

"Perhaps," said Thaydor.

She frowned, jittery with nerves. There had to be something here that would give them a clue about what had happened to Lord Eudo while he'd last been here.

Thaydor had said that if they could manage to uncover a definite lead here, then he could find a way to bring the information to the king, to warn him privately.

"There's something," Thaydor murmured, pausing.

"What is it?" Jonty quickly turned to look.

Wrynne also stopped and followed her husband's nod.

"Dead animal."

She grimaced at the deer carcass lying on the grass. She instantly thought of Urmugoths. And dead squires.

Queasiness pulsed through her, but she shrugged it off.

The deer looked like a fresh kill—the traces of blood on the torn fur and antlers still crimson, not brown. The bones, however, had been picked clean.

"Well, *some* sort of predator is here," Thaydor said.

"I'm fairly sure the Harmonists keep a herd of tame deer in the park." Jonty's usual jovial tone had turned taut. "It's one of Efrena's totem animals, if I am not mistaken."

"I'll go have a look. Maybe I can figure out what might've killed it," Thaydor started, but Wrynne suddenly drew in her breath.

*"Don't move."*

Both men froze.

Thaydor glanced at her in alarm. "What is it?"

"Look to the trees," she uttered.

Jonty cursed under his breath. "Rocs! I don't believe it!"

"So that's why this place is closed down," Thaydor mumbled, sounding vaguely like he had just been punched in the gut.

"*That* little sign for man-eating birds?" Jonty said in outrage through gritted teeth, reminding them of the placard on the road. "They could have been a bit more specific!"

"What do we do?" Wrynne whispered, half terrified, though, so far, the rocs were thankfully minding their own business, just sitting in the high branches of some huge, old trees.

Nobody answered.

"What in the world are they doing this far south? Don't they usually keep to the Bronze Mountains?" Jonty asked.

Thaydor nodded, not taking his eyes off them. "They're a hundred miles from home."

"Maybe Eudo summoned them," Jonty said.

"Why would he do that?" Wrynne whispered.

"We can puzzle it out later." Thaydor moved his body between her and the rocs. "Let's just get out of here without getting eaten, shall we? Everybody, move very slowly. And don't make a sound."

"Bloody hell, first dire wolves, now rocs? Never a dull moment with you two."

"Stop talking!" Thaydor ordered the bard in a wrathful mutter.

Wrynne's mind spun with questions while they moved as a unit, inch by inch, back the way they had come. She could only hope the rocs were sated from their feast of venison.

A whimper escaped her as one of the huge birds launched out of the treetops and flew over to investigate them.

"Steady," Thaydor murmured. "Hold your ground. Whatever you do, don't run."

The roc soared closer, its wingspan twelve to fifteen feet wide, easily. Its glossy black feathers resembled those of a crow, but it had the bare black head of a vulture, with leathery skin, a hooked beak, scarlet throat markings…and blood-red eyes.

When it landed on its sickle-claw feet right in front of them on the grass, it stood as tall as Wrynne.

Indeed, she was on eye level with the terrifying creature.

It blinked and cocked its head.

"Nice birdie," Jonty murmured as they continued backing away slowly.

The roc flicked its massive wings in a warning display like an annoyed shrug, and squawked at them. This brief, aggressive movement made plain its displeasure about their intrusion on what was apparently now the flock's territory.

"I think we're done here," Jonty said brightly.

"Agreed," Thaydor said. "Don't worry, we're leaving," he assured the monstrous creature in a low tone.

Not that the roc could understand.

It tossed its ugly head belligerently and squawked again.

"How's your aim with that thing, wife?"

"Accurate enough. He'd be hard to miss, big as he is."

*As long as my hands don't shake too badly.*

"Be ready to fire, but only on my mark."

"Don't shoot him," Jonty protested under his breath. "If he screeches, they'll all come flapping over. Maybe I should sing to him. Music soothes the savage beast—"

"No. They're known to be very curious birds. You'll risk drawing the rest of the flock to come and investigate," Thaydor muttered. "In which case, all of us will end up like that deer."

Wrynne bit back a shriek as the roc hopped closer.

But to her relief, it seemed satisfied with backing them away.

"Why isn't it attacking us?" Jonty whispered.

"We're taller than him?" Thaydor suggested.

"Not by much," Wrynne whispered. "Maybe he's not hungry."

"Good thing we didn't bring the horses," Jonty remarked.

They both looked at the bard.

He shrugged.

The roc just stood there in the middle of the road, staring broodingly at them with its malevolent crimson eyes. Thankfully, however, it made no effort to follow them any farther once they started retreating down the hill.

While Thaydor fixed his attention on the bird in case it decided to attack, and Jonty kept an eye on the road behind them, Wrynne scanned the trees as they went, worried that more members of the flock might be lurking in the forest shadows.

Suddenly, she spotted something in the woods that she had missed before, on the way up the hill. A very big something...

"Look!"

Jonty did, but only briefly.

Thaydor didn't dare. "What is it?"

"One hell of a nest," the bard said in amazement, then he watched the road behind them again as they continued inching back down the drive.

"It's huge." Wrynne estimated that the rocs' nest was as big as the bed she had shared last night with Thaydor at the inn—and probably home to a mated pair of the birds. "I wonder if there are any eggs in it."

"Wonderful," Jonty mumbled. "Babies."

"And protective mother birds," she added.

Tucked away on the forest floor between a large boulder and a clump of trees, the nest looked empty from this distance, but its brushy walls were built up high, so it was hard to be certain. She did, however, notice a curious plant stuck to it, wedged between the side of the nest and the trunk of the massive oak that held it in place.

The plant gave her pause even more than the nest itself had. As well versed as she was in apothecary herbs and the vegetation of both woodland and field, she had never seen such a thing before. She certainly would have remembered something like that.

It looked like a giant burr, brown and dried out. No—rather, some monstrous breed of thistle, she mused.

But instead of being the normal fist-sized bloom, like a milk thistle, or even its larger cousin, the artichoke, the seed head was nearly the size of a barrel or a full-grown pig.

She stared at it in fascination. Bristling with prickles like a knight's mace, it looked stuck to the tight, twiggy weaving of the roc's nest. Its spiny leaves, though dead, had a reddish-orange tint. The globular seed head itself was hideous, wrapped in a white, cobweb-like layer of something resembling spider's silk, while the dried-out plume of brushy petals sprouting from the top of it were a deep, dark red.

But the strangest part of all was the bizarre sensation that the thing was...watching them. As if each small, dark-colored seed tucked into its bristling bracts were so many beady little eyes following their every movement, tracking her and Thaydor and Jonty as they passed.

She swallowed hard. She could have sworn she sensed evil emanating from the thing. It seemed to pulsate with pure malice, aware of them somehow.

And it hated them.

*Impossible*, she scoffed at herself, even as chills swept through her. There was no such thing as a sentient plant! She, of all people, should know that. This species was merely foreign to her. The rocs must have brought it down from the mountains with them, she reasoned. One of them must have eaten a seed of it in their homeland and shat it out here, where it must have taken root.

Which was a shame.

For these were beautiful gardens, and that thing looked like an invasive weed species that could be very hard to destroy. Nasty and sharp. It had all the charm of a thornbush in winter and probably no beneficent uses.

Thankfully, they regained the road without further incident and all breathed a sigh of relief.

"What are those creatures doing here?" Jonty asked as they rejoined the horses behind the sanctuary spell.

"No idea." Thaydor sheathed his sword with a grim metallic *zing*. "We were lucky to get out of there alive."

"Did either of you see that bizarre plant stuck to the rocs' nest?"

"No. What about it?"

"I could've sworn… Oh, never mind," Wrynne mumbled, shaking off her silly imaginings. "What do we do now?"

"Good question," said Thaydor.

"I want to know why both of you were sensing evil," said the bard, untying his horse. "This is quite a mystery. Rocs are dangerous, of course, but can mere animals ever truly qualify as evil?"

"A few." Thaydor shrugged. "Most dragons."

"I've seen an evil dog or two in my day," Wrynne added. But Jonty had a point. She glanced at her husband. "Maybe the evil we were sensing was simply coming from the Harmonist cult itself."

He considered this. "You're probably right."

The idle flick of Jonty's dark eyebrows told them he had no desire to get into a philosophical discussion with a pair of the Ilian faithful. He let out a sigh and leaned against his horse. "Well? I'm not sure we accomplished anything at all here."

Wrynne frowned. "Maybe the oracle was wrong."

"Maybe *I* was wrong and we've wasted our time coming here," Jonty answered, then frowned. "Maybe it's some other knowledge in my head that's of importance…"

"No, this is all very strange," Thaydor said. "You would think that if the Harmonists knew the rocs were here, they'd send men to kill them."

Wrynne shrugged. "Maybe they don't know."

"But they have to. They put the sign up warning people away," Jonty pointed out. "Maybe they just decided to leave them be for a while."

Thaydor snorted. "Sounds like something the Harmonists would do. Whatever's easiest."

"Now, now," Wrynne scolded with a smile. "I will say one thing, though. The overall experience here does seem related to the general unpleasantness surrounding Lord Eudo."

Thaydor scowled and looked away. "If only there was some way I could get in to meet privately with the king and warn him not to trust that blackguard."

"No!" the other two said in unison.

"Don't even think about it," Wrynne added. "You'll be arrested on sight. As your wife, I forbid it. One dungeon rescue was enough, thank you very much."

"I'll second that," Jonty said. "Besides, His Majesty won't listen to you, anyway. You and I both know from firsthand experience that the king no longer tolerates those who speak anything other than what His Majesty wishes to hear."

Thaydor's frown deepened. "I suppose you're right. But if I can't speak to Baynard myself to warn him to be wary of Lord Eudo, at least my brother knights will listen to me, surely. We need to go to the barracks."

"That's awfully close to the palace," Wrynne said with a worried glance at him.

"It's actually attached," he admitted. "But don't worry. We knights have our own private entrance on the side. We'll go in that way."

"It's not a bad idea," Jonty admitted. "That way, Thaydor can warn the knights to watch out for Eudo. If they keep their eyes open around the palace, maybe someone will see something to help us figure out what he's up to. Before it's too late."

Thaydor's face was etched with more than its usual resolve as he nodded toward the road. "Let's go."

They led their horses back through the woods, pausing at the roadside to glance around at the treetops and the skies. When they were certain no rocs were circling above, Thaydor helped Wrynne into the saddle. Then both men swung up onto their horses' backs, and Polly fell into line behind Avalanche.

Ahead of her, Thaydor urged his steed into motion.

Before Wrynne could think of a way to dissuade her overly brave husband from walking into the lion's den, they were already galloping down the hill away from Silvermount, heading for the capital.

Where all three of them were wanted by the law.

\* \* \*

An hour and a half later, they paused in the foothills and looked down on the plain below, considering their approach to Pleiburg.

The kingdom's capital city had been founded centuries ago at the confluence of the wide, placid River Sevock and the narrower but faster-running Drard to form Veraidel's principle waterway, the mighty River Keo. The Keo, in turn, ran another sixty miles through the green, fertile lowlands of the south, watering the country's richest farmlands on its way to flow into the Dragon Sea at the rowdy — and pirate-ridden — port town of Keomouth.

One of Father's companies had helped to build the docks and the customs house there, not to mention several chief buildings in the capital.

The thought of the big, loud, crude Building Baron made Wrynne's heart clench with missing him — missing *all* of them, maddening as they were. Staring down at the city where she had been born — and where her family still resided, no doubt wondering what had become of her — she felt her heart lifting with a blend of fear and excitement.

She had lived in sleepy, rural Mistwood for so long now, it seemed ages since she had walked the busy avenues of the capital or browsed the shops with her sister, Juliana. As much as she loved the quiet of the North, she supposed Pleiburg would always be home.

Torn between fond nostalgia and the dread of being arrested, she let her gaze travel over the familiar, hazy outline of the city. It was jagged with palace turrets, and the bell towers and clock towers of hulking stone cathedrals and fancy guildhalls. The wizards' spire jutted up amid various temple domes and aristocratic mansions; near it, the crown of philosopher statues posed along the edges of the Great Library's roof. The round theater beckoned from beside the Sevock River, where innumerable ships' masts bristled.

Jammed into all the nooks and crannies in between lay the endless hodgepodge of timber-framed houses and shops of the ordinary folk, countless chimney pots smoking. There were scores of inns and almshouses, schools and training halls, market squares, livery stables, animal pens. Plazas and monuments, graveyards and parks. Roads of all sizes, from the wide Royal Boulevard to a labyrinth of back alleys with sorry names like Dead Man's Jaunt and All-For-Naught Row.

From this distance, they could just catch a whiff of the city's many smells on the breeze and hear the Ilian cathedral's carillon intricately ringing in the noon.

She turned to Thaydor. "Do you think we'll have time to visit my family? I so want them to meet you. And you, too, Jonty," she added.

Thaydor frowned in apology. "As much as I want that, too, I do not think it's safe yet—for them or for us. Reynulf will have figured out by now who you are. Your family's home and your father's offices are probably being watched."

She stared at him, paling a little. "You don't think they're in any danger, do you?"

"As long as we stay away from them, probably not. Your father is an important man, after all. That helps him."

"I see." She swallowed hard.

Thaydor reached over and squeezed her arm gently. "We won't let anything happen to them, demoiselle."

She tried to smile. "Well, my mother would probably make a scene if I went home, anyway. I can't even think what she's going to say when I see her. Getting married without even telling her? She's going to wring my neck."

"It couldn't be helped," Thaydor reminded her.

"Ah, nonsense," Jonty interjected, lightening the mood with his droll tone. "What mother wouldn't be delighted to learn that her daughter had just married the chief outlaw of the land?"

He flashed a grin at Thaydor, whose answer was a leonine stare. He then looked away with a low huff.

"Shall we?" Thaydor drawled, urging Avalanche ahead, as before.

"You shouldn't taunt him," Wrynne scolded the bard with a smile.

Jonty sniggered, pleased. "Eh, he's a big boy. He can take it."

"It's you I'm worried about!" she retorted, trying not to chuckle.

Before crossing the bridge across the Sevock into the city's triangular central district between the rivers, they pulled up the hoods of their cloaks.

The soldiers stationed by the city gates only looked on idly while the milling crowd came and went. Still, they weren't taking any chances. Wrynne smuggled Thaydor into Pleiburg with a *hasten* spell, whisking him to safety.

Once inside the city walls, the two of them waited nervously, watching around the corner of a nearby alley while Jonty rode in, leading Avalanche and Polly. They had covered Thaydor's warhorse with Polly's plain blanket in an effort to conceal the white stallion's magnificence.

To their relief, the bard got into the city without incident. Nobody recognized Avalanche or the famous bard without his distinctive Highland plaid.

Reunited, they hurried through the back streets, doing all they could to avoid calling attention to themselves.

"Are you sure about this?" Wrynne asked Thaydor when they arrived at the stone archway outside the knights' barracks and training yard.

He nodded. There was a gleam in his eyes at being back at his old quarters. "Follow me. And, er, if anything should happen to go horribly wrong, you and Jonty *hasten* out of here. And don't go to your family. You will only lead the danger to them."

"I understand, b-but I'm sure we won't need to. Right?" she demanded, grabbing hold of his sleeve.

"Right," he said in a tentative tone that gave her no comfort at all.

To their amazement, however, after all the trouble they had gone to get there, the knights' training yard was empty but for three bored-looking squires, each about twenty years old.

The first was grooming a large black warhorse, the second was oiling a suit of armor, and the third was sharpening swords. All three big, strapping lads looked extremely annoyed and put upon.

The one sitting on a long, rough-hewn table polishing armor was the first to notice them. His jaw dropped the moment he set eyes on Thaydor. He jumped out of his seat and pointed in astonishment.

"Look!" he cried to his companions.

The other two did just that as Thaydor sauntered warily into the sunny training yard. "Gentlemen," he said.

"Sir!" The boys abandoned their tasks and came rushing over to him, their eyes wide and brimming with instant hero worship.

"Sir Thaydor!"

"You're alive!"

"I knew it! Didn't I tell you, Kai?"

"They said you were an outlaw!"

"But we didn't believe it."

"No, not for a minute."

"We knew that was nonsense," the first shoved in. "We all said so."

"But some folk were claiming you were dead!"

"Are you all right?"

"What are you doing here?"

"Can we help?"

"Er, thank you, gentlemen," Thaydor said, looking a little overwhelmed at all three gushing over him at once. "I appreciate the kind words. And you might be...?"

The squires introduced themselves as Jeremy, Petra, and Kai, which, he informed them, was short of Karolus. They were brave, educated boys from good families, with big dreams of derring-do, Wrynne mused. *Just like Eadric.*

No wonder their brimming enthusiasm seemed to pain Thaydor. But for their part, they obviously worshiped the great paladin, outlaw or no.

"We should warn you, sir, if Sir Reynulf sees you—" Petra started.

"He's the new royal champion!" Kai broke in.

"Can't I talk for once?" Jeremy demanded. "I was just about to tell him that!"

"Is Reynulf here?" Thaydor prompted, barely showing his impatience.

"No, sir," Jeremy forced out before his friends could answer.

"Ho! Aren't you that famous bard?" Kai suddenly asked Jonty in excitement.

"Never mind him," Thaydor ordered. "Where are all the other knights? I need to talk to them. Where is everybody?"

The boys exchanged reluctant glances.

"Well?" Thaydor prompted.

Wrynne noticed that all three lads had started blushing.

"Um..."

"I'm waiting." Thaydor arched a brow.

"Er, well, it's just...they've gone to Fonja, sir."

"To see their lady friends."

"I wouldn't call them ladies," Kai mumbled.

Thaydor stared at them incredulously. "You must be mistaken. It's the middle of the day."

"No, sir. The king said it was all right for them to go as often as they liked. To, er, worship the pink goddess. Now that everything's…changed," Petra said with some dismay.

The other two looked sheepish on behalf of their masters and lowered their heads.

"Fonja?" Thaydor echoed with thunder gathering in his voice. "They're off rogering harlots when the kingdom's on the verge of falling apart?"

"Thaydor," Wrynne said softly.

Blue fire flared in his eyes, and he suddenly looked like he might put his fist through the nearest stone wall. He pivoted, his wide shoulders bristling, and marched toward the archway. "Let's go."

"C-can we come with you, sir?" Jeremy asked eagerly.

Thaydor paused, his face hard. "I don't advise it. Helping me could cost you your heads."

Jeremy planted his fists on his waist. "We're not afraid!"

"Please, sir! Let us do something useful! We've had loads of training!" Petra begged.

"We can't just stay here doing chores all day," said Kai.

"Tending armor is useful. So is sharpening blades and caring for horses," Thaydor replied. "It's better than spending the middle of the *day in a bloody brothel*!"

Everybody present flinched a little at his rare outburst.

The boys looked at one another and blanched, and then turned to Thaydor in a conciliatory fashion.

"Perhaps we can help, sir. If there's some *other* mission we could carry out for you in the meanwhile—"

"Oh, yes, please! You need help, surely, sir. If it's just you and the lady and the bard—"

"You need knights!" Petra insisted.

"And since our masters are…indisposed," Kai added with admirable delicacy.

Wrynne raised a brow at her husband. His lips flattened into a guarded line.

"How are you at stealth?" he asked, seemingly in spite of himself.

"Excellent! Especially Petra," Jeremy said, gesturing at his friend.

"All right, then," Thaydor conceded after a moment. "There is a house in French Square."

Wrynne's eyes widened hopefully.

"I need to know if it's being watched, by how many men, and from what vantage points. My lady, describe your father's house to our spies here."

"Spies? Yes!" Kai and Petra bumped forearms in victory while Jeremy nearly leaped into the air, fists clenched with glee.

"Very stealthy," Jonty murmured, folding his arms across his chest. He shook his head.

But the lads were too thrilled to be able to hide their jubilation at this assignment from the greatest knight in the realm.

"Are you sure about this?" Wrynne asked him.

Thaydor looked them over with a well-trained eye of a seasoned leader. "They can do it…I think."

"Oh, we can, sir! Certainly!"

"It's easy!"

"Which house on French Square do you want us to watch?"

"Wrynne, what's the house number?"

"There isn't one. It faces south," she told them, homesickness tugging at her heart as she described her childhood home. "A large, timber-framed house with stained glass in the shape of a hammer in the front bay window. The upper floor overhangs the street, with flower baskets hanging from the posts underneath. It's the home of the Baron du Mere."

"Have you got all that?" Thaydor asked.

The boys nodded eagerly.

"Good. Go there and get into position around the baron's house, and I will meet you there shortly. Take no action yourselves, but when I arrive, you'll let me know what you've found out. I'll handle things from there."

"Wait, *you're* going to my family's house?" Wrynne asked Thaydor, holding her breath with hope.

He shrugged. "I think a short visit may be all right, provided our spies do their job properly."

"Oh, we will, sir!" Petra said while Wrynne gazed gratefully at her husband and mouthed a silent *Thank you.*

"You can count on us, sir!" Kai vaunted.

"Good. We'll see you there," Thaydor replied. "Now, go."

The boys scrambled to carry out their assignment, quickly arming themselves with discreet daggers quite at odds with their grins.

"Are all baby knights that eager to get killed?" Jonty inquired after the trio had rushed off on their mission.

Thaydor sighed. "You have no idea."

From there, they set out through the city, hiding their faces in the shadow of their hoods, until they came to Temple Row. Along the broad, treelined avenue, all the main religions of Veraidel were represented. The massive Ilian cathedral with its Gothic spires and rose windows sat at the head of the table, as it were, holding pride of place at the far end of the road. Opposite it, the Greek-style Argent Temple to Efrena gleamed in white marble, domed and pillared. All along the boulevard in between were smaller shrines dedicated to less popular deities believed to rule over all sorts of random things.

Midway down the street, two large temples sat across from each other like partners in a dance: the Red Temple of Xoltheus, granite and austere, and the so-called Beehive building, dedicated to Fonja.

Wrynne had heard her builder father marvel many times over the strange, honeycombed architecture of the latter. The hive-like design had been chosen because the honeybee was a totem animal of the pink goddess.

*More like a hornet's nest, if you ask me,* Mother would usually respond, while Wrynne's brothers would snicker over the mention of the place. *They deserve to get stung for what goes on in there. Humph!*

After dismounting in an out-of-the-way corner of the Beehive grounds, the three of them kept to the shadows of a pretty copse of trees. Whatever Thaydor planned to do in there, he said it wouldn't take long. Wrynne gladly agreed to wait outside with Jonty, though the bard protested at missing out on seeing all the scantily clad harlots.

"If the king's men show up, Wrynne, you get out of here, but Jonty, come get me. As Paladin of Ilios, this is the last place I want to get arrested. It would only shame the church. If we should end up getting separated for any reason—"

"Separated?" Wrynne asked anxiously, the oracle's warning echoing in her mind.

"We'll plan to meet up again on that lookout ridge in the foothills. Remember? Where we paused before entering the city?"

"Aye, I remember," Jonty said with a sigh of weary disappointment.

Wrynne stared up at her husband's hard, handsome face. "I don't want to be separated from you."

Thaydor cupped her cheek for a fleeting moment with a tender smile, even amid his wrath at the knights. "Don't worry, my love. It's only a contingency plan. It won't happen. I'll be right back. Trust me. This won't take long."

"It usually doesn't, with those girls."

"Jonty!" Wrynne reprimanded.

"What? They *are* the experts."

Thaydor rolled his eyes.

"Those women are vile," Wrynne informed the bard.

"But who are we to judge, Sister?" He flashed a wicked grin, then looked ruefully at Thaydor. "Well, run along, then. Go and bash some heads. We'll be waiting."

"On your best behavior, I trust."

"Whatever that is," the bard replied. "But let the record note I pronounce this denial of my starved eyes cruelly unfair."

"Oh, stop pouting, you'll live," Wrynne chided as Thaydor took leave of them, shaking his head as he stalked toward the entrance of the place to deal with the absent knights.

"Easy for you to say! You haven't been locked up in prison for the past month." As they sat down to wait on the low wall around the trees, he took a large bite of an apple he had swiped from an orchard they had passed on the way to the city. "You two holier-than-thous have each other at night. All I've got is Mistress Hand."

"Jonathan Maguire!" She sat down next to him, wide-eyed and blushing. "You'd better not let my husband hear you say such things in front of me. He'll chop you into chicken feed."

The bard let out a rascally chuckle. "Ah, don't worry, my dear. Got to say, I admire you for not bein' jealous of him goin' in there."

"Jealous?" she echoed in surprise.

"But why should you be? That place might be full of naked ladies— well, not *ladies*—but if any man's impervious to a right seething cauldron of temptation, it would be your paladin."

Wrynne just looked at him, taken aback.

It hadn't even crossed her mind to doubt her husband.

Then she scowled. "You're teasing me, you blackguard."

Jonty chuckled, then offered her a bit of his fruit. "Apple, dear heart?"

"No, thank you, devil." But after a moment of trying, she could not hold her tongue. "You don't know him at all, Jonty. Thaydor could never be tempted by the likes of those harlots."

"Of course not," he agreed, his green eyes dancing with wicked amusement.

"He's too good for that."

*Besides, he's* mine.

That part, however, she did not say aloud. Instead, rather pouting now, she turned and glared at the Beehive's rounded, gold-toned doors, through which her wildly desirable husband had just disappeared.

Suddenly, every second that passed began to feel like an hour, and to her annoyance, she found herself sulking. She got up and paced, arms folded across her chest. She fidgeted impatiently, waiting for him to return.

*This is stupid.*

She plopped back down onto her seat again and gave Jonty a stern look. "He would never."

"Of course not. I agree with you completely."

"Stop it!"

"Stop what? I'm just sitting here!" he exclaimed with an innocent look.

"Stop smiling," she cried.

"Oh, relax." He relented with a lazy grin, lying back on the wall. "He's besotted with ye. It's disgustin', really."

"Dashed right, he is!"

*Humph.* She decided she would just have to remind him tonight to whom he belonged. *Provided we're not in jail by then.*

\* \* \*

The place stank of incense, but even that cloying perfume was not strong enough to mask the rank smell of stale, drunken sex that filled the place. Thaydor looked around in wary scorn as he stalked across the dimly lit space of the round, soaring entrance hall of the Beehive. The ceiling rose into a shadowed dome high above him, while the sloped walls on all sides were honeycombed with dark alcoves where visitors would be received by the temple prostitutes.

These guest chambers could only be reached by the spindly, winding walkways that wove and spiraled along the walls, like paths made by insects. They looked treacherous. The place *was* treacherous as far as he was concerned—a sticky-sweet trap. No windows let in natural light. Instead, by the intimate glow of candles, it was impossible to tell if it was night or day. There were powerful drugs and powders on offer, potions and wine, baths and music, whips and bindings and perverse toys, and many other things to make men mindless and weak.

One of the wild-haired, kohl-eyed priestesses prowled toward him from across the open space, wearing nothing but a few strands of beads, a couple of ribbons, and strange, tall, complicated boots. "Welcome—"

"Don't bother," he interrupted, holding up his hand to keep her at arm's length. "Where are they?"

"Excuse me?" Her empty eyes flickered with wounded vanity at the slight.

"I'm here to collect the knights of Veraidel."

A sudden gasp of recognition escaped her. "Paladin!"

She bit her rouged lip on a giddy grin as her smoldering gaze ran over him. Her pink animal tongue licked out. Toying with her beads, she moved closer and reached out a languid hand to finger his coat. "I knew someday if we were patient you would finally come for a taste—"

"Forget it." He brushed her off and walked past her. "I'll find them myself."

She made a sound of indignation behind him. "You cannot bring those weapons in here! It's not allowed!"

"Try to stop me," he muttered under his breath, then went in search of his colleagues.

They weren't hard to find. All he had to do once he gained the back hallway was follow the sound of hearty, drunken laughter.

And the groaning.

Thaydor could hardly stomach what he saw when he arrived at the entrance of a large, shadowy chamber. Draped panels of transparent silk lightly partitioned the sections of the room, separating sets of low couches, where twenty or thirty naked fools of his acquaintance were engaged in all manner of lewd acts with women they didn't know.

Some were using riding crops and shackles. Some were using oil. Some were using objects Thaydor didn't even know the names of.

He scanned the room in shock.

Three of his best fighters were laughing lustfully, watching Berold bend some intoxicated harlot over a couch, taking her from behind while he lightly choked her throat.

Thaydor's stomach turned at the spectacle they were making of themselves. He looked away. Pulse pounding in confusion, he almost walked out, too ashamed on their behalf to speak to them.

It seemed the knights of Veraidel had indeed abandoned the old ways and taken to heart the new religion of the self. The lusts of the flesh, the pride of the will.

They were too absorbed in their pleasures to even notice him standing there, but for his part, what he saw made him sad. He'd had no idea that his friends were such weak men. So easily deceived. The bloody bard had been right all this time. His hot-blooded warriors were fools. How could they not realize they had been sent here merely to distract them from what was really going on?

This place was not a beehive, it was a spider's web, and his friends were caught like so many idiotic flies. He glanced at them again in searing disgust.

Most appeared to be enjoying their dishonor as the venomous spider women sucked them dry. He could feel rage building in his veins. And he began to understand more deeply why the king—or Lord Eudo—had wanted him banished from the city.

He couldn't believe how far his men had fallen away from the code without him there. They would never have dared act this way if he'd been on hand to watch them, rein them in, and bring down the hammer when the occasion called.

Indeed, it pained him to wonder if this was partly his fault somehow. Damn it, some of these men had good and decent wives at home. Children...

He tamped down his fury, well aware they were likely just following the king's new, scandalous example. *To hell with this.* Their marital infidelity was their own business, but their dereliction of duty was his.

As their former captain, he was seriously displeased, yet what could he possibly say?

Caught like this, faced head-on with their shame, they would never listen. They would only defend their actions and retaliate. *Blind fools.*

No words could wake them from their carnal dreamland. But perhaps the power of the Light could make them open their eyes and *see.*

Thaydor drew his sword, closed his eyes, and lifted the blade skyward as he bowed his head. Sinking down on one knee, he humbled himself with his head down, tapping into the might of the just, all-seeing god who daily made him strong, so long as he was obedient. The god who had tasked him with the terrifying mission of standing in the gap to uphold law and order.

But he couldn't do it alone.

He slowed his breath, in and out, and felt the gathering rush of righteous anger filling his offered blade with crackling energy. His every nerve ending began to tingle and thrum with the divine strength that he usually saved only for the enemies of Ilios. Letting out a sudden wrathful roar, he slammed the lightning-touched blade of Hallowsmite into the brothel floor.

It thundered as it struck. The ground shook. The women shrieked. The wave of power flowed outward in a circle from around him and knocked the wicked off their feet.

Thaydor rose slowly, glaring at his stunned men as their midday orgy came to an abrupt halt.

"Oh, no," he said in icy rebuke. "Don't stop on my account."

Their eyes widened with shock and with shame when they saw him, jarred back to reality.

Faces paled. Heads hung.

Erections wilted.

"So this is why you could not come to my aid when I sent for reinforcements to drive the Urmugoths from Mistwood."

"We wanted to," Sagard answered from the back of the room. "We were told to stand down."

"I'll bet you were," Thaydor said in a quiet, murderous tone.

"Uh, sir?" one of the others spoke up, somewhat covering himself with the nearest drape. "W-what are you doing here?"

"Put your damned clothes on," Thaydor ordered in a steely tone. "The kingdom is in danger."

Silence hung over the shame-faced revelers. They began to disentangle themselves, avoiding one another's eyes.

He trusted he had made his point.

Sheathing his sword, Thaydor turned away to give them a moment's privacy, only to find his wife tearing down the corridor toward him from the direction of the entrance hall.

"Are you all right?" she cried, looking frantic. "What happened?" Hood down, her cloak flowed out behind her. She had her crossbow in hand. "We heard the concussion wave from Hallowsmite—"

"Wrynne, you should not be here. I'm fine. I told you both to wait outside." He glanced at Jonty in annoyance as he strode in a few steps behind her.

The bard held up his hands. "Sorry, I couldn't hold her back. Did you find the knights?"

Thaydor snorted in disgust and nodded over his shoulder. "They're in there."

When Wrynne glanced past him curiously, he stopped her from going any farther. "You don't need to see this. Go back outside and wait for me."

Her brow furrowed with a hint of stubborn protest, but he rested his hands on her shoulders and gently turned her around.

Before he released her, though, he froze.

Reynulf was marching down the hallway straight toward them.

Thaydor thrust Wrynne into Jonty's waiting arms. "Get her out of here."

"I'm not leaving you!" she cried.

"Oh, let her stay! By all means," Reynulf said with a cold smile, sword in hand. "Then she can watch you die."

# Chapter 13
# The Red Knight

"**D**on't make threats you can't keep, Reynulf."

"Not a threat, old friend, but a promise."

"And we all know what your word is worth."

Wrynne's heart was in her throat as she and Jonty backed up against the wall, while Thaydor and the assassin from her nightmare circled each other, swords drawn.

"No killing in this place. The goddess forbids it!" the half-naked priestess insisted.

"Why, look, Thaydor. Seems your luck holds. Saved by a woman once again." Reynulf's glance flicked darkly to Wrynne.

She scowled at him.

"You cannot have weapons in here!" the priestess insisted.

Jonty snorted. "Darling, do you really think the Paladin of Ilios and the Bloodletter of Xoltheus needs blades to kill each other?"

The priestess looked at the bard in dismay, then gave up and backed off to a safer distance.

Meanwhile, the knights in the large room that Wrynne could now see from her current position were hurriedly getting dressed, barely able to take their eyes off the gathering duel.

Their women seemed crestfallen at being cast aside, but the knights clearly couldn't care less.

Reynulf drew a dagger with his left hand as they continued circling, sizing each other up. "I see you've brought your little witch with you. And the bigmouthed bard. Interesting company you're keeping these days."

"I could say the same for you. I killed your Urmugoth friends, by the way. I hope you're not too disappointed." Thaydor drew a dagger as well.

Reynulf laughed. "Ah, Thaydor, I've missed you! What are you here to do, exactly? Recruit an army or merely save their souls? Can I be honest?"

"Can you?"

"It's been a relief to be rid of you, the pageboy of Ilios, and all your tedious rules. Ask the men. Under my leadership, they finally get to enjoy the rewards they deserve for their service."

"Ah, leadership. Is that what you call this?"

"What, you disapprove? There's a shock. But it makes no difference. Judge us as you please. You're a relic, Thaydor. Sorry to say the world has moved on without you and your god. You're the past; I'm the future."

"No, Reynulf, you're a traitor. And you know it."

His face hardened. "Seize him. Sir Thaydor Clarenbeld, you are under arrest for the murder of the sentries on the North Gate."

The knights just stood there.

"What the hell are you waiting for?" Reynulf barked. "I said seize him!"

None of them moved.

They glanced uncertainly from Reynulf to Thaydor and back again. No one said a word, but doubt was written on their faces.

It seemed that being in Thaydor's presence again was all it took to make them to finally question what they were being told. No wonder Lord Eudo had wanted to get rid of him. When it came down to it, he was the one they trusted. Reynulf clearly did not command the same sense of certainty.

He turned to them in outrage. "What is this insubordination?" he uttered in fury. "Sons of bitches, I'll have the lot of you drawn and quartered! I said *move!*"

"I have a better idea," Thaydor said. "Why don't you try telling them the truth about who really let the Urms in the gate? My only question is why, Reynulf? What did Lord Eudo promise you in return? Surely you did not send all those innocent people to the slaughter just so you could gain the role of royal champion. Because if you wanted it so badly, you should've trained a little harder. Then maybe someday, you might've bested me in the joust. Though, personally, I doubt it," he added with a taunting little smile, as though he were deliberately trying to push the Bloodletter over the edge.

It worked.

Reynulf loosed his rage and flew at him, driving Thaydor back a few steps with an onslaught of savage blows. The harlots shrieked and fled to the edges of the salon where the bleary-eyed knights hurried to finish dressing, barely taking their eyes off the two top warriors.

The corridor rang with a deafening clash of swords the likes of which had surely never been heard within the walls of the Beehive before. Jonty pulled Wrynne farther down the hallway, out of harm's way, but her stare was glued to Thaydor, fear coursing through her.

As Reynulf swung his blade at the level of her husband's head, she wanted to bury her face in the bard's shoulder, unable to watch, yet she couldn't look away. It was the first time she had ever really seen Thaydor fight in earnest, let alone against that rare enemy with whom he was evenly matched.

Back in Toad Hollow, fending off the royal foot soldiers, he had gone out of his way not to kill anybody. And though he had battled full force against the Urmugoths, Wrynne had only seen the aftermath of that melee.

As they hacked and slashed their way back and forth across the narrow confines of the corridor, Thaydor's eyes had darkened to a bluish black with a furious intensity. His powerful body bristled with sinewy grace, loose and ready, and yet tightly coiled, fully controlled.

Honed expertise flashed in the angle of his blade and made every step surefooted as he pressed his attack. He did not take his eyes off Reynulf, anticipating his longtime rival's every move. When the Bloodletter took another hacking blow at Thaydor's head, Wrynne ducked, biting back a shriek.

With Thaydor's parry, the tip of Hallowsmite nicked the wall a few feet away with a ringing sound and a brief trail of sparks. Reynulf attacked again and again with vicious persistence. Thaydor parried every thrust, making it look easy.

They were too well matched.

Both warriors quickly grew frustrated, because neither could gain any real advantage over the other.

"This is pointless!" Thaydor finally spat. "We should be fighting *them*, not each other! Don't you understand what's going on? You're being used, you fool! You know you're in the wrong."

"Go to hell." The red knight stood, panting, his muscled chest heaving, his eyes black and fiery as burning coals.

"Join us, Reynulf. You can still help us put things to rights."

"And go back to taking orders from you?" he exclaimed with a defiant scoff. "I don't bloody think so, you pompous pain in the arse! I'm in control now. You just can't stand seeing me win, can you?"

"You may be the champion right now, but it won't last. The king has turned, Reynulf. He betrayed me; he'll betray you. It's only a matter of time."

"You don't know what you're talking about. Ow!"

Suddenly, both men reflexively dropped their swords and daggers as if they had been burned.

"Damn it!" Thaydor cursed.

"What the hell?" Reynulf demanded.

Wrynne saw the priestess holding up her hands and realized the woman had been murmuring a spell under her breath. It had apparently turned the hilts of their weapons searing hot.

Jonty and Wrynne exchanged a glance, impressed.

But that did not stop the two warriors from fighting. They both looked at the priestess in reproach for interfering, then exchanged a scowl, kicked their blades aside, and charged each other, resuming the brawl with their fists.

Wrynne winced as Reynulf laid a crashing punch on her husband's jaw that sent him reeling. But she needn't have feared, for a few seconds later, Thaydor had wound an arm around Reynulf's throat in a brutal wrestling hold and was arching him back like a bow.

"I know it was you who opened the North Gates," he ground out, overpowering his opponent. "Tell them! You owe them that much, at least. Tell the men the truth, or I'll break your bloody neck." He wrenched him for good measure, but Reynulf, red-faced and grimacing, laughed at the pain.

"You think I'm ashamed of it?" he retorted with a wince. "Not at all! I'm proud of what I've done. For the glory of Xoltheus!" Reynulf grabbed Thaydor around the back of the neck and flipped him over his head.

Thaydor's back slammed against the floor, and he gave an angry grunt. He immediately leaped to his feet, but Reynulf had already swept backward a few steps, grabbed his cast-off dagger, and held it to the throat of the priestess.

He began backing away, dragging his hostage with him.

Thaydor paused uncertainly. Wrynne watched, riveted.

"Careful, Paladin," Reynulf taunted, breathing hard. "You don't want an innocent to die needlessly, now, do you? Well, *innocent* is probably the wrong word."

"Let her go."

"I think she's earned her place in Fonja's heaven after all the cocks she's sucked so dutifully down here, don't you? Of course, if I cut this pretty throat of hers, your witch could simply heal her, I suppose. Still, it buys me time to seal the city. His Majesty wouldn't want you to flee from his hospitality."

"Reynulf, please," the priestess whimpered, clutching the thick forearm that held her fast as the red knight dragged her slowly backward. "We've shared a bed. I know you wouldn't hurt me."

Thaydor apparently decided at that moment that Reynulf was bluffing.

"You always had a soft spot for a beautiful woman," he chided. "How many times did I warn you an enemy would take advantage of it one day?"

"Thaydor!" Wrynne insisted, at the same time Jonty shouted, "Don't goad him, he'll kill her!"

"No, he won't," Thaydor said.

The woman whimpered, but Reynulf's midnight eyes had narrowed with fury—apparently at being exposed for having some vague shadow of a soft side.

He clutched his hostage by her hair and shoved her at Thaydor when he lunged at him. Thaydor caught the woman as she stumbled into him.

Reynulf ran. Thaydor set her aside, but she fell anyway on her ridiculous spiked heels and landed in a sobbing heap.

Thaydor chased Reynulf out of the building.

Jonty let out a breath and strode over to help the woman up as Wrynne peered into the hallway down which her husband had raced off and disappeared, but there was no point in following. Gathering her wits as best she could, she swallowed her distaste toward the temple prostitute and went over to see if she could be of help. After all, the woman was still rather hysterical and had turned an ankle, as well.

A few of the other Fonjan temple girls crowded around their companion, however, and brushed Wrynne aside with scornful looks. They seemed as repulsed by the symbol on her necklace as she was at their life of willing exploitation.

They crowded around their friend.

Wrynne ignored their rejection and turned to Jonty. "Now what?"

He shrugged and shook his head, but to her relief, Thaydor came back a few minutes later, furious but unscathed.

"He got away, the coward. Disappeared into a crowd." He turned to the knights, who still looked grimly shocked at what they had witnessed and the treachery to which Reynulf had confessed.

"*Now* do you understand what's been happening around you? It's as I told you!" Thaydor said fiercely to them. "Reynulf was following orders—just like the red knights always do. Do you realize what that means? It means it was essentially the king who let the Urms in the gate, knowing full well that some of his own citizens would die. The king who allowed me to be blamed for this crime. But the king is not himself. Another wields an unholy influence over him."

"What are you saying?" one of the men asked darkly.

"Oh, for feck's sake, you idiots," Jonty burst out. "A coup has taken place right under yer idiot noses! If Reynulf's confession wasn't proof enough, ye have only to look at yourselves! Did you imagine 'twas a coincidence that all the strongest defenders of the land should be sent here to lose themselves in pleasure? Didn't that happen to ring any wee warnin' bells in yer great thick skulls?"

They stared at Jonty none too happily. Taking the rebuke from their former commander was bad enough.

"Who's this?" one of the large, scary-looking knights asked Thaydor.

"He's with us. He's the bard, Jonty Maguire."

"As if ye don't know." Jonty tugged at his jacket with an indignant huff.

Thaydor resumed. "So I ask you now, are you finally awake? Or have you ruined yourselves for soldiering for good here, lolling in the pigpen?"

They exchanged frowning glances with one another.

The large, Norse-looking fellow who had just spoken nodded. "We're with you."

"What would you have us do?" asked another.

"First, we need to get out of the city before Reynulf seals us in. We'll retreat to the old citadel, the Eldenhold, to discuss the extent of the infiltration and plan our response. Let's go." He started marching away, but Wrynne grabbed his arm.

"Thaydor, what about my family?"

When he turned to her, his eyes were still dark with wrath, the indigo of a night sky.

"You said Reynulf probably knows by now who they are," she reminded him. "We've got to get my family out of the city, too. Otherwise, the king may take them into custody and use them as hostages to force us to turn ourselves in."

He nodded, while behind them Jonty beckoned to the group of knights to hurry up.

"We'll send them to my father at Clarenbeld Castle," Thaydor replied. "Don't worry, the old War Hammer will protect them, considering he and my sister are under the same threat. He's got twenty knights at his keep and hundreds of loyal foot soldiers among the local peasants he can call up anytime. They'll be safe there," he added a little more gently, touching her arm. "You tell them what's going on, and I'll put together an escort of a few knights to protect them along the way."

"Thank you." She offered him a faint, hapless smile. "Not quite how I imagined introducing my new husband to my family, but as long as they're safe."

He nodded, still seeming hard and remote in his leadership role. "Let's go," he said to her, then nodded at the bard and all his followers.

\* \* \*

Meanwhile, a bruised, somewhat bloodied, and thoroughly furious Reynulf strode into the palace to tell the king what had just occurred. *What the hell have I got myself into?*

Damn Thaydor. Overgrown choirboy and all his infuriating virtue. Yet…he had a way of putting things into perspective that made Reynulf want to scream.

*Why* he had just given the paladin and his merry band of followers a small sliver of time to escape the city, Reynulf did not know.

He denied even to himself that he had done it. Perhaps because he was a survivor before he was a loyalist. Oh, he had ordered the city sealed, the gates closed, but he hadn't rushed to it as quickly as he might have. He hadn't even gone personally.

The chamberlain jumped out of his way and hastily ordered the doors opened before him as he marched down the long, narrow-windowed gallery to King Baynard's receiving room. When he arrived at the guarded door to the square crimson chamber, the pudgy, balding, middle-aged monarch was chatting with some courtiers.

*Fashionable fools.* They wore those stupid floppy hats that were all the rage, the two different-colored leggings, and the overlong, curly-toed shoes that were no doubt perfect for their idle existence but would have got an *actual* man killed.

Reynulf wanted to throw the lisping pair and their tittering lady friend through the window to get rid of them more speedily. The king seemed to read as much in his frank stare.

King Baynard IV of the House of Lionsclaw arched a brow, his crown winking in the sunshine.

The courtiers were dismissed and went tripping out, both escorting the velvet-gowned aristocratic lady in the strange, pointy hat.

*Thank the gods*, Reynulf thought in disgust when the door had finally closed behind them.

"Bloodletter," the king greeted him, beckoning him over and looking rather amused at his discomfiture amid the fashionable and highborn.

Which Reynulf was not.

Hell no. Everything he had in this life he had got for himself, thank you very much.

Far from being born into a line of national heroes or heir to an earldom, Reynulf didn't even know who his parents were. And didn't really care. He'd come up as an orphaned street rat, kicked around by life far more than his fair share, before he had found god in the Red Temple and learned to put his rage to good use.

"Sire." He bowed.

"You have news for me?" the king asked.

Reynulf glanced over his shoulder to make sure the rich royal chamber was empty, but to his dismay, they still were not alone. The Silver Sage, the king's top advisor, leaned in the shadows in cold, tranquil stillness.

Reynulf feared nothing, but the Lord Hierophant's insipid smile and unfailing politeness never failed to send a chill down his spine. He looked at the king. "I would rather reveal it to you alone, sire."

"Don't be absurd. I have no secrets from Lord Eudo. What is it, man?"

He managed to hide his annoyance. "Thaydor's here."

"In the city?" the king exclaimed.

"Yes, sire. And he knows about the Urmugoths."

"How could he know?" the sage snapped. "You said you left no witnesses!"

"I didn't, sire!" Reynulf assured the king, ignoring the other man. "It has to be the woman. She's some sort of seer or witch. But I haven't even got to the bad news yet."

Baynard looked at him in alarm.

"Thaydor sought out the knights at Fonja and must have given them one of his grand, ridiculous speeches."

"Oh no," the king groaned.

"I tried to stop him. I got there within minutes. Fortunately, I was just across the street offering my sacrifice for the Xolthean holy day tomorrow. I ordered the men to seize him, but they just stood there in complete insubordination!" he said, fuming. "Now they follow him. Old habits die hard, I suppose."

*"You suppose?"* Baynard shot up from his gilded throne and glared at him. The raised platform put him on eye level with Reynulf. "How could you let this happen?

"Me, sire? I'm not a sorcerer! I don't control their wills." He hesitated. "The new ways have made them lazy, just as I warned Lord Eudo that they would." He sent the Silver Sage a glare. "I told you it was stupid to let them lounge about all day. But no matter. I'll take care of it," he said grimly, unsurprised at having to take the blame as usual for other idiots' mistakes. "Believe me, when I get a hold of them, I will personally stretch each of the bastards on the rack until he screams for mercy. Of which I have none."

"Save your anger, Bloodletter. You may need it." Still cloaked in shadows, Lord Eudo sounded annoyed by Reynulf's wrath.

The feeling was mutual. Reynulf couldn't stand the old man's preternatural calm.

"So…" The king sat back down slowly. "The paladin has stolen my army. If the majority of my knights have abandoned their oath of loyalty to me and put themselves under his command, it is certain the common soldiery will follow. Put that together with the troops his father commands—"

"And the love of the people," Reynulf reminded them in a prickly tone.

The king turned to his advisor at the edge of the room, looking pale and stricken at the implications. "He must be stopped. We cannot have an uprising of these rebel knights!"

Eudo emerged from the shadows, robed in silver. "Not to worry, Your Majesty," he soothed. Gliding over, he bowed. "I already have the answer in motion. Just give the word, and Sir Reynulf shall have a new army under his command within twenty-four hours."

"What are you talking about?" Reynulf retorted. "You're going to conjure an army out of thin air?"

The Lord Hierophant gave him a skin-crawling smile. "You'll see. They can be in Pleiburg before noon tomorrow if you give the word, sire."

"I take it you mean mercenaries?" Baynard replied.

"Of a sort. Yes. But we mustn't frighten the people," the Silver Sage added. "Once our new fighters arrive, I suggest we call the people together into Concourse Square to explain the situation to the public. If you spoke to your subjects, Majesty, I'm sure it would calm them, help them not to be afraid."

"But mercenaries, Eudo?" Baynard hesitated, glancing from his advisor to his champion. "Doesn't that make me look a little...desperate?"

"Unfortunately, I'm not sure we have much choice," the sage said gently. "Are we to wait for Sir Thaydor to march in here and take your crown from you? That is what he wants, you know."

Reynulf kept his mouth shut, but he doubted that was true. If these two really knew the irritatingly virtuous paladin, they'd have realized he had no aspirations of power whatsoever.

Hell, if it were up to Thaydor, he'd probably take his psalters and his poetry books, and retire to some peaceful hermitage like the girl's woodland bower, which Reynulf had discovered near the waterfall.

"Who exactly are the mercenaries you're thinking of hiring for us, Eudo? Are they trustworthy?" the king asked.

"Sire, mercenaries are not trustworthy by their very nature," Reynulf mumbled before the old man's advisor could reply. "They fight for gold," he said in disgust. "They have no reverence for the art of war. No code."

"Good Sir Reynulf, I'm sure His Majesty appreciates that hired soldiers do rather offend the sensibilities of the mighty warriors of Xoltheus. But, my dear lad, what choice do we have? Our knights have turned traitor. Fortunately," he added, "every Urmugoth fighter is usually the equal of two or three human soldiers. Plus the fear they inspire by their appearance, reputation. I doubt we'd need more than a couple hundred."

"Hold on!" Reynulf turned to him in shock. "You want to bring an

Urmugoth force into the capital? Are you insane, man? They'll destroy the city!"

"Now, now. You know we made great progress with them in our recent negotiations. Of course, they are quite different from us in their ways and their appearance, but there will never be peace so long as we continue to assume the worst of our northern neighbors. As I see it, this is a chance to show them that we really do see them as equals."

"They are beasts," Reynulf said slowly, staring at him.

"They just want to be accepted by the other nations of the world." Lord Eudo's frown of disapproval deepened as he shook his head. "This is just the sort of outmoded bigotry that must end or we will never know peace. The Urmugoths have shown they can be trusted when they fought Sir Thaydor as we asked."

"They obviously failed. They were supposed to kill him," Reynulf reminded them. He turned to the king. "Sire, you cannot seriously be considering this. It is madness."

King Baynard looked from one man to the other, uncertain. "I realize the Urmugoths caused plenty of problems for our ancestors in bygone days. But perhaps Lord Eudo is right and it's time to put the past behind us."

"Has Lord Eudo ever attempted to fight an Urmugoth? Oh, of course not! He's against warfare. Pardon, I forgot!" Reynulf spat. "Let's solve everything by talking! Because that always works. Well, *I'm* no coward. And I *have* fought them. It is like fighting a damned bear armed with a poleaxe. You try it."

The Silver Sage looked askance at him in cold superiority, his eyes gleaming like the points of silver blades.

Reynulf met the king's gaze imploringly. "Your Majesty, the last thing we need is a royal guard made up of monsters. I still have fifteen red warriors who would never dream of abandoning their oath. Trust me, sire, the house of Xoltheus can accomplish whatever is needed for the security of the kingdom."

"Fifteen against fifty? One hundred? Do we even know how many men follow Thaydor today? How many by tomorrow?" Eudo said with withering scorn. "Sire, let me bring in a mere fifty Urmugoth mercenaries to help keep the peace."

"And how do you expect to control them?" Reynulf shouted.

"That's your job," Eudo replied icily, frowning at the way he'd raised his voice. "You're the royal champion."

"Well, I won't do it."

"Reynulf!" the king exclaimed.

"Sire, it's asking for disaster. Do you want the people to hate you?"

"How dare you?"

"I don't know what the old man is up to here, but if you could've seen the swath of destruction the Urms unleashed up north before Thaydor got there... Let's just say things got a good deal bloodier than even I expected."

Baynard shrugged in regret. "Still, they did as we asked them. At least they tried, in good faith."

"I beg you, listen to me. Mistwood has suffered. You two didn't have to see it. I was there. Sire, don't do this."

"Sir Reynulf"—Lord Eudo looked very fed up with him—"you are the greatest knight in the land and you've earned your place as the royal champion. But leave strategy to the graybeards, won't you? We've wiser heads and more experience. So, why don't you run along and do as you're told," he finished, narrowing his eyes.

Reynulf blinked at him in astonishment.

Eudo smiled blandly, clearly believing himself untouchable.

Reynulf clenched his teeth. If Eudo were not an old man—and if the king were not sitting right there—he would have killed him on the spot for such an insult.

The feeling seemed mutual, however, judging by the murderous gleam in the Silver Sage's eyes.

With a great effort, Reynulf decided to ignore him and turned to the king once more. "Sire, if you feel we must have reinforcements, let us call them from our allies in Aisedor. Even the bards of Lyragon would be preferable to Urm mercenaries. Aisedor would surely send troops to help us contain the knights' rebellion—"

"I hardly think any help will be forthcoming from that quarter at the moment," Lord Eudo interrupted crisply. "Not after the queen's displeasure about the lady Sana living in the palace. Remember?"

The royal philanderer snorted. "She did go huffing on in quite a royal snit, didn't she? Running off to her parents. I'll be surprised if her father doesn't send assassins after me. He always did spoil her." He leaned back in his throne, shifting uncomfortably at the reminder of the hurt and public humiliation he had dealt his poor wife.

Even Reynulf felt sorry for Queen Engelise. He wondered when she'd be back from visiting the King and Queen of Aisedor. If ever.

"I don't see why she took such offense, anyway," the king grumbled. "It's as you said, Eudo. It's only natural for a man in my position to expect more out of life than just one quim for the rest of his days. I'm no monk, and besides, the pink goddess is worthy of our worship, eh?"

He sent Reynulf a knowing smirk.

*The old goat,* as Sana called him behind his back.

Reynulf barely managed to hide his disgust behind a vague nod.

"Ah, well," Baynard sighed. "There's the vanity of a queen for you. I do miss her, though, oddly enough."

"Ahem," Lord Eudo said, drawing the weak-spined megalomaniac back to the matter at hand.

"Very well." The king nodded, lifting the front of his crown absently off his lined brow and wearily rubbing his forehead. "Reynulf, we have heard your doubts and have taken them under advisement. But for now, you may go."

"Sire—"

"You heard your king, Reynulf." The Lord Hierophant's thin, pale lips curved in triumph, but the smile didn't reach his eyes. "His Majesty and I will discuss the particulars and send you word once the plan is settled."

King Baynard nodded his dismissal, and Reynulf gave up to some degree. It was abundantly clear that this was a losing fight. The only intelligent thing to do was to withdraw, regroup, and figure out some new line of attack.

"As you wish, sire." He bowed and backed out of the room, heaving a disgusted sigh once he was out in the corridor.

Without further ado, he returned to his apartment in the residential block of the palace reserved for the king's most vital cohorts. He shut the door behind him and leaned against it for a moment, feeling rather defeated.

Not by Eudo. Not by the king. Not even by Thaydor.

But by himself.

Maybe Thaydor was right. *Wasn't he always?* he mused cynically. Didn't his god always tell him exactly the right thing to do? But really. Urms on the very streets of Pleiburg?

*Does Eudo actually trust them?* he wondered. *Or has he perhaps made a deal of his own with the beasts? One the king doesn't even know about?*

The possibility made his stomach clench.

Pulling off his gambeson, he crossed his chamber to hang it up neatly on its peg, but as he did so, his glance happened upon the figurine of Xoltheus atop the chest of drawers nearby.

He drifted over to the idol and stared at it. *Why don't you ever help me like Ilios helps him? Why do you always leave me on my own?*

But then again, cruelty was part of his religion. It was a part of life, so it only made sense that his god was cruel, too.

He picked up the black stone statue, its simple humanoid shape polished smooth in the primitive style. The carving represented Xoltheus as a powerful warrior with a ram's head, ready to charge into any battle. He carried a shield and a spear, and his wide, staring eyes were painted red.

One did not expect kindness from such a god. But then again, kindness made men weak. If only he could understand...

*I follow my orders, no matter how they nauseate me. I fight even when I know I'll probably lose. I've been a model knight adhering to your laws, just as Thaydor is to his. I've done all you've asked of me. So why am I constantly in pain?*

He called himself a choice epithet, then shut his eyes and tried to embrace the suffering. But he just felt empty, and if he dwelled on it too long, the emptiness deepened to despair.

*Are you even real?*

At that moment, he heard a coy little scratching at his door. Instantly on alert, he turned. "Who's there?"

The door creaked open, and a beautiful face peered through the crack. "May I come in?"

"Oh. It's you." He nodded, his tension easing for the most part, but not entirely.

Sana, the king's mistress, slipped into his room and closed the door behind her with a quiet click. Dressed in the same gauzy nothings and spiked heels as the temple girls, she was Fonja's finest, luscious from head to toe, and she knew it.

How Thaydor had resisted, Reynulf could not contemplate. *Why* His Majesty let her walk around naked like that, he could not guess. Unless the old goat wanted the world to envy him for his prize.

Reynulf had done more than envy. He wondered what method of execution they would choose for him if anyone found out.

"I heard you had a little spat with Thaydor," she said in amusement as she sauntered across the chamber toward him, wine goblet dangling from her hand. "The news is everywhere."

"And with Lord Eudo," he said with a smirk. "And with the king. And with nearly every knight of Veraidel. And with the world, more or less. Nothing new in that, pet."

"Ah, but not with me." She pushed her way between him and the chest of drawers, and draped her lithe bare arms around his neck. "Hullo, Reynulf." She started to kiss him, but he winced at the contact after taking a couple of Thaydor's punches to the face.

Annoyed, he brushed her off. "I'm not in the mood."

"Humph." Preening, she smiled and leaned her perfect naked derriere against the chest of drawers. "Very well, my naughty boy, I forgive you. To be honest, any mention of Lord Eudo has the same effect on me."

"You…!" Reynulf suddenly had an idea. "Sana! You're the answer!"

She arched a well-shaped brow and offered him her cup. He shook his head. "What's the question?" she asked.

He took hold of her arms and stared into her eyes. "I want you to do something for me."

"Oh, goody. Then you'll be in my debt. How delicious."

"I need you to talk to Baynard. Sana, they're talking about bringing Urms into the city to help defend the palace from Thaydor's knights."

She wrinkled her nose prettily in disgust. "Urms?"

"Nearly all our knights have run off after Thaydor. Eudo says we need a contingent of mercenaries as reinforcements."

"Darling, if Eudo says it's all right, then it's probably fine. He knows what he's doing. You worry too much. Everything will be well. Here. Take a drink. You look like you could use it."

"Will you help me or not?" he demanded, ignoring the offered goblet.

She tilted her head and gave him a melting look. "As if I could deny you anything." She ran her hand down his chest. "What do you want me to do?"

"Convince His Majesty, as only you can, that this is a terrible idea and will lead to disaster."

"How sweet. You're worried about the people."

"I'm not a monster, Sana," he said in annoyance. "I know full well it's Thaydor they love, but just because I don't go around making grandiose speeches like he does doesn't mean I don't care."

"You're getting me hot. So noble!" She giggled and reached out to stroke his face, but he knocked her hand away.

"Would you stop it? This is serious! Those creatures will tear the city apart."

"Yes, sir!" She gave him a teasing salute.

He stared at her. "Are you drunk?"

She flashed a pout in answer to his question and walked away with her nose in the air. "Goodbye, Reynulf."

"Will you talk to the king as I asked or not?"

She propped a hand on her slim waist, stopped strutting toward the door, and turned. "What will you do for me in return?"

Reynulf gave her a knowing look and asked softly, "What would like me to do?"

She bit her lip. "I should think you remember what I like *quite* vividly."

"Indeed." He glanced at his bed in speculation and then at her again. "Talk to the king first and then we'll see about that."

She turned to him with a seductive little smile, trailing her hand down her creamy chest and midriff. His heated gaze followed as she sauntered back toward him.

"A kiss to seal our bargain, Bloodletter?"

"Very well," he conceded in a husky tone.

She sidled up to him again, her stare locked on his. She pressed the wineglass to his chest. "Wet your lips so you can kiss me properly."

He took the goblet from her hand, raised it to his mouth, and took a sip, then frowned at the odd, faint sizzle on his tongue. He looked into the cup. "What is this?"

"A new vintage. An import from Lyragon, I think."

His mouth tingled with a bitter aftertaste. He looked at her warily. "Did you put something in it? One of your little happy powders?"

"No. Don't you like it?"

He seized her by her throat, his eyes aflame. "What did you just give me?"

"Reynulf!" She clutched his wrist as he lifted her onto her toes. "Let go of me!"

"What's in the wine, Sana? Some new drug of yours, or did you just bloody poison me, you bitch?"

She choked.

"Answer me!" He squeezed harder.

She looked shocked, but the harlot should've remembered whom she was dealing with.

"It's not…poison," she forced out, clawing at his arm as he slowly cut off her air.

"What is it, then?" he demanded.

"A potion. To make you…obey."

"Eudo put you up to this?"

Eyes wide with terror, she managed to nod despite his grip around her neck. But he wasn't quite done with her yet.

"Has he had you slipping it into the king's wine, as well?"

"No."

"You'd better be telling the truth."

"*I* make the king obey, you fool!"

"How?"

"How do you think?" she rasped, then she kicked him in the balls and he dropped her.

The instant she landed, she threw her head back and let out a shrill scream. "Help!"

The door burst open immediately, and Reynulf, still bent over his groin, could not believe his eyes as her help arrived.

*Urms.*

Three huge Urmugoth warriors flooded through the doorway into his room. In the fleeting second before they attacked him, Reynulf's jaw dropped as he realized that what Lord Eudo had posited to the king as a possibility awaiting his permission was, in fact, already a fait accompli. Eudo had somehow smuggled his Urm allies into Pleiburg behind the king's back. And behind his.

While Sana slid out of the way, still on the ground, and withdrew to the wall to watch, a sneer on her face, they spread out and approached, intent on surrounding him.

*Bloody hell.* He straightened up, his heart pounding. He glanced around at them and braced himself, battle readiness flooding into his veins.

These boys weren't Thaydor. The funny thing about the paladin was that he never fought dirty. Reynulf did. And, to be sure, so did Urmugoths.

The fight exploded—a whirlwind of chaos and pain.

Reynulf was quicker and more agile than his towering opponents, but he had to admit the barbarians were stronger than he was. At least they were stronger than Thaydor, too, which he could attest to, having been punched by both within the hour. It allowed for a convenient comparison.

He doubled over from an Urm knee like a tree trunk to the gut. His gaze shifted to a nearby chair. He grabbed it, arced up, and backed the brute off by smashing it across its ugly head.

As he turned to bash the next one with what remained of the chair leg, he briefly wondered why they didn't draw blades on him.

They must have needed him alive for some reason.

*Well, hurrah,* he thought acidly, irked in the extreme to see the chamber that he always kept in Spartan shipshape becoming a wreckage.

His furniture turned to rubble as they crashed around the room. Even the window broke when he sent one of the Urms stumbling headfirst into it. Alas, the beast did not fall out into the river, too broad-shouldered to fit through the narrow hole. The bloodied thing merely turned around looking all the more pissed off.

*Shite.*

The Urm strode toward him. Damn, but they were ugly and they smelled like pigs, crowding around him on all sides to press the fight. With their towering size, gray-tinged complexion, and bestial yellow eyes, their appearance was off-putting to say the least. Especially when they tried to look a bit more human—as these ones had done—by sawing down their tusks to the roots.

As if this could help them blend in.

You couldn't punch them in the jaw or you'd split your knuckles open on those things. The jaw was hard to reach anyway. Too high. He hated being smaller than his foes. He usually wasn't.

*Bugger!* He blocked a sledgehammer fist flying at him and wondered if he'd just taken a hairline fracture to his forearm. His breath heaved. He had to get to his rack of weapons on the wall, but there was no way they'd let him near it.

From the corner of his eye, he saw Sana looking fascinated by the no-doubt big-dicked giants. She slid her back up the wall, rising to her feet, and then she crept to the doorway, where, to his astonishment, Lord Eudo stood looking on.

The split second's startle was Reynulf's undoing.

Two of the Urms grabbed him on either side.

He panicked for a second as they seized his arms, thinking they were going to rip them out of their sockets. Tear him apart.

He'd seen the bodies up north.

"No! Wait!" He swallowed hard. "Please. I'll cooperate. Eudo, call them off."

"Aw, look at him beg," Sana taunted. "I thought you only did that for me, darling."

The Silver Sage remained at the threshold, his icy stare fixed on Reynulf while the two Urms held him in their viselike grips. "You really shouldn't question my judgment in the future, Bloodletter. You are an admirable warrior, and you are needed. But in matters of strategy, as I said, wiser heads must prevail. Perhaps now you will remember your place."

"I will," he lied hastily, ready to promise anything so long as they let him keep his arms.

"Indeed. I will make sure of it." He handed Sana a small glass vial.

Reynulf assumed it was the same stuff she had tried to get him to drink in the wine. Whatever Eudo was up to, Reynulf was shocked that the king's mistress was in on it, too.

But why the hell was he surprised? The old man had talked him into opening the North Gates, hadn't he?

Angry at himself, he couldn't believe that Thaydor could have been this right once again, son of a bitch.

Sana toyed with the vial and took off the lid with her long, skillful fingers, then approached at her hip-swaying saunter. "You should have chosen the easy way, sweeting. But somehow you just never do."

Heart pounding, he tracked her with his stare.

Perhaps he *was* a fool, as she had said. For he had never noticed till now how intelligent—and how cruel—her pretty eyes were. Like most men, he had been too distracted by the beautiful body on display.

"Pour it down his throat," said Eudo, nodding to the third Urmugoth while the other two held him captive.

The largest of the three, the leather-armored Urm, stepped over to Reynulf and unceremoniously grasped his jaw in its big gray hand.

Reynulf thrashed, the sense of powerlessness enraging him, but it was useless.

"Wait." Sana waved the big Urm aside for a moment and stepped closer to Reynulf. When she came to stand right in front of him, she gazed into his eyes for a moment, then slapped him hard across the face. "That's for choking me."

Though it stung, he managed to smirk at her. "You usually like that sort of thing."

She sneered back at him, then cupped his cheek. "It's all a game,

Bloodletter. But here's a little secret. I like winning even more than you do. Last chance now. Be a good boy for once and open your mouth for me. No?"

She sighed and shook her head. "Do it," she said to the third Urmugoth, moving out of the way.

The big Urm returned with a grunt and splayed a huge hand across Reynulf's forehead. While his clammy left palm applied counterpressure, the fingers of his right hand slowly started prying Reynulf's mouth open.

Sana waited with the potion at the ready.

Reynulf fought to no avail, and the Urm pulled harder on his jaw.

"Don't break him! We need him," Sana scolded the brute. "If the royal champion tells the people everything's all right, they'll believe it."

Well, that explained it, then.

In one horrifying moment, the ironic truth all came clear.

The whole time he had been plotting with His Majesty and Lord Eudo to get rid of Thaydor, the Silver Sage had been running another game, plotting with Sana to take power from the king. They had already got rid of the queen.

As for him, it seemed the only reason he was being spared was to help smooth the transition as the Silver Sage took power. Things had to look reasonably normal, at least for a while, or the people would riot.

Reynulf now understood that the king's life was in imminent danger. Indeed, if this potion made people obey, for all he knew, they might be planning to use *him* to strike Baynard down.

He had to get to Thaydor. Warn the son of a bitch.

Reynulf didn't bother praying to Xoltheus to get him out of this. By now it was abundantly clear that he was on his own and always had been.

Reaching down into the rage that drove his existence, he drew forth a sudden burst of strength. He wrenched his right arm free of the Urm's grasp with a low cry, snatched the brute's knife from its sheath, and stabbed the big one in the throat.

The crimson blade whipped back and forth almost too fast to see as Reynulf set about doing what he had always done, at any cost.

Surviving.

# Chapter 14

# Defiance

The Eldenhold did not look much like a citadel to Wrynne. She saw no castle, no fortress. Just stark, dramatic limestone bluffs looming over the loud, fast-flowing River Drard.

She, Thaydor, Jonty, and the large company of knights who had joined their cause had only galloped about seven miles northeast of Pleiburg, but this lonely place had the feel of wild country.

The old, forgotten citadel was located in the southernmost approaches to the Bronze Mountains, and the track they currently followed wended its way along the river, barely wide enough for two riders abreast. Thaydor, leading their company, sat astride Avalanche beside her.

Wrynne lifted her head and scanned the river cliffs. They created a claustrophobic sort of canyon, down which a constant wind whipped. The bent, scraggly pines and scrub brush seemed to have adapted to the steady, sculpting gale, but she, for one, was tired of it blowing dust from her horse's mane into her eyes. She had long since stopped trying to lift the hood of her cloak because the wind merely whooshed it back to her shoulders again.

The noisy rushing of the river made conversation difficult. Even Jonty had shut up for once. But not the three young squires, whom they had found posted outside her family home, carrying out their idol's orders to the letter.

The three young, would-be heroes chatted merrily, talking over one another, just as before. They had been awed by her beautiful sister, Juliana, and had nearly volunteered for the company of knights assigned to escort her family to Clarenbeld Castle. But in the end, their thirst for valor had won. If there was to be a battle of some sort, they wanted in.

Wrynne was a little surprised that Thaydor had allowed it, protective as he was, but it seemed they needed every able-bodied soldier with any sort of training they could rally to their aid.

She was even more surprised that he had let *her* come. With the oracle's warning not to be separated from him ringing in her ears, she had pleaded to be allowed to stay by his side—much to her mother's alarm—and he had finally relented.

As they rode along side by side, heading for this unknown, unseen citadel, she was dying to ask him what he'd *really* thought of her family. He had, of course, been polite. She had yet to hear the man utter an unkind word to anyone—unless they were trying to kill him, but even then. It was a testament to his patience that he had not taken up the habit with his new mother-in-law.

Mother had been rather brutal on the poor man.

"Darling, how could you do this to me? I've been agonizing over you!" she had wailed. She had hugged Wrynne hard, then burst into tears, barely paying any attention to Thaydor, which spoke volumes.

Her siblings had been awestruck in his presence, however. Paladin or outlaw, both roles seemed equally impressive to her brothers. Her sister had been goggle-eyed at his looks, and had squeezed Wrynne's arm in disbelief.

"How in the world did *you* get *him*?" Juliana had whispered.

"Thanks a lot," Wrynne had retorted, casting an arm around the younger girl's shoulders.

One could not grow up in such a family and still contrive to be insulted by rude questions.

But if her sister was blunt, she got it from Papa. The blustery Building Baron had demanded explanations. Unfortunately, there was so much to say and so little time.

They had to get her maddening clan safely out of Pleiburg before Reynulf sealed the city. They had been lucky as it was to catch Papa home for supper rather than having to make a second trip to fetch him at his latest construction site.

While Thaydor and Wrynne had both hastily given their account to her astonished and long-worried family, Silvertwig had flown into the room and landed joyously on Wrynne's shoulder.

The tiny fairy, arms outstretched, had hugged the side of Wrynne's neck. Then she'd whispered in her ear that she had delivered Thaydor's message to the warrior monks at their monastery in the Scythe Valley, as asked.

Before leaving that place to journey on to Wrynne's family home for their eventual reunion, as planned, Silvertwig had seen the monks of Ilios off. After making their swift preparations, they had gone marching north through the woods to Mistwood. Their mission: to go and help defend the North Gates against any further Urmugoth invasion.

In hindsight, Wrynne mused, the monks' presence there probably was pointless now that they knew the first Urm incursion had been deliberately allowed. Still, the presence of the holy warriors would surely make the people of Mistwood feel a lot better after what they had been through.

Just then, over the roar of the river, Wrynne heard the squires discussing her sister.

"Agreed. Mistress Juliana is passing fair."

"Maybe my lady will put in a good word for us?"

"Enough," Thaydor scolded with an easy smile at them over his shoulder. "Nobody asked your opinion on my sister-in-law's looks."

"Oh, sir! No disrespect intended!" Jeremy said, aghast.

"None at all!" Petra chimed in.

"At ease, lads," Thaydor said with a laugh. "You did well today. Don't ruin it."

"Sorry, sir. Sorry, my lady," Kai mumbled.

"No apologies needed. Not from you three, anyway," Wrynne answered, glancing back at them. "I may be the one who should apologize. For my kinfolk." She sent Thaydor an arch smile. "I'm wondering how my husband is feeling after that ordeal. How was it, meeting them? Worse than fighting Urmugoths or about the same?"

He gave her a cautious smile, the wind riffling his blond hair.

"Well?" Wrynne teased. "You might as well share your reaction. What did you think of them? Be honest."

Holding the reins in a light grip, he glanced at her with a twinkle in his eyes. "They're all fine folk. I guess I'm just not used to quite so much...hysteria."

She chortled. "You *get* used to it, believe me."

"I can see why you'd want to go live on a nice, quiet mountain after that," he admitted.

Laughing, she leaned across the empty space between their horses and swatted him playfully on the shoulder. "You're naughty."

"You asked for the truth! Now *you* tell me. Your mother hates me, doesn't she?"

"No, she'll come around. You are an earl's son, after all. That's something, at least."

"I take it that's a quote?" His eyes danced when he glanced over at her again.

Wrynne shrugged. "Sorry."

"Funny, I used to be considered a good catch," he said wryly.

"Times change, you brigand," she said with a laugh. "If it makes you feel any better, at least my brothers were awestruck."

"Personally, I can't wait to hear what *your* family thinks of my father. If your poor mother is expecting the courtier type of earl, she's in for a massive shock."

"I wonder how long it will take them to reach your father's castle, considering it took a hundred years to get Mama out the door."

"She had to bring her *things*, Wrynne." He sent her a knowing wink.

She grinned at him in return, adoring him all the more for taking the everyday chaos of the du Mere clan in stride. The way her sister had ogled him, her brothers had crowded him with the usual hero worship, her father had grilled him, and her mother had frosted him out had all been more than a little embarrassing. But, thankfully, it seemed their marriage would survive it.

"Just a little farther," he assured her, as if he could read her mind.

"Good." She was more than ready to get out of the wind and off this horse.

Behind her, the boys could barely contain their excitement.

"This is incredible. I never thought I'd get to go to Eldenhold!"

"I still don't see a fortress," Wrynne remarked.

"But you'll see the opening to a cave just around the bend," Thaydor replied. "The cave turns into a tunnel, at the end of which stands a pair of massive iron doors. Behind the doors, you'll find the citadel."

"Oh." Wrynne glanced up curiously at the cliffs. "The fort is inside the mountain?"

He nodded, peering upward. "You can't really see the archery windows, but they're there, hidden in the rock face above us, disguised as crevices and chinks in the stone."

As they rounded the bend, he pointed out an ordinary-looking cave mouth situated about twenty feet up the steep, dusty slope at the foot of the bluffs before the rock face angled up vertically. But what was outside the cave mouth instantly made Thaydor rein in. He raised a hand to halt the whole company.

Somebody else had got there ahead of them.

"Who the hell is that?" Jonty muttered from behind them.

A black-haired man lay facedown on the ground, unmoving. A large black warhorse stood guard over him. The man looked unconscious. Indeed, he looked dead, but the tall, glossy steed seemed familiar.

"That's Sir Reynulf's horse!" Kai exclaimed.

"Are you sure?"

"Yes, sir. It's Hecaterus. I just groomed him this morning."

Thaydor studied the inert figure of the man who had just tried to kill him at the Fonjan temple. "What is he doing here?" he asked under his breath.

"It's probably a trick," Jonty murmured, scanning the bluffs above them for archers. "Is he playing dead?"

"That's not his style. He may actually *be* dead, though." Thaydor swung down off his horse. "Stay back!" he ordered everyone.

"Be careful. He's capable of anything," Wrynne warned.

"Reynulf?" Approaching with caution, Thaydor marched up the slope, then murmured a few soothing words to the massive horse. The animal was trained for combat, after all, and looked ready to protect its fallen master from enemies.

While Avalanche lifted his head and sniffed the air, Hecaterus did the same and obviously smelled a friend. Satisfied that Thaydor did not have hostile intentions, the big black horse stepped away, allowing Thaydor to go to Reynulf's side.

"At least his horse likes him," Jonty muttered.

Heart pounding, Wrynne gripped Polly's reins in nervous hands as she watched. The red knight didn't move as her husband crouched down warily beside him. Taking hold of his shoulder, Thaydor turned the man over. It was only then that they could see Reynulf was in far worse shape than when he had fled the Fonjan temple.

She could see her husband talking to him but could not hear the words at this distance. As Thaydor propped him up, Reynulf clasped his forearm with an air of desperation. He seemed to be trying to talk, but his face was all bloodied and swollen.

Wrynne and Jonty exchanged a puzzled glance.

"What do you think?" the bard murmured skeptically.

"That he got what he deserved."

"I wonder who did this to him."

"It couldn't have been just one man," one of the boys whispered. "The Bloodletter fights like a demon. Sir Thaydor was the only man who could ever best him."

"Wrynne!" Thaydor suddenly looked over his shoulder. "Come here!"

She furrowed her brow but started to dismount.

"My lady." One of the boys held her horse's bridle as she jumped down from Polly's back, smoothed her skirts into place, and then strode up the pebbled incline toward the pair.

"What is it?"

"Heal him."

She stopped in her tracks. "What?"

"He's badly hurt, and he's brought us vital information. He can barely talk." Thaydor scanned the other knight's battered body. "Whoever did this to him broke his jaw. I need to hear what he has to say. He's also got a stab wound in the side. White as a shroud. He's lost a lot of blood."

He rose and stood back, beckoning her over to the Bloodletter with a hurried motion.

Wrynne did not move. She looked at the assassin from her dream, his coal-black eyes glazed with suffering. Then she turned to her husband, stared hard at him for a second, and said, "Absolutely not."

Reynulf shut his eyes with what might have been a wry, pained smile of *I knew it. You Ilian fools are all hypocrites.*

Thaydor's blue eyes, however, locked on to hers with a gaze that turned flinty. "Do it."

"No," she said flatly. "He's an animal. Let him die."

The whole company of knights stared as the young bride of the top warrior in the land openly defied her lord in front of all his men.

"My lady," he clipped out, "you appear to have mistaken my words for a request. Heal him."

Her cheeks colored with her acute awareness of some fifty knights and one startled bard looking on. The atmosphere in the canyon turned exceedingly tense.

Nevertheless, Wrynne held her ground. "He brought this on himself. It's probably the punishment of Ilios upon him." She looked coldly at the Bloodletter. "I suggest you review your choice of deities while you still have time."

She turned around to march back to her horse, but Thaydor's voice froze her. "I gave you an order."

She lifted her eyebrows and pivoted slowly. "Excuse me?"

His stare was every bit as steely as his armor. "You are my wife. I am your lord and commander of this company. If you cannot obey orders like everybody else here, you will be sent to Clarenbeld. With the civilians."

She lifted her chin a notch in astonishment. *Well!*

She had encountered every other aspect of her husband, but she had never seen him in warlord mode before.

It was decidedly…intimidating. She faltered, trying to read a little leeway into his stare. She saw none, and now it was her turn to be embarrassed in front of everyone.

Was he joking? Or merely making a point to show his men that their mighty leader would not be ruled by a female?

Her heart pounded as she expanded her argument beyond a simple refusal. "What you ask of me is wrong. You cannot compel me to use my gift for such an evil man. He doesn't deserve it."

"I did not ask you if he deserves it. I asked you to do your part. That is why you're here."

They stared at each other, neither backing down. Wrynne's heart pounded. *Our first official fight. What fun.*

She could have fought anyone or anything by his side, but facing off against the paladin herself was another matter.

*This isn't about Reynulf. It's about you and me*, his piercing blue eyes seemed to say. *Do you trust my judgment or not? Can you do as I ask, even when you hate it?*

"He tried to kill you, and would've killed us both! He let the Urmugoths in. Have you forgotten what they did? To my patients? To your squire?"

"Vengeance does not belong to us, as you well know," he said with maddening, calm control. He lowered his voice to a husky and intimate warning. "If you refuse, you and I are going to have a serious problem, wife."

"Because I won't follow orders?" she retorted, trembling with ire.

"Because I did not know you could be this hardhearted. He is dying. You're a healer—"

"So are you. You heal him, if he means so much to you."

"You know I don't have the skill for wounds this bad."

"So let him die. Sorry, husband," she said icily, "I'm not as merciful as you. But then, *you* didn't deliver the baby girl who died smashed against a wall by Urmugoths, all because of this blackguard's treachery!" she said, leaning down to scream the final words in his face.

The red knight actually flinched.

"Sunnhild. We called her Sunny," she told him. "She was three months old. A beautiful, innocent baby, and her blood is on your hands, you foul, wicked thing."

If he had anything to say for himself, he could not share with his jaw broken. His pain-glazed eyes were fixed on her, but Wrynne returned his gaze with hatred.

She straightened up again and turned to her husband. "Let him rot in hell where he belongs."

Thaydor stared at her like he was wondering if he really knew her at all.

"Just hold on," he started to reassure the wounded man, but when he glanced down, they both saw to their surprise that while they had been arguing, Reynulf had reached into the stab wound at his side. Taking some of his own blood on his finger, he was scrawling words on a nearby rock: *eudo urms pleiburg.*

His arm flopped to the ground again.

Thaydor stared at the crimson letters, then looked at him in alarm. "Eudo is bringing Urms into Pleiburg?"

Reynulf nodded with a look of suffering.

Wrynne shook her head. "He's lying. We were just there. We didn't see any."

Thaydor suddenly turned to her in fury. "You do as I told you. *Now!*" he thundered, the echo of it rolling down the canyon.

Reynulf's horse spooked, and every knight went stock-still.

Wrynne's eyes widened. Then she dropped her gaze, seething with humiliation at being scolded and ordered around like a child by her husband. Unfortunately, she got the feeling this was her last chance.

At least in his eyes.

If she refused to do what the paladin deemed the right thing, she did not know what effect it might have on their love.

She despised him in that moment for forcing this on her, but with the oracle's warning of her pending betrayal ringing in her ears, she gave in.

*Very well*, she tried to say, but her voice was too strangled with the bitter task of swallowing her pride and her hatred of the red knight that she could not get the words out. All she could manage was a curt nod, avoiding Thaydor's gaze.

*Whoever he kills next, it's on you, husband.*

Aware of all the men's worried eyes on her, she turned to Reynulf and lowered herself to her knees beside him, glaring at him. She doubted her abilities would even work in this state.

His night-black eyes met hers with a gaze that brimmed with soulful repentance, but she wasn't fooled. Such a man would feign any useful emotion to save his hide. He was an assassin.

"You owe my husband your life for this. Don't forget it," Wrynne murmured. "If it were up to me, I'd leave you and the crows would peck your eyes out—"

"Sweet Ilios! He's losing blood, woman! I need his information!"

"Fine. Let's get this over with," she muttered.

Reynulf closed his eyes.

While Thaydor looked on with a stony expression, Wrynne lifted her hands. "Make sure he doesn't stab me when my eyes are closed."

Thaydor did not dignify her rebellious mutter with a response.

Feeling very much like she was in over her head with all these inscrutable warriors, and suddenly doubting the wisdom of having insisted on coming along, she dutifully cupped her hands a couple of inches away from the wound on Reynulf's side.

Then she closed her eyes. She sought the power of the Light within her, but it was rather dim at the moment.

The patient groaned.

"What?" she snapped and sent him a harsh glance. "Quit whining."

"He's fading. Hurry," Thaydor urged.

She gritted her teeth. *If it were anyone else asking me to do this, I would never even...*

*Oh, never mind.*

Trying to shake off her vexation, she finally succeeded in tricking herself into ignoring the fact that it was Reynulf.

*Just an ordinary patient in need...*

Well, she supposed he was no worse than the criminals she'd had to treat in Blackport Dungeon. Then she begrudgingly admitted that the blackguard *had* come here and warned them of this fresh danger. That stab wound in the side must have made the ride over this rough country hellish, which at least gave her some small satisfaction. She wondered how he had known they would come to Eldenhold, but he was one of the knights, so…

Finally, all her unsettled thoughts faded as she managed to connect with her gift. The moment the Light rose in her, it seemed to shine a harsh, exposing light on her own reluctance to forgive. She felt herself chastened not just by her husband but by Ilios himself, and her heart sank.

*Ah, Thaydor.* What woman wants a man who's always right?

But once more, he was.

Very well, it was not her place to judge or punish anyone. No mortal could ever see the contents of another's heart.

It dawned on her as she concentrated on drawing up the healing power that she had never sensed actual evil coming from Reynulf. He was wicked, to be sure, but for those with the spiritual gift of discernment, true evil always gave itself away by the cold, sickening feeling it inspired, almost like a fetid smell.

She had sensed it strongly from the dying Urmugoths on the night she had found Thaydor, but not from the red knight…

With that, she felt the draining flow of power rush out of her tingling hands and flood into his well-muscled body. The Light closed the seeping wound in his side, and then she cupped her hand almost tenderly near his face and healed his broken jaw.

But when she reached to cure the worst of the scrapes and bruises, he brushed her off with a defensive air and sat up swiftly. "That's enough."

"Hooray, he can talk," Wrynne said, stung by the way he held up a bloodied hand to ward her off.

Reynulf probed his side, found it fixed, and then eyed her in wary astonishment. "Thank you," he said gingerly, even as he edged back from her a bit, as though he half expected her to add a curse to the healing just for fun.

She might have, if she'd known any curses.

She scoffed at him. "I'm not a witch."

He grunted skeptically, watching her.

She rolled her eyes and shook her head.

"Feeling better?" Thaydor offered him a hand up with his usual princely magnanimity.

Wrynne found it rather vexing at the moment.

Reynulf looked at him and seemed to decide on the spot to give up their rivalry, clasping the paladin's hand.

Wrynne eyed the sword at the Bloodletter's waist. "Maybe you should take away his weapons before you get too close to him."

"Never mind that. What news?"

At her husband's dismissive answer, Wrynne spun on her heel and headed back to her horse.

"My lady!" Reynulf called after her.

She paused, fought with herself again, and then begrudgingly turned around.

He lifted his hands slightly. "I am sorry about the babe."

"That's all you're sorry for?" she cried.

"Wrynne, don't start," Thaydor warned. "I need to talk to him. Details?"

"Eudo's gone mad," Reynulf said. "He's got a company of Urm mercenaries marching into Pleiburg tomorrow morning, about a hundred strong. Some are already there."

"What?" Thaydor breathed.

"They're meant to replace the knights who've sided with you, to put down what he calls your rebellion. There's a gathering in Concourse Square tomorrow morning to let the people know the Urms are here with the king's permission and not to be afraid."

"Baynard actually went along with this?"

"The man's a jellyfish, Thaydor! He has no idea what's really going on, that Eudo's just imported his own praetorian guard. A few Urms are already lurking in the palace, under Eudo's command. I know because they paid me a little visit."

"You weren't aware—"

"No! If I had known this, I wouldn't have opposed you. Eudo wanted me to stand up as leader of his Urms so the people wouldn't panic. They tried to pour some witch's brew down my throat to make me obey. Sana's part of his conspiracy. I fear the king's a walking dead man. He just doesn't know it yet."

"You did the right thing coming here."

"First time for everything," Wrynne drawled, keeping her distance.

Reynulf looked regretfully from her to Thaydor. "All your lady said of me is true." He glanced around. "I had my orders. They wanted Thaydor out of the way. Kill me if you think I deserve it, but I'm here to help now however I can."

Thaydor gave him a searching look, needing no words to communicate what would happen to Reynulf if he betrayed them again.

Reynulf's face was still defiant, but he dropped his gaze, silently acknowledging that Thaydor was in charge.

Thaydor clapped him on the shoulder with a guarded nod. "Best go get your horse." Then he beckoned to his men. "Come on, open the gates! Let's go inside and get everybody settled. We've got work to do!"

As he turned, waving them toward the cave mouth, his gaze met Wrynne's. He gave her a hard look that warned her she was in more trouble than Reynulf had been.

But of course. For her, the paladin had higher expectations. A knot promptly formed in her stomach as she wondered what her warlord would say to her in private.

# Chapter 15
# Uncloak

The next morning, the gates of Pleiburg had been reopened but were heavily guarded. That hadn't stopped Thaydor from getting into the city, of course.

He moved through the crowd gathering in Concourse Square to hear the king's proclamation, planning his next move. He couldn't stop thinking about Wrynne, though, and hoping he hadn't been too hard on her last night.

She had sat through his lecture in stiff, wifely obedience, but he had seen the mutiny in those pretty gray eyes, tracking him as he paced back and forth, commander-like, outlining his expectations. She hadn't argued, which worried him a little, in hindsight. Instead, she had expressed her opinion of his rules by denying him her body for the first time in their marriage.

He hadn't liked that. It had quite startled him, in fact, but he was not fool enough to insist. *As if she doesn't enjoy it, too*, he grumbled mentally. *But so be it. Let her have her sulk.* Hopefully by tonight when he returned to the Eldenhold, she'd be over it and things between them could return to blissful normal.

He pressed on through the throng, his face hidden by the draped hood of his pilgrimage cloak. He kept his head ducked a bit, trying not to draw attention to his height.

Once again, he wore chain mail under his civilian clothes. Likewise, he was sensibly armed in case of trouble, but took care to keep the jeweled hilt of Hallowsmite from sight. He had also brought five of his most trusted knights with him from the Eldenhold, similarly garbed, and the Runescar Trumpet.

The bard had insisted on coming along. "I canna miss this! I've got to *be* there to document whatever stunt these sneaky bastards try to pull off next."

Reynulf had offered to come, as well, but Thaydor had ordered him to remain at the citadel. The Bloodletter was too recognizable—and too valuable, given the eyewitness testimony he could bring to bear against the Silver Sage. In their discussion of the situation, Reynulf had revealed that it was Lord Eudo, in the presence of King Baynard, who had given him the order to let the Urms in the gate.

Thaydor only hoped he had not made a mistake, leaving Wrynne and Reynulf alone in the same building. He did not want any fighting when he was gone, and his dainty little wife bore the Bloodletter a hatred of dragon-sized proportions.

He could understand why, but in such times, they did not have the luxury of indulging their personal feelings about someone offering crucial help. Besides, as he had told her in his gentle scolding last night, it was a tenet of their faith to forgive those who were genuinely sorry for whatever they had done, no matter how distasteful. All were to be given another chance if they were sincere, and Reynulf seemed so.

In any case, there were more than forty knights left back at the Eldenhold to break up any feuds his bride might start with the deadly warrior. They'd all be busy enough as it was. Thaydor had ordered the men to spend the day in spiritual purification to prepare their souls for battle. As a Daughter of the Rose in good standing, Wrynne would have a role in that, leading all knights willing to participate in the prayers and oblations of atonement in the rock-hewn chapel deep inside the Eldenhold.

Attendance in the ritual was not required, but for the truly penitent, Thaydor had also suggested they fast. Frankly, they would never defeat the foes arrayed against them in the degraded state in which he had found them. Ilios, as far as he knew, was under no obligation to help those who chose to live like pigs.

Thaydor still could only shake his head at how he had found them debauching those women—willing or not. Chivalrous knights should know better. The girls of Fonja were sadly misguided. For all their flaunting of pleasures, he had never met one who seemed happy—and now the king himself had taken up with one of their kind. Sana was the worst of them all, plotting with Lord Eudo, as Reynulf had reported.

Thaydor took up a position at the west corner of the square, where he had a good view of the royal balcony and the crowd. He leaned against the wall of a house there, eyes and ears alert.

His men were arrayed around the square in other advantageous spots, and he exchanged nods with them across the wide space. Sirs Ivan and Gervais had fanned out on his left, Richeut and Godefroy to his right, while Hugh had wandered up the middle, getting as close to the front as he could.

Marking their positions, Thaydor wasn't sure where Jonty had disappeared to, but he returned his attention to surveying the crowd, calculating the various exits from the square if violence broke out.

He was one of the few, after all, who already had a fair idea of what the king was going to say when he came out onto the balcony any minute now.

How the people would react to the introduction of the Urms as the new palace guards was hard to predict. Most citizens had never actually seen one of the creatures before, and most people's first impression of the ogre-born race was flat-out terror.

There could well be a panic, which could turn into a stampede. People could be hurt, even killed, if all this went badly. Scanning, Thaydor noted countless children in the crowd and many old people, too.

He was worried. He had told his knights to be ready to speak up and try to keep order if the crowd ran. But he suspected that the silver-tongued bard would have even more of an impact on panicking people than his knights would.

Warrior though he was, Thaydor knew full well that the right words at the right time were far more powerful than any sword. He just hoped this didn't turn ugly. The square was packed with two, maybe even three thousands souls by his estimate. People overflowed into the surrounding streets, peered out the windows, sat on the roofs, and crowded onto the balconies of the houses that had views of the square.

Despite the occasional undercurrents of uncertainty over what all this was about, a festival atmosphere presided. As it happened, he overheard several conversations around himself as the citizens of Veraidel speculated on what the king had to say.

"Maybe the queen's finally pregnant."

"Pah! She's barren. More likely they'll announce another war."

"I hope not! We can't win without Thaydor!"

"Well, he's abandoned us and turned outlaw," somebody muttered.

Thaydor frowned.

"Maybe Their Majesties are getting a divorce," some matron

suggested to her neighbors. "She left him, after all. Serves 'im right!"

"Nay, I'll bet she's back from her parents, and they've thrown that tramp of his out of the palace," an optimistic female assured those listening.

She was laughed at.

"Maybe they've finally decided who'll be successor to the throne, since they got no children. That's it! I'll bet they'll tell us who the next king will be."

"Care to make a wager on that?" a grinning man tossed back to the aproned shopkeeper who had spoken.

The latter waved him off with an easy laugh. "Not a gamblin' man, sir."

"Oh, I know!" someone else piped up. "I'll bet they're going to announce that they finally took Sir Thaydor into custody!"

The grinning man scoffed. "Ach, they'll never catch him unless he wants to be caught. He's too clever."

"Why would he want to be caught?" someone asked.

"Because Sir Thaydor always does what's right," a young girl piped up earnestly.

"Daft chit," some robed scholar sniffed, looking uncomfortable amid the press of so much humanity. "What, just because he's got a handsome face?"

"You ask me, he couldn't've done what they said. Not 'im," the shopkeeper declared.

Thaydor kept his head down but was gratified to hear many people agree with the man.

An old woman sighed. "All I know is things used to make a lot more sense around here back when he was royal champion."

No one disagreed.

Then a sudden blast of trumpets proclaimed the arrival of the king on the royal balcony.

"What lies have you got for us today, Your Majesty?" Jonty murmured, appearing out of the crowd to lean against the wall beside him.

Thaydor looked askance at him. "Where have you been?"

"Oh, here and there. Why? Did you miss me?" He flashed a grin.

Thaydor's lips twisted as they both joined in the clapping for the sake of blending in. He returned his attention to the royal balcony, where various attendants of the king were stepping out. But he had to admit the bard had grown on him, especially since Jonty had left off making fun of him.

For the most part.

Then the proceedings began as King Baynard held up his jeweled, pudgy hand to quell the obligatory applause. "My dear subjects, I am so grateful for your loyalty in these trying times. You may be wondering why I called you here today. Well, I regret to say some very disturbing news reached the palace yesterday afternoon. As many of you know, our former champion, Sir Thaydor Clarenbeld, has sadly turned traitor to the kingdom."

He clenched his jaw, hard-pressed to maintain his implacable outward calm.

"What a load of shite," Jonty muttered loudly enough to be heard by several surrounding townsfolk.

"Yesterday," His Majesty continued, "we found out that matters have just got a good deal worse."

The crowd went very quiet, worry suddenly palpable in the air.

"Through some misguided sense of loyalty to Thaydor, nearly all my knights and military officers have defected to side with this outlaw against the Crown. Now, do not fear," he hastened to assure them. "We do not feel you are in any immediate danger. However, we believe the knights *are* planning some sort of violent rebellion. War may come to the very streets of Pleiburg."

Murmurs of alarm ran through the square.

"You have our word that these traitors will be found and brought to justice. But in the meanwhile, until the rebel knights can be replaced, their defection has left the palace and, indeed, our city undefended.

"So, on the wisdom of my top advisor, Lord Eudo, I have made arrangements to install new defenders who can easily repel any attack Thaydor and the knights might try to mount against our city."

"*Repel* being the key word," Jonty muttered.

"Now, I don't want any of you to be alarmed when you see the fierce countenances of our new soldiery. They are not going to hurt you," the king said slowly, emphatically. "Some of you may doubt this, since the Urmugoth tribes were once the enemies of our kingdom. But that was centuries ago."

The reaction of the crowd was instantaneous.

"Wait, what?"

"Did he say Urmugoths?" the people said to one other.

"A new age has dawned," His Majesty continued. "An age of peace and hope, trust and mutual understanding, as the Silver Sage, in his wisdom, has long taught us to expect. Well, my dear people, the age of peace starts with each and every one of us."

Jonty made a gagging sound.

"Therefore, until other arrangements can be made, these fine Urmugoth warriors are here to help with the defense of our palace."

"Urmugoths? In the city?" a nearby woman asked in alarm.

"And we should all be grateful," the king added. He turned to the doorway behind him. "Gentlemen? Will you please come out and let the people see you?"

A collective gasp of horror rose from the crowd as six huge Urms—probably including the ones who had beaten up Reynulf—trudged out onto the royal balcony to show themselves to the citizenry in all their gray-skinned, yellow-eyed, tusk-jawed glory.

The crowd recoiled at the sight. A few people screamed, and several children burst out crying. The expletive Jonty uttered was particularly blue, even for his foul mouth.

"Now, I charge you, citizens of Veraidel, do not be alarmed by the appearance of our new friends!" the king shouted, holding up his hands to try to calm the frightened crowd.

His voice was nearly drowned out by the exclamations of dread.

"What you do not know is that we have quietly been conducting trade negotiations with our northern neighbors for some time now! The Urmugoths have become our allies. You have my word as your king. They are only here to keep everybody safe!"

None of the courtiers on the balcony seemed bothered by the fact that the Urms towered over the king, made old Eudo look extremely frail, and caused the two human palace guards flanking the doorway to cower a bit. But much worse than the ones on the balcony with the king were the line of them marching out into the square to stand guard along the exterior wall of Lionsclaw Keep. About thirty Urms lined up on either side of the palace gates.

The beasts' nearness to the crowd after what he had seen them do to the peasants of Mistwood tangled Thaydor's stomach into knots.

His knights looked over at him from their posts in various degrees of shock and disgust.

Hearing from Reynulf that the king was going to allow this was one thing; seeing it firsthand was quite another.

Thaydor's heart pounded. *He's lost his bloody mind.*

"Excellent!" Baynard congratulated his subjects from his perch on high. "Very good. You show great courage, my people. Ah, now, no tears," he fondly scolded the few screaming tots with an oily smile from above. "At this time, Lord Eudo would like to say a few words. I want you to know that you can and should trust him just as much as I do. Heed him well."

While the king stepped back and beckoned the old man in silver robes to the fore, Jonty shook his head at the Urms. "You killed how many of those things?"

"Twenty," Thaydor said, his stern stare fixed forward.

*"Yourself?"*

"Through the might and mercy of Ilios, Jonty." He did not take his eyes off the creatures.

"Well, hang me," the bard said wryly. "Paladin of Ilios... You're the real deal, mate. Imagine my surprise."

"Shh! I want to hear this."

Jonty leaned against the wall again, drumming his fingers idly, as he was wont to do.

The whole crowd was full of whispers while the Silver Sage looked around at everyone with a lizard-like smile.

"Your Majesty. My fellow citizens of Veraidel, Urmugoth friends," he began. "I feel very sure that all the gods are smiling this day to see our peoples united, and I am ever mindful of the trust that has been placed in me." His smooth tone seemed to soothe the people. "But as His Majesty has said, these are serious times," he continued in a lulling voice. "We know you find these developments as disturbing as we all do, but we ask humbly for your trust.

"You see, it is not always possible for us to tell you what choices we must make on your behalf behind closed doors. Some secrets must be kept for a time. But believe us, everything we do is for your own good, and for the safety and security of you and your families."

"Who could ever doubt it?" Jonty drawled.

"Of course, there are some secrets that not even His Majesty knows," the Silver Sage quipped, turning to their ruler.

Nervous laughter rippled through the crowd as some tried to accept what was going on, needing to believe their leaders knew what they were doing.

But from where he stood, Thaydor saw that something in the Lord

Eudo's brief glance had left even the king looking puzzled.

As he turned back to the people, Baynard's bushy eyebrows knitted into a line across his brow. Uneasy. Still, his mouth tried to hold on to a public sort of smile, as though he were half expecting to be given a statue in his honor.

Nausea turned Thaydor's stomach. He could smell treachery in the air. Arms folded across his chest, he braced for whatever came next.

The Silver Sage paused for a moment. "All secrets must be revealed in time, however. And today, it gives me great pain to reveal the one I've kept, even from His Majesty."

Baynard arched a brow, but Thaydor knew his king well enough to recognize the glint of terror growing behind his thinning smile.

Lord Eudo gazed out over the crowd, his bony, gnarled, harmless-looking hands resting on the rail. "My dear people…it breaks my heart to share this awful news with you. But I am sorry to inform you that Queen Engelise is dead. Her husband had her *murdered* on the road to Aisedor," he boomed, pointing an accusing finger at King Baynard.

"What?" Jonty cried.

The thunderous announcement rocked the square down to its very flagstones. The instantaneous reaction from both the king and the crowd was gigantic. Even Thaydor was shaken, standing up, away from the wall at once while a wave of shock and horrified grief surged through the people.

"*Sanctus solis,*" he whispered, narrowing his eyes, while screams and cries erupted here and there. Which was strange, since Queen Engelise wasn't even that well liked. The general view of her was that of a mousy, stiff, unsociable woman.

Still, a royal death caused enough of a stir when it came by natural causes. *Murder* in the royal family was all but unthinkable.

It struck the kingdom like an earthquake.

And everyone was too shocked to question it.

The whole kingdom had heard or seen His Majesty, after all, doting on his beautiful, young, mostly naked mistress.

Baynard's face was beet red with fury. He still didn't seem to have quite absorbed that he had walked into a trap. "This is outrageous! I'll have your head!"

Lord Eudo ignored him. "King Baynard, by the laws provided under the Right Noble Charter of Veraidel, you are under arrest for the murder of Her Majesty, our rightful queen."

"This is absurd! You treacherous— My wife isn't dead! She went to visit her father!"

"No, sire. She never made it there, as you know full well." Lord Eudo shook his head with a look of outrage. "Her Majesty is slain, along with every member of her traveling party, save one. One soldier from her royal escort survived, escaping the onslaught to bring us the terrible news. But he is only one of several witnesses against you, sire.

"He told us under oath of perjury that the attackers of the traveling party were dressed as brigands, but this was only a disguise. He saw the leader's face and the tattoos on his arm, marking him none other than Your Majesty's current champion, the Bloodletter of Xoltheus, Sir Reynulf."

"Damn," Jonty said. "Good thing you left him back at Eldenhold."

"Oh, he is not going to be happy about this." Thaydor shook his head, stunned at the depth of this perfidy.

The king looked frazzled as he yelled, trying to convince anyone who'd listen. "This is impossible! I would never do such a thing. Reynulf would never do such a thing, and I am sure my wife is alive and well at her father's castle!"

"No, Your Majesty," Lord Eudo said sadly. "She is right here. Look upon your handiwork with your own eyes!"

Two Urms carried out something that looked like a long, narrow table covered by a tablecloth, but when Lord Eudo yanked the white fabric away, they beheld a glass-topped coffin.

And there was Queen Engelise, lying preserved under the lid.

Dead on display.

The crowd contracted with a unified gasp of horror at the sight of their late queen, and then swayed as a wave of shocked agony moved through them. Only the Urmugoths stood stoic.

"Engelise!" Baynard fell upon his wife's coffin with a disbelieving sob. Then he turned viciously to Eudo. "What have you done? I'll kill you!"

He lunged at his supposed advisor.

"Arrest him!" Eudo howled.

Two of the Urmugoths grabbed the king by the arms.

Despite the fact that he was too far away to be of help, Thaydor tensed and reached for his weapon, remembering when the monsters had taken hold of his young squire in the same manner.

But they did not tear Baynard apart. At least not physically. They merely looked to Eudo for their orders.

"Well, old Eudo's certainly got a flair for the drama," Jonty murmured, but Thaydor ignored him, for the panic he had feared would come was slowly taking over the crowd.

He could feel it building all around him. The people were losing control of their emotions, hysteria prevailing.

Unfortunately, his former worry about the threat of a stampede was nothing compared to what would happen if the sixty Urmugoths lining the palace wall took it upon themselves to cow the crowd into obedience.

Then there would truly be bloodshed.

People around him were crying and shaking and cursing in confusion. "How can this be happening? The queen's dead, and Urmugoths in Pleiburg? Has the world gone mad?" they asked one another. But nobody had answers. "War with Aisedor? They're to be our enemies now, and the Urms are our friends?"

"What will become of us? The king will hang! He's got no heir!"

"It's all right!" Thaydor could not help himself from saying to the wild-eyed people around him. He stepped away from the corner, trying to calm them and stave off the panic, looking around at them. "Take courage! Everything will be well. Trust in Ilios."

They weren't listening.

"Father Ilios has abandoned Veraidel on account of King Baynard's idolatry!" the old woman cried, the same one who had defended him before. "The king's cursed! The paladin tried to warn him! But he wouldn't listen. And now we'll all pay the price!"

"People, be calm! You mustn't lose hope," he was saying, when Jonty suddenly grabbed his arm.

"Would you stop it before someone recognizes you?" he whispered fiercely.

"We have to keep order!" Thaydor replied. "You're the bigmouth— talk to them!"

"You're my chief concern right now. Your wife made me promise to look after you. Let's go!"

"Jonty, you don't know what these Urms will do to these people if things get out of hand."

"I can guess," he retorted. "*You* forget what they'll do to *you* if you're captured, Villain of Veraidel."

"Wait," Thaydor said. "Eudo's not finished."

The Silver Sage was holding his arms up, waiting for the crowd to settle down. "Now, I realize how terrible we all feel right now," he soothed while the two Urms held the dazed, listless king in their grips.

Baynard was clearly in shock. He just kept staring at the body of his wife, as though he'd lost the will to fight.

"The public funeral for the queen will be held tomorrow here in Concourse Square. Her Majesty will lie in state for two days, and you all may come back and queue up in an orderly fashion to pay your last respects. In the meanwhile, we shall hold the trial for His Majesty tonight. There is no need to drag out this painful process."

"You devil!" Baynard suddenly wrenched out, then he broke down, bawling without even trying to hide his unmanly tears. "I loved her!"

"Be that as it may, we believe that when your wife added leaving you on top of her failure to produce an heir, you took matters into your own hands to be rid of her, sire. Freeing you to marry again—this time to a fertile woman. In fact, we have witnesses to prove as much."

"No, you don't! How can you? It's a lie!" he wailed, tears streaming down his face.

No one could blame him, but it was embarrassing to see it all the same.

"Who bears this false witness against me?" he cried.

Eudo turned to the doorway and beckoned to someone in the shadows.

Out stepped Sana, dressed as demurely as Wrynne, all draped in pilgrim's gray.

*You bitch*, thought Thaydor, shaking his head. If there was one thing he could not stand, it was evil masquerading as good. But that seemed to be the theme of the day.

The former temple prostitute proved quite the actress. She came out with a long white handkerchief trailing from her hand, dabbing away false tears.

"The king's own mistress was the one who exposed his treacherous plot," Eudo said. "Speak, woman."

His tears interrupted, Baynard stared at Sana in astonishment.

She looked around at the people. "The king told me...w-when we were alone...that he would soon be rid of his wife. He offered me the chance to marry him once he was 'free' if I bore him a son. He said we could easily lie about the child's birth date on the court records to make it legal." She paused for effect. "But I would not hear of any harm coming to Her Majesty!" she insisted with a fetching stare full of sincerity, before lowering her head. "I know what I am, and I'm not worthy to be queen."

Her virtuous refusal of a crown seemed to make her instantly credible in the eyes of many in the largely unlettered populace.

Jonty let out a low whistle of amazement, but Thaydor was seething at this mockery.

"Go on," Eudo urged her when Sana paused to dab at her eyes.

"I feared if I refused to go along with it, the king would have me killed, too. So I pretended to cooperate, but at the first opportunity, I fled to Lord Eudo and exposed the whole plot. Unfortunately, it was too late by then. Sir Reynulf had already been sent out with his men to murder her. He was very well paid for it."

"Sana." Baynard finally found his voice, staring at his mistress. "How could you?"

She turned her back on him and hurried to Lord Eudo's side as though frightened.

At last, the incredulous king seemed to come back to life and started struggling against his captors. "People! Not a word of that is true! You have to believe me!"

"Judge and jury will determine that, sire, just as they do for any other citizen accused of murder. All are equal under the law," Lord Eudo countered. "Guards, take the accused inside. He will stand trial at once so the citizens of this good land need not suffer under his misrule any more than they already have."

Then he addressed the crowd again. "You see, ladies and gentlemen, as soon as the dreadful news reached me, I used my role as royal advisor to order a full investigation of the matter. I kept it hidden from the king in strictest secrecy. I had no choice. I knew he would only thwart me to hide his guilt, but at the same time, my greatest fear was that his evil deed would bring down the wrath of the kingdom of Aisedor upon us.

"We cannot risk going to war with the nation that has long been our strongest ally and lose thousands of brave young men, all because of one royal marriage disintegrating.

"I promised Aisedor that I would get to the bottom of it as quickly as possible. My investigation has been ongoing for a fortnight. I assured Queen Engelise's parents that if our king had indeed done this to their daughter, he would be punished like any other criminal. And so he will."

"How could you do this to me, Eudo? I trusted you!" the weeping man shouted, his crown askew. "He's mad! Do you hear me? Don't listen to this!" he screamed at his subjects. "I'd never kill my wife!"

Sana shook her head dramatically and kept her eyes down.

Thaydor marveled that she could so coolly betray a man she'd lain with for the past year.

All around him, meanwhile, the people were growing all the more bewildered and devastated as the situation sank in. Their whole world had just gone topsy-turvy.

Lord Eudo forged on, apparently determined to show he had everything well in hand. "You will be granted lawyers to argue on your behalf, sire, but your trial will take place this very night. The complete findings of our investigation will be revealed, and if you are found guilty, justice will be swift."

"Oh, you will hang me? You and what army?" the king roared.

The Urmugoths growled and pushed back the crowd.

Answer enough.

"No, sire, the punishment for murder is beheading, as you well know," Lord Eudo corrected him.

"You bastard!" As they started to pull him away, Baynard looked frantically over his shoulder. "Somebody find Thaydor! Tell him what's happened! He's no outlaw! It was all lies—"

His confession of having framed his former champion was silenced as he disappeared, abruptly dragged inside.

Jonty huffed in disgust while murmurs about this new revelation raced through the crowd. "Can you believe that blackguard just assumes you'll still rescue him after what he did to you?"

Thaydor glanced at him in surprise. "Of course I will," he said. "I took an oath."

The bard, for once, was speechless.

# Chapter 16
# Citadel

**R**estless tension filled the dramatic limestone caves of the citadel under the mountain as everyone waited into the night for Thaydor to return.

Only Jonty had stayed with him in the city to await the verdict in the king's trial. The rest of the knights who had set out with them this morning had come back by late afternoon and recounted all the awful news.

Wrynne sat in a high rocky nook with a narrow window that overlooked the starlit road below and grieved for her country. She prayed that the Urms did not start butchering people in the city. But one thing was clear. With such troops under his command, who would dare protest Lord Eudo's rise to power? Most of the simple folk of Veraidel would not even recognize it for a coup until it was too late.

Thankfully, the knights saw it all quite clearly now that her husband had shaken them out of their torpor. Their collective fury thrummed through the Eldenhold's labyrinth of tunnels and caves. But they neither shouted nor raged. Not even Reynulf, despite being blamed for murdering the queen.

Looking at him now, slowly sharpening his sword, Wrynne realized that she had not seen the Bloodletter truly angry until now. When he'd heard the accusations against him, Reynulf had retreated into himself with dark, brooding patience. His icy silence made him ten times more frightening. Thaydor had warned him his masters would betray him, and once again, the paladin was right.

The whole place was eerily quiet with the warriors' grim anger.

Only the three boys vented their outrage, taking up their swords and training hard. Kai, Petra, and Jeremy clashed with surprising ferocity.

Wrynne was impressed. The squires were more dangerous than they looked.

The older and more experienced veterans saved their strength, however, waiting for their captain to return with news and a plan. They merely readied their armor and their horses and rested as best they could ahead of the coming battle.

Wrynne had done her best, too, earlier today in the chapel to help them prepare their souls for the possibility of death.

The thought of the looming confrontation made her shudder as she sat peering out the window into the canyon. It was hard not to worry, knowing that when the time came, her husband would be the one in the thick of the fight. It certainly put their tiff into perspective.

Listening to the wind and the night birds, and ever searching the pale ribbon of the road, she ached for his solid, steadfast presence.

*Where are you?*

She missed him, and she didn't like the way they had left things this morning. The oracle's warning not to let herself be separated from him was ringing in her ears. What if something had already happened to him? What if he'd gotten caught in the city?

She had been so vexed at him last night, subjecting her to his stern talking-to, as though she were a child. He had scolded her once before—at that cave where they had first kissed—and it had irked her just as much then.

*Never lie to me again,* he had said that evening.

Well, he had added several more rules for her last night. Arms folded across her chest, she had sat there seething, mentally sticking her tongue out at him, while he had lectured her.

*Thou shalt not defy me in front of my troops.*

*Thou shalt not disobey a direct order in matters of strategy.*

He was the chief. Yes, she understood perfectly. She was a neophyte to all this war business, lower than the squires, and he had put her in her place.

Of course, all the while, she had wanted to strangle him. Especially when he'd had the nerve after all that to ask for sex!

*Unbelievable,* she had thought, staring at him in astonishment, still stung by his dressing-down. She had huffed at him, rolled over, and feigned sleep.

In the morning, when he had ridden off for Pleiburg, she had glared after his broad back, thinking, *Yes, please. Go away for a while. I need a break from you.*

It frightened her to wonder if this was the *Kiss of Life* spell wearing off. But with every hour that passed, her anger at him seemed less urgent...even unfair. She didn't like being told what to do, but in hindsight, were his requests really that unreasonable? Wasn't he only trying to keep order and cohesion among his fighting force?

The disapproving looks some of the knights gave her suggested they would have never tolerated such open rebellion from *their* wives. Indeed, she got the feeling that many of these "head-lopping warriors," as Jonty called them, would have probably answered similar defiance from their own spousal chattel with a backhand rather than a speech.

At least she had perfect faith that Thaydor would never hurt her — or any female, for that matter.

By the time night came and he still failed to return, gnawing worry had overpowered her hurt pride. It didn't matter. She just wanted him back safe.

Even her indignant rejection of his lovemaking last night seemed petty to her now. What if they never got the chance to make up properly?

She hoped Jonty was looking after him, as she'd made him promise...

Suddenly, she spotted motion on the road. With a swift intake of breath, she leaned forward.

The moonlight revealed three riders coming around the bend.

*Three? Gracious, has he already rescued the king by himself?*

It sounded typical of him. Perhaps a battle could still be avoided.

"It's Thaydor! He's coming!" she called over her shoulder to the men.

One of the big, rough head-loppers rushed over to verify this. The word of a mere female was apparently not enough.

Wrynne frowned.

"She's right! Open the gate!" he hollered.

Before long, Thaydor was striding into their midst, his tall, confident posture rejuvenating the men at the mere sight of him and sending a thrill through Wrynne down to her toes.

*Thank you, Ilios.*

She ran down through the dim, winding tunnels to see him, eager to feel his arms around her and confirm for herself that he was unscathed.

When she arrived in the large underground cavern that served as the citadel's great hall, he was just walking into the warm, gold glow of the lamplight, Jonty safe and sound a step behind him.

He greeted his men, who crowded around him with a hundred questions and blocked her path to him like a mighty forest of so many thick, towering trees. She tried to push her way through, but it was Thaydor who made them clear a path.

"Where is she?" she heard him ask. "Where's my lady? Is she all right?"

"I'm back here!"

A pair of big fellows parted to let her pass. "Oh… Sorry, milady."

As soon as Thaydor saw her, he offered an intimate smile, his blue eyes glowing with hopeful affection at the sight of her. "There she is."

Wrynne rushed forward to launch herself into his arms but stopped short at the sight of his prisoner—a tall, burly man in peasants' clothes with a sack tied over his head, his hands bound behind his back.

"Who's this?" she exclaimed.

"Oh, sir, you didn't already rescue the king without us, did you?" Kai asked, sounding extremely disappointed.

"Hardly. The king's still in the dungeon under Lionsclaw Keep. I'm sorry to tell you he was found guilty at that mockery of a trail they just held for him."

"Big surprise," Jonty said ruefully.

"His Majesty is to be beheaded in the square tomorrow morning. But of course, I don't intend to let that happen. Which is why we nabbed *him*. Gentlemen, allow me to present our guest." Thaydor pulled the hood off his prisoner. "There you are. That better?"

Blinking in the light, the scruffy-faced man scowled at him.

"Who the hell is that?" Reynulf asked.

"The royal executioner. But tomorrow morning, I'll be taking his place. Instead of dropping the blade, obviously, I'm going to get the king out of there, and all of you will be in place to cover my retreat with him when the Urmugoths attack. Which they will."

Wrynne closed her eyes. "This, for the man who's spent the past six months trying to have you killed?"

"I told you she wouldn't like it," Jonty said to Thaydor.

"The man who framed you as a traitor to your country?" she persisted, flicking her eyes open angrily.

"Darling," Thaydor said in a long-suffering tone.

She checked her temper, determined not to restart hostilities between them. "It's just— One wonders why you don't just let him die, my lord. Is he really worth it?"

His blue eyes flickered with amusement, acknowledging her effort to be a most agreeable wife in front of his men. "Tell her, bard," he said with a narrow smile.

"He took a vow," Jonty said wryly. "Oath of loyalty, y'see. They all did. And you know Thaydor."

The bard's humor helped defuse the brief tension at her protest.

"So I do," she said, offering her husband a knowing smile. "I suppose that's what I get for marrying a hero."

"And here we thought you'd be cross," Jonty said. "In fact, we brought you something to cheer you up! A souvenir from our day." He reached into his pocket and pulled out a length of white-and-silver cloth.

"You brought me a handkerchief?" she asked dubiously, taking it from him.

"It's an armband," Jonty said as she inspected it.

"Er, gallant. Thanks," she said, confused.

"We took it off the arm of a dead Urm." Thaydor clapped the bard on the back and grinned. "Jonty killed one today."

"What?" she cried.

Thaydor nodded proudly at his companion while the squires cheered with equal parts envy and enthusiasm. "We ran into one while we were running around the city after curfew, figuring out our battle plan."

Reynulf arched a brow. "Curfew?"

"Lord Eudo ordered everybody off the streets by nine," Thaydor explained. "He's got Urms patrolling the city to make sure of it. Came around the corner, and there he was."

"Gods, they're big. And smell like a pigsty," Jonty muttered in disgust.

"You should've seen him. The bard actually *can* fight."

"Oh, aye, I'm full of surprises," Jonty drawled. "I have been on quests, you know."

The squires gasped with envy, but Wrynne wrinkled her nose and held up her present. "You got this off a dead Urmugoth mercenary?" she asked. "Thanks *very* much."

"Well, I could've brought you the head, but I didn't think you'd want it," Jonty said, his green eyes dancing.

She gave him a droll look.

"Enough chatter. We've all got to get into position by dawn."

Thaydor clapped the executioner on the back. "Get this fellow some food and drink. Lock him in one of the chambers where he can't escape, but see that he's made comfortable. You can untie him once he's secured in a room. He's our prisoner for now out of necessity, but I gave him my word he'd be treated well and that he'll be free to go once all this is over."

Two of the knights led the executioner away.

"You must be hungry, too," Wrynne said, going over to Thaydor and slipping her arms around his waist.

"Starved." He pulled her close and curved his arm around her shoulders. "Did everyone behave for you today?"

"Oh, yes. It was uneventful here. We all finished supper hours ago, but sit down and I'll conjure a meal for you and Jonty."

Now apparently great friends, much to her amusement, both paladin and bard sat down at one of the long, wooden tables in the giant cavern.

"More tricks! Is this magic food safe to eat? I mean, if I eat it, I won't be doomed to stay in this cave forever or anything, will I?"

"She's not a sorceress. It's Ilian magic, Jonty. From above."

"If you say so."

Thaydor shook his head, but Jonty sent Wrynne a cheery wink to show he was only teasing.

While the rest of the knights took their places on the tables and benches around Thaydor to hear the specifics of their battle plan, Wrynne retreated to a quiet corner to work the *Feed the Hungry* spell.

"So what is the hour of the execution?" Reynulf asked.

While they started discussing the mission, Wrynne closed her eyes, connecting her awareness inwardly with the Light. It was strong in her today after all the hours she had spent in the chapel helping the knights repent for their shameful behavior. She knew she shouldn't judge, but it was still a bit difficult to look at some of them and not see them drunk and half-naked, acting like a bunch of satyrs. She was so glad Thaydor never conducted himself that way.

With deep breaths in and out, she felt the power flow through her, and within moments, the meal manifested into being on a platter before her.

She carried it over to Thaydor and set it down in front of him rather proudly.

Jonty looked at her in amazement. "Hang me! Can I order whatever I want?"

She laughed and set her hands on her waist. "No. All you get is that." She pointed at the loaf of bread, hunk of cheese, and roasted chicken breast on Thaydor's plate. "It always comes out exactly the same. Don't worry, it's quite good."

"She makes chicken. Magic chicken." The bard elbowed Thaydor. "You definitely married the right girl. Why not steak? Have you ever tried? What about mincemeat pie?"

"Oh, be quiet!" She swatted the laughing bard on the head.

"Be glad she's here," said Thaydor. "I can only make an apple."

"No, thanks."

"I wasn't offering!" He snorted. "At least my horse appreciates it."

Chuckling, Wrynne withdrew to work the spell a second time, delighted to see the two men getting along so well.

After setting Jonty's meal down in front of him and mouthing a discreet *You're welcome* in answer to his small bow of thanks, she sat down next to her husband, savoring his presence, but only half listening while the men talked strategy. She was eager to speak to him in private and let him know she was sorry for their fight. One look in his cobalt eyes had already told her he was sorry, too. Unfortunately, it was always business before pleasure with the paladin.

She bit her lip, trying to focus on the men's conversation. She did not like thinking about the violence to come. And dawn was only hours away... Which of these men would die? she wondered, letting her gaze travel around the room.

While Thaydor and Jonty ate, Reynulf and several of the other men debated different possibilities of how to launch the attack once Thaydor had whisked His Majesty off the execution platform.

Wrynne had an idea, too. She tapped her husband on the arm and whispered, "Maybe I should stay near you when it all happens so I can *hasten* the king out of there. Would that be safer?"

"Not for you!" he exclaimed, and washed down a mouthful with a swig of the ale one of the lads had brought him. "No, love. It's too dangerous."

"It might be safer for the king."

"Your safety matters more to me than his does. You'll have a small role to play ahead of time, which I will soon explain, but you'll be long gone from the city by the time the fight breaks out. I don't want you anywhere near that square tomorrow."

"You're going to let me help?" she murmured, pleased, but he was already answering another question from one of his men.

*So I'm even more important to him than the king. How sweet!* Warmed by his protectiveness, indeed, relieved by it after their quarrel, she snuggled against him on the bench, eager to find out what her job would be.

For now, she turned her attention to her morbid "present." The two-foot length of Urm's ribbon made her shudder, as it suggested the massive circumference of the gray-skinned biceps around which it had, till recently, been tied.

On closer study, she noticed an insignia embroidered on it in silver thread. She furrowed her brow and stared at it, then tapped Thaydor on the shoulder.

He was still in the middle of speaking. "Obviously, the civilians there will be a liability, but perhaps there's some way to channel them out of harm's way. Yes?"

Wrynne pointed to the symbol on the armband. "What *is* this?"

His gaze flicked down to it, then back to her. "I believe that's the crest Lord Eudo has adopted for himself. Do you know what this is?" he asked Jonty.

The bard shook his head. "Eudo had all the Urms wearing those armbands. I assume to make the people feel better about the creatures' presence in the city. Probably as a visual reminder that, as horrid as they look, they're under his command and they're not supposed to hurt anybody. Well, except us."

"But what does it *mean*?" she persisted.

"Well, it's got the silver and the white to represent Efrena," Thaydor offered.

"That much I figured, but what does the symbol look like to you?"

"I don't know." Jonty shrugged. "Flame of knowledge, maybe?"

"It's not a flame. Thaydor, doesn't this look familiar?" She held it up to him.

He shrugged. "Looks like perhaps some kind of flower or plant."

"Exactly! I've seen this before," she told them.

Thaydor elbowed the bard. "Did you know she's an expert in botany? Grows the plants, then turns them into medicine. Very clever, my wife."

Jonty looked at her. "I've been listening to this all day. Do you realize that? It gets a little tiresome."

"No, it doesn't," Thaydor said with a grin.

"Thaydor!" Wrynne insisted.

"Yes, love?"

"Listen to me! I've seen this before. The actual plant, not the symbol. At Silvermount!"

He gave her a blank look.

She frowned. "You didn't see it. Oh, that's right—you were too busy keeping us from getting eaten by the rocs."

"Rocs?" all three young squires exclaimed at once.

Wrynne ignored the boys. "It was this huge, bizarre species of thistle that was stuck to the rocs' nest. I've never seen such a thing before, and I had to learn every species of plant that grows on the continent in my studies at the Bastion. I'll bet you anything that's what this insignia portrays."

"Huh," said Thaydor, as though he didn't really see her point.

"I know it sounds strange, but this was not a normal plant. I could've sworn the thing was…staring at me."

Everybody laughed.

"I'm not joking! I really think I should go to the Great Library and do some research on it."

"Ahem, anyway," said Reynulf. "How are we going to get into the city with all our weapons and equipment without being noticed?"

"We had a talk with the sentry unit in charge of the West Gate," Thaydor answered. "The captain there is loyal. He and his men have agreed to help."

"Turns out more people in the city are on our side than you'd expect," Jonty added.

"Good!" one of the knights said with a snort.

"I'm not surprised," said another.

The bard nodded. "They seem to be waking up."

"Finally," Thaydor muttered.

Wrynne was doing her best to hide her exasperation at being brushed off by a bunch of head-loppers planning their battle, but she couldn't take it any longer. "What about this symbol?" she cried.

Thaydor caressed her back. "Darling, we'll sort it out once we've got the king out of harm's way. One thing at a time."

"But we still don't even know *why* Eudo is doing all this. Doesn't it strike anyone as strange in itself?" She looked around at them. "The Silver Sage has been in court circles for *years* and never showed any such lust for power before the past year or so."

"Power corrupts," Thaydor said with a shrug. "Perhaps these nefarious desires started growing in him years ago. Hidden and festering."

"Or maybe this plant had something to do with it," she insisted. "Maybe he's using it for medicinal purposes, o-or maybe it released some kind of poison that affected him. You heard what Eudo's handmaid told Jonty about how different he was when he came back from his retreat."

"Look, I'm not that worried about Lord Eudo at the moment," Thaydor said. "I'm worried about the Urms amid the populace and the king getting his head chopped off. And by the way, as I said, you've got a role to play in all this, too, so you'd better pay attention, lovely."

"I'm all ears." She was so pleased at being included rather than tucked into a blasted strongbox somewhere for safekeeping. "What shall I do to help?"

"Didn't your father's construction company work on the new wing of the royal palace that was built a few years ago?"

She nodded. "Why?"

"I need whatever architectural plans he might have of Lionsclaw Keep. There are sections of the palace I've never seen."

"He might well have something like that."

"Good. Any sort of map of the building that might reveal an easier way to rescue His Majesty before they ever lead him out onto the execution platform tomorrow."

"You'd spare him even that?" she asked softly.

"I'd spare the people having to see their king so degraded."

"Well, if Papa does have a detailed scheme of the palace, it would be in the vault in his office. It's always locked, but I used to help him around the office before I studied at the Bastion, so I know where he hides the key."

"Excellent. We'll see what we can find among his papers. Then there's the matter of getting me into the palace, and I need your help for that, as well."

"*Hasten* spell?" she asked, holding his businesslike gaze.

Thaydor nodded. "I'll appoint a few of my men to protect you." He glanced around the hall, weighing which ones he could spare in the battle ahead for the sake of ensuring her safety. "You'll come with us when we head into the city shortly. We'll see what your father's vault might yield, then you'll *hasten* me into the palace, as close to the dungeon as we can get. That way, even if I can't manage to get His Majesty out of there beforehand, at least this will put me in position to play my role as executioner when the time comes."

He met her eyes, unblinking. "As for you, once you've got me into the palace, you'll pop right back out again to your guards, do you hear me? They'll immediately bring you back here to the Eldenhold, where you'll be safe no matter how the battle goes."

"I'm happy to do my part, but I want one alteration to the plan," she said.

Reynulf's lips twisted at this new attempt to get her way.

"After I get you into the palace, I want to go to the library before coming right back to the Eldenhold. I need to research this plant." She showed him the thistle insignia again. "I just know in my bones that it has something to do with whatever's affecting Lord Eudo."

Thaydor narrowed his eyes at her, considering her request with a smile toying at his lips. "You drive a hard bargain, lady."

"Well, I am the daughter of a great merchant, aren't I? Come, it's a *library*, Thaydor. How much trouble can I really get into amongst the bookshelves? It's not as though the Urmugoths are going to be there studying. Plus, it's on the opposite side of the city from Concourse Square."

"She might be right about the plant," Jonty pointed out with a shrug. "Maybe it is poison. Stranger things have happened."

"Very well, if you think so, then you can go with her," Thaydor said to the bard. "You boys, as well."

The squires were horrified at this assignment.

"Oh, sir!" Kai protested. "Play nursemaid?"

"And miss the battle?" Petra cried.

"Please, no!" Jeremy begged him.

"You heard me. This is a very important mission, keeping my lady safe. Serve with honor and I will remember it for next time."

The boys glanced at one another, looking completely disgusted. Wrynne hid a smile.

"I'll *never* get to kill an Urmugoth," Jeremy huffed under his breath.

Reynulf leaned over and gave the lad a mild smack in the back of the head. "Just shut up and follow orders."

Thaydor then chose three very large and scary-looking knights as her bodyguards. Unlike the boys, these stood stoically and did not argue with their orders.

Only Reynulf was annoyed. "We can't spare three of our best men for this. Let her wait until afterward."

"I'll give the orders," Thaydor said matter-of-factly. "Or maybe we just need one, Bloodletter. Care to volunteer?"

"No!" Wrynne and Reynulf exclaimed in unison.

Thaydor snorted. "I thought not."

Reynulf sighed and looked away, shaking his head, but Wrynne touched her husband's arm softly. "Thank you."

"Perhaps if all goes smoothly, you won't even need to return to the Eldenhold. Then you'll be closer at hand when the battle's over," he murmured with a meaningful stare.

She blushed and dropped her gaze, well aware of his preferred way of celebrating a victory. Cheeks blazing, she peeked at him from beneath her lashes, more than happy to oblige. It seemed they'd have to wait until later to really make up. He gave her a discreet wink that assured her he'd be looking forward to it, too.

* * *

Before long, it was time to go.

As the wee hours of the night crept on, they carried out the plan just as Thaydor had described it. The loyal sentries posted at the city's West Gate let them in; the company of rebel knights streamed through without a word.

Once inside the city, they split up into their designated teams. Wrynne took Thaydor, Jonty, the boys, and her three designated bodyguards to her father's office. They slipped into the building quietly. Wrynne moved around the offices in the dark until she located her father's vault key under a loose brick in the fireplace in his office. In all these years, he'd never moved it, she thought in amusement.

*Oh, Papa.*

While her guards kept watch around the building outside, the boys carried in Thaydor's suit of armor, a couple of shields, and extra weapons for safekeeping.

Thaydor meant to leave the items here until they were needed tomorrow. The location of her father's company offices was close to Concourse Square. It would serve as a convenient retreat once he had played his role disguised as the executioner and rescued the king.

He intended to bring Baynard here as a brief first stop to get him out of immediate danger. Then he would quickly don his armor before conducting His Majesty to the greater safety of the Eldenhold, if necessary.

The boys marveled over Hallowsmite in the midst of their task, while Wrynne led Thaydor and Jonty down into the cellar to open her father's vault.

Once they were below ground, Jonty lit a candle and held it up for her so she could see what she was doing. Thaydor had forbidden it upstairs, fearing the light would shine out between the shutters and their presence would be noticed.

Unlocking her father's strongbox, she quickly sorted through the papers inside and unrolled several scrolls until she finally found the one she was looking for. "Lionsclaw Keep. Here it is."

"I'll bet he wasn't supposed to keep this," the bard remarked.

"Probably not," she admitted as she unfurled it fully and laid it on the rough worktable in the center of the dim room. "But men like my father have a way of looking out for their own interests." She put paperweights around the edges of the architectural drawing to keep it from rolling back up again.

Just then, the boys joined them, noisily clambering down the wooden steps to the cellar.

"Did you find it?" Kai asked, joining them at the table.

"We did," she answered, while Thaydor spent a few minutes scanning the sketch and memorizing the castle's layout.

"All right. I've got it. We'll go to the wall right about here." He tapped a particular line on the drawing and then looked at Wrynne.

She nodded, and they set out once more.

The city was dark and still and eerie, the moonlight silvering the outlines of buildings and walls. Wrynne found the silence of the normally bustling capital unnerving, but it was nothing compared to the dread that stole her breath when they spotted a pair of Urms on patrol farther down the very street where they were headed.

Their whole party ducked out of sight. Wrynne shrank into the shadows behind Thaydor, who put his arm out to guard her, but the creatures marched past without even noticing them.

Exhaling en masse, they pressed on.

A little farther along their stealthy trek through the sleeping city, they passed one of the streets leading into Victory Plaza, where the queen's body would lie in state, just a few blocks away from Concourse Square.

Wrynne stopped in her tracks at the sight of two white banners erected on posts on either side of the lane feeding in to the plaza. The banners bore the same silver thistle-shaped symbol as the Urm's armband.

She poked Thaydor in the side and pointed at them. "*Now* do you believe me?" she whispered.

He furrowed his brow, glancing at her with an air of distraction. "Come on, we're almost there."

She said nothing more as they hurried on.

At last, they arrived at the spot by the wall that he had chosen for his entrance point. Thaydor gave a few final instructions to the knights assigned as her bodyguards, and then offered the trio of squires a brief word of sympathy. "Don't worry, they'll be plenty more battles to be fought when you're older."

"Yes, sir," they said, still rather crestfallen.

He turned and offered Jonty his hand.

The bard clasped it heartily. "Good luck in there."

"Thanks. Look after her for me, would you?"

"Do my best."

Thaydor clapped him on the shoulder, then turned to Wrynne. "Ready?"

Now that the moment was upon them, she had to bite her tongue against the urge to beg him not to go. But she knew he had to do this. He was the Paladin of Ilios.

Somehow she found the strength to give him a cheerful nod, and spine straight, she walked by his side over to the massive outer wall of the castle. Based on her father's plans, they had determined the dungeon lay just on the other side.

They looked at each other as they stood in the moonlight.

"Well, here we go again," she said. "Two wanted fugitives breaking *into* another dungeon. We must be mad."

He smiled back with far more feeling in his eyes than there was time to express. "This time it's my turn." He took her hand, the moon's glow shining around his golden hair like a halo. "Are we all right, then, you and I?" he asked.

"You tell me. I'm not angry anymore," she confessed in an earnest whisper.

"Neither am I." He paused, searching her face. "I'm sorry if I was too hard on you. I can be such a Clank sometimes."

"No, no, you were right, anyway. You always are."

"No, I'm not. Not always."

"Usually."

"Usually," he admitted, one corner of his mouth lifting in a rueful smile. "As long as you still love me. That's all I care about."

"Thaydor...I'll always love you. No matter what." She moved closer and embraced him.

He wrapped his arms around her and held her tightly, resting his head on top of hers. She squeezed her eyes shut, wondering how she could help him do something so suicidal.

"I love you so much," she breathed, her cheek pressed to his chest. "I know you have to do this—it's who you are—but *please* be careful. You're everything to me."

"You're everything to me, too, my sweet demoiselle." The fierce intensity in his whisper belied the softness of the kiss he placed on her head as he held her. "Don't worry. This will be over before you know it. But in the meanwhile, just know how much I love you."

He pulled back just a little and lifted her face with a tender touch under her chin. She looked into his eyes.

"You are my joy, Wrynne. My vision of all that's beautiful in the world. You're the very embodiment of everything I've spent my life fighting for. That's why you have to promise me that you'll be careful, too. I need you as I need no one else."

Tears sprang into her eyes at his heartfelt words. It took a moment to find her voice.

"Ah, don't fret for my sake, husband," she forced out with a teasing smile. "I'll be wary of all those menacing books."

He tapped her on the nose. "I mean it. If you run into any trouble at all, *hasten* yourself out of there. Don't stay behind to see about the men— not even those idiot boys. They've got training. They can fight their way out if it comes to it. You're what's important. As long as I know you're safe, I can do whatever needs to be done."

She held his gaze, her arms around his lean waist. "I'll be safe, I promise. Just get through this in one piece, all right? Then we'll celebrate your victory. Privately."

"Mmm, you do know how to bribe a man." He bent his head and kissed her. The silky glide of his tongue parted her lips, then plunged into her open mouth, deep and hot and wet, an unspoken promise of what he'd do to her later.

When he finally released her, she leaned on her walking staff to keep herself upright, dizzied with delicious arousal.

A breathless giggle escaped her. "Well then! Let's get this over with, shall we? Go save the king and win the battle so I can give you your prize."

"*You* are my prize," he growled, running a smoldering glance over the length of her body. "And don't you forget it."

She turned bright red. "Such wickedness from the paladin!" she whispered.

He raised a finger to his lips. "Shh."

She shivered with anticipation at the hunger in his eyes.

"And now I become Monsieur Death. Don't scream," he added wryly. He pulled the grim black hood of the executioner on over his head and presented himself. "How do I look? Scary?"

She arched a brow. "Terrifying, dear. Here. Take my hand."

He did, firmly.

"Into the dungeon with you now."

"And for you, right back out again and straight on to the library. Either head back to the Eldenhold as soon as you find what you're looking for, or just stay there till I send for you. Your guards can decide which seems best at the time. They're seasoned warriors, Wrynne, and good men—despite their antics at Fonja. Either way, you'll be quite safe."

"Which of us are you trying to convince now? Stop worrying, I'll be fine." She paused and looked at him. "Except for missing you."

"I love you," the new executioner replied from beneath his ghastly death's hood.

Wrynne gazed at him, a little unnerved by his costume, then shook her head at the strangeness that had become of her life.

"Ah, well. Here we go." Holding tightly to his hand, she banged her staff on the ground and put their plot into motion with a whisper. "*Hasten.*"

# Chapter 17
# Fidelis

Once Wrynne had gone, safely whisking off back to her bodyguards outside the castle walls, Thaydor glanced around at the torch-lit dungeon.

Thankfully, the corridor where they had landed was empty. He adjusted the executioner's hood a bit to improve his field of vision, then stalked down the dim stone aisle to get his bearings. His pulse pounded with a dark excitement at the danger. Dawn was just an hour away. It wouldn't be long now.

He found his way to the dungeon's small armory, which the real executioner had described. He stepped in and scanned the array of axes and swords for him to choose from for his supposed task. He took a nasty-headed axe off the wall and tested it.

He had a dagger in his boot and another on his waist. He wished he had Hallowsmite, but to bring his famous blade on this mission would have, indeed, been pushing his luck. The axe would have to serve as his weapon of choice on the platform. Satisfied, he took it with him as he walked through the mostly empty dungeon searching for the royal prisoner.

Any questions about how Baynard would meet his death were answered when he found the king's cell.

The man he had served, the man who had made him royal champion only to betray him, lay sobbing quietly on his ratty cot. Thaydor wondered which loss His Majesty regretted more—his wife or his throne.

Staring at his disappointing liege lord through the eyeholes of the black hood, he indulged a moment's brief, bitter musing. How satisfying it would be to actually drop the axe tomorrow and take that traitorous, empty head off Baynard's shoulders.

The king suddenly noticed him standing there outside the bars of his cell. Perhaps *lurking* was the word.

He left off sobbing with a small gasp. "Is it time?" he spluttered, sitting up in his wrinkled nightshirt, looking bewhiskered and quite common, frightened and aged by several years overnight.

Thaydor shook his head but said nothing. He did not want His Majesty to recognize him by his voice. Oh, it would be an act of mercy to let the royal captive know that his rescue was at hand. But he didn't want to risk the fool inadvertently giving him away. That could ruin everything.

Besides, at the moment, he wasn't feeling all that merciful, considering that if the king had got his way weeks ago, it would have been Thaydor in that cell. *His* head destined for the chopping block.

And Wrynne's.

His eyes narrowed behind the hood, and he thumped the handle of the axe against his opposite palm, enjoying the king's wide-eyed look of dread.

Just a whiff of revenge.

Then he pivoted slowly and stalked off to wait in the shadows for the executioner's summons.

* * *

"Finally!"

When the Great Library of Veraidel opened its massive, carved doors later that morning, Wrynne and her unlikely band of armor-clad research assistants rushed in.

The old librarian watched them pass in surprise.

Wrynne led the way, her staff in hand, her cloak flowing out behind her. Jonty strode confidently beside her, followed by the knights. Bearded Berold, scar-faced Sagard, and Humphrey, with the long, gold, Norse-style braids, could no doubt kill anything that came at her, but somehow she got the feeling they had never set foot in the library before.

She flicked a glance over her shoulder at them. Prowling along behind her, they scanned in all directions as if they were walking into hostile territory. Fortunately, it appeared they had the place to themselves today.

And no wonder. Most of the populace was swept up in the great matters of the day—either weeping over a queen they had not cared about till now or seeking a good spot from which to watch King Baynard's execution.

The one that wasn't going to happen.

Meanwhile, in the back of their party, the three young squires were still mumbling complaints about the unfairness of having just completed their studies, only to have to return here again.

"Pardon." Jonty stepped toward the clerk's desk. "Could you point us to your section on matters botanical?"

"It's all right. I already know exactly where it is," Wrynne interrupted. "Follow me."

The men obeyed, hurrying deeper into the library.

The morning sun lit the vast atrium from on high, shining through windows six lofty stories above them. Mighty stone pillars spanned the length of the place on all sides, from the marble floor up to the vaulted ceiling. Lacy iron railings ran between the pillars, and behind those lay endless rows of shelves packed with priceless books and scrolls on all realms of earthly knowledge—and a good deal on unearthly realms, as well.

"This way." She led bard and bodyguards into the stairwell, where they hurried up the zigzag stairs to the third floor.

From there, she wove through the labyrinth of bookshelves until she reached the aisle filled with all the classic tomes on botany that she had studied day and night as a student.

"Here we are." Stopping midway down the aisle, she began busily pulling reference texts off the shelves and handing them to her helpers before it occurred to her that perhaps not all of them could read.

But it turned out they could, so she put the head-loppers to work, too. Berold got *The Compendium of Plant Life, Beneficent and Baneful*. Sagard took *The Herbal Arcana*. Jonty helped himself to *Fey Wisdom of the Flowers*, while the boys perused *Secrets from an Apothecary's Garden*.

For herself, Wrynne reserved *Botanical Brews for Witches & Healers*. She quickly opened the thick book. "What we're looking for is probably in the same family as thistles and artichokes," she told them.

They all started flipping through pages to find that section in their various tomes.

Jonty soon rattled off some choices. "Milk thistle, musk thistle, star thistle, sow thistle, blessed thistle, common thistle, globe thistle, cotton thistle— Hold on! What's this? Fire thistle. Also known as a firechoke."

"Let me see that." Wrynne exchanged books with him. "Hmm.

Hmm," she repeated in a lower tone as she scanned the page. "Well, that's not good," she mumbled.

"What is it?" Kai asked, staring at her.

"It says the fire thistle falls into the dread category of the *fleurs du mal*."

"Flowers of evil?" Jonty asked in surprise.

She nodded. "Also known as flowers of hell."

"Fonja's knees," Petra murmured.

She read to them from the tome. "'The fire thistle is occasionally found in the lonely places of this world, but it is not of this earth. It blows in from the Infernal Plane—'"

"What?" Sagard exclaimed.

"'Blows in'?" Jonty echoed.

"'Carried on the solar winds,'" she continued reading. "'Its seeds are known to be a great delicacy to rocs—'"

"We saw them! At Silvermount. That *must* be what it is!" Jonty said.

"Shh! Rocs are the least of the dangers associated with the fire thistle, according to this," Wrynne reported. "'As one of the commonest flowers of the lower planes,' it says here that 'the prickles of this sentient plant bear a venomous poison'— Ha! I knew that thing was staring at me!"

Jonty squinted at her. "Did you say *sentient* plant?"

She pored over the page. "It has a base form of consciousness, so yes, according to this. Well, many plants do," she added, glancing at him. "That's why they grow better when we talk to them. But this one is unique."

She read on. "'The firechoke seeks a higher level of consciousness by taking over human beings in something akin to demonic possession.'"

"Are you saying Lord Eudo's possessed by an evil flower?" Sagard asked slowly with a frown.

"Possibly?" At a loss, Wrynne looked down at the book again. "'The fire thistle seeks to infect people with a seed of evil through the dispersion of its thistledown.'"

"You mean like dandelion fluff?" Jeremy suggested.

"Somewhat similar. But larger and sharper, judging by the sketch." She studied the article herself for another couple of minutes and then summarized for them. "It seems that if a human being is hit with one of the bits of thistledown, the seed penetrates through the skin. The evil stored in the seed dissolves into the person, corrupting him or her. The victim is slowly taken over by the consciousness of the fleur du mal."

She winced. "There is no known cure. It says the more innocent the individual who becomes infected, the faster and more potently the poison works. 'As a sentient organism, the fleur du mal is an agent of darkness, after a fashion. The base consciousness of the fire thistle *hates* all that belongs to the Light. It wants to dominate and destroy the good, and to extend its control as far as possible through the ones it infects.'"

"Well, that could explain why Lord Eudo would've sought to target someone like Thaydor...if it especially hates the good," Jonty said in a guarded tone. "And to get control of the king."

"According to this, having once been infected, Eudo's evil will only grow and intensify until the firechoke venom ultimately kills him." She looked around at them anxiously. "He might not be the only one who was struck by a piece of this nasty thistledown, though. We need to find and burn this thing before it infects anybody else."

"You stay here," the bard said. "I'll see to it."

"But Jonty, I'm the one who knows where it is!"

"If anything happens to you, Thaydor will have our heads on pikes."

"Nothing's going to happen to me. Let's go together. We need to destroy it—"

"You can't," a new voice broke in abruptly.

They all looked over.

A tall, broad-shouldered silhouette loomed at the end of the aisle, blocking the exit. The mysterious man standing before them had a sculpted face, long black hair, and brooding silver eyes faintly lined with kohl. The midnight cloak dripping from his shoulders bore the fiery crest of Okteus, Lord of Shadows.

"If you have truly seen a fire thistle in our world," the stranger said, "the only way to get rid of it is to open a portal to the Infernal Plane and push it back into Hell."

Wrynne stared dubiously at him. "And you are?"

"Stand back, my lady," Berold said. "Look there, on his cloak. He's obviously a sorcerer."

The boys gasped and quickly backed away, making hand signs against the evil eye.

"He was spying on us!" Kai uttered.

"No," the stranger retorted, while Wrynne noted the wand tucked into a black leather sheath by the dagger at his lean hip. "I was sitting right over there, grading papers," he informed them, and her eyebrows arched high at this response.

*He's a teacher?* It seemed so unlikely that it nearly made her laugh. It was easier to imagine this exotic wizard fellow summoning dragons and roasting cities from astride one's back than grading tests.

He frowned at them in annoyance, then returned his gaze to Wrynne. "Your friends make enough noise, lady, to be heard in the Bronze Mountains. I couldn't help but overhear your discussion, and it's fortunate I did. Obviously, none of you have any notion what you're dealing with. Where did you see a fire thistle?" he demanded.

"How do you open a portal to the Infernal Plane?" she countered.

"*You* don't," he clipped out. "But I can."

Jonty grasped her arm. "Wrynne, if this man is truly a disciple of the Dark One, he can't be trusted."

"We might not have a choice. Sir, what is your name?"

He eyed her as warily, as she did him. She watched his gaze land on her necklace, identifying her as a follower of the Light. He gazed deeply into her eyes for a second, as though trying either to read or hypnotize her.

"I am called Novus Blacktwist," he finally admitted, but then Wrynne remembered that sorcerers never revealed their true names. "Now tell me where you saw the firechoke."

"Tell him nothing, mistress! He probably wants it for an ingredient in some vile potion," Berold warned.

Novus let out a weary sigh. "I'm trying to help you here. This is a very serious situation."

"We're aware of that." Wrynne held him in a penetrating stare, trying to gauge how strongly she sensed evil from the man. It was always hard to be certain, especially since Oktean mages could cloak their true intents from Ilian magic.

But given his dark expertise, Novus Blacktwist undoubtedly knew what they were dealing with better than she did.

"Well?" he prompted.

She concluded on the spot that he did not give off any stronger presence of wickedness than Reynulf. Definitely dangerous, but a little less than sinister.

"'Twas at the Harmonists' retreat of Silvermount," she conceded. "There were rocs there. We couldn't understand why at the time, but this makes sense. It would also help explain Lord Eudo's behavior for the past year. If he was infected—"

"Shh!" Novus hushed her, moving closer with an impatient wave of his hand. "Don't keep mentioning that name! He has spies everywhere. Do you want them to hear you?"

"He does?" she asked, wide-eyed.

The handsome wizard scowled at her.

Wrynne tried not to stare at him, for he was quite a novelty—not just because she had never dreamed a sorcerer could possess such striking good looks, but mostly because this was the closest she had ever stood to a follower of the Dark god. According to the pagans, Okteus was the god of night and magic, evil brother to Ilios, and the wicked uncle of Xoltheus, the war god.

"I don't understand," Sagard muttered. "How could this fire thistle thing just 'blow in' from the Infernal Plane, like the book says? Portals between dimensions don't just open by themselves."

"Well, er," Novus said, discreetly dropping his gaze and folding his arms across his chest, "I *may* know something about that."

"*You* did it?" Wrynne exclaimed.

"Hardly," he said with disdain. "But I recall hearing a rumor about a year ago or so concerning a few of my students. I tutor a small number of gifted young adepts at the Wizards' Spire."

"I see," Wrynne said, barely able to fathom what subjects he taught.

"Nobody confessed, but I heard that a few of my wee geniuses got into a spat with a group of young Efrenists," he said with a long-suffering air. "The Silver Sage's disciples enraged my adepts by claiming there was no real difference between good and evil, as they are wont to do. I only became aware of the prank when I overheard one of my students boasting of how they had set out to show the Efrenist students there was a large difference, indeed. I believe they might've opened up a portal at Silvermount to give their foes a firsthand view of Hades."

"How incredibly stupid," Wrynne said.

"Try teaching them." He sighed and shook his head. "Well, it's not wise to enrage a wizard. Not even a spotty-faced apprentice."

"I'll remember that," Jonty mumbled.

"Well, Professor Blacktwist—"

"Novus, please," he said.

"If you're the one who taught them how to do this little trick, then I think you should be the one to fix it."

"Why else would I be standing here?" he asked.

"Mind your tone in speaking to milady," Humphrey warned the prickly fellow. "And don't try turnin' anyone into a newt."

Novus looked askance him. "Honestly."

"I propose we go to Silvermount immediately. The sooner we get rid of the fire thistle, the sooner Lord Eudo might return to normal, call off the Urms, and stop this madness."

Novus shrugged. "Getting rid of it won't cure him, as I said. But it might loosen its hold over him. Anything is possible."

"How do we know we can trust you?" Jonty asked.

"Do you think I want Urms in the city, master bard? I have to live here, too."

Wrynne gave her friend a glance. *Satisfied?*

Jonty shrugged.

"Knights, how do you feel about battling rocs?" she asked her big, gruff bodyguards.

They exchanged wry glances, looking intrigued at the prospect of such sport, especially the young squires.

"Good. You'll keep the rocs at bay long enough for Novus to open the portal, then Jonty and I will carefully shove the fire thistle through it and send the awful thing home."

"But my lady," Petra spoke up, "shouldn't we ask Sir Thaydor first if it's all right for you to go?"

Wrynne looked quizzically at the boy. "He's a bit busy at the moment, don't you think?"

* * *

Indeed, he was.

As Thaydor stood on the platform in the square, the morning light glinting on the axe in his hands, he couldn't help wondering what manner of man set out to make his living as an executioner.

It seemed an odd choice of vocations by anybody's standards. Not that he could talk, he supposed. Being a knight *did* involve killing people, too. And monsters. And creatures in between...

Urmugoths, for example.

Eudo's hired Urms with the silver armbands stood in a ring around the platform, their broad, leather-armored backs to Thaydor.

He figured he could take a couple of heads off from behind with a well-placed swing of the axe. Make a hole in the wall of beasts flanking the dais. Rush the king out of it. His blood thrummed with anticipation.

On second thought, perhaps he should not mock the executioner, for they were not so different. What manner of man enjoyed the holy rage of battle as he did?

Meanwhile, Lord Eudo was speechifying about the necessity of making himself regent, since the king had no heir.

Baynard stood in chains in his nightshirt and braies, the very sketch of misery, staring at the chopping block and the large wicker basket below it, meant to catch his severed head.

Thaydor couldn't help feeling a little annoyed seeing the old man looking so desolate. *You bloody royal dunderhead. You ought to know me better than that by now. You think I'd let you die?*

But the doomed monarch was in his own world, perhaps contemplating joining his dead queen in the next world and having to account for himself on how he had betrayed her.

Through the eyeholes of his grim black mask, Thaydor scanned the area. Just out of sight, around the corners of the four streets leading into Concourse Square, and hidden for the moment by buildings and alleys, he knew his so-called rebel knights waited, in position.

As for the square itself, thankfully, it wasn't too crowded. Still, one had to figure that despite his men's best efforts, a few civilians would probably die. It couldn't be helped. They were in the wrong place at the wrong time and either hadn't heard or had ignored the rumors he had spread through the city: that there would be trouble and nobody ought to attend.

*Ah well.* Now they'd pay the price for being the sort of people who found a public execution entertaining.

"And now, Your Majesty, any last words you wish to share with your former subjects?" Lord Eudo asked. He was not quite able to keep the glee out of his voice while the white banners with the silver thistle insignia flapped in the breeze all around the platform.

Baynard raised his chin and looked around with tears in his eyes. "I have failed you all, and I am sorry."

Eudo smirked. The aura of evil pulsated from him, sickening and cold.

Even now, it puzzled Thaydor. He had known the Silver Sage for years at court, and while there was no love lost between them, he had detected no such palpable malevolency as he sensed in the man now. If he had, he would have seen him barred from court years ago for the king's own safety.

Maybe Wrynne was on to something with her theory about some

sort of exposure to a poisonous plant. He supposed stranger things had happened.

Having made his simple and obviously heartfelt apology, the king stepped forward to the chopping block, unasked. He knelt with a clank of his chains and laid his neck on the designated spot.

The sight of his liege lord waiting to be murdered brought the battle rage quickly into Thaydor's veins.

The moment was upon them.

Lord Eudo spoke some condescending prayer to Efrena over him, then nodded at Executioner Thaydor.

As he took the few slow paces over to the king's side, the three drummers began to pound a noisy rhythm meant to cover up any screaming. Their beat served as the agreed-upon signal to his knights that it was time—and matched Thaydor's driving pulse.

He raised the axe.

Seconds from taking full power over Veraidel, Lord Eudo seemed practically orgasmic. He watched, riveted.

But when Thaydor took an unexpected step forward and swung the axe horizontally rather than straight down, two of the Urms' ugly, yellow-eyed heads went flying. He had already grabbed the king and yanked him to his feet before the bodies hit the ground.

The knights charged in, and chaos broke out.

Thaydor whipped off the mask and turned to the king. "Follow me, sire!"

*"Stop him!"* Eudo screamed.

And the drums thundered on.

\* \* \*

Except for the knights' banter, the same eerie silence Wrynne remembered hung over the Harmonists' retreat.

"Bet it tastes like chicken," Berold murmured.

"Soon find out," Sagard rumbled in reply. "Roasted roc breast with a nice cream sauce, maybe?"

"Might be good with vegetables," Humphrey chimed in from behind her.

"Milady, did you know Sagard can cook?" Berold asked merrily.

"Soothes the nerves after a hard battle," the burly head-lopper admitted.

"Shh!" Wrynne whispered.

"Would you please be quiet?" Jonty also insisted. "The birds might hear you. If they're still here."

"I hope they do," Sagard mumbled. "I'm hungry."

The boys snickered, but Wrynne shook her head. "Watch how fast you change your tune once your 'dinner' shows up. *We* might be the ones on the menu."

"Nay, mistress," Humphrey assured her. "We'll keep ye safe."

They had left the horses farther down the mountain to avoid attracting hungry rocs. Still, the men kept Wrynne in the center of their company, the better to protect her.

Though it wasn't quite the same as having Thaydor there, she felt relatively safe with two massive knights and one wiry but very determined squire ahead of her, two squires and a knight behind her, a bard on her left, and a wizard on her right.

Of course, she was prepared to defend herself, as well. She gripped her crossbow in one hand, her staff in the other, and continuously scanned the underbrush for the huge nest that she had seen before. She just hoped the fire thistle stuck to its side a few days ago hadn't blown away to some new destination, where it could infect more innocent people.

So far, the whole place was just as she remembered, overgrown and haunting. She spotted a few pigeons roosting on the giant Efrena statue's head and shoulders, but still no sign of the rocs. Perhaps the monstrous birds had moved on or returned to the mountains. Somehow she doubted she and her companions would be so lucky.

At least they didn't find any fresh deer carcasses this time.

"Ho, look at that!" Kai said from his spot between Sagard and Berold.

Wrynne tensed as the lad ran a few yards ahead of them and bent to pick up something off the ground.

He laughed as he held up a huge black feather. "Jonty, do you want this? You could write some *really* epic tales with a quill pen this big."

"Give me that," Novus snapped, reaching for it.

"You have a use for it?" Wrynne asked, glancing at him.

"Actually, I know of several potions that call for roc feathers. They're very rare."

Jonty gestured that the sorcerer could have it.

Wrynne suddenly gasped. "There it is!"

They all looked over and saw the grotesquely oversized thistle clinging to the side of the huge bird's nest.

Wrynne stared at it, a chill shooting down her spine. She did not know if the others sensed it, too, but as mad as it sounded, she could immediately feel the malice emanating from the dried-out seed head, as before.

All the more so now that she knew what it was.

The dark base of each bulbous seed seemed to study them like the many beady eyes of Argue, the monster of legend, covered in eyeballs.

The fire thistle's otherworldly evil charged the air around them with tension. The group stopped and gazed back at it uneasily.

"Is it just me or is that thing watching us?" Petra muttered.

"Aye, and it hates us all, remember that," Jonty said. "It would kill us if it could."

"Some more than others." Novus glanced at Wrynne and then at the relatively innocent youths. Then he took out his wand and reminded them of their assignments while he strode ahead.

"You lot," he said with a gesture to the knights and squires, "keep your eyes open for those birds while I open the portal. And you two, mind you don't touch that thing when the time comes to shove it through the portal, unless you want to end up evil."

Wrynne and Jonty nodded.

As they walked closer to the nest where the firechoke was trapped, Wrynne shuddered with the sensation of pure hatred pouring out of the bizarre plant.

Such a thing did not even seem possible…but wasn't evil always like that? It always took good by surprise, because its motives and its ways were so alien to the way that good creatures thought and felt and acted.

The things that came naturally to evil never even occurred to good, which was why it was always so shocking when the twisted works of evil came to light. It might as well have come from another world, another plane of existence, she mused, for evil *was* absolutely *other*. At least, it seemed that way to her.

When they all stopped near the tree line, about ten feet away from the nest and the firechoke stuck there by its prickles, Wrynne looked around at her companions. The knights and squires got into position, standing sentry on the lookout for rocs.

Jonty glanced at Wrynne, a trace of wry, graveyard humor in the twist of his mouth, while Novus stood nearby and closed his eyes. Taking a deep breath, the sorcerer lifted his hands, his wand in his right, and began his dark chants invoking the Lord of Shadows.

Wrynne furrowed her brow, wondering if their plan was quite all right with Ilios. She hoped this wasn't a mistake.

Novus chanted on, his voice growing louder.

When she glanced uneasily at the Firechoke again, she found she could not look away from its blind, malignant stare. She felt queasy being near the thing. It was as though the fleur du mal were pulling her in somehow, luring her under its influence…so it might destroy her.

She almost felt sorry for Lord Eudo, being subjected to this unpleasant presence within him for the past year and a half.

A ball of flame appeared in the air a few feet in front of Novus. He chanted louder and more powerfully, ugly words with harsh accents. The fiery orb widened and grew into a circle, and a hot wind blew around them. Novus's black hair waved in the gale he had stirred up.

"It's working!" Jonty exclaimed over the chaos of the supernatural breeze.

All of a sudden, an explosive ripping sound rent the air, and the circle of flame that hung before Novus tore open into a hole between dimensions.

Wrynne was not prepared for what she saw beyond it—a glimpse into the underworld. She took a stumbling step backward, and thankfully, Jonty caught her before she fell on her backside.

Terrible roars of beasts and the howls of the damned reached them distantly from beyond the portals shredded edges, deep in the heart of Hell.

Wrynne cowered, irrationally fearful that she would be pulled into it. She wished with all her heart that Thaydor were there with his unfailing aura of goodness. Her Golden Knight. But he had never seemed more far away…

At that moment, a piercing screech filled the skies above them.

"Here comes supper!" Berold boomed, lifting his sword and shield. The other knights did likewise; the squires waited in position without flinching.

Jonty glanced up worriedly as the shadow of a huge wingspan swirled over their entire company.

When Wrynne looked into the late-morning sky, so bright and blue, it seemed filled with rocs, black as night, their red eyes glowing with fury at this intrusion.

She hunkered down a little where she stood, though she knew Thaydor's knights would protect her with their lives, if it came to it. She vowed that it would not and brought up her crossbow, ready to fire if any of those creatures came too close.

"Novus, how are you holding up?" she called.

He didn't answer, deep in trance. Sweat beaded his face, though whether that was from the oven-like heat pouring out of the Infernal Plane or the surely superhuman effort of keeping the door between dimensions open, she could not say.

Arms lifted, he was swaying while the chants tumbled from his lips.

"Right," Jonty said. "I'll do this." He grabbed a long, broken branch off the forest floor. One end fanned out into many smaller twigs. "This should serve as well as any garden rake."

He hefted it to make sure the wood was strong and wouldn't break. The last thing they needed was for the firechoke to escape their hold and roll away. Satisfied, he stepped toward the nest.

But then the first roc dived at the knights, signaling the whole flock to attack. Wrynne looked on in alarm. Her mind spun as she tried to grasp hold of a new plan.

*That's it!*

"Jonty!" She lowered her crossbow and took the branch from him, instead. "Let me do this. Try your music! You said last time that you thought that it could calm them."

He started to protest, but when he turned and saw Sir Sagard's hoped-for dinner fighting savagely to turn the tables on the would-be chef, the bard nodded. "All right. I'll see what I can do." He slipped his lute off his shoulder. "But please be careful."

"I'm a trained gardener, Jonty. I think I know how to use a rake," she teased, trying to sound braver than she felt. "If you can lull those beasts into a trance, maybe we can all get out of here in one piece."

"Daresay I've played for tougher audiences." Armed with nothing but a musical instrument, the brave red-haired bard stepped toward the flesh-eating birds and struck up a soft chord.

Then he began to sing.

# Chapter 18
# Infernal

eanwhile, back in Pleiburg, Concourse Square had become a battleground. All around them, the heave and press of the seething crowd threatened to separate the dazed king from him.

"Stay behind me, sire!" Thaydor yanked the hapless man closer by the front of his soiled nightshirt and then continued his mission of hacking and slashing a path through the forest of swinging blades and roaring warriors.

The din of clashing metal and screaming civilians filled his ears. He parried a blow from the nearest Urm on the handle of his axe, then buried the blade in the brute's chest. It had never been his favorite weapon, but his father had made sure he knew how to use one since the age of nine.

"Thaydor!" the king shouted.

"Don't worry, sire! I'll get you to safety."

"It's not that. Wait!" King Baynard tugged urgently on the back of Thaydor's black executioner's coat and pointed. "Look!"

"Your Majesty! Sir Thaydor!" a shrill voice screamed from behind them. "Oh, wait for me, please! Let me come with you! Get me out of here!"

Panting and blood-flecked, Thaydor paused in his labors to steal a brief glimpse over his shoulder. The king stretched out his hand and pulled a crying and terrified Sana toward him from amid the jostling sea of violence all around them.

Thaydor narrowed his eyes and growled at the traitoress. "Get back!"

"Oh, please, help me, I'm so frightened! Let me come with you, Thaydor! Don't leave me here with these animals! You know what they'll do to me!"

"Stay away from the king," Thaydor ordered her, taking a step in her direction. "Forget her, sire. The woman's a snake. Her lies were what condemned you."

Sana cried harder, terrified tears running down her oh-so-pretty face. "I didn't want to say those things! Lord Eudo made me do it! He threatened my family if I didn't cooperate."

"You see?" Baynard insisted.

"I don't have time for this. Sana, leave him alone."

"But Thaydor! You are the Paladin of Ilios. Doesn't your god command you to forgive—"

"Look out!" He shoved the king's head down forcefully and ducked as a huge Urmugoth swung a halberd at them, snarling.

Unluckily for the Urm, the blade bit into the wooden edge of the platform and got stuck for a moment. In the fleeting heartbeat while the beast tried to yank it out, Thaydor countered. Sweeping upward, he dispatched the Urm with a backhanded chop of his axe. Then he reached once more for the king and pulled him up again.

"Let's go."

Baynard looked up at him with a strange, frozen astonishment in his wide, staring eyes.

"Sir?"

The king staggered forward and suddenly crumpled into Thaydor's arms.

As he fell, Thaydor found Sana standing behind him with a cold smile of satisfaction curving her lips.

Then he spied the knife hilt sticking out of the man's back.

The air left his lungs in a whoosh. "What have you done?" he whispered.

"Go to hell, Thaydor. I've been waiting to do that for weeks. You try sleeping with him. Repulsive old goat." Sana glanced over her shoulder to where Lord Eudo was making his escape surrounded by a ring of Urm bodyguards. "You think we'd let him live after we've gone to all this trouble? Sorry, but we couldn't leave that little task unfinished. Aw, have I upset you, Paladin? What are you going to do, strike down a poor, defenseless female?"

As she started backing away, moving toward Lord Eudo, she produced another dagger to ward him off.

The king groaned. Thaydor hesitated, glaring at her in fury, but he quickly decided the king was his priority. *I'll get him to Wrynne*, he thought. *She can heal him. There's still hope.*

Ignoring Sana, he put his arm around the wounded king's waist to hold him up. He could hear her laughing behind him, jeering at him.

"Oh, such chivalry! You were too scared to bed me, and now you're even too good to kill me? Righteous fool!"

"Thaydor!" a deep voice rang out in warning from somewhere nearby.

He turned just in time to see Sana draw back her arm to hurl a second dagger at him. But instead of throwing it, she dropped the weapon and suddenly started screaming. A grimace of pain contorted her face. She flailed her arms in wild terror, trying to reach the expertly thrown knife in her back.

As she collapsed to the ground, only to be trampled in the fray, Thaydor saw Reynulf's sardonic nod to him, as if to say, *You're welcome.*

Thaydor arched a brow. Hmm, perhaps there *was* an advantage now and then in having friends with looser notions of chivalry than his.

And less exacting scruples about how to win a fight.

Thaydor did not think he could ever kill a woman, but Reynulf's shrug reminded him that Sana *had* set the Urms on Reynulf in the palace. With that, the red knight turned away to battle another Urm.

With a grim twist of his lips, Thaydor held the king up, then forged on through the crowd, seeking the nearest safe haven.

\* \* \*

"Keep playing, Jonty! It's working! Well, at least on some of them," Wrynne amended.

Several rocs had surrounded the bard, lured by his music.

While the knights and squires battled the rest of the vicious flock attacking their party, Wrynne marveled at her friend's steel-nerved concentration. Jonty played his lyre and sang to the birds that gathered around him, standing nearly as high as his shoulders. The power of his beautiful music lulled those nearest him to stop their attack and listen intently.

Some hopped closer. Others cocked their heads. Wrynne was terrified on her friend's behalf. If his music failed or even faltered, he would probably be torn to shreds before the knights could even reach him.

Meanwhile, Novus was still chanting in his trance, using his will or his magic or whatever wizards used to hold the portal to the Infernal Plane open. The hot wind coming up from that volcanic landscape blew his hair and robes, as black as the glossy feathers of the rocs. Sweat poured down his face.

From beyond the portal, the screams of souls in torment, the roars of the demons, and the crackling lake of fire were things no faithful follower of Ilios should ever have to witness, but here she was. She didn't know how much longer Novus could last.

*Let's get this over with.*

Using the long, rake-like branch Jonty had found, she got to work, gingerly prying the hideous seed head of the fire thistle away from the giant nest where it had been stuck for who knew how long.

Heart pounding, her every move was cautious as she got the treacherous thing onto her makeshift rake and then held it in place there with her staff. She could not risk letting a breeze catch it away.

She wondered absently how Thaydor was doing in the square.

If he had been caught in his disguise as the executioner.

If he was still alive.

She shoved away a chilling reminder of the oracle's warning not to let herself be separated from him, then concentrated impatiently on her task. It was too unnerving to wonder if something had happened to her beloved.

At the moment, she had enough problems of her own.

"I'm bringing it now," she told Novus, though she wasn't sure he heard her in his trance.

As she started carrying it toward the portal, she could feel how much the fire thistle hated her. It seemed to watch her with all its countless seed eyes, and with whatever otherworldly evil it possessed, she could feel it whispering in her mind:

*Human, weak and puny, you are worthless. You are nothing without me. I can give you power. I can make you mighty. Give yourself over to me, and you shall be a goddess in your own right.*

Wrynne gulped, inching toward the portal with it. Gracious, she had always talked to the plants in her garden, but none had ever talked back.

Walking slowly and ever so carefully with it clamped between the branch and her staff, she froze and drew in her breath when, from the corner of her eye, she saw one of the rocs lift Jeremy off the ground in its talons.

The lad screamed.

"Jeremy!" his friends shouted, but none could go to his aid, each already embattled with other members of the flock.

Jeremy kicked his legs as the roc flapped higher into the air, its talons grasping him under his armpits. "Help me!"

Berold dispatched his feathered opponent and ran to him, jumping to try to grab the squire's ankle and pull him back down, but, despite the knight's impressive stature, the bird flew out of range. It climbed toward the treetops, clearly intent on hurling its prey from a height sufficient to kill the boy.

Wrynne choked as the thing succeeded before her eyes.

Kai and Petra screamed their friend's name as Jeremy plummeted to earth.

When he hit the grass, he did not move again. Berold stayed planted over the boy's body as the roc returned to feast on its now unconscious prey.

The second the monstrous bird flew into range of his sword, the big, bearded knight let out a roar and struck its head off with one mighty blow. An arc of blood spurted from its neck, and its body flapped around a moment longer, like that of a chicken meant for the stewpot.

*Concentrate*, Wrynne told herself, shaken to the marrow. If the boy was still alive, she could heal his broken bones. *Just get rid of this thing.*

She pushed on. As she carried the fire thistle toward the portal, she noticed Novus beginning to slouch with the exertion of his task. The sorcerer looked exhausted, and the bard was now surrounded by sinister, overly curious birds.

"Somebody, please kill these things," Jonty sang out louder, in a taut but still pleasant tone, coolly strumming away. "My audience is about to eat me."

"Sagard!" Wrynne shouted.

"On it!" the chef-knight yelled back, hacking off a roc's wing and then its beak, with which it had tried to tear out his innards. "Keep singing, bard! I'm on my way!" Sagard yelled as he started running toward him.

Jonty played for his life.

*Whack!*

"Dinner!" Sagard said cheerfully as he struck the head off the nearest roc that tried to stop him.

Humphrey was helping Petra fend off two large, nasty ones. Kai stabbed his feathered foe through the heart with a ferocious war cry, then stalked to help Sagard rescue Jonty.

"Maybe barbecued?" the lad jested with taut, forced graveyard humor as he joined the older man, using humor to steady his own nerves.

"We could try that," Sagard agreed.

*Whack!*

Bone-chilling screeches.

"Or maybe in a soup. Lots of parsley."

Jonty laughed at their mad banter as he strummed his lyre and made up a song on the spot just for the rocs. "You hideous fiends, I hope you all die, hey, nonny-nonny…"

Wrynne shook her head. She would never understand men. How they could joke around at a time like this?

A bead of sweat ran down her face. Just a few more steps to the portal. "Hang on, Novus. I'm almost there."

Unfortunately, the rocs finally figured out that the music was somehow causing them to die.

She heard a jangle of lyre strings breaking and a garbled shout.

She looked over in horror as her friend fell. *"Jonty!"*

Ashen-faced, he clutched a wide talon slash across his abdomen. Kai killed the roc that had just nearly disemboweled him, but it was too late.

"Uh, healer?" the bard choked out.

She stared at him, aghast, when Petra suddenly shouted and pointed toward Novus.

"Hurry, my lady, get rid of that thing! The portal's closing!"

* * *

The king wasn't going to make it all the way to the Building Baron's offices, so Thaydor brought him into the tavern on the square. A few knights hurried in to be of service, but most of them, under Reynulf's command, closed ranks outside the place, lining up to protect it.

The aproned innkeeper hastily shooed his patrons off to one side of the pub and offered a cushioned bench, where Thaydor set the wounded king down.

Baynard's lined, dirty face was ashen, and blood was seeping from his back. Thaydor helped His Majesty recline on his side, but he dared not remove the blade. He knew from personal experience that that would only make the blood flow faster.

"Take courage, sire. Just hold on. My wife is a healer. Try not to move too much." He glanced at his men.

Sirs Richeut, Gervais, and Ivan awaited his orders.

"One of you, go to the Great Library! Tell my wife I need her here, now! But I want guards by her side at all times. And keep her away from the square. I don't want her anywhere near those Urms. Bring her through the back door when you return." He pointed at the pub's back door, which was down the small aisle at the far end of the building. "Now, go!"

"Don't bother," the king rasped even as Richeut went racing out the back door of the pub. "I don't want to live. Not after all I've done."

"Sire! You mustn't say that."

He shook his head weakly and beckoned to Thaydor. "Come closer."

He crouched down beside the man, waiting.

"You really are a marvel, my lad. After all I did to you, you still came to my rescue."

"An oath of fealty is no light matter, Your Majesty."

"It was to me. I have failed you all."

"You will have time to fix it. As soon as my wife gets here, she will make you well again."

"Married. How nice. I am happy for you, lad. But no. I don't deserve it. Let me go to my wife."

"Your Majesty—"

"Don't." Baynard shook his head with a pained grimace. "Please. I was blind and stupid. Never saw through Eudo's scheme until it was too late. Not even after what he did to you. Or had *me* do to you, I should say. I am sorry, paladin. If you could forgive me. I was not worthy of your service. I see that now. I've brought this kingdom to the brink of ruin, all for a woman I knew from the start would be my undoing."

"Sana's dead, sir. If it's any comfort."

"No. The fault was mine. An old man's vanity."

Thaydor offered the king a sip of water, but Baynard shook his head painfully.

"There is, however, one last service you could do for me," he ground out.

Thaydor leaned closer, instantly ready. "Yes, my liege?"

"Take this for me." The king pried the thick gold ring that bore the royal seal off his finger and dropped it in Thaydor's hand.

His fingers closed around it. "What shall I do with it, sire? Take it to

Aisedor and explain to Their Majesties for you—"

"Be quiet!" He started laughing wearily. "Put the damned thing on, lad."

"What?"

"I am appointing you...my successor."

Thaydor stared blankly at him. "Sir?"

"It is my right. I trust you will not shirk your duty."

Thaydor looked down at the ring and then stared at the king in disbelief, but made no move to put it on.

The knights gazed at him, wide-eyed.

"Well, you heard him," Ivan murmured.

"No!" Thaydor whispered.

"You would not disobey your king's command, would you, paladin? I want witnesses to hear me. People!" Baynard called weakly to the staring citizens crowded into one side of the pub.

The innkeeper beckoned them closer, and they all leaned in.

"Hear my dying wish," His Majesty said, pausing to cough up a spume of blood. "You know I have neither son nor daughter to survive me. But by the ancient decree of the Charter, I exercise my privilege to appoint my own successor. And I hereby make Thaydor Clarenbeld your king. Noble bloodlines. Impeccable record of service. Years of experience. Proven sound judgment. Heed him. He's the only one I know can be trusted," he said, and just like that, he died.

Thaydor stared at the old man's stark, frozen face in astonishment.

"The king is dead!" Gervais suddenly shouted, lifting his sword and turning to the people. "Long live the king!"

Thaydor looked up at the crowd blankly.

"Long live the king!" they cried in unison at him, and to his even greater shock, they went down on one knee around him.

Thaydor shot to his feet, aghast. "No! Don't do that! I-I haven't agreed to this!"

"Sire, you heard your lord's dying wish. How can you refuse him?" Ivan countered, looking highly entertained by this turn of events.

Thaydor scowled at him, bewildered.

"The old man was wise—on occasion," Gervais said. "Who else could govern Veraidel better than the Paladin of Ilios?"

"Sir Thaydor, if I may," the innkeeper ventured with a humble bow. "Your people need you. You've rescued us so many times before. And now, this. Look at all we've been through." He gestured to the battle taking place outside the window.

His heart sank. "I-I don't know. I must seek to learn if it is…truly the will of Ilios."

"Why else would He have preserved you through all your quests if not for this?" some plump, cheeky townswoman piped up. "This has to be your destiny—Your Majesty!" She grinned to be the first to say it.

In fact, they all started grinning, and then the smiles broke out into laughter and cheering.

He was utterly nonplussed. "I, at least, need to discuss this with my wife!"

"Oh, she'll hate being queen," Ivan jested.

Thaydor shook his head in frustration. "I don't have time for this right now! First, I need to rid this city of Urmugoths, and then we can see what might be best. Knights! One of you, attend me as armor-bearer."

"Yes, sire!"

"Don't call me that," he muttered at his men as he stalked off.

"Should His Majesty really be going into battle?" the townswoman protested. "I mean, if he's the king now?"

"Try to stop me," he retorted, pausing. "And by the way, when my wife arrives from the library, tell her she's too late to save His Majesty. And tell her guards I said to keep her out of trouble until I'm done here."

"Yes, sire!" the innkeeper said, bowing again.

Thaydor gritted his teeth at the honorific and stomped out the back of the building, passing *Wanted* posters with his face on them as he went.

* * *

Jonty was dying. Jeremy might be dead, as well. Wrynne didn't know.

But while the knights and two remaining squires labored to dispatch the rest of the rocs, she concentrated on getting the fire thistle through the portal.

It was narrowing by the second.

Clamped between the branch and her staff, the fleur du mal strove mightily to infiltrate her mind. She could feel it prying into her awareness.

Ilios, the noxious thing was not just sentient. It seemed to have some form of telepathy, no doubt the better to torment the condemned souls in its native homeland.

The Infernal Plane waited.

"Careful!" one of the knights warned from behind her.

"Stay back!" she commanded. "I've almost got it…"

She raised the two sticks gingerly and thrust the fire thistle through the hole. Just as she unclamped them to cast the fleur du mal back into its hellish homeland, the hot, sulfur-laden breeze pouring out of the Infernal Plane blew a puff of thistledown loose from the seed head.

She drew in her breath in horror as all the floating bits of thistledown flew into her.

She bit back a scream and looked down at herself with a gasp. At once, she tried frantically to brush the seeds off, but their prickly fluff made them stick to her clothes, and when her hands touched them, they penetrated her skin.

She whimpered, powerless, as she watched the pieces instantly dissolve into her flesh and disappear as if they'd never been.

Panic spiraled through her. It happened so fast, she wondered if maybe she had imagined it. She didn't feel any different.

She didn't feel evil. Just scared out of her mind.

Barely a fraction of a second had passed when the portal zoomed shut with a thunderclap. Novus dropped onto his hands and knees. Berold went over to him to see if he was all right.

She looked over her shoulder and realized all the rocs were dead.

Dear, charming Jonty, however, was bleeding his guts out. Literally.

She had to save him. Pulse pounding, she swallowed hard, feeling sick with the panic of it all.

*Maybe it's all right.* She was not sure if the others had seen.

"My lady, quickly! The bard needs you!" Kai shouted.

Gathering herself, Wrynne hurried over to help Jonty, while Novus lay panting on the ground, spent.

"Stay with him," she ordered Berold, but as she ran over, she cringed as she knelt down beside her friend.

"Ow," he attempted to jest, but his beautiful voice had turned to an agonized rasp, and his face was white with suffering.

And blood loss.

"Let me see it," she whispered.

"Darling, if I let go, my guts will fall out," he ground out through the pain.

"All right, then. Stay as you are. This will only take a moment. You'll be fine soon. I promise." She touched his shoulder to comfort him, then closed her eyes.

She bowed her head, searching inside her for the Light.

Her frantic state made it rather difficult to center herself, but she took a deep breath, let it out, and waited…

Nothing happened.

She tried again, concentrating harder.

Still nothing. No Light. Not even a spark.

*No.* To her horror, a black wall of cold, dark emptiness blocked her from connecting with any sort of Light that may have lived in her before.

*No, no, Ilios, no.*

"What's wrong?" Kai asked her quickly.

"Nothing! Just wait." She tried harder. "I'm having a little…"

"Hurry, my lady! He's dying!"

"*I know!* Ilios?" she wrenched out, lifting her gaze to the empty sky. The blue of it seemed so cold, so far away.

Unreachable. Unpleasable.

Like Thaydor. Her too-perfect husband.

"Uh, Wrynne?" Jonty croaked.

"It's all right, I j-just need a moment," she vowed, but not even she believed it now. *It won't come.*

*Father, please!*

Petra drew in his breath, the first to realize. "My lady, did the fire thistle touch you?"

"Shut up and let me concentrate!" she snapped at the lad.

"Hurry, mistress! You have to heal him!" Kai insisted.

"Aye, and then heal Jeremy! If he's still alive," Petra added.

Sagard laid a firm hand on her shoulder. "My lady, answer the boy's question. Did the fire thistle touch you?"

"How dare you? Take your hands off me." She shrugged off his touch and tried once more to heal Jonty.

"Oh, Wrynne," the bard said softly, mournfully, his green eyes welling with tender understanding.

"No. I can do this." She was shaking with horror. "If they'd just stop talking!"

Kai shot to his feet and rushed off. "Wizard! Can you heal?"

Novus sat up and shook off the grogginess. "What's happened?"

"I think milady got stung. Her healing power's not working and the bard's at death's door. Come on!" Kai pulled him to his feet.

Novus looked sharply at Wrynne.

Her eyes welled with tears. "Help him. Please. I'll do anything you ask."

He scowled at her words as he strode over to her and Jonty, who had just lost consciousness. "You shouldn't make such offers to a wizard of Okteus, pet. Didn't your paladin ever teach you that?"

"Can you save him?" Sagard demanded.

"Healing's not my forte. But I think I've got something that will work…"

Shrugging his shoulders as if to loosen them after the effort he had already poured out, Novus crouched down beside Jonty and began chanting more spells from the realm of shadows, moving his outstretched hands back and forth a few inches over the bard's inert form.

Shaking, Wrynne laid her hand on Jonty's shoulder and tried to will whatever residue of healing power she still retained into him. Of all the times for her gift to fail her!

*Oh, Jonty, please, come back. I don't know what I'll do without you and all your silly jokes.*

She hadn't known him very long, but in that short time, he had become like a brother to her.

Novus's strange brand of healing magic levitated Jonty off the ground. Wrynne watched in trepidation as a cloud of churning smoke hid him. Novus spoke verses in some arcane language, and suddenly, the bard dropped out of the cloud of smoke and plopped onto the ground, coughing.

Wrynne leaned closer and looked at Jonty's stomach. There wasn't a scratch on him. Even the bloodstains had vanished. She gasped, looked at him, and laughed aloud through her tears.

The others let out exclamations of grateful relief, except for Novus, who just knelt there, eyeing Wrynne in brooding suspicion. Avoiding his gaze, she hugged her friend with all her might.

"What happened?" Jonty asked, sounding dazed.

"You scared us half to death, that's all," she said with a sniffle.

"Bloody hell." He glanced around at all the roc carcasses around him and grimaced. "I'll never eat chicken again. Not even Wrynne's magic chicken, and especially not yours, Sagard."

If her healing gift could fail her, Wrynne didn't know if she could even still work the *Feed the Hungry* spell, but she was so relieved that Jonty was all right that she cupped the bard's face between her hands and kissed him soundly on the forehead.

"There, there. I'm all right," he insisted. "You healed me."

Her laughter broke off as she realized he must have been in shock from his wounds during their exchange. She just looked at him and then at Novus, whose piercing silver eyes seemed to see right through her.

"Professor, sir," Petra ventured, "what about our friend, Jeremy?"

"What about me?" a cheerful voice replied.

Wrynne looked up. *"Jeremy?"*

"Jeremy!" his two companions cried in shock.

The formerly unconscious squire was standing there with his hands propped on his waist, curiously watching the goings-on around Jonty. "Looks like you got everything well in hand without me, then."

His astounded friends jumped up, rushed over, and embraced him, clapping him on the back and checking him over for injuries, but he seemed unscathed.

"You're alive, man!"

"We thought you were dead!"

"Nah," he scoffed with a wave of his hand. "This thick skull? Blasted bird must have knocked me out when he dropped me. Lucky, though—nice soft turf where I fell. So, what did I miss?"

He looked around at everyone with an eager grin, but nobody had the heart to answer.

The silence was grim.

Novus rose to his feet, then offered Wrynne a hand up.

She took it, but when she stood, he held her captive by her hand and searched her face for a long moment. "What happened?"

"Nothing."

His penetrating stare unnerved her. "Then why couldn't you heal?"

"How should I know? I never said I was perfect."

"Did you see how many pieces of the fire thistle hit you?"

"None of them did!" She yanked her hand out of his hold and turned away. "Now stop bothering me about it! Gods! Leave me alone! Just take me back to Thaydor. I want my husband. This company grows tiresome."

She snatched her staff from the ground and stalked off, angrily ignoring the worried looks her companions exchanged.

# Chapter 19
## Temptress

The rout was complete. Thaydor and his men had retaken the city, and those few foes that still eluded the knights were on the run. Reynulf was seeing to them.

Thaydor, flush with victory and flecked with Urm blood, strode into Lionsclaw Keep, ignoring the hails of all the people insisting he become their king. He looked askance at them as palace doors opened in succession before him.

He just wanted his wife. In every way imaginable.

He had accomplished his mission, and he wanted his reward. He'd received a message she had been brought here once Lord Eudo had been taken into custody, his bodyguards slain.

"Not now," he brushed off some dignitary who stepped toward him as he marched through the center of the great hall. Everybody in the kingdom seemed to want to talk to him or ask him questions, or even curry favor already, or set up some important meeting about one thing or another.

He simply didn't care about any of that until he laid eyes on Wrynne. He had to see her, make sure she was safe.

A foreboding feeling had been gnawing at him all day. True, he tended to worry overmuch where she was concerned, doting husband that he was, but no matter. He'd be fine once he saw she was all right. This very violent day in the heart of his home city had merely rattled his protective side.

By Ilios, he had never been happier to hear the cheer of victory go up among his men than when the last Urm in the square had fallen. They were not the brightest creatures, but even Urm mercenaries should have known that Eudo was inviting them to their doom.

With the clash over, the city secured, and the feast already being planned, couriers were currently racing to every corner of the kingdom to tell the people that King Baynard was dead and had appointed the Golden Knight as his successor.

Yes, the foremost outlaw of the kingdom had just become their ruler. What they must think of that, he could not fathom. He hoped they had never bought into all those lies about him. Otherwise, they might think *he* was the one who had carried out a coup.

Thaydor still had not officially accepted the post. To be honest, he did not know if he really had a choice, but he at least had to ask his wife if she'd mind becoming queen. Perhaps it sounded droll, but he had been around power all his life and knew it was actually a very serious commitment and a burden of duty that few in their right minds would desire.

If she didn't want this, then he wouldn't do it. He could not ask that of her. He'd serve some other way. Devise some other form of rule for the kingdom. The bards of Lyragon ruled over themselves, for example—to the extent that bards of any kind were capable of discipline, he thought with a twist of his lips.

His full armor clanking with each pounding stride, he put all the concerns of the day out of his mind, just wanting—no, needing, nay, *aching*—to take his woman in his arms and lay her down. Let her love drain him of the ferocity that still lingered in his veins.

"Where is she?" he asked when he reached the upper hallway of the residential wing.

A pair of footmen snapped to attention ahead, then bowed as they parted before one of the gilded doorways. "In here, sire."

He frowned again at the honorific as he went toward them. It was horrid enough being called a hero everywhere he went. If somebody called him *Your Majesty* again before he got to Wrynne, he reckoned he very well might punch the fellow.

"Allow me, sire," the obsequious little footman simpered.

Then the door opened before Thaydor to a sumptuous, gilt-trimmed apartment that overlooked the sweeping confluence of the rivers.

"Her Majesty chose these as your rooms, if it please you, sire. Your chambers connect." The servant pointed to a door on the wall to his left. "Shall I send your armor-bearer?"

"I'll let you know if I need any assistance. You may go."

The servant whisked out, bowing low and walking backward. He pulled the door shut behind him, and Thaydor let out a breath.

*Finally.*

"Oh, darling, I'm home," he called rather wryly as he sauntered toward her door.

"Come in!" she replied from within her chamber, but when he opened the door and saw her, his jaw nearly hit the floor.

His dainty little Wrynne leaned against the nearest post of the canopy bed, wearing a short, transparent wisp of fabric that she might as well have robbed from the dead Sana's wardrobe.

It looked *much* better on her.

His heart slammed in his chest as his gaze traveled over her. He was not a man easily tempted, but this…

Her nipples strained against the petal-pink gauze, and her long hair spilled like dark silk all around her white shoulders. A thin, jeweled belt dangled around her slim waist, the dark tuft of hair at her mound barely veiled by the tiny chemise. Her long, creamy legs were crossed at the ankles where she leaned against the bedpost.

He wanted them wrapped around him. Now. She looked taller, too, but that was because she had on intriguing heeled sandals with crisscrossed lacings that ran up to her knees.

It was by no means her usual garb, but he could not deny it all looked good on her.

Very good.

And since it *was* his darling bride, it did not raise the usual defenses in him forged from years of discipline and virtue.

"Well, well. Don't you look fetching…"

"I've been waiting for you," she purred.

He went to her without a word, and then he took her mouth. She kissed him hungrily, her tongue flavored with sweet wine. He hooked his arm around her waist, pulling her against his metal-clad body. Dazed with her beauty and his own breathless yearning, he barely remembered he was still wearing his armor gauntlets until he ran his hands down her curves and could not feel her soft, yielding flesh.

She seemed to enjoy the feel of hard metal touching her, but it quickly frustrated him.

"Help me," he panted, showing her the fastenings at his wrist. "I need to touch you. This is just cruel."

With a curve of her kiss-swollen lips, she passed a seductive gaze over his face and undid the strap, then carefully took his right gauntlet off him. He was already caressing her with his right hand as he offered her his left. She bared it, as well.

"You…look…delicious," he said as he kissed his way down her neck.

"So eager. Why don't we undress you?"

"Mmm. Let's."

But first she pulled him down with a firm grip on the back of his head and consumed his mouth in another fiery kiss.

His heart raced. He could not wait to have her.

She began taking off the pieces of his armor one by one. She knew how. She had done it before. The time she had saved his life.

Engrossed in watching her, he waited as patiently as possible, already hard for her and so very needy.

"Did you win, then?" she whispered, nibbling his ear as she unbuckled the hidden straps around his shoulder.

"Of course I won," he answered.

"Good boy. Sit."

"What, am I a dog now?" he jested softly, but he obeyed anyway.

"You're my dog," she said wickedly. "Would you like a bone?"

"I have one for you," he countered.

She giggled. "Thaydor Clarenbeld, did you just make a dirty joke?" She flicked the tip of her tongue playfully against his cheek. "That's a first."

He grinned, enchanted. Then he got to work helping her remove the many pieces of his armor. "Did you hear they want me to be king?" he inquired as he waited.

"I did."

He watched her face for her reaction. "What do you think?"

She shrugged. "Seems obvious to me. Who else is going to do it?"

He arched a brow. "You don't seem very surprised."

"No, the oracle told me of this weeks ago."

"What?" He looked at her in astonishment as she lifted away his breastplate. "You didn't tell me!"

She laughed idly. "I don't tell you everything. What fun would that be?"

"Oh, you're keeping secrets from me?" he scolded, pulling her down onto his lap. "I won't have that."

"I wasn't *allowed* to tell you. Come, how can you be so surprised? Of course you are the king. You were obviously born for this."

"I doubt that."

"Well, I don't." She leaned her head against his shoulder and toyed with his chest. "Think of all the great things you'll do. Things Baynard never would've dared. You'll be the greatest ruler Veraidel has ever had. You...with your skill. And your courage. And with how the people love you. Almost as much as I do."

She changed positions from sitting draped across his lap to straddling him, and though she smiled at him, there was something strange in her gray eyes.

He searched her gaze. "So you don't mind, then?"

"Mind?" She laughed at him. "Husband, you could take over the world. And I'll help. But for now, you're all mine."

Then she dragged the coat of chain mail off over his head. It fell to the floor with a jangle. She opened his gambeson and ran her hands down his sweaty bare chest.

He tilted his head back, savoring her touch. It made the whole savage day worth it to feel her hands on him.

She leaned closer. "Why don't you show me that big, hard lance of yours, paladin?" she whispered, nibbling at his ear.

"You naughty girl. Don't you want me to bathe first?"

"No. I like you dirty and smelling like a man," she growled in his ear. "I want your scent all over me."

"I have some blood on me."

"I don't care. I married a warrior. You kill so well. No one can defeat you. It's one of things I find most incredibly...seductive about you, my love."

"Seductive? Me?" he asked wryly.

"Oh, very. We can bathe together after. I need you now. I've been wanting you all day."

"Well, then, let's not keep my luscious queen waiting."

She slid back a bit on his lap and hurried to untie his braies.

"I think I like you like this," he confessed.

She leaned to kiss him and laughed against his mouth. "You like me every way."

He caught her by her waist and looked into her eyes. "No, Wrynne. I love you," he whispered. "I'd do anything for you. Do you know that?"

"I know." She set her feet on the floor and stood astraddle him, offering her nipples. Intoxicated, he took hold of the wispy garment clinging to her and parted the deep V-neck of it, kissing her silken chest.

He caressed the curve of her low back. She arched it and moaned, moving against him as he sucked on each swollen, pink crest, feeling it harden in his mouth. She ran her fingers through his hair.

Thaydor forgot all about the battles of the day, swept up in his desire for her. Freeing his cock with one hand, he drew her to him. She stroked him only briefly before he had to take her, and then she lowered herself slowly onto his massive erection.

"Oh, that's so good," she breathed, quivering in the most bewitching fashion. "Thaydor."

She licked her lips as she sank onto his lap, finally taking him all in. He was impressed. Large as he was, she wasn't always able to do that in this position. But now…

He shuddered at the pleasure of her hot, drenched passage giving him such a lavish hero's welcome. They enjoyed their joining in stillness for a moment. He paused to tear off his gambeson and get rid of his shirt. She trailed her fingers over the planes of his shoulders and down his biceps, then she kissed him fiercely, her tongue delving into his mouth, her hand clutching the back of his hair.

*Sweet Ilios.* He knew she was a passionate woman, but today she was on fire. He clutched her soft backside in his hands and lifted her gently up and down, helping her ride him. She was breathless, sweaty.

Staring into his eyes with glittering need, she was so hot for him that he suspected her supple, young body was in season. Which only made him harder.

He feasted on her neck with his kisses and got a little naughty with her, slipping the tip of his middle finger into a hole he'd never played with before. She liked it. He knew by the breathy little gasp that escaped her. Then she bit down on her lower lip. He brought her to climax a few minutes later, but to his surprise, the lady was not yet satisfied.

"More," she panted.

His senses blurred with desire. He was surprised but pleased by the invitation as she crawled off his lap and slid to the carpeted floor beneath them. Moving onto all fours, she sent him an utterly wanton look over her shoulder, licking her lips, and arching her back to entice him.

Thaydor needed no encouragement. The rest of the world had disappeared. Heart pounding, he abandoned the chair for the rosy lure of those smooth, rounded cheeks. He could not resist.

Kneeling behind her, he reached between her parted legs and smeared his trembling fingers into the teeming heat of her passage. Then he replaced his fingers with his cock and pressed into her, holding her hips.

She groaned, quivering and tightening around him anew. Thaydor closed his eyes and lost himself in taking her. He wrapped a length of her silky hair around his fist like horse's reins and rode her into a lather. With his free hand splayed across her hip, he gripped her in place so she could not escape him even if she wanted to.

"Oh, yes. Harder!" she wrenched out.

He rammed her with all he had, no longer able to carry the worry of hurting her. There was so much need in him, raw and hot and wild. So much more than he ever wanted to confess. But she could fill it. She always had. Only Wrynne. Only his darling.

She screamed out with pleasure rather quickly, but he continued without pausing. *So close.* He gritted his teeth. *Don't make me stop*, he pleaded mentally. "You asked for it."

"Come for me." She reached back to clutch his hip and show him it was all right, that her body was his plaything.

In a trance of throbbing lust, Thaydor permitted her a momentary respite, but only so that he could turn her to face him. He pushed her onto her back on the carpet.

Towering over her on his knees, he mounted her right there on the floor and continued her ravishment in near-mad hunger.

"Yes. Don't stop," she said fiercely. He was amazed. She just kept eating up whatever he gave her.

She clasped him between her thighs, gripped his buttocks, and hooked her dainty ankles behind his knees as if she couldn't get enough. Indeed, his every thrust only seemed to inflame her desire the more. Then he was undone. Unable to hold back a second longer, he clutched her to him with a stark groan of ecstasy, and even as convulsions of release racked him, his seed coursing deep into her body, he claimed her mouth, plunging into her with his tongue and his cock, until he was utterly spent, shaking all over.

"Oh, Thaydor," she groaned, holding him.

He panted, having lost the power of speech.

"No, don't take it out. Stay inside me." She caressed his legs with her own while her hands ran dreamily up and down his bare back.

He could feel her heart pounding in her chest, smashed against his.

"That was good," he rumbled in an almost drunken tone.

"Yes," she purred, "let's do it again."

He laughed softly. "Right."

"I'm not jesting." She twirled her fingers in his hair. "I'm not done with you yet." She kissed him and lifted her hips as she whispered feverishly against his skin, "Come on, Thaydor, keep that big, delicious prick hard for me."

"At least give me a minute, all right?" He winced and laughed, a bit confused. "What's got into you? And since when do you use such language?"

She shrugged. "Well, it's true. It *is* big. And delicious."

He winced as her movements had the desired effect. "I only meant it's not very ladylike."

"Did you really want a lady this afternoon?" she whispered, squeezing his nipple.

He moaned, forced to concede she had a point. But when she giggled knowingly and gave him a love bite on his shoulder, he furrowed his brow and pushed her back just a little, so he could look into her eyes. "Don't take it amiss, sweet, but have you been in here drinking all day?"

"Not all day! Why? Do you want some, too? There's another bottle in the cabinet."

Before he could answer, a loud knock at the door made them both look over from their spot, still entwined on the floor.

"Beg your pardon for the interruption, sire, but there is a wizard here who says he simply must speak to you!" the servant called, sounding rather frantic. "That Your Majesty might be in danger."

"What?" Thaydor asked wearily.

"Please forgive me, sire, but he says it's very urgent!" the man added.

Wrynne let out a throaty laugh. "I'll bet."

"Er, he also says he'll break the door down by magic if Your Majesty will not come out and hear his news!"

"Oh, really?" He looked at Wrynne. "Well, that rather killed the mood, didn't it?" he muttered as he sat up.

"Not for all of us." She giggled and closed her eyes, still lying on the floor. When he withdrew, she ran her hand down her body as though tempted to please herself if he did not hurry to indulge her again.

His male instincts were instantly aroused by her wicked playfulness in spite of himself. "Ilios, what's got into you today?" He grabbed her hand to stop her and kissed it. "You'd better wait for me, you insatiable little beast."

"You promise?"

He heaved himself to his feet and refastened his chausses again as he went to the door. "What is the meaning of this intrusion? I don't like being threatened," he said upon opening the door, "and I do not speak to sorcerers."

"You will this one," Jonty said sternly, waiting for him in the hallway, much to Thaydor's surprise.

The bard was there with some rather sinister-looking fellow with long black hair.

"Where's Wrynne?" Jonty demanded.

"She's in here." Thaydor could not help grinning. "She's a bit busy at the moment."

His two visitors exchanged a guarded glance as Thaydor stepped out and pulled the door shut behind him. He did not fancy them seeing his wife in her current, odd state, let alone dressed like his own little harlot of Fonja.

Come to think of it, perhaps he was fortunate to escape the bedchamber for a few minutes before the lovely little wanton decided to eat him alive.

He took a step forward into the hallway to avoid her overhearing their discussion. She'd already been through enough for one day.

Jonty spoke first. "Look, I know how you probably feel about practitioners of the dark arts, but this is Novus Blacktwist. He teaches at the Wizard's Spire. You can trust him."

"I'll be the judge of that." He flicked a glance up and down the sorcerer's person, wondering if he'd need his sword.

"He saved my life today," Jonty said firmly. "And more to the point, he's got an important message for you. About Wrynne."

The bard suddenly had his full attention.

"What about her?"

Jonty looked expectantly at the servants.

"Go," Thaydor commanded, and they scurried away.

When they were out of earshot, the Highlander lowered his gaze, searching for the words, as though even his silver tongue failed him at what he had to say.

"What?" Thaydor demanded.

"You say you were just with her. Did she seem at all...strange to you?" Jonty asked with great delicacy.

Thaydor stared at Jonty with an unsettled feeling. "Maybe a little.

Why?"

"Turns out she was right about Lord Eudo's strange insignia. It was a fleur du mal called fire thistle—that plant she saw up at Silvermount."

"The thing she wanted to look up in the library?"

Jonty nodded. "Yes, and she was right. It *was* the cause of Eudo's corruption."

"How's that? Was it poisonous?"

"Worse." Jonty gazed at him wistfully. "Evil is such a strange force, Thaydor. Sometimes it's just a small thing, some petty, personal failing. But there is another kind—pure evil."

"Tell me about it," he said with a snort. "I've been fighting it my whole life." He looked from one man to the other in deepening confusion. "But I know you didn't come here to philosophize with me. So somebody tell me what the hell is going on."

"We believe you are in danger," the newcomer informed him, echoing the servant's earlier claim.

"Another day, another foe that wants to kill me." He let out a cynical sigh. "Who is it now? King of Aisedor? Or the leader of the Urms? Tell 'em to get in line."

"No, Thaydor. This time it's Wrynne," said Jonty.

Thaydor stared at him, then frowned and turned back to the door. "Right. If you'll excuse me."

"This is no jest," the sorcerer informed him.

"We think the fire thistle might have stung her today when we went to Silvermount."

"Wait. You took my wife back to Silvermount?" he exclaimed, pivoting. "What about the rocs?"

"They're all dead," Jonty hastily assured him. "Unfortunately, that was not the greatest danger on the premises."

"What did your wife tell you about today?" the sorcerer pursued.

Thaydor looked at them blankly. "Nothing. I only walked in about an hour ago. And we weren't really…talking."

"Oh, perfect," Jonty muttered to his companion. "You see what this means?"

"It's already using her to try to get control of him." Novus shook his head. "Especially now that he's king."

"She didn't by chance try to kill you in there, did she?" Jonty asked, seeming to holding his breath.

Thaydor looked from one to the other, bewildered. "Have you two lost your bloody minds?"

Just then, Reynulf came marching into the corridor.

"Oh, good, Thaydor, there you are. What do you want me to do with Eudo? Do we bother with a trial or can I just kill him?"

"Not right now," he said, waving him off.

Suddenly, the chamber door opened behind him, and there stood Wrynne, dressed just as he had left her. Which was to say, barely dressed at all.

Indeed, she looked like the very embodiment of sex.

Skin flushed, lips swollen, hair tousled, and every curve of her magnificent body on full display, she leaned in the doorway as the other three men gaped at her for a heartbeat and then swiftly averted their eyes.

As well they might, if they valued their lives.

Thaydor stared seethingly at them, making sure none was peeking, then he turned to her. "What are you doing out here? Did you need something?"

"Oh yes." A radiant smile broke out across her face, but she stared right past him. "Reynulf!" she purred, running a feverish gaze over the man who had once given her nightmares. "Bloodletter, such a bad boy," she teased, twirling her hair, then she bit her lower lip. "Are you busy right now?"

Thaydor's jaw dropped.

# Chapter 20
# Poison

"*Rrright*." Reynulf looked around uncomfortably at the others. "Is she drunk?"

"No," Jonty said, while Thaydor moved angrily to the doorway, looming over her.

"How dare you?" he thundered at her, red-faced. "Get in the room, *now!*"

"Easy, man!" the bard warned, launching over between the two of them, as though he feared Thaydor might do her some act of violence. "This isn't her fault!"

"Get out of my way." Wrynne pouted, trying to peer past them. "I want to see Reynulf."

"Leaving." The red knight lifted his hands in surrender and backed away, looking bewildered.

"Oh, don't go! Mmm." She ogled Reynulf's rear end from under Jonty's arm as he retreated.

Reynulf shot her a look of incredulity over his shoulder, then shook his head and strode away.

Thaydor never took his eyes off her. "Why is my wife acting like a harlot?" he asked through gritted teeth.

"That's what we're here to explain, and why we've spent the past *hour* trying to get a meeting with you. They wouldn't let us see you!"

He glared at the bard. "You have my attention. Now, talk."

"The simplest way to put it is that she's sort of, well…possessed."

"I just had the best sex of my life with a *possessed* woman?" he shouted in astonishment.

She laughed gaily. "It was good, wasn't it? But I'm only getting started. Come on, boys, who's next? Thaydor couldn't satisfy me. But I'll bet one of you can. Or both of you."

"Why, you little—"

"Not her fault!" the bard insisted again.

"Jonty! My darling," she moaned, turning her dewy-eyed attentions to the Highlander, slipping her arms around his waist.

Right in front of Thaydor.

"Won't you sing for me, Jonty?" she asked, her lips skimming the bard's earlobe. "Your voice *melts* me."

"Stop that before you get me killed!" he scolded, his cheeks reddening as he slipped out of her grasp and backed away. "Wrynne, you're not helping yourself here. You've got to fight this."

"Fight what?" she asked prettily. "Oh, hullo, Novus."

"Don't look at her!" Thaydor barked.

"We're not!" Jonty cried. "I'm sorry, dear, but this is for your own good." With a scowl, he shoved her none too gently back into her chamber, pulled the door closed, and held it shut while she protested, pounding on it.

"Let me out! You can't make me a prisoner! Oh, please. All of you are so boring!"

*Possessed?* Thaydor walked away, stunned, utterly confused, and pretty well humiliated, too. He looked at them in shock. "What the hell happened to my wife?"

Novus took over the task of holding the door shut so that Jonty could go over to him and attempt to explain.

"She's under the influence of a very dark magic right now. The venom of the fire thistle turns a person wicked. The more time that passes, a perfectly nice person can begin turning into a very devil."

"Or a whore?" Thaydor asked coldly, angry at himself for allowing her to sway him where all the Fonjan harlots had failed—and even worse, for enjoying it so much.

He should have known.

Jonty looked pained by his bitter question but forged on. "According to our research, the more innocent the victim, the less immunity he or she has to something like this. In such hosts, it takes hold all the faster and has a more powerful effect. Listen, we don't have much time."

"Fine. We'll get the Golden Master to perform an exorcism—"

"That's not going to do the trick! Thaydor, listen to me. I know you feel betrayed right now, but it's not her fault. I'm afraid your wife's condition is very serious."

"Ahem, if I may." Novus used a spell to lock the door and joined them over by the window at the end of the hallway.

"By all means," the bard muttered, gesturing to him to take over the explanations, and looking rather at his wit's end with Thaydor's hardheadedness.

As Novus turned to him, Thaydor eyed the exotic-looking stranger skeptically, unsure if he trusted him.

Novus returned his gaze with equal wariness.

To be sure, there was no love lost between the followers of Ilios and Okteus. On the other hand, Thaydor did not sense a particular aura of evil around him.

"Blame me if it helps," Novus said, addressing him as though he were still simply paladin and not king.

It came as a relief.

"I took the group of them to Silvermount," he continued. "I needed their assistance to send the fire thistle back to the Infernal Plane so that no one else might become infected."

"But someone did," Thaydor said coldly, quietly.

"Your lady insisted on coming despite your men's protests, because she alone knew where the firechoke was."

He clenched his jaw. It certainly sounded like Wrynne, launching herself into the thick of the danger.

"We had her well protected," Jonty said in dismay. "All her guards were around her, as were Novus and I. Then Novus opened the portal to the Infernal Plane, as planned, and I was to have cast the fire thistle through it. But the rocs attacked, and Wrynne suggested I use my music to calm them, which I agreed to because I was afraid the three lads would die."

He looked away as another wave of anger washed through him. "So, they were with you, too?"

"They did well, Thaydor! The point is, Wrynne ended up with the job of throwing the fire thistle into the portal. Handled carefully, it didn't seem that dangerous. Especially for someone who's an expert on plants. And don't blame Novus, despite what he says. He was in a trance with the effort to hold the portal open and stop any demons from coming through. Nobody saw exactly what happened, but we soon suspected she got stung. Novus asked her flat out and she denied it. Lied to his face."

"Tell me she wasn't acting like this with all of you earlier today?" he asked in a strangled tone.

"No, no, this is new," Jonty said grimly, glancing over at the door, where she still knocked and scratched and begged to get out, occasionally calling them all bastards for locking her in.

His little Wrynne, cursing like a fishwife!

"What made us suspect she'd been infected was when I got wounded up at Silvermount," Jonty said with a flicker of horror passing behind his green eyes at the memory. "Wrynne tried to heal me but couldn't. Her ability was gone."

"What?" he breathed.

"Novus had to do it. And then she lied about that, too," Jonty added.

"And now this," Novus said. "As you can see, it's escalating quickly. Taking hold. Very soon, she'll be out of control. You need to be careful around her. Because just as the fire thistle made Lord Eudo target you, it will likely cause your wife to do the same."

"That's impossible. She loves me."

"But the evil that's taking over in her *hates* good, Thaydor," the bard warned, shaking his head in regret. "You're known for being, well, rather ridiculously good. Ergo, it hates *you*. Weren't you the first one the Silver Sage marked for death?"

"Because I spoke out against him and his influence over the king."

"Of course you did. You make my point for me."

Thaydor heaved a frustrated sigh, his mind spinning. "Well, it sure didn't seem like she hated me in there."

"Oh really?" the bard countered. "She wasn't using you? Wasn't manipulating you?"

"He's obviously not used to being treated the way the rest of us are by females," the sorcerer muttered.

The bard snorted in cynical agreement. "You need to be on your guard around her," Jonty repeated.

"I don't believe this."

"Thaydor, right now, Wrynne is turning dark. You must be prepared to expect treachery from her until we figure out how to save her. Just remember, what you're seeing isn't really her. This isn't her fault. You mustn't hold this against her."

Folding his arms across his chest, he was silent for a moment, staring at the floor. "So what do we do? How do we cure her?"

Novus and Jonty exchanged a grim glance.

"What?"

"There is no known cure," Jonty forced out.

Thaydor turned white. "Then find one! Make one!"

"I wouldn't know where to begin," Novus said. "This thing is very rare. It is said that even on the Infernal Plane, these plants only bloom every hundred years. The chance of one escaping Hell is miniscule. There haven't been enough cases for study, and in the few that have been found, the patient ultimately—" He stopped abruptly.

"What?" Thaydor demanded.

"Dies." Novus's quicksilver eyes were difficult to read. "The poison of the fleur du mal kills the spirit first and, later on, the body."

*Ilios.* Thaydor turned away, feeling as though he'd been struck in the gut, and spent a moment trying to gather himself.

"Very well," he said with difficulty at last. "You have the first case available now. Experiment on Eudo if you must. But you have to save my wife. I order it. As your king."

His innards felt like cold porridge as he faced the reality of the task set before him. He had been hesitant about taking the reins of power, but this changed things. To save Wrynne…

*Very well.*

"Spare no expense. You have the resources of Veraidel at your disposal. Just name it. Heal her." Thaydor looked from one to the other, sickened by the thought of how many people Wrynne had healed, including him, but now that she was the one dying, they dared say there was no cure?

"If you succeed, you shall have whatever you want as your reward. But if you fail," he said to Novus, "I promise you, there will be hell to pay."

"Thaydor, don't threaten the man!"

"It's all right," Novus mumbled to the bard.

"And you!" Thaydor turned on Jonty. "How could you let this happen to her? Never mind the idiot knights, I told *you* specifically to protect her!"

The sorcerer came to Jonty's defense. "It was a little difficult for him when the rocs ripped his guts out and nearly started eating them—sire."

Taken off guard, Thaydor fell silent.

Jonty looked away.

Thaydor dropped his gaze and strove to get his rage under control. There was no need to take it out on them. "I'm sorry," he finally managed in an awkward tone. "I'm sure you did your best. It's been a very trying day."

"No, you're right. It *is* my fault," Jonty mumbled, head down, and obviously distraught. "I should have found a way. It should've been me it happened to. You told me to protect her and I failed."

"We all failed," Thaydor said. "I should have never let her out of the Eldenhold. But it's just, when she asks me for anything…I can't say no."

"Even if you had, do you really think she would've stayed put?" Jonty asked, and they both knew the answer to that.

Not that the realization helped.

"She is to be my queen." Thaydor swallowed hard and tried to check his rising wrath, to little effect. "I need her by my side. If I lose Wrynne, I don't give one damn what happens to this kingdom or anyone else in it. Do you understand me?"

"Perfectly," Novus replied, looking quite tranquil. "That's probably what the evil in her had in mind all along."

Thaydor looked at him in angry surprise.

"Destroying her destroys you. Two birds, one stone."

"No, a whole flock, actually," the bard said.

"What do you mean?" Thaydor countered.

Jonty shrugged. "Say you refuse to take the kingship because of what's happened to her. Chaos ensues. Rival warlords take to the battlefield to vie for power. Of course, they'd probably have to hunt you down and kill you, just to be sure you didn't change your mind and try to come back."

"So?" Thaydor replied darkly. "Without her, I don't care if I live or die."

"Well, Reynulf would probably come out the winner in a struggle of this magnitude. Sorry," Jonty said, "but he'd make a terrifying king."

"Of course, if you were dead," Novus said, "the Lady Wrynne herself could claim the crown, as your wife. What then? Are we to be ruled by a madwoman?"

"Perhaps Wrynne and Reynulf would reign together," Jonty persisted. "Bloodletter and the Mad Queen, now there's a match—"

"Enough!" Thaydor wrenched out, even though he saw what the two were doing, trying to goad him into doing what the world asked of him.

The bard shrugged. "That, my friend, is what happens if you choose now, of all times, to walk away from your duty."

"You've made your bloody point," Thaydor grumbled, closing his eyes for a moment to steady himself.

He could hear her scratching at the door and wheedling him to unlock it. It sounded like she was crying. "Why are you doing this to me, Thaydor? Why are you being so cruel? Don't you love me anymore?"

He flinched at the question and finally nodded at the men. "Very well. Do whatever it takes. Anything you need to help you find this cure, you have only to name it."

Novus inclined his head in a token bow. "I'll go get started."

"Bring me any word of your progress."

"Wait, what about Wrynne?" Jonty interrupted. "What are we going to do with her in the meantime? When we make her better—and we will—she'll be horrified at how she acted. She needs to be protected. From herself. And from others who might take advantage of her, er, peculiar state."

Thaydor blazed with sudden rage at the thought of any man daring to accept one of the little maniac's lustful invitations. But again, he checked his urge to smash cities at the thought.

"You're right," he said with grim, forced calm. "I will not let my queen become an object of mockery. If it's evil at the root of her…disease, then we should transfer her to holy ground, where the Light can help protect her."

He nodded to himself as the answer came clear. "I want her taken to the Bastion and watched around the clock by the nuns and clerics there. Tell them I want prayers and orisons said for her continuously until she's healed. Can you go with her?" he asked Jonty. "I'm needed here. Perhaps your music will help the sisters keep her calm."

"Certainly. Whatever you want me to do."

"If she tries to tempt you, Jonty—"

"Please. I do have one stray moral here and there." He glanced at Novus, who was still waiting to see if there was anything else.

"I'll be on my way, then," the sorcerer said.

"Novus," Thaydor called after him.

He glanced back in question.

"Thank you," Thaydor said.

The longhaired sorcerer gave a curt nod and then strode off, his black cloak flowing out behind him.

* * *

A while later, having quickly bathed and dressed, and having made the arrangements for Wrynne's safety, Thaydor approached her chamber again and braced himself. Behind the door, he could hear her raging at the servants who had been given the task of dressing her and packing her traveling trunks.

The poison was taking hold of her quickly.

"Take your hands off me, you swine! Who do you think you are? Don't you know I am your queen? I demand to see my husband! Where is that pompous lout?"

"Right here, darling," Thaydor said in an agreeable tone, stepping into the room before she started pulling clumps of the servants' hair out.

Or her own.

"Don't you look pretty," he said softly, which was true, except for the wild, harsh glitter in her eyes.

"I don't want to go. Why are you forcing me to leave? Are you casting me aside so quickly? You think I don't see what's going on?" She pushed her way past the servants, striding toward him. "I helped you gain power and now you're done with me. Is that it?"

"Well, your propositioning Reynulf right in front of me could have a little something to do with it," he said with a taut smile, though he knew he probably shouldn't bring it up.

She let out an unpleasant laugh. "So possessive! How dull. Don't you know only insecure men bother getting jealous? Is that what you are in your armor, Thaydor? Just a big, empty shell?"

The servants gasped with horror at her words, but Thaydor merely dropped his gaze, stung. *Wonderful.* She was already moving from being lust crazed to plain nasty. *It's not her fault,* he repeated to himself, but truly, it seemed his commitment to Ilian virtue would be tested.

He smiled gently and drew her into his arms. "Come here, my love." He embraced her, ignoring her struggles. He caressed her hair and whispered "hush" as she tried to shove him away.

She quieted for a moment, leaning against him as though exhausted.

"I'm sorry I couldn't protect you today at Silvermount," he whispered as he stroked her head and her back in fierce protectiveness. "I wish you would've waited for me. I never wanted you to put yourself at risk, but I know that you probably did it for my sake."

For a fleeting moment, she was her old self again and clung to his waist, her cheek pressed against his chest. "Help me, Thaydor. My head's all a tangle. I don't know who to trust. I'm scared."

"I know, sweeting. But it's going to be all right. I'm going to save you. We're going to find a cure for this, I promise. Whatever it takes," he finished in a choked whisper.

Holding her tenderly, he closed his eyes, sent a desperate prayer up to heaven, then kissed her on the head. "Come back to me soon. You must go to the Bastion for a while. I want you to cooperate with your doctors."

"You're driving me away," she wrenched out, pulling free of his hold. "You don't love me anymore."

"I love you. And because I do, I'm sending you somewhere you'll be taken care of properly. You like the Bastion," he reminded her. "It's very beautiful there, remember? The gardens?"

"No, that's not it." She shook her head and backed away from him as the shadow reclaimed her. "You want me gone. You're cheating on me, aren't you? Of course you are. Everybody wants you. The great paladin! Well, I don't care if you're the king. You're mine. Do you understand me? You touch another woman and I'll kill you in your sleep."

*Damn,* thought Thaydor, but he kept his expression impervious. "There is no other woman, Wrynne," he promised. "There is only you. Forever."

The words were the last he could manage with the lump in his throat, seeing the unnatural hatred of him gathering in her eyes.

He nodded in farewell, then turned around and walked back to the door that opened onto the corridor.

To his astonishment, a vase smashed near his head against the lintel as he reached for the latch.

"What was that for?" he exclaimed, glancing back at her.

She flung a sneering laugh in his direction. "Oops."

He clenched his jaw, refusing to be baited. "You're charming when you're possessed. Be as evil as you please. I still love you."

She hissed at his answer like a feral cat with very sharp claws.

He stepped out while her servants scurried back into her chamber, but his taut smile faded as soon as he pulled the door shut. In the corridor outside her room, a world of work and duty awaited him. He shut his eyes, more shaken than he had let on.

Indeed, he was nearly queasy over what had befallen his precious bride. His best ally. His one indispensable friend. Pain and utter dread pulsed through him. *Please, I can't lose her...*

Somehow he steeled himself. When he flicked his eyes open, they gleamed with a hard light. For he knew then that if his prayers went unanswered, if he did *not* get her back, the world might yet discover that the Golden Knight had a dark side, after all. If evil wished to turn his wife into a Fonjan harlot, then why should he not likewise unleash the war god within himself?

He would make the entire world pay.

* * *

*Bastard...*

About a week had passed, but Wrynne lost count of the days. She had heard her caretakers saying her condition was worsening faster than expected.

Well, perhaps they would not have been surprised if they could have spent one second in her skin. Agonized confusion had become her normal state. She couldn't stop thinking about Thaydor. Her love for him was becoming a cold, gnawing obsession.

It was strange how quickly love could turn to hate, like a flower tossed carelessly along on an ill wind. The warmth of their love felt like another lifetime.

Somebody else's. She felt cast aside, used up and rejected.

*Well, you were never good enough for the paladin in the first place,* her fears whispered. Really, what had she expected? For Thaydor Clarenbeld to content himself with *her*? A mere merchant's daughter? Her own sister had barely believed it. He was, after all, the son of an earl, a national hero—and now the king.

He could do a *lot* better than her on his worst day. No wonder he had locked her up here so he could go and find himself a proper queen...

Such were the fears tormenting her at every hour of the day. She tried to put him out of her mind like the doctors had told her to, but thoughts of him kept creeping back in, the snake. Continually, she wrestled with herself over what she would do to him if he were in the room. Have her way with him again because he was *so* good, and then run him through?

The fool would probably *let* her kill him. She plotted his death in various ways even though he was king. Succeeding would cost her her life, but if they hanged her or sent her to the executioner...

*Ha! So what?* she thought in black humor. Life was nothing but a stupid game, anyway. She hated it, she hated him, she hated everyone—herself most of all.

Still, she tried to keep herself amused as best she could throughout the day.

*Whack!*

She slapped her scroll of Jonty's rolled-up music sheets down hard on the table, but Silvertwig flew out of reach again with a little shriek.

The bard sighed. "Wrynne, stop trying to splat the fairy."

"Mind your own business. The little pest is bothering me. Why won't it go away?"

"Silvertwig is your friend," he said, sweetly strumming his mandolin.

"It's not her fault, Silvertwig," Jonty reminded the tiny, silver-winged fairy, who now crouched in the rafters with a wounded gaze and watched Wrynne pace back and forth restlessly across her sun-filled chamber.

Her *jail* was more like it.

"I don't understand this. Why can't I leave? Why is everyone treating me like a rabid dog? Don't they know I happen to be the rightful Queen of Veraidel? Why the hell won't anyone listen to me?"

"You're not yourself," he said gently as his clever fingers skipped up and down the neck of the instrument. "But Novus is working on a cure. We must be patient, love."

"You do love me, don't you, Jonty? You're the only one who hasn't abandoned me." She stopped pacing and gazed out at the window, where the monks were tending their hops vines in the warm, golden light of afternoon. The murmur that escaped her was bitter. "I used to cure people."

"Yes," Jonty said encouragingly. "Tell me about that. All the people you used to help…"

"I cured Thaydor once. And this is how he repays me," she uttered bitterly, staring out the window. "Putting me in jail." She whirled around. "I got *you* out of jail, and all you do is sit there and play that blasted—thing! Would you stop and do something useful? You're driving me mad!"

"It's not me making you mad, Wrynne, it's the firechoke venom. But I'll stop if you wish." He put his instrument aside, rose, and walked over to her, laying his hands on her shoulders. "Thaydor loves you, lass. That's why he had you put here where you'll be safe. Try to understand."

"But it's so boring." She pouted, gathering a handful of his shirt and pulling him closer. "I know a way you and I could pass the afternoon. Come on, bard. It'll be fun. Take my pain away, my wild poet," she whispered, pressing herself against him. "I'll bet you're a wonderful lover."

"Aye, that goes without sayin'." He pried her away with a frown. "But you belong to Thaydor, who is my friend and also happens to be king."

"Don't mention him to me! I despise him!" she hissed.

"No, you don't. You adore him as much as he adores you. Me, I've written many a love song, Wrynne, but I'll never know the kind of true love you two have. Yours is a match made in heaven—literally." He tapped her on the nose. "You must hold on to that somewhere in your heart, where you're still *you*. The man needs ye, lass. Now more than ever."

"I don't care what he needs. Stupid Clank!" she scoffed, though she ached at the memory of his face. "The great hypocrite. He probably spends all day at Fonja now!"

"Ach, don't tell yourself these lies. He's always faithful to you. Even now."

"Of course you'd say that. You work for him now, don't you? That means you'd lie for him, too. Why are you all against me?" she wailed.

He looked at her for a moment, then shook his head. "Let's try something else." He changed instruments, tuned a string, and then sang to her as he played. The lyrics seemed oddly familiar:

> "When the nightingale sings,
> The woods waxen green,
> Leaf and grass and blossom springs,
> In April, to be sure;
> But love is to my heart gone
> With one spear so keen,
> Night and day my blood it drinks,
> Until my soul cannot endure…"

Wrynne felt herself pale, remembering where she had heard them before. She suddenly burst into tears.

Jonty kept playing, singing the next verse. After all, her falling into hysterics was nothing new. But this time was different. Thaydor and his little poetry book...

She remembered him reading these very words to her in their brief time at her woodland bower. The memory of discovering his sweetness, discovering love for the first time, made her cry harder. She withered onto her bed and drew her knees up, curling into a ball. It was as though her very heart shattered.

"Help me. I'm losing myself, Jonty. It won't stop," she sobbed. "Everything's all jumbled up inside. I don't know where I am. It hurts. I want my husband. Where is Thaydor?"

He didn't answer, because *he* knew that *she* knew exactly where Thaydor was, and had only asked the question out of her madness. She clutched her head. *What is happening to me?* She used to be so calm even in a crisis, but now she could not control her wild moods, could not stop weeping. *I'm disintegrating.*

*Ilios!*

But if the god she had been so sure of all her life answered now, his words could not get through the black walls that had imprisoned her within herself, like a maiden trapped in a tower.

Silvertwig flew down cautiously and stood across from her in somber concern, but Wrynne was alone in the dark. As she lay curled up sobbing on the bed, bewildered and utterly in pain, Jonty played on, as though, in his wisdom, the bard knew his music was the only medicine they had right now for her.

No matter how much it hurt to take it.

Aye, the song brought back exquisite memories so sweet they made her want to die. Something about floating over a winding brook on her Aladdin stretcher with the blue-eyed man who had taught her the meaning of love.

"Where is he?" she asked, dragging her tear-filled eyes open to gaze in agony at her friend. "I need him. I need him. Tell him to come to me. I'll die if he won't see me."

"Do you promise you won't try to kill him?" Jonty asked softly. "Because we need him, too, Wrynne. He is our king now. We must protect him. People who get what you have usually try to kill Thaydor."

"Oh." The reminder came like a punch in the gut.

But she remembered Lord Eudo and King Baynard and how they had set Thaydor up to die, and in the fading ray of light that Jonty's song had allowed into her darkened mind, she nodded desperately. "Of course. You're right. Keep him away from me. I love him so much, Jonty.

Keep him safe. Don't let him near me." Her fists clenched. "I want to hurt him."

"I think that's enough music for now." He put his lute aside and stood, walking over to offer her a handkerchief. "Dry your eyes, love."

She rolled onto her back and gazed at the ceiling in despair. "Jonty, I don't want to be the Mad Queen."

"I know. Don't worry. You'll be better soon." Gazing down at her, he offered a hand up, but she just lay there, too depressed to move.

"Hmm." He and Silvertwig exchanged a worried glance. "Why don't we see if they'll let you walk in the garden a bit? That used to make you happy. I'll bet it still would."

"Can I?" She sat up with a sniffle and looked at him hopefully. "My hands in the dirt...but I suppose that's not very queenly."

"At this point, who cares?" he mumbled. "Silvertwig." He pointed to the rafters.

The fairy flew to safety while Jonty left Wrynne briefly unsupervised, stepping out of her chamber to check with Brother Piero and Mother Superior to see if she was permitted to go outside.

*Perhaps they'll put me on a leash.* But she made an effort to dry her tears and thought about gardens, struggling to remember what bloomed this month and how many average inches of rain there would be.

When they finally took her out, there was no leash, but she was well guarded on all sides. Like a mad queen should be. She knelt in her velvet gown in the dirt and focused on picking dead leaves off the flourishing plants.

It was surprising how much better it made her feel. She mumbled the ancient *Prayer of the Nine Herbs* for Jonty as she worked.

But still, she could not resist wrapping her hand around the most beautiful red rose bloom they came across and crushing it in her fist. She welcomed the pain of the thorns digging into her hand, and smiled cruelly as the rose gave off its dying perfume.

"Why did you do that?" Jonty asked.

"Do what?" she asked pleasantly.

He let out a weary sigh, shaking his head.

She walked away, mincing down the garden row alone and holding up her soiled skirts, when, suddenly, amid the many herbs, her gaze happened upon an old friend.

Deadly nightshade.

She stared at it, then bit down gently on her lower lip, a secret, murderous thrill of inspiration running through her.

As she had told Thaydor in her garden up at Mistwood, used in small doses, it was a key ingredient in several common medicines. In large doses, it could kill a man.

Even a king.

*That'll teach you to get rid of me.*

"Should I be worried?" the paladin had teased her upon finding it growing among her apothecary herbs.

*Oh, yes, darling. Most definitely.*

For beside it grew the equally infamous bloodbane.

And then her inspiration was complete. It was much better suited to her uses than the nightshade.

With a furtive glance at her keepers, she saw the annoying monks and nuns were distracted for a heartbeat. Taking care not to touch the residue on the deadly berries, she broke off a sprig of the bloodbane and slipped it into the pocket of her gown.

# Chapter 21
# Paladin

"Ah, there's my good-for-nothing son! Finally made something of yourself, eh?"

"Father," Thaydor answered with a broad smile.

Gray-haired but still hearty and hale, the grizzled old Earl Clarenbeld strode to him down the long, gilded great hall of the palace, where Thaydor, for his part, could not bring himself to sit on the throne for more than thirty seconds.

He still felt like an imposter who didn't belong there. Especially when the queen's throne next to his remained empty. He missed her so much sometimes he couldn't breathe.

"Son." His father gazed at him with surprising tenderness for a man who'd earned a nickname like War Hammer in battle.

Thaydor embraced him and held on to his father's brawny frame hard, a lump in his throat.

"I'm so sorry, lad."

Thaydor took a shaky breath. "We're working on a cure."

The brusque old warrior pulled back and looked into his eyes, so like his own. Despite the fact the son was now taller than the father, his sire looked at him with pained, futile protectiveness, as though Thaydor was a ten-year-old boy again, bawling over his beloved horse, Northstar, who'd had to be put down for a terrible leg injury.

"She'll be all right," his father whispered, squeezing his shoulders.

But of course, the old man knew exactly what he was going through, or close enough. His own wife had died unexpectedly, snatched away from him when he and his two children had needed her most. Thaydor had no words as his father held his stare in knowing sadness. He didn't even have a child from Wrynne to keep and comfort him if this infernal poison robbed her of her life.

"Easy," his father murmured, but Thaydor shook his head and sat down on a nearby bench, overwhelmed.

He was able to keep his emotions at bay when various officials, strangers, needed him for the endless range of tasks and decisions to be made every day. But with those who knew him best, those who could take one look at him and see how much pain he was in, it was hard to keep up the act. He was frankly falling apart and didn't care to live if his beloved died.

With a downward stare, he braced his elbow on the table beside his chair and held his head in his hand for a moment, struggling for his composure. His father gave his shoulder a comforting squeeze and stood in position to block him from view in case anyone came along who should not see their king teetering on the edge of despair.

"Be strong now, boy."

"She's everything," he wrenched out.

"I know. Get up, son. They're coming."

"Clank?" a pert voice burst in on them.

He quickly hid his heartbreak as best he could and rose as his sister came running into the great hall, lovely as ever, but woefully lacking in decorum, despite her being seventeen and of age to be making her debut.

*Typical.*

"Thimble." He smiled, cleared his throat, clapped his father on the shoulder in thanks, and stepped around him, ready to continue with the charade. All flying blond tresses and whooshing skirts, the exuberant Lady Ingrid Clarenbeld raced to him and launched herself into his arms.

He lifted her off her feet with a big hug. As soon as he set her down again, she stepped back and beamed with sisterly pride. "Look at you, all kingy-like!" she teased. "Dressed properly for once, too. Nice tunic, King Clank!"

He gave her a droll look.

Her blue eyes danced. "But where's your crown, brother?"

"I don't get it until the coronation."

"Oh. Do I get a tiara?" she asked with sudden eagerness. "After all, I *am* the only sister of the monarch. Does this mean I'm a princess now? Another thing—if I give you ideas for laws, will you pass them? Because I have a few ideas."

"I'm sure you do." He laughed at her question and hooked his arm around her shoulders. "I've missed you, little hoyden. How've you been?"

"Not bad. Bored as usual. But finally, something interesting has happened!"

"I guess you could say that. Are you getting on with the du Meres?" he murmured, looking askance at her.

"Oh, Juliana and I have become great friends. But her mother...sweet heaven, how she nitpicks!" she whispered with vehemence.

Thaydor arched a brow but did not disagree.

"The Building Baron's very jolly. He and Father talk on and on for hours like they've known each other for years. Lord du Mere has made a few suggestions about improvements to the castle. Did you know the foundations of the north tower are cracked?"

"Really?" Thaydor asked in surprise. "So that's why it leans."

"He says he can fix it. For free. Which obviously means a great deal to Father. You know what a cheapskate he is."

"Am not!" the earl retorted, overhearing.

"Yes, you are, Papa."

"Why, because I won't buy you the moon?" he muttered.

Thaydor hugged his sister again, already cheered up a little in spite of himself. "How I've missed your prattle."

She pushed him away with a scowl. "Excuse me, but I don't *prattle*! I say very important things. You should heed them!" She punched him lightly in the arm.

"Sorry. Of course," he said. "Don't mind me. I'm a little off these days."

"Oh, I know, my poor, dear brother." Ingrid gazed up at him in sympathy, then caressed his arm. "The du Meres are all beside themselves, as well. But I keep telling them, have faith, she'll be all right. I mean, she has to be! I haven't even got a chance to meet her yet. Don't worry, Thaydor. Ilios listens to you and I'm sure you're praying for her, just like the rest of us are."

He kissed her on the head. "Thanks."

"But in the meanwhile, just remember one thing."

"What's that?"

She pulled back with another pert smile and poked him in the chest. "You may be the king now, but you still can't tell me what to do."

He smiled ruefully. "I'm not naive enough to hope for that. Just try not to call me Clank it front of the Earls' Assembly, if you don't mind?"

"Hmm, blackmail," she said with a twinkle in her eye.

Thaydor tugged a lock of her golden hair with affection, then moved past her as his in-laws presently arrived under the tall, arched doorway of the great hall.

He instantly saw that Wrynne's mother looked a wreck.

"Where is my daughter?" Lady du Mere demanded, marching down the narrow red carpet toward him. "I must go to her at once."

"My lady." Thaydor bowed to his mother-in-law, and offered a handshake to the fat, ruddy-cheeked baron, whose portly jowls were pushed upward by the small ruff around his neck.

"Your Majesty," the baron said, unable to mask his delight at calling his own son-in-law that.

"No need to stand on ceremony, please. You are all most welcome," Thaydor added, nodding to Wrynne's three worried siblings as well.

Her mother started right in, shaking her head at him. "You're her husband. How could you let this happen to her?"

"Mother!" Juliana exclaimed, rather horrified.

Lady du Mere pursed her lips and continued glaring at Thaydor. "I want to go to her. Where is she?"

"Wrynne is at the Bastion. But I don't think that's a good idea right now."

"Of course it is! I am her mother. She needs me!"

"Wrynne is not herself right now, my lady. The smallest things can send her into a rage."

"Saint Wrynne? Rage?" her sister uttered.

"I don't think she'd want her family seeing her in her current condition."

"Well, I don't care what she wants. I am her mother, and I am entitled to see my daughter for myself! I've tended her in illness since she was a babe, and I'm warning you—"

"Enough, woman!" the baron broke in. "If that's what her doctors say, we have to listen."

He shook his beefy head at Thaydor in exasperation.

"I have an idea!" Ingrid spoke up brightly. "Perhaps we all could take a tour of the royal palace. Wouldn't that be interesting?"

"Yes! Mother, that's a fine idea, isn't it?" Juliana seconded, taking the frowning baroness's arm.

Thaydor sent his sister a meaningful glance. *Thank you.*

*You owe me,* she mouthed back. Then she skipped over to the royal chamberlain and sweet-talked him into taking them on a tour of Lionsclaw Keep.

"You want me to stay here or go with them?" Lord Clarenbeld asked.

But before Thaydor could answer his father, Novus Blacktwist came striding into the great hall, brushing off the footmen by the door.

Thaydor turned to him, forgetting all else. "What news?"

"I've got something." He had been working round the clock and it showed. The dark circles under his pale eyes came from more than just the kohl liner around them, now smeared with sweat after hours in his laboratory. Dispensing with all court propriety, he strode into the throne room with his black leather gambeson unlaced partway down his chest, the sleeves removed, exposing the esoteric tattoos twining all down his arms.

Lady De Mere, on her way to the palace tour, huffed in disapproval at the wild and dangerous-looking fellow as he passed them in the doorway, but both young girls turned to stare.

Novus ignored them all, no doubt used to such reactions. His black boot heels pounded out an urgent rhythm as he marched in carrying a small vial of bright green liquid. "I ran my final tests on Eudo last night right before he—er, well, died. Sorry."

"You killed him?"

"Of course not," he said as he joined him, then lowered his voice. "The fire thistle poison must have run its course, but I was close. If I had got to him sooner, maybe...but he was already too far gone."

Thaydor felt himself turn white at the implications. So, the firechoke venom *was* indeed a death sentence.

Novus read the dread in his face. "No. Listen to me. Your wife is young and strong, and we caught it right away. Eudo was an old man and had it in his system for a year. She has only been infected for eight days. This should do the trick."

"Should?" Thaydor studied the Oktean sorcerer intensely, weighing the question now that it came down to it: did he trust him with Wrynne's life?

*Damn it.* He hated the situation he was in. The greatest warrior in the land—the very king—powerless to save his own lady. Instead, he had to rely on this enigmatic servant of the Dark One.

Novus held his searching stare matter-of-factly.

"If it were your wife—" Thaydor started.

"I would pour this down her throat, whatever it took." Novus tilted his head, striving for patience. "I understand your hesitation, believe me. We are different, you and I. But that doesn't mean we can't work together. You have to trust me. I am trying to help you here. I don't want to see this kingdom turn to madness."

"I know you are acting in good faith. It's just…"

"She means the world to you," Novus said. "I understand. I loved once, myself. Unfortunately, our window of opportunity is closing. I interviewed Eudo's whole staff in depth. Several of them gave independent confirmation that there was a marked turn in Eudo's condition about ten days after his return from Silvermount. They remembered because it was one of those feast days when Efrena becomes a man," he added. "Anyway, based on my research, I strongly suspect that this ten-day window represents some kind of turning point…beyond which, I'm not sure there's any coming back. We are nearing that threshold with your wife. We have to give this to her as soon as possible. I've already run all the tests on it I can think of. But time is running out. She needs to drink it."

Thaydor shuddered at the thought of losing her permanently. "Very well. So that's all? I make sure she swallows this, and then I get my wife back?"

Novus nodded. "The sooner the better."

Reynulf had just walked in and heard the tail end of their exchange. "Hecaterus is already saddled; I can ride now. Do you want me to take it to the Bastion and have the monks administer the medicine?"

"No," Thaydor answered, glancing around at them. He clapped Novus on the back in wordless thanks. "I'll take it to her myself. I want this done as gently as possible. She's already been through so much. She's not going to like it. If she has to be forced to swallow it, then it should be by my hand."

"Be careful around her," Novus reminded him.

"She won't hurt me." No matter what anyone said, Thaydor could not bring himself to believe she would try. Not after all they'd shared. His face set with grim resolve, he strode out of the great hall, carrying the precious vial of potion.

"Saddle Avalanche!" he barked at the palace staff, and the whole flock of them scattered into motion to convey this message to the royal stables before he got there.

"Where are you going, brother?" Ingrid asked as he marched past their families, whose dawdling on the tour had only got them as far as the anteroom.

He didn't answer the question. "Pray this works," was all he said as he gusted out the door.

"Honestly! Where does he think he's off to?" he heard his mother-in-law complain in his wake. "Doesn't he know he's the king now? He just goes barreling off as if he's still a knight errant out to slay some dragon!"

Thaydor paid her no mind.

Within minutes, he was on his horse, the potion safely tucked into his breast pocket. He urged Avalanche into a gallop and rode hell for leather to the Bastion.

It was time to claim his queen.

* * *

"You have a visitor, Your Majesty," Mother Superior said kindly, opening her chamber door.

Wrynne rose and stared at the tall blond man who stepped into the room. *Finally.*

A smile curved her lips, but not because she had missed him.

*I am going to enjoy this.*

"Thaydor."

For a second, as he met her gaze, his blue eyes glistened with unshed tears. "My darling," he answered in a strangled tone.

Why, her warrior-king looked quite distraught at their little reunion, but Wrynne was wintry cold.

His tousled, sun-streaked hair and wind-kissed cheeks belied the haste with which he'd ridden here. *But for what purpose?* she wondered as she watched him guardedly, folding her arms across her chest. What perfidy was he scheming now?

While Mother Superior withdrew and pulled the door shut to leave them in privacy, Wrynne kept her distance on the far side of the room.

"So. You finally show your face after abandoning me." She paused. "What do you want?"

Thaydor swallowed hard and took a step toward her. "Novus found a cure. You have to drink this."

He held up a vial of some ghastly green liquid, and everything in her recoiled at the sight of it.

"Not bloody likely." She backed toward the wall, keeping her canopy bed between them. "You think I don't know how much you hate me? You have a lot of nerve coming here, paladin," she spat.

His lips parted with an intake of breath at her cutting tone. Then he lowered his gaze as though reminding himself to be patient.

Because, of course, Thaydor was all that was good and kind and virtuous, she thought with a sneer.

He gazed at her again. Like a wounded pup. "You're everything to me, Wrynne. That's why I'm here. I love you. I need my wife back. I don't want to play any games; I don't want to have to trick you or restrain you. Please just drink this. Trust me."

"Why in the world should I do that?"

He looked baffled by the question, obvious as it was to her.

"What?" she taunted, enjoying his confusion. "Don't try to look innocent. You're the one who had me locked up in this cage. I'd rather be in here alone than with you, anyway." She turned her back to him, gazing out the window with a bitter sulk.

"You don't mean that," he said softly, painfully.

"Did you bring Reynulf?" she taunted with a coy, wicked glance over her shoulder.

She caught the flicker of wrath in his gaze before it dropped to the floor. "No."

"Too bad. He's not boring like you. Or a pompous hypocrite. Or naive." She was enjoying hurting him, pounding on his very heart with her words like some crazed Urmugoth with a mace, battering him in his armor.

Only, he had no armor when it came to her, she knew full well. No defenses. How she enjoyed that. The power it gave her.

She was the one dragon he could not slay.

"I wish I never married you," she said, enjoying how he faltered at the words.

He clenched his jaw, took a deep breath in and let it out slowly, and, in his eyes, she could almost see him mentally resolving to forgive her with his sheer, maddening, unconditional love.

It only made her hate him all the more.

*"Who do you think you are?"* she screamed.

He ignored her raging and lifted the vial toward her. "Come drink this, sweeting."

"Why don't you make me?" she countered coldly.

"Please. I don't want to be rough with you or force you. I'm never giving up on you, Wrynne."

"Oh, look at the king beg."

"Please," he whispered again, shamelessly. "I love you. Nothing's going to change that, no matter what you do."

Now it was her turn to flinch as though he had smote her with the flat of his famous sword. Only teaching her a lesson so far. But those sweet words stung her skin as though he had doused her in acid.

His stare glowed like a blue, celestial beam of light pouring out from Elysium. Pouring out from the sweetness of his breaking heart. For, oh yes, she knew his secret. The one the rest of the world had never guessed. The firechoke had showed it to her.

It was Thaydor's love that made him mighty.

His love for his god, his family, his country. His love for the people and all the little children, like those who had flocked to him instinctively the day they had visited the plundered village. His willingness to lay down his life for them if necessary, without blinking an eye. His devotion to all that was beautiful and righteous and good.

And his love, most of all, for her.

She shrank from him, suddenly unsure if there was enough hate in Hell to overcome the likes of him. His Light shone so brightly it nigh blinded her.

"Come back to me, Wrynne," he insisted with soft implacability. "Drink your medicine of your own free will, and show me you at least want to get well."

"Stay away from me! I hate you!"

His face hardened. "Then you leave me no choice."

He seemed to fill the room then with his sheer determination. She had rejected the lover, and so now she would have to deal with the large, angry knight.

He crossed the chamber in a few strides until she was driven back against the writing desk, with nowhere left to flee.

"Let go of me, you brute! Help! Jonty! Brother Piero!"

"Scream all you want, love. Your king ordered everyone to stay away, no matter what they heard."

She looked at him in dread.

And indeed, nobody even peeked in. Of course, it was partly her own fault. She had already used the trick of crying wolf on her keepers in her endless attempts to escape before she had given up and laid her trap for him instead.

Looming over her, Thaydor captured her and held her fast against his chest, his left arm clamped around her waist. With his right hand, he caught hold of her face. "Open your mouth for me. Come on!"

She refused, sealing her jaw shut and glaring at him as she continued trying to push him away. She might as well have shoved a mountain.

"Wrynne, don't be difficult. You're acting like a child." With calm, maddening patience, he bent her backward, partway over the desk, trying to pry her jaws apart.

"Stop fighting me!" he said through gritted teeth. "This is for your own good!"

"I *despise* you!" she wrenched out in seething, volcanic passion, but that was all the chance he needed.

He forced her mouth open wider the second she spoke and poured the medicine down her throat.

She choked a bit.

He quickly covered her lips with his hand to stop her from spitting it out. "Swallow it. Now."

She glared at him in rage, holding the vile liquid in her mouth.

"Wrynne. Swallow the medicine. Do as I tell you, now. There's a good girl."

*I hate, hate, hate you*, she told him with her eyes, but he just smiled, as if he knew he had already won. Then he clamped his fingers gently over her nose, squeezing her nostrils shut.

Her eyes widened to think her own husband would actually cut off her air. Now she'd *have* to swallow the medicine to gasp for breath through her mouth.

"Sorry," he said with a slight shrug.

*You will be*, she thought. For while he was distracted, waiting for her to swallow and watching hopefully for any sign that the foul-tasting stuff was beginning to work, her searching hand found the handle of the top desk drawer.

Without a sound, she pulled the drawer open just a bit, reached into it, and sought the illicit weapon she had prepared and hidden there. A nasty little penknife she had fashioned by breaking off one of the metal sunrays in the religious sculpture hanging on her chamber wall.

Working under cover of darkness the past few nights, she had coated the metal file with the juice of the poisonous bloodbane berries she had carefully collected from the garden.

The idiot monks and nuns thought it was simply walking in the garden that had cheered her up and calmed her down, but this was not the case. The reason for her better state of mind in recent days was that she had hatched an excellent plan.

To rid the world of Thaydor.

And as her fingers closed around her little blade, the time had come to strike.

She did, plunging the makeshift dagger into his side, even as the need for air overcame her.

She swallowed the mouthful of medicine at last, while a small cry of pain escaped him. She let go of the blade, abandoning it in his side to let the poison do its work. Her husband released her from his viselike hold and looked down at the sunray of Ilios sticking out from between his ribs.

"Rather poetic, don't you think?" she gasped out, panting for air.

"Oh, Wrynne," he said mournfully, and moved away from her, a crimson stain spreading at his side.

What was that the oracle had said so long ago?

*You will betray him.*

He deserved it.

Her stare fixed on him, she wiped the taste of his hand and the residue of the medicine roughly off her lips. The potion he had forced down her throat tasted foul on her tongue, but she took satisfaction in knowing she had paid him back in full.

"You're hard to kill, love, but that should do the trick," she said.

He pulled the metal file out of his side and sent her a grim, defiant smile. "I've had worse."

"Oh, I know, dear," she said sweetly. "That's why I tipped the blade with poison."

He stopped, paling. "What?"

As Thaydor glanced down in alarm at the blood on his hand, a wave of nausea suddenly overcame her.

"But it seems you've poisoned me, too," she rasped.

"Wrynne!" He reached for her as she dropped to her knees, clutching her stomach.

"What have you done to me, you bastard?" she ground out, spittle dripping from her mouth as she dry-heaved.

Everything inside her was burning. She started shaking. The room was spinning. She let out a scream of pain and convulsed.

"Wrynne! No, I'm sorry, I'm sorry... Sweet Ilios, I'll kill that sorcerer…" Thaydor knelt beside her, covering his own wound with his hand, blood flowing out between his fingers, as he looked on in panic, asking her what was happening.

In a moment, she was barely aware of him. He dissolved out of focus. She curled into a ball, panting, her eyes squeezed shut, and when the next wave of blazing pain tore through her innards, she screamed. The agony was so intense it reminded her of the night she had relived his mortal injuries through the *Kiss of Life* spell.

And just like then, once more, she simply blacked out.

\* \* \*

He gradually brought her back with a kiss. His lips lingered atop hers, silken and warm. She became aware of a large, trembling hand stroking her hair. His whispers wove into her addled mind.

"Please come back to me, demoiselle, so at least we can say goodbye."

*Goodbye?*

When she opened her glazed eyes in confusion, blinking against the light, her temples were pounding. Her head rested on Thaydor's thigh.

The room was waving with sickening slowness, and behind him, the ceiling seemed to stretch a hundred feet tall.

But she instantly noticed she felt different. Like a fever had broken. She felt cleaned out inside. As if she had vomited out some meal of putrid food that she had eaten by mistake. The residue of the medicine still tasted foul on her tongue, but the blessed emptiness within told her the stuff had killed the parasitic evil that had nested inside her.

Thaydor was stroking her head, watching every expression on her face. "There you are," he breathed, a catch in his voice.

As her vision cleared, she noticed he didn't look so well. His tanned, outdoorsy complexion had gone pale.

"Thaydor?"

"Wrynne." He took her hand, twining his fingers through hers. "Are you back?"

She stared at him…with no idea what they were doing on the floor or how they had got there or what was going on. "Where are we?"

She looked around the room and recognized it as though she had only seen it in a dream.

Then her gaze happened upon the bloodstain on the side of his shirt, and instantly, it all came flooding back.

She sat up with a gasp of horror. "I did this to you!"

"Shh, it's all right." He cupped her cheek and shook his head, gazing tenderly at her. "It's not your fault."

"But I-I tipped the blade with bloodbane!"

"It doesn't matter. Kiss me."

She stared at him, her own complexion nearly as ashen with dread as his was, with the wicked work of the poison in his veins. He leaned closer and brushed her lips again with his own, but she refused to kiss him goodbye.

Instead, she reached for his shirt and lifted it with practiced hands, though they were shaking.

"Quickly—I can heal you."

"Wrynne, I don't think—"

"Let me try! Now that I'm better, maybe…" Disoriented as she was, she cupped her hand over the hole she had punctured in his smooth, muscled side, and drew on her power.

Nothing happened.

"No!" she cried. "I can't. My gift— It didn't come back."

She tried again, squeezing her eyes shut, grimacing with the effort, to no avail. It was useless.

This was so much worse than her failure with the bard.

"Stay here." She started to get to her feet. "I'll get Brother Piero. We can send for one of the healers—"

"Wrynne, I don't think there's…time." He clasped her wrist. "Don't leave me. I don't want to die alone."

She looked at him in shock. His face was ashen; his breathing sounded strange. "No…"

"I've been close enough to death enough times to know when I'm actually dying," he whispered wearily, and for the first time, she saw real fear in his eyes.

"No, no, no, Thaydor." She jumped to her feet, ran to the door, and started screaming for help, but he needed her. She went racing back in a state of shock and dropped to her knees beside him. Shaking, she cradled him in her arms on the floor and covered his face with tears and with kisses. "No, no, no, you can't leave me. Please—I love you. I need you."

"I think I was always meant to die in your arms, as I should have done that first night," he panted. "But you saved me with your kiss. And I got to learn what love means. The poems…don't do it justice." He shivered, the cold of death settling into him.

Aghast to find her otherwise-invincible warrior slipping away—by her own hand—she lowered her head and tearfully kissed him hard on the mouth, willing every ounce of love she had into him.

She couldn't even remember now what all she had put into the poison. She wouldn't have known how to begin making an antidote. But at his mention of the *Kiss of Life* spell, something tugged at the back of her mind.

She suddenly pulled back. "Thaydor!"

"Hmm?" he mumbled, already beginning to fade.

"The *Kiss of Life* spell! It transferred my ability to you—"

"No, I was never the healer you were."

"I mean the power to heal *yourself*. Oh, why didn't I think of it before? That was the sacrifice I had to make, the gift I transferred to you! Remember? Darling, stay with me now. You must try! Quickly!"

"What do I do?" he mumbled.

"It's just the same as if you were healing someone else." Heart pounding, she gripped his shoulders, pulling him upright, heavy as he was. "Hold your hand above the wound. Close your eyes. Make contact with the Light."

He looked doubtful but he tried it. As a low-level healer, he knew the simple procedure. With his hand cupped above the place where she had pierced him in her madness, he closed his eyes and bowed his head a bit.

She leaned her forehead against his and sought the Light from which she had been so desolately cut off under the fire thistle's curse. It was there for her now, even though she could not heal.

*Please don't take him from me. I beg You. We still have a destiny left to fulfill. The oracle also said we'd have a son.*

Fresh tears rose behind her eyelids. But as she joined her silent, desperate prayers with his, love rose around them, the purest form of Light itself, enveloping the two of them in a sphere of warmth and tenderness.

She could feel Thaydor's goodness flowing through him, pure and strong, like a wave of bright power pouring out of the unseen realms to a dark and hurting world.

The brilliance shone between the palm of his hand and his bleeding side—a blinding flash—then it vanished.

"Did it work?" she whispered.

It took a heartbeat for her dazzled eyes to adjust, and she looked down at his side.

The dried blood was still there, but the wound had closed and disappeared. There was not a scratch left on him, and when she looked up from his side to his face, his color was already improving.

"How do you feel? What of the poison?" she asked quickly, pressing her fingers to his brow.

He swallowed hard, looking disoriented. "Better," he said tentatively. "I think…I'm all right. Wrynne—it worked."

She threw her arms around him with a sob.

He pulled her closer. She hugged him harder. He held her for a long moment, but she couldn't stop crying, clinging to him. Nearly losing him was even worse than nearly losing herself.

"Shh, I'm all right, love," he assured her with a kiss on her cheek. At last, he took her face between his hands and stared into her eyes, drinking in the sight of her, his face full of stormy tenderness. "Do we really have each other back?"

She nodded for all she worth. "But how can you ever forgive me?" she wrenched out.

"Darling, you saved me. With the sacrifice you made for a dying man all those weeks ago, asking nothing in return, I'm all right. It's over now. Dry your tears."

"But I can't. I nearly k-killed you."

"Shh." He kissed her on the forehead.

"Oh, Thaydor, I'm so sorry. You deserve so much better than me."

"Don't say such a thing. You are my love, and you always will be."

"The awful things I said… I didn't mean any of it."

"I know. Shh, don't cry, sweeting. Everything will be well. None of this was your fault."

"Even so!" she cried, furious at herself. She pulled back and stared at him in tears. "It's too horrible. I can't believe I stabbed you a-and poisoned you. You could have me hanged!"

"Never," he whispered, wiping away a tear.

"Y-you should shun me! Or b-banish me or throw me in the dungeon!"

He tilted his head with a fond gaze. "Then who would be my queen?"

"Don't smile at me," she said wretchedly. "I don't deserve it."

"But I must, when I'm looking at my happiness."

"Oh, Thaydor." She hung her head as she gripped his hand. "You can't possibly still want me after that. You have every right to hate me. I really wouldn't blame you."

"Ah, you know me, demoiselle." He wiped away the tear rolling down her cheek, then lifted her chin on his fingertips. When she met his gaze, his cobalt eyes were full of love, his voice slightly choked with emotion. "I am nothing if not steadfast."

A shudder of devotion racked her at his sweet, familiar words. She'd heard them before.

At the cave the night he had first insisted she become his wife. He had lived up to every heartfelt promise he had made to her that night, and by now it was clear that though their love might've been born in the *Kiss of Life* spell, this magic they shared was never going to wear off.

If it could survive this, it could survive anything.

"I love you so much. You are...everything that's wonderful, Thaydor," she whispered. "Please, never, ever leave me."

"Leave you? Are you jesting, woman?" He firmly wiped a tear off her cheek, then gave it an affectionate pinch. "I'm not letting you out of my sight, now that I know you have this penchant for rushing off to perform noble deeds that only land you in trouble."

Her tears stopped abruptly as he arched a teasing brow at her.

"Well, you do the same thing," she pointed out.

"And that's why we're perfect for each other." His dazzling smile widened. He lifted her hand and kissed it. "So, are you ready to be my queen? Because if you don't want this, Wrynne, I'll step down. Believe me, I don't mind. I don't need a crown. I could be happy anywhere as long as I have you."

For a moment, she couldn't even answer, amazed at the sheer size of his golden heart. His generosity. His ability to forgive and forget. She had nearly murdered the man, and yet he was doing all he could to comfort *her*.

"Well?" he prompted.

"Of course...if that is what you want. If you'll still have me."

"I can't do it without you," he said earnestly, which she very much doubted, but *he* seemed convinced that this was true.

She lowered her head. "Then I'm all yours. Do with me as you will...my king."

"Hmm." A wicked sparkle glinted in his eye.

He suddenly jumped to his feet and swept her up in his arms with a roguish laugh. Breathless, Wrynne clasped her fingers behind his neck and kept her stare locked on his handsome face as he crossed the room, kicked the door open ahead of them, and marched out of her chamber, carrying her out into the golden sunshine and long shadows of the early evening.

"Where are you taking me?"

"Home," he said. "I seem to recall promising you a palace before all this was over, and, you know, I always keep my promises."

"Yes, you do," she whispered.

He paused and kissed her soundly before setting her upon Avalanche's back. Then, joining her in the saddle, he wrapped his arms around her waist, grasped the reins, and urged the stallion into motion.

Riding at an easy canter through the rosy light of sunset, neither of them spoke for many miles. Just being together was a balm for both their battered souls.

Wrynne laid her head on his shoulder, still feeling unworthy, but lulled by the horse's rocking gait. In truth, she was dazzled. What *wouldn't* this man do for her? With Thaydor's arms around her, she had never felt more loved and protected. Indeed, cherished...

Prized.

# Epilogue
# Elysium

**P**ealing carillons proclaimed the occasion of the new king and queen's coronation.

The Golden Master conducted the ceremony in the great Ilian cathedral of Pleiburg. Wrynne and Thaydor were dressed in sumptuous finery, from the white satin brocade of her gown and his belted tunic to their long, red ceremonial robes of ermine-trimmed velvet.

Thaydor knelt before the altar with Hallowsmite at his side and one hand on the holy book as he swore the vows of kingship—to uphold the Charter, be subject himself to the laws of the land, and to defend the realm from all enemies, both within and without.

The aged prophet anointed Thaydor's head with oil while the attendants sang the chants to procure divine protection upon him and swung censers of frankincense.

The Golden Master asked him a series of ritual questions, ending with the oath from Thaydor. "On my eternal soul, all this I solemnly vow. So may it be."

"So may it be," the congregation gave the solemn refrain.

Wrynne whispered it, too, her heart pounding as she then watched the old man set the thick, jewel-encrusted gold crown on her beautiful husband's head.

"King Thaydor of Veraidel," the old man proclaimed.

Cheers erupted from inside the cathedral, so loud they could have shaken the building to its massive stone foundations. The bells rang louder.

Thaydor rose and sent her a discreet wink as he moved aside.

She was next.

The ceremony was repeated, though the vows were slightly

different. She was trembling with terror, or at least awe, the whole time, knowing how fallible she was. But she swore to herself she would never let evil darken her thoughts as it had during her enthrallment by the fire thistle. And she would certainly never pass judgment on anyone else again, especially not the Fonja girls, because now she knew personally how the wicked suffered.

Yet for all the noise outside, within her, the deep, profound stillness of the Light had returned, washing her with the inner peace that had always sustained her. True, her healing power had been lost, possibly for good, but it was a small price to pay to have at least got *herself* back.

Besides, what more could she ask after her sacrifice in the *Kiss of Life* had paid off in the most vital and unexpected way?

She had not lost Thaydor. If her murder attempt on him could not put a dent in their bond, then nothing could, she supposed, as she watched him with a private smile.

He looked more kingly by the second. He truly had been born for this, whether he knew it or not. Clearly, everybody else did.

Then the Golden Master lifted the queen's crown off the velvet pillow and said the prayers over her. Her crown was fashioned on slimmer, more graceful lines, with diamonds inset all around, but light as it was, the weight of it on her head gave her pause and made her stand a little straighter.

"Queen Wrynne of Veraidel," the prophet announced her to the people, as though she were a bride.

Thaydor took her hand and helped her rise, then they turned to face the congregation side by side. They gazed at each other as the official proclamation was made.

"Their Majesties, King Thaydor and Queen Wrynne of Veraidel!"

From that first moment of their shared rule, the cheers resounded from one end of the kingdom to the other. Thaydor leaned down and kissed her cheek, then smiled at the people.

In the front row of the church, Wrynne's mother was weeping. Their beaming fathers shared an illicit toast from flasks hidden in their pockets. Their sisters were holding on to each other and jumping up and down in excitement, while behind them, the three young squires flirted with the two pretty girls, leaving off only to join the company of knights in sending up hip-hip-hoorays.

One voice—a particularly deep and melodious one—could be heard above the others cheering. Jonty blew Wrynne a kiss, then pressed his hand to his heart with a courtly bow to them both.

Brother Piero was clapping so loudly he could've been heard in the Bronze Mountains. Even Novus was there, frowning in distraction. The solitary sorcerer glanced around, looking a trifle uncomfortable in the throng—not the least because he was a follower of Okteus sitting in an Ilian church. Perhaps he was looking out for lightning bolts.

Well, she thought, he might feel that he didn't belong here, but he was wrong. The man had saved her life. She wasn't sure if the brooding sorcerer quite realized he had just become the most important mage in the kingdom.

The only one who wasn't there was Reynulf.

Wrynne still cringed when she thought of him, though the red knight had laughed off her apology for her wanton propositions.

"You think a woman's never thrown herself at me before?" he had teased. "Please. It happens every day, and who can blame them?"

Though he'd had the grace to spare her pride, his past crimes were a more serious matter. Given his role in letting the Urms through the North Gate and killing those poor sentries, Thaydor knew that as soon as he took the oath of kingship, he'd be required to bring charges against Reynulf. True, the red knight had only been following orders from King Baynard's own lips, but he still bore culpability.

On the other hand, Reynulf's actions in helping to expose the machinations of the Silver Sage *and* his skillful fighting on Thaydor's side against the Urms in the Battle of Pleiburg, as it was being called, were mitigating factors. Not to mention he had personally saved Thaydor's life when Sana had moved to stab him in the back.

For his part, Thaydor had not wanted to send him away—Reynulf was a valuable ally to have on hand—but justice had to be answered. He could not start off his rule by making special exceptions to the law for his friends.

So banishment for a period of eight years had been suggested by the Crown's lawyers as a fair compromise in weighing Reynulf's good deeds against his wicked ones.

Reynulf seemed to understand and accept the court's judgment. He was too proud a warrior, and honorable in his way, to deny what he had done. Instead, he took the blame for his actions with his head held high.

Wrynne was rather surprised but very relieved he wasn't angry. They had already had a taste of what it was like having Reynulf for an enemy, and she did not want him out there somewhere on the loose in the world holding a grudge against her husband.

Where he would go or what he would do from this point, not even Reynulf knew, but one thing was certain. He had abandoned his worship of the war god. He had told them he no longer believed that Xoltheus even existed, and if he did, Reynulf said he'd like to put a dagger in the god's lying heart.

"Kill a god? Leave it to Reynulf," Thaydor had murmured after they had bade him goodbye.

Wrynne just hoped the world out there would be safe from Reynulf without Thaydor on hand to keep him on the straight and narrow.

At least he hadn't gone alone. Some of the other red warriors had followed him into exile; taking orders from Reynulf was apparently too strong a habit to break. Wrynne had heard that a dozen or so of the Fonja girls had wanted to tag along with them as camp followers, but they weren't invited.

Wrynne and Thaydor had watched Reynulf ride off at the head of his caravan, heading for the coast and a ship to take him who knew where. He had waved farewell with a promise to let them know where he landed, but had scoffed when Wrynne had asked him to promise that he'd stay out of trouble.

Just then, a few officials beckoned to her. Her recollections of the past few days whooshed away as she and Thaydor were hurried on to the next phase of coronation day.

When they stepped out of the cathedral, the broad avenue was teeming with humanity and resounded with the deafening roar of the crowds. They got into a gilt-trimmed open carriage pulled by white horses and went in a grand processional to Lionsclaw Keep, waving to the people as they went. Their fellow citizens littered the road before them with flower petals.

"This is a lot to live up to," Wrynne whispered.

"Tell me about it," Thaydor muttered, then sent her a sideways smile. He was used to such attention and all the pressure that came with it.

When he took her white-gloved hand and raised it to his lips, the people went nearly mad with cheering. After the last king's betrayal of his wife, seeing how much the two of them loved each other seemed to hearten the populace somehow.

Later, they again waved to the crowds from the balcony overlooking Concourse Square, where King Baynard had been rescued by his executioner. Before they retreated to the great salon behind the doors, it was time for the release of a hundred white doves.

All the cages were opened at once. The people watched the white birds go fluttering aloft and agreed it was a beautiful sight and a good omen.

At length, the sea of humanity took to their own feasting, and all those in the palace crammed with guests did the same.

Across Veraidel, from Mistwood to the coast, songs and celebration filled the pubs and village squares. Bonfires burned. Games and contests abounded. Even the smallest hamlets had costumed performers reenacting Thaydor's past exploits as paladin.

Crowds laughed as other actors dressed up as Avalanche and carried the great knight around piggyback, chasing after their fellow mummers dressed up as Urmugoths or even dragons, beating on them with silver-painted models of Hallowsmite.

Of course, the real Thaydor was used to all the fuss. Wrynne watched him introducing his father to various dignitaries, and she couldn't help smiling to herself.

No, the hero treatment would hardly turn his head now after he'd been subjected to it for years. She had to admit King Baynard's final act had shown wisdom, naming the famous paladin as his heir. It was a relatively easy transition for the people, too, since they already knew and trusted him. Command sat easily on those broad shoulders.

The night waned as more elegant entertainments than those in the provinces were brought before them—dances, acrobatics, the dramatic reading of poems. Wrynne stayed at the feast for as long as she could keep her eyes open, but near midnight, she was exhausted after the long day's whirlwind of activity.

Her head was spinning as the reality of her new role in life finally started sinking in. She took leave of the gathered company after Jonty's beautiful song in their honor.

Of course, rascal that he was, he could not help but sprinkle a few droll jibes in among the praise. Recalling the bard's stated mission of keeping an eye on the powerful for the people's sake and taunting them when necessary, Wrynne gave him a big hug when he was through. She and Thaydor both welcomed their friend's intent to keep them honest.

"Thank you…for everything," she said earnestly, looking up into his twinkling green eyes. "You are very dear to me, you know."

"Likewise, lass—I mean, Your Majesty." He winked. "And you are most welcome."

Fondly pulling away from him for now, she went to thank the contingent of ambassadors from Aisedor for coming.

They still looked a little dour at the tragedy that had befallen their sovereign's daughter, but since the man who had engineered it was dead—namely Lord Eudo—they seemed mollified by Thaydor's earlier talk of trade advantages that he could offer as a token of his thanks for not declaring war on Veraidel in retaliation.

No doubt, the king of Aisedor would be watching closely to see what manner of man had risen to the throne in their neighboring country.

The bards of Lyragon to the east had also sent a merry contingent. They had talked nonstop to Jonty, and indeed, to everyone, and by now, they all were especially drunk.

Jonty had whispered to her and Thaydor earlier that he had officially been invited to Lyragon to act as a judge in the annual bardic competition. This rare honor seemed to amuse him greatly, though he tried to keep a serious expression, assuring them it was a cutthroat contest. Only the most respected of minstrels were chosen to join the panel of judges responsible for determining who would be named the best bard in all the land.

Still saying her good nights, Wrynne thanked the slurring Lyragonians for coming, and was treated in return to a flamboyant litany of the loftiest compliments any queen had ever received. Her eyes were stars shining through a sea mist, her lips were summer roses, et cetera, et cetera, along with the courtliest of bows.

One of the bards actually fell over as a result of too deep a flourish, and promptly passed out on the floor.

Thaydor arched a brow.

Jonty looked at his colleague and shrugged. "Been there."

She chuckled, then went and hugged each member of her family. She smiled at her mother's fussing, well aware the woman couldn't help herself. She laughed at her father's jolly bear hug. As she curtsied to her gruff, scar-faced father-in-law, she tried not to let the old warrior notice that she still found him utterly intimidating. Yet every time the War Hammer opened his mouth, he said the sweetest things.

Like father, like son. She supposed she'd get used to him soon. Then she said farewell to her siblings and the bubbly Lady Ingrid, as well.

"I'll be there soon," Thaydor promised as he walked her to the doorway.

The entire banquet hall rose when she stood to leave, then a whole entourage of servants, footmen, ladies-in-waiting, and guards—led by none other than bearded Sir Berold and scar-faced Sir Sagard—escorted her through the palace to her gilded apartment in the residential wing.

Two maids assisted her in unfastening and lifting away her heavy brocade gown. They started taking all the pins out of her elaborate hairstyle, once her crown—her *crown!*—was removed. This was set safely back on its pillow to be returned to the royal vault until it was needed next.

She stared at it as they whisked it away. Never in her life had she ever thought she'd own a *crown*, diamond-crusted or otherwise. She had never wanted greatness or riches. She had only wanted peace.

Love.

And she had definitely got that.

He walked in the door shortly after she had dismissed her attendants. They had left her with her hair hanging loose over her shoulders and her tired body wrapped in a simple silk dressing gown over her white shift.

In the mirror's reflection, she watched her darling husband step into the room. Thaydor let out a weary exhalation as soon as the door had closed behind him. She rose from her stool at the dressing table and went to him.

"There she is," he said fondly as she slipped her arms around his waist. "Alone at last."

She sighed with happiness as he leaned down and kissed her.

"How are you feeling?" she murmured.

"Fairly worn out," he admitted.

"I'm not surprised." She undid the sword belt around his waist for him. "But that's not what I meant."

As she went and set the dress sword aside, he looked at her curiously and started unbuttoning his coat.

"I meant do you feel any different, now that you are officially the king?"

He shrugged. "Not really."

She returned and helped him slip the coat off his shoulders. "I see. Steadfast."

"That's me. King Clank, according to my sister."

"Well, if you ask me, a kingdom could do worse than have a lawful, good, serious, responsible, just, virtuous Clank for a leader."

He laughed. "When you put it like that, the damned bard might be right. I really am just a boring stick, aren't I?"

"Oh, not at all!" she scolded with a chuckle, sliding her arms around his waist. "Especially not to me."

"Are you sure?" he murmured with a taunting gleam in his eyes. "You wouldn't rather have your good friend Reynulf here with you right now?"

"Not on your life!" she exclaimed, turning bright red.

"Good." He wrapped his arms around her, pulled her against his chest with a roguish tug, then he lifted her off her feet and carried her over to the bed. "Because here's a secret for you, sweeting: I'm not always that virtuous."

"Oh, I know," she whispered, a thrill running through her whole body as he laid her down. "Neither am I."

"Believe me, I remember. But let's just keep this between you and me," he said as he nuzzled her earlobe. "We wouldn't want to scandalize the world, now, would we?"

"Leave them their illusions," she breathlessly agreed, then she closed her eyes in dreamy delight as he began kissing his way hungrily down her throat.

He took her breast in his hand, flicking her nipple with his thumb. She cradled his head against her neck and arched her back in yearning under his possessive touch.

"Oh, darling, I want you so much," she whispered, trembling for him.

"I'm all yours." He raked his fingers through her hair and claimed her mouth again almost roughly.

He drove her wild, consuming her lips with his hot, wet kisses, his tongue filling her mouth. Wrynne caressed him everywhere, shivering with anticipation for her ravishment. Her body burned for her mate with unquenchable fire. Her fevered hands glided over his silken, sculpted abdomen, up his muscled chest and then down to his rampant manhood, stroking, teasing him until he couldn't bear it anymore.

With a low, seductive laugh, he pinned her hands to the mattress above her head. She could feel his heart pounding against her body as she wrapped her legs around him and pulled him closer with a needy moan. "*Take me.*"

"Yes, Your Majesty," came his wry, husky answer.

Then he did—with great gusto and quite heroic valor, of course.

What the servants in the corridor must have thought at the way the headboard banged against the wall, she barely dared imagine. But neither of them cared. The starlight streaming in through the window silvered his sleek, powerful silhouette as he rode deep between her thighs, giving her everything—it was the only way Thaydor knew how to love.

And that night, when he conquered her completely once again, she conceived a son.

Just as the oracle had promised.

*Coming Soon!*

## AGE OF HEROES, BOOK 2

# Muse of Fire

Bard, charmer, and adventurer Jonty Maguire travels to Lyragon, where he soon suspects his bardic brethren have fallen under the sway of a necromancer. To break their dark thrall will require a song more potent than any he has ever sung before, and to bring it forth, he will need the help of the most powerful muse he can find.

The legendary fire muse, Capricia, beautiful and deadly, swims like a mermaid in the lava of a volcano on the edge of the Dragon Sea. But a dream has been growing in her heart of flame…to become human, live a mortal life, and experience for herself the passion she has inspired in others for a thousand years.

When the handsome Runescar Highlander arrives seeking her help, the muse offers Jonty a deal fit to strike terror in the heart of any wayward, womanizing bard. *I will give you your song if you'll show me your world—and teach me the meaning of love…*

To be notified when *Muse of Fire* and other books by Gaelen Foley are released, please visit www.GaelenFoley.com and subscribe to her Author Mailing List.

*Romance fans!* While you're waiting for Jonty's book, I welcome you to check out my twenty previous bestselling historical romances. But if *Fantasy* is more your cup of tea, I've got more of that for you, too!

Separate from my romance books, I also co-write "clean" all-ages fantasy adventure novels with my husband, a former teacher, under the pen name E.G. Foley. Our Gryphon Chronicles series is suitable for Ages 10 and Up. Set in a magical version of Queen Victoria's England, it's as much fun for grownups as it is for kids.

## Book 1: THE LOST HEIR

*Strange new talents…*

Jake is a scrappy orphaned pickpocket living by his wits on the streets of Victorian London. Lately he's started seeing ghosts and can move solid objects with his mind! He has no idea why. Next thing he knows, a Sinister Gentleman and his minions come hunting him, and Jake is plunged headlong into a mysterious world of magic and deadly peril. A world that holds the secret of who he really is: the long-lost heir of an aristocratic family with magical powers.

But with treacherous enemies closing in, it will take all of his wily street instincts and the help of his friends—both human and magical—to solve the mystery of what happened to his parents and defeat the foes who never wanted the Lost Heir of Griffon to be found…

*"A wonderful novel in the same vein as Harry Potter, full of nonstop action, magical creatures, and the reality that was Queen Victoria's England."* ~The Reading Café

## Other books in the series:

# ABOUT THE AUTHOR

 Noted for her "complex, subtly shaded characters, richly sensual love scenes, and elegantly fluid prose" (*Booklist*), Gaelen Foley is the *New York Times*, *USA Today*, and *Publisher's Weekly* bestselling author of twenty historical romances from Random House/Ballantine and HarperCollins. Her award-winning novels are available worldwide in seventeen languages, with millions of copies sold. Gaelen holds a BA in English Literature and lives in Pennsylvania with her husband, Eric, with whom she also co-writes family-friendly "PG-Rated" fantasy adventure novels for kids and adults under the penname E.G. Foley. (Book one in their Gryphon Chronicles series, *The Lost Heir*, has been optioned for a movie!)

Visit www.GaelenFoley.com and sign up for her mailing list to be notified when her latest books are released. Subscribers also receive access to sneak peeks, bonus extras, and other exclusive content—plus a chance to win prizes in monthly giveaways.

*Thanks for reading!*

Printed in Great Britain
by Amazon.co.uk, Ltd.,
Marston Gate.